O

MINI-THINs

o

o

MINI-THIN^S .: ·· _{BY} ·· *TZVI PECKAR the THIRD*

---

a POLYMORPH productions PUBLICATION•

In Memory of Dave Young,
who would have fucking loved this book.

o

GhOSTie[s]
A TYLER GOODMAN AUTOBIOGRAPHY
My Teenage Tragedy

~

chapter ONE

*d*avey and I got kicked out of some motor-hog, house party in the bum-fuck of Sonoma County, all for punching the quarterback in the nose.

—Why are there jocks here in the first place?

It's 1991—

Davey wanted to come to this pecker show of a drunken rampage for no better reason than not going home. So, I walked right in the backdoor with my *VHS* camcorder, a *Panasonic*, suction cupped to my eye and in the middle of the kitchen is the cross-town's, obnoxious as all hell, quarterback-cock-jock in a *Pearl Jam* shirt, rockin' on the *Tupperware* hollering *Even Flow* and Davey just snaps, socks the guy right in the nose, and the negative 20 I.Q. goes all ape shit reaching for my camera lens. He's got a bloody nose, but this doesn't faze him. This pigskin catcher has had a billion busted nostrils in his short lifetime.

"WOOOF, WOOF!" the jock barks, mouth splooge splashing all over my lens, and my camera angle shifts, a *Twilight Zone* transitional pan blur. I'm suddenly on the ground, tackled, being dragged backwards. Davey's got me by the collar of my worn *Butthole Surfers* shirt, and these hicks of cow-town are calling me a "Fag Fuck" as I'm being towed through the kitchen door into the living area. The door swings right back at my army-green *Doc Martin's* and I dropkick that door so hard it keeps swinging open and closed— *Swoosh, Swish* —my back's being chafed by the crappy carpet, then I'm sliding out the frontdoor, down the stairs, my back cracking along each step, and along a dirt path that leads to the house. Davey releases my collar, but it's not D, it's a 6 foot motor-hick who's dragged me out. Where's Davey? "Stay the fuck out," the beast tells me as he steps over my torso, struts back into the home, punches fists and slappin' fives with the other wasted motor-head-cowboy youth of *Sonoma County* who have gathered in this front yard for a night of boozing, cigars, country crack cocaine, and the few skaters that showed up because there is really nowhere else to fuck off tonight. The general attendance of this here party are all good people, it's just that the cock-jocks showed up unannounced, and that's just annoying. Davey squeezes out the front door, approaches my flattened ass and reaches out his hand, "That had to be stopped."

Davey's this skin tight, bleached blonde, already naturally blonde, nearly shaved, skinny twig of a punk, who always wears this oversized, leather, motorcycle jacket, decorated in safety pins, and covered in white, paint pen, hand written, band names such as the *Specials, DK, NOMEANSNO, LARD, Dead Boys,* etc. He's sixteen years old; I'm a few months older. "You're gonna get a beat down for that camera one day, Red," Davey advises me as he yanks me up from the moist dirt; the fog is thick tonight. There's dog shit on my pants from the gnarly grass, and I'm soaked from the beer people had tossed on me as I got 86'ed from this generally lame party.

The owner's monster of a half-pitbull, half-alligator barks at us as we pass by his bin, a chain-link fence, sectioned off in the front yard. Davey kicks the fence. The dog, teeth and all, leaps at the barrier, grapples with the wire he's grabbed with its muscular jaws. "Fuck you, *Cujo*," Davey scowls as he punches the dog in the face, tears up his knuckles on the fence, and grabs me by the shoulder, forcing us to run off the property to the main road.

My eyes try to focus on the faded white line along the asphalt that separates the road from the ditch. Ditches define *Petaluma CA*; ditches line all the country roads out here. Tonight, this ditch is decorated with roadsters, hogs, rotting-rusted *Toyotas* that are missing letters, and— BAMM — Davey intentionally leaps into the side of a white pick-up truck, denting the muddied side panel. The truck's back window has a *49'ner* football sticker, *A's* stickers, 2nd *Amendment* stickers, and a *Bulldog* stencil. Basically, your run of the mill *Nor. Cal* hick propaganda, and now we're really hustling to get out of here.

> *—I don't want to die by the hand of a Jock tonight.*
> *Davey doesn't care.*
> *Figures he'll die a violent death someday.*
> *Today would be just fine.*
> *A martyr for the Luman Punks.*

Davey starts singing his anthem, *"We've lost sight of all our goals - Just given up or so it seems. And now we depend on a new generation to realize our dreams."* Lyrics from a homegrown *Petaluma* ska band appropriately name *The Conspiracy.*

o   •   o

We finally reach my car that we parked like a quarter mile down the ass-dark, country road. I acquired this mini-heap of drivable metal, my very own *Little Red Civic*, last month when one of my cousins was shipped off to *Iraq (Part One)* for a day; *George Bush Senior* promised a swift and clean fight. He was right. Yeah, for him. My dumb-ass friends and I took to the high school lawns in protest of that coming war; hippies and punks united as rebels against the *Republican* establishment! That shit lasted like overnight, but I still got the car.

Davey and I climb in my *Little Red Civic*, plop our asses onto the fake leather seats, unlock the manual steering— CLONK —make sure I'm in first gear, pop the clutch, accelerate, get it up to second— putt, putt —and we're roaming at a whopping 30mph, so I jack it up to third; stick-shifts rule.

○　　　　　•　　　　　○

We hit up *Denny's*.

I order a cup of coffee for each of us, ponder an order of fries, repetitively flick the corner of the plastic menu, as Davey digs through his pockets mining for gold. Last week Davey literally got up out of the booth, dug into his back pockets, a real performance, only to find a match book, and a stub from the county fair, from like a year ago. "Shit man, I'm broke," he had deducted. Another time he even suggested he might have some dough still in his bag, the bag he left at *7-Eleven* while we were playing a tumultuous round of *Double Dragon*...when we were fuckin' ten.

"Dude, stop looking. You want fries?" I offer.

"Nah my stomach feels kinda wonky from all the *Mini-Thins*," he says, putting an end to the petty money hunt. I calculate that we've popped at least four to six *Mini-Thins* since the party started. It's a bit much on the stomach. *Bronchial dilators*, trucker's speed, the party pill of the *Petaluma* Punk.

"Remember when I pissed in the coach's office in exchange for a *Moons over My Hammy*?" Davey reminds me.

"Last week dude. That was last week," I tell him.

"Got detention for that shit. You owe me fries," he says.

"I thought you didn't want no fries," I refute.

"Check it out," Davey points toward the front of the diner. Through the reflection of Davey's *Operation Ivy* pin I spy the glass doors open, but I can't really make out the faces of the three figures that pass through the checkerboard graphic on the pin. I don't lift my head, I'm more dramatic than that. I'm *Matt Dillon*, a *Rumble Fish* as I shift to the side, slide one leg out of the booth, drape my arm over the blue, faux-leather booth, squint my eyes, bite my jaw, and watch the *SRL Laboratories* styled freaks coming in for a table. I don't really know them all that well, but it's Jessica Doheny, Mitch Danefski, and Brad Elbourne, a.k.a. Loosey, Mu'cus, and Mitch the Bitch, and they got a band like everyone else who lives in the surrounding area; their band's called *Knee Shot 3*, and nobody likes their music, but they've replaced *The Morticians* as the staple *Denny's* loner crew, so yeah.

"Loose is lookin' pretty haggard, eh Red?" Davey chimes in.

"Come on," and I turn back to him, "Stop calling me Red."

"Don't be a tight-ass."

•

○   ○

People who don't know Davey generally assume he's just a faggy, angry, hateful, mischievous punk, but mostly he's strictly discouraged. Those other things are merely subplots, subplots that line up, single file, and topple over like dominoes with a birthday wish. Yawn, he's really just another festering countryside punk who's been sold a *Live-and-Let-Us-Yell* sort of anarchism from the *80's*, blended with this *Northern California* live for today, love-love, public service, waxed *Volvo*, happy, hippie, rising yuppie culture. Dare to bring this kind of analysis of public garbage up around Davey and what you'll get is a face full of shit-rants about his older sister Kelsey, who has got this, "get off your rebel ass and stop jerking off," locked in the closet higher-than-thou *Catholic* sort of attitude towards him and his friends which deeply bothers the guy. First, because he's not gay, and second, he really used to like his sister. Loved everything about her that wasn't corrupted by all the newly found churchy shit. Kelsey goes to *St. Vincent's*, the private *Catholic* high school in town. Davey's academic performance is not worthy of that sort of funding, so he goes to *Petaluma Public High* with me. *St. Vincent* isn't all that hardcore, but they do wear uniforms. *Petaluma High* on the other hand is jock central.

"Kelsey's a Cath-Aholic-Cunt," Davey blurts out, as he toys with his mini cup creamer. He uses a safety pin from his leather to punch holes in the top of the aluminum cover, and then he lets the milk dribble out; one micro dot at a time. My scalp still tingles from the *Mini-Thins* as I slide my fingers through my hair to induce even more nervy-tingles, and all the while, my eyes fixate on Davey as he uses one hand to re-poke the safety pin back into his sleeve. He continues, "I

8

got back from hooking up with Annie at eleven, eleven thirty last night and Kelsey the Jesus-bitch is on the couch waiting up for <u>me</u>. Waiting up, Red? What's that shit?"

"I don't know, man? Maybe she loves you," I say, my ears widening, another strange *Mini-Thin* spasm.

"How do you spell that?" Davey snidely asks.

"I-N-C-E-S-T," I spell it out for the dunce.

"Gross. Kelsey won't even touch her own slit when she pees," he eloquently explains, "She's not so perfect. I hear her on the phone, hardening up her guy." —Yank, yank gesture.

"She's still calling Danny her boyfriend?" I ask, push the subject, intentionally try to get Davey all riled up as Mitch gets up from his band's table and struts his way to the john.

"Daniel's a dweeb," Davey says.

"A Sunday Schooler," I push.

"A fucking blue-balled Christ-cock."

"Ha, you think he anals your sista?"

"I think he anals your *Rabbi*," Davey strikes back.

"My *Rabbi's* got a big dick, with no foreskin," but that's all cut short because Mitch's heading back this way, and Davey seems to have some business to attend to. "Hold up, I gotta ask Mitch something," and he hands me the *Half n' Half*, slithers his lanky body out of the booth, and trails Mitch back to his booth, farting.

—I'm still bothered about being called Red.

Three, four weeks ago, I don't remember, I thought it would be cool to dye my hair red, like fire red, super-hot. It was not cool, and they all started calling me Red, even after I died it black again. I thought that was over by now. My revenge? Tonight, I maturely pour out a mini creamer all over the booth where Davey's destined to sit back down. I wait. I wait with the *Mini-Thin* jitters. I have to do something with my hands. There is a loose piece of black electrical tape on my camera's record light. I fidget with that.

Davey, grinning like he got his dick sucked, heads back. I'm gonna film him sit in milk splooge. He's gonna be so pissed. I raise my *Panasonic*, focus it on the booth as Davey slides in, wets his pants, leaps back, bashes his knee under the table, jerks from the shock, whacks his elbow, scoops up his glass of ice water, and flings it directly at my lens. Tilt and Cut as the glass shatters against the cash register behind us. "HEY!" yells the waitress behind the counter. I toss $2.50 on the table and Davey's pushing my ass out the front door, through the parking lot, directly to my *Little Red Civic*, and the waitress bursts from the door howling, "I'm gonna call the police you fuckers of shit of shit heads!" as I fumble with the camera trying to get the car keys out of my pocket. "Shit of shit heads? What does that even mean?" Davey asks.

I get the key in the door, and now the *Denny's* chef has made his way outside as well. *Knee Shot 3* are still inside, pressed up against the window, laughing at us. Davey's suddenly gotta pee, and doing a little peepee dance. I get the car door open, slide in, pop the passenger side, yell, "Get in!" but Davey's turned his back on the car and unzips his pants as the chef rushes towards us.

—*Oh, please don't.*

Davey whips it out, and yup, starts pissing towards the cook. The burley dude backs off, and Davey slides in the car with his dick still dangling out, pulls the safety belt, looks me right in the eye and says, "Were gonna die." I pop the clutch and my *Little Red Civic* hops forward and stalls. Davey's watchin' the cook through the rearview mirror, "Red, he's coming back."

"Why did you piss on him?!" I question in anger.

"Drive, fuck face! GO!" he yells shaking his dong at me. I realize the problem, release the parking break, turn the key, and bounce out at a ripping 20miles per hour. Davey's howling with laughter, "Oh god, so funny." I shift into third, order my friend to, "Put your dick away, man," and continue to *Jew* complain as we pull onto the boulevard, and make our way down death row; a short strip of faux highway lined down the middle with massively thick oak trees, oak trees that have taken many a head-on collisions since *George Lucas* shot *American Graffiti* here forever ago. This small town of ours is just 45 minutes north of *San Fran*, first stop out of *Marin County*, and the first town in *Sonoma County*;

Wine Country, but our town, *Petaluma*, is surrounded by hills so we're exempt from this fine, intoxicating, fruit juice that yuppies enthusiastically call a hobby.

○   •   ○

Ex-Chicken Capital of the World, that's what people historically know about this town, but we're also the proud home of the *Wrist Wrestling Championships*, the *Polly Klass* kidnapping, *Winona Ryder, Elijah Wood*, and the *Phoenix Theater*; *Tom Waits* is rumored to live right outside *'Luma*, and yet we are a humble community, named after it's little hills. That's what *Petaluma* means in *Native American*; little hills.

Near the turn of the Century, late 1800's, we invented the incubator, which soon after, was scooped up by the *East Coast* farmers who in return stole all of *Petaluma's* business, but that was like two million centuries ago and no one raises chickens here anymore. Dairy farms are what scatter the countryside now. Dairy farms and veal.

All of my friends and I seem to be locally obsessed about how white-redneck-settlers ousted the Indians with small pox blankets, and created the bloody soil of our stomping grounds, the darkness that lurks under us as we sleep, and the town museum that displays the inhumanity of our past. To top it all off, there's a new mural that illuminates the history of the *Little Hills*, minus the panel for respiratory failure among the *Native Americans*, and this, this keeps our angst strong and justified. "We've always been cool to your people though, Red," Davey once said amid some teenage group of white hatred jabber to what I simply replied, "You don't have to defend your ghostly pale kind; us *Jews* just go where it's safe." Back in the day a ton of *East Coast Jewish* families migrated to *Sonoma Valley*. They liked how vast it all was and the autonomy away from the big cities, where the farming environment still allowed for intellectual pursuits without jobs supplied by racists. We have a small temple in town and there are like six *Jewish* kids at my school, yet I haven't been to temple since my *Bar Mitzvah*. Every other year my parents get the strange irrational motivation for us to attend the *High Holidays; Rosh Hashanah*, and Starvation

Day aka *Yom Kippur*. *Jack London* spent his last years just a few miles away up in *Glenn Ellen*. "We've staked our claim, but you Davey, your kind, the white man, stole the red man's livelihood, so fuck off, we don't want your poisoned handouts."

"Fuck whitey," is what D retorted.

—Duh?

o   •   o

Davey and I stop at the gas station in the heart of town, just across from *Walnut Park*, and right around the bend from *Foster's Freeze*. Davey is about to get out of the car when he turns to me with those, "I have a shitty life and my parents give all their money to my crazy *Christian* sister, not me," eyes, and simply asks, "Wanna get one last pack of *Thins* before we go home?"

—Shit,
I'm not doing anymore tonight,
we got school tomorrow and
I got swim practice.
Just say no.

So, what do I do? I dig into my pocket and pull out a couple of sweaty bills and hand them to him. I'll spend the next 5 minutes waiting for him to pee and get the trucker's speed. During that time, I will concoct a suitable act of payback for loaning him the 2 bucks to purchase a packet of six asthma pills, and Davey's back with a new pair of purple, rectangular shaped, black rimmed sunglasses, instead of our *Mini-Thins*.

"Dude they got the same glasses for a buck cheaper. Two bucks. We don't want no more pills, night's done, your dollars are better spent on these," he rationalizes as he puts the purple sunglasses back on, "*Thins* only last one night; these'll last me a lifetime."

"Dude that's not why I gave you the money."

"Rules and Regulations make people liars. I told you I

bought the glasses. Don't be a *Republican*."

•

•

•

•

•

•

•

•

•

•
•
•
•

chapter TWO

*L*ung *Butter* opened for *Victim's Family* at the *Phoenix Theater*, and this show is killer until *Ralph Spight* snaps another guitar string. This time he cuts the whole song. *Spight* ain't stressing as the sweat drenches his oversized, dark blue, plain T-shirt. The crowd, a humble three to four hundred post-punk, funk-punk teens, and twenty-somethings, all grind to a halt. Some slip and bite it, bring the pit to a panting, stagnant pause; testosterone nervously pumping through the anxious legs of the youth, who are all well aware we are hyperventilating in the hub of a new music scene at the turn of the decade. You can have *Seattle*, but before *Limp-LipStick* and *Bakersfield's Candy-Korn* totally corrupt anything good about this scene, we are going to have this year; a step before we all gotta go *Raving* instead.

o　　　•　　　o

I'm on the outskirts of the moshpit surrounded by shirtless long-haired hickory-punks, all with bone cut physiques from farm work, and wreak of mud hog perspiration. In the darkness of the *Phoenix*, I have to eject the mega-plastic *VHS* tape from my *Panasonic* and keep a hold on the camera, all the while ripping at the shrink wrap of a fresh cartridge with my chompers; my messenger bag's strap has slid down to my elbow and I hope it's not sitting in spilt soda.

POP— *Spight's* plugged back in, spits, and calls for the audience's attention— feedback —while I'm still not filming. It's a rambled sort of message as *Spight* suggests another ditty entitled *Sinatra's Mantra*, and I have about three seconds to get that tape in the cradle. I'm balancing the *Panasonic* on my knee, perched like an ostrich, propped up against some girl, who's obviously trippin' her tits off. I toss the cardboard sleeve onto the sticky hardwood floor, slide the tape into the carriage, blink, and the crowd, in unison, cheers for *Victims Family*, and the girl asks, "You got fifty cents?"

—What the fuck?

From the corner of my eye I can see, in absolute slow motion, *Spight* signal to the drummer, *Devon VrMeer*, and not only do I have to put the finished tape in my bag and turn the camera to record mode still, I still have to find some new footing because I'm being shifted by the moving crowd right into the heart of the mob. The song has begun and I can't see shit. I'm too short, so I lift the camera over my head, shoot aimlessly at the band as they play the one song I've had on loop on my record player for the past week after Davey and I found the 7inch at the *Music Coop, Petaluma's* only indie-record store. I haven't seen Davey all week? He likes *Victims Family* enough— it's *Alternative Tentacles* approved.

—Where is he?

I stop myself from caring about my pal as soon as I'm pushed by some douche-bag sporting a mullet in a *Forty-Niners* jersey, "Film fag," he calls me as he gives me a direct shove into oncoming traffic of the pit.

—Okay, now there's jocks at our shows, too?

The spiraling pit has got me by the balls, a constant flow of muscle, bone, molten skin; I figure the only way out is to start filming, hope they all want to be on camera, do their silly little punky-funk dance moves, slow down, make space, let the guy with the camera out alive— BAM —a knee whacks my lens which shoves the eye piece into my socket. I swish around, cover my eye, use my good eye to see, and there's my gal pal Cindy making a hole in the human wall for me to slide through, past the crowd, and up the carpeted aisle. My eye's sore as hell, *Victims Family* is still playing and I'm missing this whole song.

○　　　　●　　　　○

Upstairs— The *Phoenix Theater's* boys' bathroom is my next stop. Check out my eye, maybe take a leak? The walls are head to toe filled with paint pen tags that have been overwritten by paint pen tags times a hundred. Thirteen-year-old Stephan and his Junior High sidekick Jax-a-million, a rich kid who gets Fs, are trying to decipher how much of the oddly shaped tab of *LSD* they should take. "They dab the juice on with a needle, right? Like a micro-dot in diameter. So, what's it matter how big the thing is?" Jax tries to calculate. I figure this kid has no idea what he's talking about, but neither do I; I'm pretty much *straight-edge*.

Stephan, using his grubby fingernail, gently flips the octagon tab over in his palm, squints his eyes, x-ray vision, he's *Superman,* except he isn't. Jax just wants to see Stephan's *Mr. Bungle OU818* shirt animate out on acid, wants to see the swirling psychedelic, melting monsters, jerk off, and splooge into each other's mouths.

"What if there's more than one dot on here?" is all Stephen can conjure 'til he looks up at Jax, and just says, "We'll just split it."

Jax-a-million picks up the tab with his equally grubby fingernails, raises the micro-paper to his teeth, parts his lips, reveals his pre-pubescent tobacco stained teeth, uses his front teeth to rip the tab in half, catches his piece on the tip of his tongue and hands the other half to Stephan. For amateurs that was some serious footwork.

"Dude, you can't man-handle the shit," Stephan's disappointed, thinks all the touching and tearing will rub all the chemistry off. "Sorry?" Jax feels, kinda bad? Stephan takes the half tab, "Well it's your fault if your skull explodes," and down the hatch goes Stephan's part. These idiots don't even realize I'm there filming their whole discussion in the door-less stall.

The two children nonchalantly strut out of the toilet. "What up?" Jax says in passing. I've lowered my camera, I got two to three years on these kids; I'm their elder. I haven't tried acid yet, but if I'm gonna punch myself full of something, acid's the one experience that appeals to me. I just wasn't gonna do that shit when I was raw young like those nits. My friends have always tried to get me to go south on my straight-edge lifestyle. It's not like I'm not philosophical about it, just hesitant I guess. Besides, they usually don't have a good sales pitch, save for the acid.

Munts- "Weed makes you dumb-hungry and funny."

Davey- "Cocaine? Makes you an asshole. Speed's alright in fractions, too much and poof, ya turn into a thief."

Tenderloin- "I drank way too much, but I'm not gonna puke..." and then he puked; on my shoes.

Cindy- "Acid's like running down a black light world with neon hallways, molten visions, riding kaleidoscopic camels."

I will try Acid.

•

"Don't do drugs," I lecture Stephan & Jax as they leave.

•
○   ○

My eye still pulses from the knee jab in the wonder pit of sweat metal. I followed these kids out of the bathroom and now I'm looking over the railing, downstairs. I don't think Cindy's in the lobby anymore. I figure that's okay cause Cindy's not really all that sexy, but it's nice having a girl around to keep your boyish juices boiling until you have someone you can call your own; but again, she's not hot. Not to me at least. We've never hooked up. No plans. *Victims Family* is still raging and as bad as I want to ditch my *Panasonic* in the theater office, I'm pretty sure it'll get swiped, so I consider running it home since I'm the guy who actually lives a few blocks from this place; last corner of downtown. I'm taking the stairs down thinking on it. Stairwell's clear tonight, rare.

○   •   ○

Davey's waving at me from outside the *Phoenix*. I can barely see him through a sliver of the glass doors that are covered in photocopied concert posters. He's smoking a menthol, wearing some new black stocking cap and, as always, his leather jacket. I know why he's outside; basically, he has no money and even though *Tom Gaffey*, the theatre manager, would let him in anytime, because Tom's cool like that and looks out for the eighteen hundred *Phoenix Orphans*, Davey only asks when Davey asks, and tonight Davey did not ask; I guess? Better see what he wants although I already know how this is going to go.

—I'm going to ask him—
"Why you cutting school all week when you got detention,"
and he's gonna be all nonchalant and uninterested as he explains,
"I go to detention, I just don't go to class."

—And I expect this because Davey's been doing this shit since 7th grade and even though he thinks he's got it all figured out he's just *"Too Far Gone"* to realize that everyone knows Davey's deal by now. That the faculty just doesn't care about him, that *Petaluma High* hasn't hired any *James Olmos* types to get the fuck-ups to *Stand and Deliver*.

And my future wife will roll over in bed
and ask me,
"T.V. lied to us, didn't it?"

Absolutely.

○　　　•　　　○

I'm exiting through the *Phoenix* doors covered in those fliers, *Skankin Pickle, Hoodlum Empire, The Conspiracy*, Friday January 28th' —I'll go to that. Davey's already walked away towards the three-story car lot just adjacent to *Thriftys* and I'm wishing *Petaluma* didn't close at 8pm so I could get a scoop of choco-ice-cream at *Swensens*, the *Phoenix's* #1 neighbor, or at the least a *Milky Way* from *Thriftys*. Davey sees me cross the street, "What up?" he barely projects as he nervously pulls out another smoke. Some thirty-something dreadlocked-deadhead is stepping up to him with a waft of patchouli oil, asking, "Can I bum a smoke?"

"Fuck off hippy!" Davey bitches, steps away and grabs me by the arm, leading me toward my *Little Red Civic* parked on the first floor of the lot. He says nothing, so I ask, "Where you been all week?" D rolls his eyes, flicks ash onto my car's hood and obnoxiously complains, "Too many questions. People are right 'bout you, Tye. Smoke a little weed and maybe you wouldn't be so talky-talky."

"What do you want?" I ask, but his eyes say, "Don't judge me," and defensively actually says, "I don't need a lift, I don't need money, I just want to hang, cool?"

"Tom always let you in for free, dude?"

"I didn't say I wanted to go inside. I said I wanted to hangout," and offers me his cigarette that he knows I won't smoke.

"Dude?"

"Whatever, ya never know? Hey, you see Cindy in there?" he asks as he leans his boney thin body along the driver's door, "She still going with Jonathan? Is the show almost over? Do you have a penis? What time is it?"

I'm not listening to him; I'm opening the trunk, ditching my camera. "Really, what time is it?" Davey asks. I make my way to the driver's side, pop open the door, key the power, and the blue digital clock flashes 00:02, "Twelve," I yell and he asks again, "Why do you drive here if you live like 30 seconds away?"

"So, we can go to *Dennys* afterward," the obvious answer.

"What a *Saint*. Is Cindy in there?"

"Yeah, she's in there, man. What's the deal? What's the sudden interest in Cindy?" I ask.

Davey zones out looking through the open wall of the lot across the street at a clique of seven to ten dirt-punk-hippies passing around a blunt that some miscellaneous hip-hopper rolled. "Nah, I'm from the *East Bay, Oak-town*," the random black guy tells some hippie chick who's never seen a black man in person before, "I'm here 'cause my cuz's getting married next week so I'm up to support, share the love, see the countryside." Her innocent mind wants to know all about his plight and wonders if it's true what they say about black guys, which she suddenly regrets because that's a stereotype and the junior high schools are pounding the kids with seminars and musical teen squads about the inaccuracies of stereotypes and racism and I'm just waiting on some sort of human response from Davey. He twitches.

•

o   o

We end up at *Lyons* around 1AM. Davey doesn't like *Lyons*, calls it the sub-par *Dennys*, but in fact it is a whole shit tier up from *Dennys*. Besides, we've been banned from *Dennys* now. D's waiting in the aisle as our cohort files into the booth. D prefers the end seat, and I'm squished into the center with Cindy sifting through her tote bag to my right and Erin Sonwik, a drama club member who wants a sex scene with *Dennis Hopper* before he croaks. She's a brunette semi length, brown lipstick, big blue eyes, B-cup on a tiny 4'11" physique and even I tower her in the booth. To Cindy's immediate right is my other super buddy Munts. He's all bitter because somehow, he got seated next to the un-sexy Cindy and now he's going to have to talk across the table to get anywhere with Erin, the actress, so instead of being social he pulls out a small black leather-bound sketchbook and pen, to start doodling something. I'm not paying attention because Munts is always sketching something and Davey's still not sitting down as he eyeballs the *Lyons'* crowd that has gathered after the show. Davey spots Trish my first ex sitting with some dude who keeps stroking his elongated un-groomed vagina monkey on his chin. "There's Trish," he says. "Fuck Trish," I respond. "You didn't," Munts jokes. "Yeah, yeah," and Eric Conway's entertaining Henley, Karen the Creamer, Charles the Stick, & some dude I don't know with jokes about the boobalicious waitress who's going on sixty-five, sick and tired of childish beasty boys offering up extra bucks to see her tits. Then there's Jimmy-the-Germ and his *sick-punks* brooding in a back booth debating whether they leave or stay and when Boobalicious asks if they are going to order anything, they all just grimace as the Germ licks his 6inch switchblade and spits on the table. She doesn't have time for this and moves along to the next table of rotten youths who'll tip her a penny on the dollar if anything, other than unscrew upside-down, salt shakers & sugar dispensers. Boobilicious takes down an order for the next table, "Fries, plate of eggs, scrambled not soggy, slice of cherry pie, coffee all around, oh, and water."

No one seems to interest Davey here, but then again, I'm not really sure who he might be looking for, or even what's on his mind tonight; obviously something's stirring in that nervous brain of his. He finally slops backwards into the booth, slides off his purple sunglasses, and then puts them right back on. Cindy asks, "Whatcha hiding from, Davey-dukes?" Without acknowledging anyone else at the table, Davey leans into Cindy's ear and whispers, "Could you spot me a cup of coffee?" Cindy, unsure why he's whispering about it, "No problem, dude, coffee's like fifty cents." I'm trying to scoot my butt around hoping to get both Erin and Cindy to give me a little room as Munts rips his drawing out of the sketchbook and slides it over to his crush. D's waving over Boobalicious and I try to see what Munts has drawn, as it passes me by into Erin's hands. She gets all dramatic, coveting the illustration, throwing the back of her hand to her brow as if she'll faint and turns away from the art, "Oh how can I look upon such of gift? How can I cherish such an outpouring of emotion and self-expression?" performs the terrible actress.

"Can it, *Baby Jane*. What's the drawing of?" I ask. Erin gently lays the sheet back down onto the table and covers it with her hands, slowly parting them to reveal a donkey with a warhead penis, with a *Grateful Dead* gummy bear sticking out of its ass and taking hits off a bong. All the while, space aliens destroy a high school in the background with a caption that reads, "All's well that ends well."

—Shit, he drew that fast.

Erin gives Munts a shit eating grin as Cindy slides the drawing to her side to get a better look, and Davey's sitting right there in the booth, his back to us as he continues to try and get Boobilicious' attention. Even behind those purple glasses where Davey's two blue eyes stare into the modern diner filled with peers, it is as if Davey's not really here and we'd all be pretty worried 'bout it, if we gave a fuck, but Davey's not asking us for sympathy for his devils, so we continue to be our jolly-dumb-selves talking *Smurf* logic, and other wasteful brain poop that we'll reflect upon as seniors looking back at the Junior year calling today the good old times, but not really, and yet, "I prefer *Max Headroom* to *Robotech*," spurts Munts. "What's a *Robotech*?" asks Erin.

o   •   o

After *Lyons* I carpool everybody home, a habit my friends have adopted, and a *mitzvah* that my father despises. I always do my best to get them to understand they have to stop bumming rides from me, that they should all get their own cars, but then again, it's kinda like they're all just too fuckin' lazy, or at least uninterested in even getting a driver's license. This is what I'm dealing with here. This is what my Dad's dealing with internally and externally, and projecting into my face every weekend.

Davey's been pretty much mute this whole night. He's in the passenger seat just watching the shadows of the night pass by as we wind around the country roads lined with dark oak trees, giant eucalyptus, and farms, all the way out to Cindy's house in the deep countryside of *Bodega Ave*, about ten to fifteen minutes out of town. The girls have been chatting up something about the difference between shaving your legs and waxing. "*Hollywood*, or Hippie-ville?" but I can barely make out this talk about the hygienic needs of teenage girls over the bootlegged audio cassette of *The Dwarves*, which according to Davey is still the best selection I have in my car, but D-man's never really looked through all my tapes. Typical Davey research entails skimming his finger across the three rows of my tape cassette briefcase— clack-clack-clack-clack-clack-clack —*Bungle, Violent Femmes, Alice Donut, Residents Live, Naked City* (which he despises), *Cat Stevens*, two mixed tapes, the *Butthole Surfers—Self-Titled & Locust Abortion Technician*, more *Alice Donut, DK, Blatz, Circle Jerks, Tom Waits, Nomeansno, English Beat, Operation Ivy, Fugazi, Crispin Glover* songs (which he threatened to run over with my very own car), *Cheech and Chong* outtakes and the embarrassing shameful *I Touch Myself* from the *Divinyls*, because when I was fourteen I thought it was funny, but Davey never bothers to read them and/or comment on the few fine pieces of punk rock I do have, it's just *The Dwarves*, and I swear it's because there are naked, bloody chicks on the cover— "HERE!" Cindy cries out from the back, pulling on my seat, which jams my seatbelt, constricts against my chest, "TURN!" she yells again. I'm seatbelt trapped, unsafe, tied up, frantically jerking my torso back and forth to get the belt to release, and *The Dwarves* are blaring at full volume, and I'm trying to cut the turn at forty miles an hour on the black night country road, choking on the muther-fuckin' seat-belt, and I finally get the car to turn, and think I'm good so I try to jerk forward and back again to get the seatbelt to release, but my foot slides off the gas, and I'm not jammin' down on the clutch and the fucking car stalls, buckles into a spin slide and we nearly grazing the street sign, stopped cold sideways in the middle of the road, and Davey finally starts laughing like a human being again.

Outside Cindy's single story, five bedroom, mild green paneled, flat roofed house, and standing in the front walkway lined with sleeping *California Poppies* illuminated by the low level garden lights, is Davey and Cindy, friendship distance apart, nothing sexy going on, and if we could actually see their faces we'd notice the conversation is pretty heavy, borderline personal, maybe even tragic, but we can't see their faces and it's probably none of our business so

Erin, Munts, and I start coming up with a new late night *Cable Access* talk show idea— "People can call in. Davey'll be a side kick to some *Redneck Nazi* Host who cuts down all the guests; even paraplegics with elephantiasis," but I'm *Jew* sensitive to the *Nazi* thing so I suggest a straight up Redneck Hairy Hen from the truck depot, but Munts says, "No *Nazi*, No Rednecks," Erin interrupts, suggests, "Meatball Jones the overweight gas boy."

Davey's buddy punchin' Cindy on the shoulder, but Cindy goes in for the big hug. Even in the dark you can feel the chilling cold that is fogging off Davey's soul as Cindy's arms wrap around his twiggy little mini-thin of a body, pulling him tight, cradling his neck as her body feeds him warmth and love, friendship, and common support against the cold worn leather skin that drapes the brittle bones of Davey Collins. The stars are bright, but Davey's still wearing his purple shades.

•

○   ○

D reaches over and switches off my headlights as we approach his country home in the middle of a strip of closely built, low-income, family homes, white-boarded, muddied, and fenced in. Davey's house is the one with the three pine trees in the front yard. The bushes along the fence are so overgrown and dead that you know possum families have been nesting in there for generations. I'm always forced to stop the car before I roll up on his house. He never wants his parents to know when he gets home. "Yea, what up?" I say. Davey finally removes the purple sunglasses and in the dark of my *Little Red Civic* hatchback, he looks right into my soul and says, "I want to kill everyone in the world," and we both burst into hysterics because this is 1991, and people aren't blowing away their classmates around the clock quite yet, this is the safe-*America*. I stop laughing first, catch my breath, roll down the window a half crank at a time, and Davey's calmed down, slipping his shades back on, and drapes an arm over my seat. "Hey, did you guys hear what me and Cindy were talkin' about?" he casually inquires, which I figure is the real reason for the intimate pause.

"Nah man, we were coming up with some lame talk show—" Davey cuts me off, "I want to tell you, man. You were one of my first real friends. I mean I respect you," Davey's still got more to say, "Outta anyone in this shitty town I really respect you, man. I like that you don't do drugs, take all the college-prep classes, that swim team stuff's gay, but it's alright, at least not fag-fuck-football, and you like, <u>like</u> your parents and shit, and yet still grew up kinda cool."

"Uh, thanks?"

"Don't get a swell head, I'll take some of the credit for that," he clarifies.

> —*You've gone off the deep end buddy.*
> *What are you getting at?*

"It's cool, T. You got a cool life, yer lucky," he concludes, but that gives me nothing; why tell me this, what's the agenda. Davey continues, "I don't want to bring you down anymore. I don't want to bum rides or money, I don't want to influence you anymore, man. I'm an asshole and if we're close, like because we know each other forever, then, like I'm going to take advantage of that, and you'll do it 'cause you're a good person, *Speedo*. And I just can't do that shit to you."

> —*Really? You just called me Speedo?*
> *Jocks call me Speedo.*
> *Not funny, not now at least.*
> *Lame.*

"Don't be a dick Daaaave. Who the fuck do you think I am? What makes you think you <u>influence</u> me?" I snap, slam my fist into the roof of my car; *Tyler Tantrums*, I have a few.

"Chill, bro—" he says. I'm almost panting pissed as Davey continues, "I'm the one that just fucks everything up."

"What are you talking about, dude? Where were you all week?" the tantrum has dissipated as quick as it had risen.

"Look, dude, I'm done. I'm gonna take the *GED* then do something else. I guess thanks for always being cool to me?"

Davey gets out, closes the door, doesn't look back at me— in his mind he will never look back —and I flash on my headlights and he flips me the bird, and I drive back to town wondering what the fuck he was talking about, and *how many trees I can run into before my car won't drive anymore; Horrible Thoughts.* I gotta talk to Cindy after homeroom Monday. Ask her about what she said to him. And I haven't actually pulled away yet, I'm still watching Davey walk home, and I'm sure he's bound to not show up at school again, and I'm fucking sixteen years old and all the movies are already seeming to come true— all of them, even *Alien.* My future wife was wrong, but then again, this isn't the future, yet.

-

-

-

-

-

-

-

-

-

-

-

-
-
-
-
-
-

chapter THREE

*S*unday. I think I wake up on my own, but it's Mom that has woken me from my slumber, without warning, no intro, just a bombastic request for information from behind my door, "Do you want to get bagels from *Arham's* with us? Are you awake yet?"

—Are you kidding me?
This is my only day to sleep in.
What time is it?

The clock reads 7:46am, crazy, I pull the comforter over my head, but Mom's not done yapping, "Okay Tyler, but don't sleep your life away. Bye!" She sounds disappointed. Guilt trip. Mom gets touchy when her only son doesn't want to play house. I'm usually there for her. At least I can jerk off in the shower while they're eatin' faux *New York Jew* bagels in cow town *Cali*.

Shower, sourdough toast, feed the dog, call Davey, don't call Davey, today's a Tyler day. I'm at the privately owned *Kozey's* Video Store. *Blockbuster's* all the way across town, suburbs, eastside. I'm westside— Cross the tracks from the track-homes and white trash hillbillies living in the not-so-city. The Westside is populated with *Victorian Hertitage* homes and actual hillbillies. I rent three movies: *Hellraiser 2:*

Hellbound, Quadrophenia, and *Pump Up the Volume.* The VHS
tapes make that clackity, clack sound in the plastic bag
wrapped around my wrist all the way back through the
Heritage Home district. These streets are lined in oak,
redwoods, some pine, with collections of other tree stuff.
The sidewalks burst and crack from their roots, and
everybody has a lawn. I'm closing in on the town blocks
again as I pass the *Old Historic Library,* the *Comic Book Box,*
even a *Christmas Store* that would have you think it snows
here. It doesn't snow. It gets to 48F in the winter mornings,
frosts all the car windows, causes hypothermia in your toes,
but snow it does not. I'll walk front side of the King's castle,
the giant *St. Vincent's Catholic Church,* with a bell loud
enough to be heard countryside. I'm almost home, hope the
folks went to buy some plant life for the garden or such so
I'm alone. Today I prefer a Tyler day.

   I dub *Hellraiser* and *Pump Up the Volume* and wait to
watch *Quadrophenia* with Pops. I call the Davey. D-man's not
around, "When's he getting back?" I ask. Kelsey, bitchy as
usual, responds over the receiver, "Never. Call back."

   "When?" I squeeze in there.

   "Tyler, I'm not in the mood. Later," and she hangs up.
I call Munts.

   "What's up?" Munts answers.

   "Munts, it's Tyler."

   "Yup, what's up?"

   "You stoned?" I ask.

   "I'm at home dude," he responds, monotone.

   "What are you doing?" I have nothing to say.

   "Drawing."

   "Tyler we're home!" I hear Mom yell from the side
entrance. I turn from the kitchen window too nothing but a
bushy tree my Father carries, pushing his way past Mom,
and intentionally whacks me with it. "Bring that through the
back! Why do you have to— Ow that hurt." Now he's
stepped on Mom's toe, "Munts, I gotta go."

   "Later," Munts says.

   "Late," I hang up. "Dad, give me that; Why you always
gotta do that to Mom?" I try to take the tree from him, but
he's persistent and won't let go, thrashes it back toward

himself.

"She's always in the way," he says as he heads for the sliding glass door to the yard.

"Hear the way he talks about me?" Mom complains as she hands me a tray of marigolds, "They're your favorite," she says as she turns back to the door to get her purse. Mom says things like they're thoughts in the wind, you can almost miss the last few words. Smoke rings in the air. By the time they get to you they are so thin and transparent. Davey always jokes with her, pretends he hears her.

•
o   o

I check the time on the *VCR*, 7:32pm, we've eaten dinner, Dad was all about this month's swim meets, always doing his best to remind me that I'm not a deadbeat artist, that I'm a dedicated sportsman. Yeah, dedicated to not being yelled at by him for being a loser with no future. How swimming and my future connect, I have no idea, but to him it goes hand in hand. *So be it*. Maybe I'll start my own pirate radio station, call it, *Today with Tyler's Fuck Ups*, and make up stories about pimping on the streets of *Petaluma*. Probably won't.

I like looking at the time. I look at the time all the time. No, that's not true, I don't do it because I like it and I'm not watching it pass. No. I'm thinking about what's coming next. What do I have to do next? What's on the list? How do I get out of here? Get out of *Dodge*.

I watch the *Disney Hour* and rub boogers into oblivion under the couch as Dad helps Mom clean the dishes, then he's ready for *Quadrophenia*, but gets up halfway through. Mom's made a stink about some missing receipts for the quarter, and Dad's gotta go find 'em, and I'm an only child, and *Sting* reminds me of Davey, but he really isn't like him, just looks like him. Davey's the *Quadra* kid, slipping through time, looking for heroes, but that was yesterday; today I wonder— *who do I relate too? Who am I in the story?*

-
-
-
-
-
-
-
-
-
-
-
-
-
-
-

chapter FOUR

—a *day* *in* *the* *life* *of* *me.*

5am— Dad pulls the comforter off of me, "Time to get up!" School's a six-block walk, but Dad always drives me to morning swim practice.

5:30am— Swim practice. Fuckin' cold. You're outta the lockers covered in a *Speedo* and straight into the pool, trying to avoid the 52 degree air, opting for the 78 degree heat of the steaming pool. Toes frozen from the puddles that nearly freeze on the deck, and you're doing laps to stay warm.

6:30am— I've set my schedule up tight; I always book an early photography class. I like it, partially my art, and it gets me outta the pool 35 minutes early. I am the envy of my teammates.

7am— Chow down a *Hostess* chocolate pie, stop at a water fountain, run the water, one-one-thousand, two-one-thousand, three-one-thousand— no mono fo' me —lower my head, sip— SPLASH —my face is suddenly wet and I'm quick enough to stop myself from being impaled by the metal faucet. Some fuck-ball has shoved me and I see him when I turn around. Wandlebrant is walking off in his purple and white *Trojan Varsity* jacket— football patch, baseball patch, butt plug patch —he's hollering 'bout me to his ape-torage, "MV-Penis pees in his *Speedos*. Woof, Woof."

7:05am— At my locker, get my photography book.

7:07am— Always have to pass by the sports display case, a glass shrine to no real accomplishment, no future *NFL* players, no *Major Leaguers*, just a few homecoming wins, a quick tour to state for the girls' volleyball, and a picture of me in my *Speedos* with a plaque that reads *Petaluma's Youngest MVP Varsity Athlete*. This is what I have to live with. This is my father's curse.

7:09am— I slide into class just in the nick of time. Most of us know each other from the scene. The girls like to shoot in the cemetery. I like to shoot in the alleys and dead chicken coops. Nobody talks to each other this early in the morning. Nana walks by me, "I swear it's a conspiracy making the smart kids wake up this early. They want to stunt our balls." Same shit every morning with her, but she still comes to class, she's a senior, she's taken photography since freshman year to get away from her Mom in the morning. Nana's Mom gets home from work at like 6:30am and is loud as fuck when she cooks her breakfast/dinner, yaps on the phone with her co-workers, and makes her Dad bang her before going to bed. They all work nights on the docks in *Richmond*, so sleep is always interrupted an hour too early for little old Nana and she rather zombie into school early than wake up to hell. Ask her, she'll lay it all out for you. I think she has a manuscript about it all.

7:10am— Bell rings, we all settle in. 15 minute lecture about depth of field.

7:25am— We're outside by the rubber track, snapping photos of the early PE class.

7:30am— We're in the dark room to develop our rolls of film in their round handheld carousels.

7:50am— Bell rings and we have 21 minutes until everybody else's school day actually begins.

8:00am— I'm in the parking lot with Munts. Something super normal about today, but I can't put my finger on why or what makes it all feel so bland. We watch everyone come to school.

8:05am— Munts asks, "Dude, lunch?" I reply, "Why not?" We part.

8:08am— I'm early for homeroom. Why am I early for homeroom? One more class until I can prod Cindy 'bout what hemorrhoidal bug that's crawled up Davey's ass this weekend.

8:11am— Bell. We settle, the homeroom schedule is barked over the loud speaker. The Vice Principal announces some winter dance, another lie about social tolerance, a short list of new programs for spring term, house cleaning, baby making, and *Lego* construction; I'm obviously not paying attention to him in the least. I know he's reading this shit from some *post-Regan California State* playbook and could care less about how bad the jocks beat down on the other team last Friday. At least the country voted those fuckers out of office this year.

8:21am— Biology starts. Today we mutilate a frog. I'm partnered with Karen. Karen's the heavy one on the cheerleading squad, long brown hair, plump face, very cute. She hasn't truly realized her sexy as of yet. The boys won't touch her, maybe rape her before schools out, but touch, hell no. They tip cows for cum squirts, not screw 'em. Karen's genuine enough, cheerleading's just a preoccupation with body image. She's cool enough all the same, she don't judge. I really barely know her, she acts like we've been close for years. Inclusive, that's what she is.

9:02am— Bell!! The halls flood with us. I'm straight for

American History with a teacher who is an A1 prick-asshole. He's the Football Coach, junior varsity, raised the tight ends to be what they are today. I'd prefer to gag on my own athlete's foot than go to this class, and that is why I cannot be— MOVE PEOPLE! —late.

9:04am— Coach isn't even here yet. Shit, Cindy's late. I'm too early, suspicious. Maybe I'll just read. People are coming in, lots of, "Hey's" & "What's going on's?" Replies like, "Hey," & "Nuthin," or "You remember what chapter we're doing this week? We skipped a few, right?" Out of the corner of my eye I see Coach Menson step in and Cindy follows. Great, she doesn't even look at me. I gotta catch her after class. The Coach is a big guy, lanky but built, with his forty-eight-year-old beer gut that hangs low. He picks up the book from his desk.

9:06am— Bell rings "Chapter Nine," he garbles, and flips through the pages of his book. In unison, we all pull out our textbooks. The thud of heavy paper and hardcovers hitting the wooden desks is much like the start of a hardcore show, but it's just shitty History class. Some people flip page by page to chapter nine, others scoop a guesstimated wad and flop them over. Another thump accompanied by a whoosh of air as the pages slide into place. Words on a page make no sound at all. "Let's skip 9," Menson instructs, "Everybody knows about that stuff, and we'll start at the Civil War." I look down and as I flip through chapter nine, images of black slaves chained and hoisted onto boats, along with paragraphs filled with words such as, "unclean, illiterate, rape, money, hate, death, alien, niggers," pass on by.

> —*This racist football ass-fuck has us skipping slavery?*
> *I hope Mr. Menson gets caught*
> *screwing some cheerleader,*
> *gets fired, goes to jail.*

"Who wants to start reading?" Menson comes back into focus. I see him scan the room for a target. Menson's tiny eyes lock onto my forehead, just above my strong brown.

This guy never looks me in the eye, and yet so eloquently says, "*MVP*, page 105 *President Lincoln*."

—Suck a football, shit-fuck.

9:43am— One minute 'til break, one minute until I grab Cindy by the arm and ask, "Davey? What up?" but she's already got her bag on her desk, she's packed up, she's gonna make a b-line for the door, I can see it in her eye, her face directly nose to nose with the doorknob, her eyes watching Menson, her ears perked, watching, listening, waiting for the bell, ready to dart...9:43.50...9, 8...

9:44am— Bell tolls. The class rises like fire, I'm already pushing down the aisle, I can't see Cindy, can't catch her, she's fucking gone, I'm fucked, who cares— 15 minute snack break —she's not even in the hall by the time I'm outta class; girl moves fast, fuck it, later. I meet up with Munts at the snack bar line. He gets a *Twix*, potato chips, and decides against the *Skittles*, he's only got, "Sixty five, Seventy, oh, uh, ninety five...I got some pennies," he pours the change from his palm onto the counter and digs into his pocket for the copper. "Let me get a Chocolate Pie," I say to the clerk as Munts figures out his financial portfolio. I drop three quarters in her hand, she says, "A dollar during school hours." I'm stunned; this is why I don't buy shit at snack break. "You're a slave to the system lady," I hand her another twenty-five cents, all nickels. Munts is still three cents short, but she takes the pennies and waves him off. We eat at the side of the snack shack. "I'm so fucking horny," says Munts. Bell tolls.

9:59am— Espanol, which I suck at.

10:39am— Bell Tolls, "Hasta la vista, baby."

10:48am— AP English, finally a break, a sanctuary in the educational system, and yet today it's a substitute, no Mr. Lovette, and I bet this bitch's going to want to try to teach us something today. Lame.

11:38am— Lunch. Munts meets me in the parking lot, his stomach is set on going off campus for *Donuts and Chinese*. Two blocks away from school is two worlds away from school. An oasis of freedom to fools like us. The white noise tends to disseminate along the *Victorian* homes leading to the grocery store with the neighboring *Chinese Food and Donuts* place; the grocery store banned kids years ago. The Donut shop's empty today. We take it to go, chow mien and a chocolate bar. Munts gets a cream pie.

1:00pm— Algeblah. Zero to the A and I don't know.

1:45pm— I'm out as early as I'm in, I don't have to take PE, the perk of being a *MVP*.

1:57pm— I'm home, Mom's at the bank, Dad's at work in the city. I watch the tail end of *Tiny Toons*, jerk off to *Crimpshrine* with *Baywatch* on the screen— read some *Frankenstein*.

3:50pm— I'm back at school, boys' locker room, and prepping for swim practice. Pauly with his blonde flat-topped out, who used to have *Thor* locks, gives me another copy of *Metallica's Master of Puppets*. Pauly's been feeding me music since I was six. He started with *Van Halen*, but I was an easy ear, so he moved me up to the hard stuff loaning me *Iron Maiden's Killers* on record, before tapes. "Thanks, I lost mine," I say, and he's all guru like saying, "Stop listening to *Jane's Addiction*, jocks stole that pansy shit and they don't even know the rest of the album…doesn't matter. Hey you're still not listening to *Nirv*…" Pauly spits into the floor drain allowing me a moment to clear the air before he completes his embarrassing question, "No, no *Nirvana*."

4:00pm— I don't want to jump in the pool; so I drop in, the water's brisk, the water's always brisk, my balls cower inside my belly, I push off, a few butterfly kicks, and rise to the surface throwing my arms into a stroke, circulating my blood, the only way to forget the freezing aqua shock. There's the wall and I'm doing flip-turns after flip-turns and my mind races with stories and characters and I find myself frustrated that I'm in a pool and can't get these ideas out of my mind and those *Horrible Thoughts— A chlorine malfunction, too much of it, turned poison, melts all of our lungs, green puss and phlegm fills the pool, our guts dribble out of our assholes, the coach commits suicide at the sight, and the school is shut down; permanently—* Flip-turn, the girl swimmers, in full piece suits, come off as A-sexuals— flip-turn —I totally didn't get to talk to Cindy today, I have to pee, Coach hates when we hop out to pee. Here comes Scotty on the left, I should pee as he cruises by. He's gonna whip my ass if I do that, oh shit I did it, I knew I should have stopped thinking about it. Coach's fault, makes us feel guilty. When this set is over Scotty is sure to pants me in retaliation? Shit he looked at me that time. He tasted it. I'm a dead man.

4:15pm— Warm ups over. I nervously await the Scott attack, what lane is he in now? Where the fuck is he? Amy's on the wall beside me, she taps my shoulder, I turn, I'm a dead man, I can feel my dick against the water and I can feel the sudden loss in the appendage's gravity, and I see rising to the surface, my *Speedo.* Scotty pops up in the lane beside me, laughing. I grab the suit and submerge. Lesson of the day, don't pee in the pool on your pal.

6:00pm— Weight lifting. Three sets of ten, all around the weight machine. Lats, Triceps, Legs, Thighs & Calves, Chest, then the pegboard —Up, over, down, over again— two more times, drop, no shower, go the fuck home.

6:20pm— I'm freezing, shivers from the chill, Mom's baking some chicken, the heater blows hot air into the living room, I roast up against the gust of heat, recall my assignments for the night; algebra, history essay, the thesis statement, *Max Headroom,* couple chapters of *Frankenstein,* call my girlfriend— that I don't have.

6:36pm— In my room reading a *Zap Comic, Issue #3,* Munts had loaned it to me a couple weeks ago. Probably forgot. Mine now.

6:78pm— Maybe if I was loaded.

7:15pm— Algebra sucks so bad.

7:16pm— *Black flag*? *Jane's Addiction, Steel Pole Bathtub*? *Apocalypse Now* on VHS? *Violent Femmes*? Gotta listen to something. Silence is deafening. If I had a sibling, maybe I wouldn't need sounds on all the time.

7:25pm— I'm try to re-spool my dubbed *Lookout Records Compilation* cassette with a ballpoint pen, but it keeps slipping around. The pen can't grip the teeth of the cassette. I need a pencil to do this.

7:32pm— I'm back to Algebra problems. Turn on *MTV* very low, *Kurt Loader* talking about *Vanilla Ice*, talking on how *George Michael* might make a special appearance with *Aerosmith* on the *MTV Video Awards* and I so want to puke, and I'm solving the problems with great focus thanks to the murmur of the TV, hypnotizing me, reminding me I am still alive. The silence can get eerie for me, I don't want to forget that I'm still alive; TV fixes that fear. TV creates a flow of sound and moving images that keep me thinking I am actually alive.

8:00pm— Dinner. "Mr. Menson's a Racist," I inform the folks. "He's the football coach? Worse than cops," Dad says. Dad hates cops. Calls them, "Assholes who grew up to be Legitimate Assholes, with a badge that says they're assholes; assholes."

9:00pm— *Max Headroom*

10:00pm— Ugh, History thesis. I'll do it on "Black slavery then and now." Suck on that, dick.

10:30pm— *Frankenstein*, for fun. Love this book.

11:00pm— Sleep, no morning practice on Tuesdays and

Thursdays until spring and this means I get an extra hour of dreamtime.

MINI THINS

-

-

-

-

-

-

-

-

-

-

-
-
-
-
-
-
-

chapter FIVE

$e$verybody's meetin' at *Putnam* Park in the heart of downtown, old buildings, banks from the early 1900s or so, now antique stores, old western facades, a couple of dive bars, two bakeries, cold cut delis with pickle jars, pig ears for the dogs, but my kind spend their time at the nothing of a park, and a few coffee shops after school. Coffee is becoming a thing now a days, again I guess, with punks instead of beatniks in suburban hickville. Twenty, thirty minutes past the school bell and the pathetic park swarms with teenage trash. Anyone with sports value or farmhouses don't show face downtown after school. Downtown's a punk rock sanctuary from 3:30 – 6 o'clock. The *Petaluma* Po-Po will cruise through to scatter them after 6. Can't have human trash loitering once the sun goes down, at least not during the week.

These kids are going to lay out on the grass, mingle around the six-foot in diameter stone fountain, Kelly, Kendrick, and Kiley, all pale as day, hippied out in seed necklaces, dual layered, paisley patterned, sun-skirts, all the way down to their *Birkenstocks* showing off their *Henna* tattooed toes, will make their way down from *Copperfield Books*, kiss and hug their friends, then wander off to the docks along the *Petaluma River*, spark a J, get weeded, head back to the park. We've knicked named them the KKKs 'cause of that untanned skin, and because it pisses them off. Tenderloin's been making some musical dealings at the *Toadstool*, the instrument shop, he'll show up to the park, long legged strides, pegged jeans, sixteen-hole black leather *Docs*, probably with some sheet music under his thin arms, baby face, 17, his tender thin torso buried in his black leather covered in white paint-pen doodles and band names with *The Cure* in block letters on the back, waist band, and the *Butthole Surfers* scribed in his underarm. For the record, none of us, but SJ, even have a motorcycle. And Tenderloin'll start asking for Davey's whereabouts, but no one will know, might assume the *Brady* house, and Tenderlion'll say something like, "Dude, that guy owes me money."

Ten to fifteen more people show up; a few skaters, a couple of Hippies-for-Death Metal, Jimmy-the-Germ's being a jerk calling on Allison with a pig call, "Soooie?" But some games just have to played when you're sixteen, drunk on warm beer, and looking to score— and Allison will actually leave with Jimmy, and no one can believe it, and it's hilarious, and it is fucking crazy, "If I knew that's what she liked I might have had some baby backs sooner?" some metal head, long hair, *Alice n' Chains* shirt, torn jeans, cowboy boots, yup, toothpick in his mouth, guy will say about her. Allison's over-weight. She also has a big mouth. Allison is not what one would call the life of the party. It's not because she's unfit, who cares, lots of people tote the lard, she's just obnoxious; an attention whore.

Jimmy's escorted Allison to the alley. He'll lean her up against the brick wall, immediately slide his hand down her laced, black skirt, and lick on her neck— sweat beading from her excitement and weight; so hot —now Allison is up against the dumpster, Jimmy whispering in her ear, "Soou-ie, soou-ie." She'll try to kiss him, open her chapped, flabby, dark purple lips, her cow tongue salivating, flopping against her gums in an attempt to entice the Germ. "You can suck my dick, but I'm not kissing that asshole of a face," is how Jimmy'll charm the girl. Allison'll roll her eyes, and escort Jimmy, a human walking nest of crabs, to her *Chevy Nova*, the only remotely cool thing about this desperately, obnoxious sow of a girl, and Jimmy's actually got her not talking, for once, not talking about nonsense no one's interested in, and they'll go at it in her backseat and Jimmy'll whip out his pin prick of a penis and Allison'll be totally disappointed, spit in her hand and pretend to suck him off, using her lubricated spit-fist to simulate fellatio, and just as the Germ is ready to pop one off she'll pull back, but he's too quick and Allison'll get squirted in the eye. "Thanks, asshole," and Jimmy'll look at her rubbing the salty-goop from her eye, "Stings," she'll complain, smearing her eye shadow. "No hoe, thank you," he'll say. No one has ever considered Jimmy a romantic.

"You want to fuck me, Jimmy?" already Allison's back to talking, and about stuff nobody wants to hear, "I'll let you do me backwards if you don't like my face. Is that why you didn't kiss me?" Jimmy's zipped up and already opening the door, "I'll be your, MooMoo." He'll pause, silent, maybe he actually likes this girl, maybe Jimmy's not a total scumbag, just doesn't understand his feelings; highly unlikely.

"Not today," is all Jimmy'll say, get out of the car, leave the door wide open, fix the collar to his shoddy leather covered in bad penmanship, all punk, *DRI, Skitzo, Lung Butter, Plainfield,* crossed out mess-ups, or blacked out bands he thinks have turned commercial, *Bad Religion, Offspring,* and the entire jacket is barely held together by the rusted safety pins that have replaced nearly all the seams. He'll return to the park to score some *Crystal Meth,* because that's all that'll matter now, "Then find that ass later, haha," and finally get arrested for stabbing some *Jeep* driving jock outside the movie theaters crosstown because they called him a freak, which he is, which we all are. Allison will still be in the car touching up her face. She'll take her time then squeeze out of her *Chevy Nova* to head back to the park 'cause she ain't got no self-esteem, shitty grades, actually works at *Burger King,* can't lose weight, has no desire to be anything anyone wants her to be, and was caught when she was 12, in Junior High, giving some eighth grader a hand-job in exchange for his History homework— She's told us this all before, "Sex makes me feel alive, like I'm doing something right," and she really seems to want us all to know she is sexually active and I just think she's a sci-fi malfunction. Allison knows exactly what people think of her, so she continues ignoring this fact and acts like everyone is her best buddy, that we all love her, and I guess that's why almost everyone has stuck something of theirs inside of her, well everyone except most of us. I don't generally have a *Horrible Thought* about Allison, she really is her own *Horrible Thought*, and it's fucking depressing.

Over the phone, Munts finishes telling me this whole elongated story about the nothingness of the park party I missed, because I always miss it, 'cause I'm trapped in this young male sports body and I got to go to fucking swim practice after school every muther-fucking day; yeah for me. Munts rambles on, "Nothing else really happened. Went to the *Phoenix* for a minute. Tom's gonna let people paint up the walls next summer. Said I could do a doorway or something? What you been doin? Prunin' your balls with flip-turns?"

"Every day," I say.

"Not Sundays?" Munts has nothing better to say.

"Yeah, not Sundays, whoopee. Bye," I hang up.

○　　　•　　　○

I scurry through the loose papers of my crappy phonebook. I had started categorizing people with nick names and that was a disaster, so I tried to remember everyone's real names and that was futile, so it's all just a game of memorize it or find it. I don't have Cindy's phone number memorized, but I'm lucky and I find it, Cindy 707-Bla-Blah. Cindy needs a nick name; then I remember that's the whole joke, her nick name is Cindy her real name is Belinda, but she hates the *GoGos*, like completely, totally despises them spoon gaggers, so we started to call her *Cindy Lauper* in seventh grade and by freshman year it was just Cindy; whoa time flies, and soon Davey's anthem will ring true for all of us— *"we're all gonna be, too far gone."*—Some more lost than others. Some will find refuge in the general swing of things when they attend Community College, find a gig or a job that's, like, kind of steady in town, a starter, a receptionist, maybe a clerk, probably a clerk. Living with the family will keep some of them in touch with each other. A few of us will actually get out of Dodge. Go to *LA, East Coast, Colorado,* maybe even *Portland.* Davey'll join the military, and then he won't. Hopefully Munts will become the new *Crumb* while I'm the more artistic *Oliver Stone.*

○   •   ○

"Yeah is Cindy there?" I ask Belinda's Mom on the other end of the line.

Cindy's Mother isn't amused by the nickname, "You mean Belinda? Let me see if <u>Belinda's</u> still awake. It is 10 o'clock; you know that don't you?"

"Sorry, it's homework."

"Give me second."

I doodle a diddy of a snowman's anus as I wait for a go sound from the phone.

"Make it snappy; I don't like boys calling you on school nights," her Mom reminds her.

"Hello?" Cindy has not been properly informed on who is calling.

"Cindy it's me, T. What's up?"

"Oh, hey how's the tan line?"

"I get you in trouble with your Mom?"

"No. Shit, Tyler, I'm not a child. My Mom's just being a mom. Why are you calling me?"

"Nuthin; no reason."

"You're not going to ask me out or anything, are you?"

"No, chill, wait why would that be so bad?"

"I don't date sports stars."

"Ha, ha. So, what's up Davey's butt?"

"Nothing. Look, I gotta go, Mom's still standing in the hall. I guess you ticked her off. You didn't ask for *Cindy,* did you?"

"Maybe?"

"You can be a real idiot when you want to be. I'll see ya at school. Laaaater."

"Wait!"— Click.

46

MINI THINS

-

-

-

-

-

-

-

-

-

-

-
-
-
-
-
-

47

chapter SIX

*C*indy— Second period, every day, not literally, she's not that uptight, unless she's being uptight. I'm on it from now on, not gonna miss her before class, not going to take my chances, I'm waiting at the door, I'm gonna get an answer about Davey, "Where is Davey?" that's the plan, every day. So, the rest of the week goes by and there's "Hello's" and "Howdy's" at first, then *Belinda* gets chattier towards Weds, but she's dodging the Davey topic, and she's good at it, she's quick, so I ask, "Davey?"

"He said he was all about going to *LA* next summer to see a *Black Flag* reunion or something. I don't like *Black Flag*, I want to go to *LA* though."

○   •   ○

Thurs—
"Cindy, I really need to talk to you about Davey?"
"I know. I'm gonna tell you later. Did you finish the chapter?"

○   •   ○

Friday—
"What's up chloroform?"

"Chlorine?"

"You always smell like it. People should call you Chloey or something, not *Speedo*; *Speedo's* degrading."

"Yes, *Speedo* is highly degrading."

"I'm on my period."

"Thanks for that."

"Gotta tell someone," and poof she's gone. Oh, she's good, so fucking good.

o   •   o

I think she's a lesbo. I just don't get that same look in her eye that I get in other girls, straight girls. Other girls are always scamming, been awhile since I have felt well scammed, at least a welcomed scam, the kind of scam that goes hand in hand with a girl that I actually want to hook up with. I'm over the lack of girlfriend prospects at this school. I'm more curious about a couple girls I've seen outside *Lyons*. Munts told me to talk to this other kid from *Casa Grande*— the *East Side* high school of *Petaluma* —Bret, Bret Eding, Bret the punk-rock poet. Bret tells me, "Those cats go to *Casa*. I think one of em's a freshman, the other's a junior." This kid was sporting a suit jacket over an *Operation Ivy* shirt, blue-jeans with a brown patch, brown suede *Doc Martin* shoes, "Where'd ya get the shoes?" I asked.

"*Berkley; Telegraph Ave*. My Dad lives there, Professor of English Lit, smartass my Dad. You want me to hook you up with those girls? I can find someone who knows 'em."

"Later," and I left it at that. I didn't know this guy, and there was something way too pompous 'bout him hatin' on his intellectual Dad. That shit comes across pretty anal retentive to me. I guess like father like son. Bret likes to be helpful, likes to be the guy, and continued, "I think the blonde's Colleen, Candice or something, and the redhead's Amanda; that I know. They're in the Drama department, maybe you could put 'em in a movie, kid?"

Okay this guy's not up on things. I'm not using Drama girls in my movies. That's a line I just won't cross. The Drama department's kinda big in our town, well at least the kids in the drama departments think Drama's big; *Winona* went to *Petaluma High*, *Lloyd Bridges* went to *Petaluma High*, *Elijah Wood's* off making *The Good Son*, *Tawd b. Dorenfeld* will become a director, his illegitimate twin brother *Tzvi* will be an out of work novelist, *Amy Beardsley* will become a *Ghost Hunter*, *Aaron Machado* will be a *San Diego* radio personality, *Sean Stepanoff* will design *Eminem's Animated Slim Shady World*, *Daedalus Howell* will produce *Abe Levy*, who will marry *Silver Tree*, who will go on to produce the show *Suits* and direct episodes of the *Mick*, and a shitload of other talent'll pour out of *Luma*, and I'm not going to speculate to my own success, but talking like that makes me sound like Bret and really all I'm presently concerned about is Davey and that's purely driven by a manic need to know the story, 'cause I know Davey's going to get through it, whatever "It" is; the elusive It everyone's so hyped up on teenagers' finding and figuring out. He'll be fine, but I might miss the ride. I don't want to miss Davey's ride. Davey keeps me connected to living.

Munts side swipes me in the gut and I turn away from my mindless gaze, I think I was looking past the cluster of freshman girls comparing new lipsticks. "What up Munts?" I foster.

"Nothing. I feel like getting stoned."

"You got any tests today?" I ask.

"Zip."

"Homework this weekend?"

"Nada."

"Crabs on your balls?"

"Sixteen."

"Do they itch?"

"Only when you scratch them."

"Do you scratch them a lot?"

"I said when <u>you</u> scratch them."

"I'll be gentler next time."

"You better be."

"Whatcha losers yapping about?" Erin, in full drama gear, a princess outfit for her scene from *Romeo and Juliet*.

"Munts' balls."

"You have two, right Munts?"

"I don't count that high. Could you help me out?"

"Nice," we slap palms, "I'll leave you two mathematicians alone," and I start to scoot through Munts & Erin, "Movies. Saturday night. Munts, my place."

Munts shakes his head no, uncool, not going to happen, "I can't smoke weed at your house. Come to my place, crab scratcher."

"Ew, does Tyler have crabs?" Erin's curiosity perks.

"Tyler's got crabby parents," Munts corrects me.

Erin grabs Munts arm, "You gonna cut class and come see me kiss Gay Gerry in our scene today?"

"I'm not sure if I'm up for that," Munts is not all so comfortable with her come on.

"Homophobic much?" Erin playfully asks.

"Uh, not really, just that..." Munts stumbles, "I got *Algebra*?"

"Sucks, maybe another time? Maybe you'll get me stoned?" Erin starts walking off backwards, drifting, into the void of the future of the day, "Maybe you'll call me? Maybe. Maybe. Maaayyyyybeeeeeeeee," Erin steps back into the sloth of a Courtyard Guard, "Oh sorry, Miss Newman."

"Watch where you're going," Sloth Newman scans Erin up and down, the princess costume is just so very loud, "And that getup is not appropriate for school?"

Bell Tolls, a warning that we should all head to class. Erin responds to the Sloth, "Would you like me to find one in your size?" Munts dies laughing, Miss Newman turns right towards us, Erin pulls the bell of her dress up from the ground so she doesn't trip and die; runs. Munts and I leave the other way.

○　　•　　○

"I think Erin just told me to ask her out?"

"Good for you, Munts."

"Is she a virgin?"

"Yes."

"Oh."

"Oh, as in, oh not good, or oh, as in oh yeah?" I ask.

Munts is unsure how to answer.

"Which is it, I gotta go to class."

"Do you think she's going to want to fuck?" Munts asks with great trepidation.

"No. Besides yer a first-class virgin, dude, I think you both better really like each other before you guys mess up the whole sex thing because you don't know where to stick your dick," and I give Munts a little pat on the ass, scaring the be-jeezus' out of him; and I'm off to class, "You'll be cool. Go south!" I holler, my words echo through the empty hallways as I hustle down the linoleum to *Spanish*, for which I'm going to be late, for which I'm getting a fucking D. If I don't get my shit together in this *Taco Bell* class I'm going to be going to *Community College* instead of a real school in a real city. Munts is totally going to be late for class too. I bet he cuts, yeah he's gonna cut.

And that's exactly what Munts did, cut class and headed directly to the auditorium where Drama was performing their mid-semester scenes. Munts stops at the metal plated baby blue double doors. He knows how loud these doors are. He knows someone's going to notice him. He knows he's fifteen minutes early to see Erin kiss the one gay guy in school. Munts pulls his black hoody out from under his jean jacket covered in *Sharpie* doodles, no words, covers his head, and makes his way along the underbelly of the benches alongside the auditorium walls to watch his crush and Gay Gerry do their scene from *Romeo and Juliet*—no kissing. Sucker.

o   •   o

"Como esta el senior Goodman?"
"Se lama, Tyler Goodman."
The class laughs in unison.

o   •   o

Erin, catches a glimpse of Munts hidden under the bleachers. She smiles, happy that Munts actually showed up, thinks he's sooo cute. And Munts watches the entire performance, and Erin's not all that bad, and Munts likes the feeling of fantasizing about the girl on stage, the actress, the star, the hot one, and then he realizes, he's stuck under the bleachers throughout the entire class. Within' fifteen minutes, Munts is rolled up in a ball, weeping into his hoody. Not really, but Munts will eat the bud he's got; the bud he was saving to smoke after school— *Choose Your Own Adventure*, Munts.

And I'm in a shitty mood for the rest of the day from being singled out in *Español*, and honestly I'm getting worried about Davey because yeah, he really hasn't shown up to school, he's totally lied about going to detention, and why the fuck doesn't he want to be my friend anymore? And my mind won't stop spiraling around about it. I don't want to go to Munts' place to watch movies tonight, I'm tired, and practice is going to really wipe me out like always, or just make me horny thinking about girls in swim suits, and I don't mean the ones on the team, I mean the ones that the girls on the team inspire us to imagine— hot ones with curves —and that shit becomes all fantasy, flip turn, and fantasy is a lot hotter than reality, and you can't get the image of—

> *—a pair of size D's on a thin waist,*
> *and the flush lips*
> *that turn to take a breath*
> *as they pass you by in the lane,*
> *and you start to thicken up*
> *and you have to tell yourself,*
> *"Don't get no wood in the pool, in your Speedos,"*
> *but the thought, accompainied by hormones*
> *take hold of your nearly naked body,*
> *with girls all around you*

Flip-turn —

In order to stop getting the hard-on you have to think about not getting a hard-on and that in itself actually induces a hard-on. Life has gotten so much more complicated since I was ten.

•

o   o

Mom's made cornflake chicken, baked potatoes, broccoli, and I'm finished, excused, and in my room funneling through my *Zap Comics* trying to find the one Munts loaned me last week, *Issue #5*; I think it might still be in my locker? I pick up the hard plastic, flesh-toned, semicolon shaped telephone and peck the illuminated neon-green, thin plastic numbered buttons, "Hell-o," Munts answers.

"Can't you get stoned at home and just bike over tomorrow?" I ask, trying to get out of going to his place.

"What? Come on," Munts pleads.

"Dude, I'll be fucking bushed, man, I wake up at..." I'm saying, but he finishes my thought—

"Five in the *Speedo* morning, I know, I get it, you like to lower your sperm count early," he says.

"Exactly, so don't make me drive all the way to the other side of town to watch a fucking movie at your house, so, <u>you</u> can get stoned."

— Call waiting clicks —

"Shit, call waiting, hold on," I push the hang up shark fin that's sticking out of the base of the phone, and release, "Hidey-Ho?"

"It's me," Erin says in her best *Betty Davis* impersonation.

"Well hello, I'm talking to your lover-boy right now," I tease.

"Call waiting?" Erin asks.

"Yup."

"Your parents are so yuppified."

"Are not."

"Are too."

"Are not."

"Are...this is stupid, what do you want?" I ask.

"Is Munts a virgin?"

"Uh, I gotta go," I say. Wow this girl's got a nut for the Munts.

"Come on, tell me. Is he, like, a virgin or something?" she begs.

"Look, I can't talk about this shit with you, and what the fuck do you mean by or something? If the guy ain't a virgin, then he ain't a virgin. There is no, or something," I kindly lecture this naïve, young Drama student.

"So, who did he lose it too?" She asks.

—Call waiting clicks—

"Oh shit, I think Munts just hung up," I gotta get off this phone call, "Hey you know where Cindy went today? I saw her leave early? Is she hanging out with Davey or something?"

"I don't know, man, maybe she is, or something?" Erin terminates all form of rational conversation.

"Goodbye. I'm calling Munts back, you can call him in like 10 minutes," I instruct.

"I don't call guys," Erin says.

"Byyyye."

"Bye. Oh, Tyler?"

"What?"

"Does he like me?" she asks, bashful. I hang up the phone and call Munts back.

"Yo, call your girlfriend. I think she's in heat," I hang up.

o   •   o

Friday night, now what, no good show at the *Phoenix*, and no girlfriend. My parents are downstairs watching some sports game Dad taped. I should pee out the window.

o   •   o

I check my wallet for a *Blockbuster* coupon I've been saving, *Two for One*; tomorrow I think I'll rent *The Brood*, and...I'll figure it out. I play *Metroid* on my *Nintendo 64* for three hours, listen to the *Dead Kennedy's Plastic Surgery*, *Blatz's Fuck NY*, *Tom Waits Swordfish Trombones*, eat ice cream, imagine fucking *Pamela Anderson*, imagine *Pamela Anderson* fucking me— I'm the best she's ever had and sure to pass along my digits to *Ms. Samantha Fox* —and I'm passed out, sound asleep.

o   •   o

Why is Saturday morning practice at 6:30am? My Saturday morning's ruined at 6:30 as much as it would be at 8:30, even 9:00. Shit, my friends don't even wake up until eleven, so why am I wide-awake, restless, watching cartoons by 9 after practice? I'm gonna protest this shit, I want a time change. Maybe some other day, coach doesn't seem in the mood. I'm not barking up Davey's tree either. Munts is probably hooking it into the Erin, and I'm not really in the mood to call my other friends, and instead opt to catching a flick with Ma in *San Francisco*. I'll convince her to have a partial day in the city. I can drop her off with Dad at work. She and Pops can dine in the big city nightlife. I'll head back to *Luma* and Dad'll drive Mom home. Mom bites and pays our way to see *Bad Lieutenant*, then gets me a cappuccino at *Steps of Rome*, buys me *Cities of the Red Night by Burroughs* at *City Lights Books*, and I take her to Dad's work, top floor at *Macy's*; he's in the TV department. My Mom's fucking cool. "Love ya," and I head back to town.

○　　　•　　　○

The east side of town is weird. It's a full track home community made up of various generations of track design that dates back to the late 50's. That general mentality of replication is just plain old weird to me. Who wants to be a carbon copy of the guy next door? I don't. Do you? The 60's tore those original homes down and replaced them with new replications, *Brady Bunch* style, stone walls, wooden panels, walkways up through the front yards, no porches, two car garages built directly into the home, cement driveways, two stories, three variations to create the illusion of variety. By the 80's people began installing above ground swimming pools. The gardens vary from plain bushes to rose gardens, desert settings, plain lawns, the rare big tree, and accentuated with basketball hoops, hand built skate and BMX bike ramps, cats & dogs locked up behind fences; shit like that. Cruise through the neighborhoods on a Saturday or Sunday and every other garage door is wide open with men and their boys blasting *Metallica* as they work on their trucks, bikes, jet-skies, lawnmowers, etc. Always *Metallica*, sometimes *Guns N Roses*, never *Bon Jovi*, unless it's a cheerleader carwash in a cul-de-sac of bikinis, lots of suds, and a line of *Broncos, Chevys, Rabbits*, and *Jeeps* filled with jocks of the *Vanilla Ice* persuasion. Munts lives in one of these neighborhoods, but he's on a non-tracked street where some guy developed privately and luckily made a series of single story homes that all look different.

I'm outside Munts' front door. The front yard has been fully neglected. The grass is dead, patched with dandelions, weeds, lined with the skeletons of bushes, and a single tree pushes itself up against the front of the house for support. Munts' little brother, Pat, answers the door. He's a little guy who has grown out his red hair, *Viking* style, and wears an iron-on shirt with a metal robo-hawk that bursts through an *American Flag*. Pat gives me an eye of suspicion, and drills me on musical taste, "You listen to the new *MegaDeath*?"

"No."

"You come to get Munts?" he asks.

"Yeah we're gonna watch some movies?"

"Mom and Dad went to *Santa Rosa* for a night out. You guys gonna smoke some pot?"

"Why you got some?" I say as I squat down and hold out my palm, "Well?" Pat's flies forward and head butts me to the ground. I drop the VHS tapes, "What the fuck freak?" and Munts steps out of the house and picks up, "*The Brood*, nice," he says, helps me up, addresses his little brother, "Leave Tyler alone," turns back to me, "What'd else ya rent?"

I follow Munts back into the house. He's quick, shuts the door, and locks Pat outside, punching, kicking and swearing to high heaven to let him in. I plop my bag down on the aged brown, four-seater couch, and follow Munts into his tiny, closet sized room, "You talk to your girlfriend yet?" I pry.

"Yes, and stop calling her my girlfriend," Munts says, embarrassed, closing his bedroom door behind me. The glass door to the kitchen can be heard sliding open, then shut, "I'm going to pee down your throat, Melvin!" Pat yells from the kitchen.

"Ha. Melvin. That's your baby name. Your mom really had it..." Melvin interrupts me, "I get it. Here," and Munts hands me this massive coffee-table book from his library of rare and highly inspiring art books, "Check this out, it's all album cover art, even gets up to the *Raymond Pettibon* and some photocopy art." Still standing I flip through the pages, pause on *Jefferson Airplane* pieces, and then continue to a whole section on *Mouse's* work. "This is awesome," and it's the late 70's that starts to introduce the carbon copy machine, and Munts pulls out a variety of other books, *Hans Bellmer*, plastic surgery operations, skin grafts, a Horror Film Encyclopedia, *Junky*, and sprawls them all over his bed; a bed that has been previously covered in sketches, comic books, cassette tapes, *VHS* dubs, torn up magazine clippings, potato chips, soda cans, broken skull fragments, and a pillow that looks more like a lump of stained pants, and I start to notice the smell, the stench that only comes from Munts room, a chemical homogeny of acrylic paint, *Sharpies*, old food, dirty underwear, and the dog hair from his family companion Franky, an ancient blue-eyed long haired *Rottweiler*. "I need a drink, can I get some water," I ask as an excuse to open his door, air the place out; anything. Munts is fidgeting with a tin, "Yeah, sure, help yourself," he says as he pops the top off, the odor of marijuana webbing itself into the *Stink of Melvin*. I go to the kitchen.

o • o

The Brood plays out, Munts is still nursing his third bowl, and the lights are off. We've covered his parent's wooden coffee-table with empty microwavable bags of popcorn, spilt boxes of *Hot Tamales*, the weed tin, a single can of *Pabst*, *GI-Joe* figures, and a *Penthouse* open to the centerfold that drapes over the side of the table. Now this is all illuminated by the blue colored flicker of a *VHS* tape run to the end. The *VCR* thumps, unlocks, and begins to rewind on it's own. Munts lowers his pipe from his lips, he has forgotten to take the hit, "I'm not so comfortable with all that kid troll shit," Munts mumbles and re-flicks his *Bic*, burns the bowl, inhales, and blows it right in my face. I move the single strand of bleached blonde hair away from my eye and stare into Munts' soul, whisper, "Don't look, but it's looking right at us."

"Who?" Munts asks, spooked, confused, and stoned.

"The Troll," I whisper.

"Don't fuck with me, man, I'm really stoned."

"Shh." In the darkness, I can spy, over Munts' shoulder a figure. It's wearing a red coat, its face covered in darkness, in its hand, a kitchen blade, the big kind. He's real threatening. I am not stoned.

"What's going on man? Is it still there?" Munts whispers back. I'm not actually fooling around here, the fucking troll from the movie is right behind him, looking at me, but I just can't see its eyes, but the blade twinkles in the blue glow of the TV.

"Okay, Munts," I whisper, "I need you to turn around; slowly," I cautiously instruct my buddy. Before he turns, he tries to blink the weed away, rubs his eyes, and takes a breath, turns, slowly, towards the troll who immediately takes three steps forward and ATTACKS! Pounces off the carpet, lands on the head of the lounge chair, his weight buckles the chair forward, then back again. The troll cackles as the chair rocks, and Munts shoves me over and hightails it to the back wall with a grip on his dick, trying not to piss all over himself, because Munts has a testy bladder. I get my shit together, turn towards the troll on the rocking lounge chair, and the Troll-Bitch looks right at me, growling. Munts freaks, pisses his pants, and the troll dives headfirst off the chair, tumbles over me, crashes against the coffee table which in turn collapses, and sends the small beast, and all our garbage onto the carpet. I roll myself up and around, and there, thrashing away in the pile of destruction is Pat removing his red hoody. "You piece of shit," Munts scolds his little brother, but it's not the time to get all testy; see Pat's got a giant gash along the side of his forehead, blood pouring down his face, and the blade has lodged itself into the kid's thigh. His left hand has been dislocated as well. It's all one big shit-fuck of a moment. Pat doesn't even realize the half of it as he laughs, poking fun at his older brother, "You so peed your pants; Bahahhaa!"

Emergency! Things get real fast, insta-quick, and it's a *Victims Family's Me vs Everything* moment in my head as

Munts rushes to change his pants, while I slip along the garbage sprawled out all over the floor, trying to get to Pat, who has just wiped the blood from of his eye enabling him to see the knife stuck deep into his thigh meat. I grab ahold him, "Don't move," but the little shit shoves me aside with the might of a hundred men; strength that comes from the extreme adrenaline rush of fear and disbelief.

Now I'm on my ass watching this poor kid bleed out on the dark green carpet. Munts has returned in corduroy pants. He stands over both of us. "What are we gonna do?" He's frozen with eyes on his little brother all fucked up, screaming bloody murder. My latest *Horrible Thought* creeps out of my subconscious— *We can't get Pat to move, he's too panicked, flails his arms, a helicopter on PCP. He kicks my jaw, snaps it out of place, teeth everywhere, blood pouring down my throat. Munts calls 911, but hangs up before they answer. "What the fuck dude! Why'd you hang up!?" Munts is spooked that we're all gonna go to jail over this. "Your brother's going to DIE! CALL THEM BACK!" I yell like hell fire, and then we hear it, a sound so penetrating to the human soul that you almost wish you were dead so you never have to hear it again, the gurgle of a child's lungs, swallowing, choking, and suffocating on his own blood. In unison Munts and I turn towards Pat, our petty argument aside, this kid is going to die. Pat has stopped making any sound, his eyes have rolled back into his skull, bubbles of blood foam out his mouth, open wide, unable to suck the oxygen in. No air at all. The kid's a goner. Next, the sound of a jail cell closing, metal against metal, we are fucked— CUT TO:*

Munts and I are lead down Death Row, accompanied by guards, a Priest, and a Rabbi. The Rabbi leans into my ear and says, "Fear nothing but G-d, Barukh Hashem you will be forgiven." The Priest leans into Munts' ear, "Proclaim Jesus as your savior and you will be forgiven my son."

We are both strapped into deathbeds, our arms spread out like Jesus on the cross. My Rabbi thinks that's a shonda. The Priest doesn't seem to mind, kisses his rosary, "I didn't know you were Catholic," I say to Munts beside me. "I'm not." I see my Mom sitting alone in the audience. Dad didn't show up. My own father couldn't stand the shame that his only son has brought upon him. Both of Munts' parents are there; they are rotten with despair. The

physician finds my vein first, slips the needle in below my elbow.
"Kid killers," he calls us under his breath.

○ • ○

I break my own silence of the *Horrible Thought*. "Help me get him to the car!" Munts squats beside Pat, "You're going to be okay. Okay?"

"I fucked up," Pat whimpers.

"Yes, you did, little fella. Let's get you to the hospital," Munts comforts him. Pat seems to trust us now as we maneuver around him; Munts gets his shoulders, I get the knifed leg. "Okay, on the count of three, we lift," I pause, "No, wait."

I run over to the front door to open them both and make my way back to Munts,

"Okay, now. One, Two, Three!" We lift Pat, he hollers in pain as the knife wiggles around. "Okay, to the car," I direct. Pat's being a pretty good sport despite Munts nearly dropping him twice. We've gotten to the car. This shit is rough. Change of plans, put him in the way back, but first we have to lay Pat's bleeding body on the hood so I can open the hatchback to slide him in. I crawl in, lower the backseats to make enough room. Munts pulls my leg, "Hurry up!"

—I AM!

It's a fucking struggle getting the kid around the car; he's suddenly not being cooperative anymore, kicking and spitting on us. Spitting blood on us, but we finally get him into the hatchback, "Ow! Fuck you!" the kid yells, and I slam the back shut, wipe my brow, and, "Let's go."

"You drive," Munts says.

"Yeah, duh?"

○ • ○

We're rolling at 65mph through the empty night streets, avoid any street light we can, run all the stop signs, and every time I shift gears Pat lets out a scream that could deafen *Helen Keller*. The soundtrack has changed since we drove out of Munts' driveway. Now all I hear between my ears coming from my meager car stereo is *NoMeansNo', I am Wrong*, yet nothing will impede me from saving Munts' little brother. Pat is quiet in the back; he's stopped yelling. Kid better not be dead. "You still stoned?" I ask my buddy in the passenger seat. He looks at me, stone cold, and says, "No."

I see the hospital just up ahead, just past the giant man-made lake. I slow down and turn into the ER lot, right up to the red zone outside the Emergency Doors. "Watch your brother," I instruct as I swing open my door, try to slide out, choke on my seatbelt, Munts chuckles. "Not funny," and I undo my seatbelt burst out, rush with huge strides toward and through the automatic doors, and I'm inside, "EMERGENCY! MAJOR FUCKING DEATH EMERGENCY!"

The woman clerk, behind the Plexiglas, leaps up from her chair slams her hands on the window, "Calm down! Where is the patient?"

I'm panting. This lady's fucking trapped behind the window, Munts' little brother is bleeding out in the back of my fucking car, fuck, where are the fucking doctors, "IN MY CAR! OH, FUCK LADY! HE'S DIEING! BLEEDING TO DEATH!" I totally lose it, stress overwhelms me, I don't know why, can't control myself, lose all sight of anything rational, think he's already dead; I have failed, and now I've collapsed onto the linoleum floor, curled up in a ball, it hurts, I feel so sorry, my gut wants to tear itself free from my spine, claws at my belly, "I'm so sorry, so fucking sorry," while four nurses stampede past my pathetic self, and I feel someone pick me up from my armpits, pull me out of the way of the passing gurney.

Little Pat's wheeled by me, out of focus, the fluorescents so bright. I compose my sixteen-year-old self, and I can see that the woman who pulled me to safety is actually Cindy, Belinda, my pal, and I don't understand why she's even here. Maybe I'm hallucinating? "Oh my god, Tyler, what happened? Who is that?" she asks.

The front doors slide open and Munts walks in, his head low, "I, I guess I got to tell them stuff," Munts mumbles.

"Yeah, man," I start, "I'm really sorr—" Munts cuts me off,

straight up tells me, "You saved my brother, dude, don't be sorry," holds back his own tears addresses our friend, "Hey, Belinda," he jokes. We all crack a little smile. Munts has that way about him, he's funny, he can lighten a moment even when it's his ass on the line. "That's your little brother, huh?" Munts nods and walks off to fill out the forms at the clerk's window. Those clerks sure got a shitty job. I couldn't cope.

"What happened?" Cindy snaps me out of my head.

"Uh, dumb stupid shit," is all I can muster.

"Accident?"

"Yeah totally."

"Is he going to be okay?"

"I don't know? It was really bad," I say and Cindy doesn't push it, she waits for it, so I oblige her silent curiosity, "Little dude was fucking around, got a butcher's knife lodged all the way through his leg."

"Oh! That's horrible," Cindy's grossed out.

"No shit. I was there. I saw it go down; saw that blade slide right through his little leg like butter. So freaky," I say.

"Oh no!" Cindy covers her mouth. Paper cut like thoughts, horrible. Horrible. I gotta change the subject, and it's so easy, "So—What-cha doing here?"

"Nothing."

—Liar.

She continues to avoid my question.

"I hope he'll be okay."

"We'll see?" and I try again, "So weird that like, you just showed up."

"Hey, what can I say, I'm cool like that."

"Were you just like leaving or something?" I ask, but she's saved from my interrogation as the ER doors open and some Doctor-dude exits, obviously looking for us. The doctor eyes me first, "Are you a relative?" I shake my head no. Cindy takes the lead, "We're his friends. That's his older brother over there." The doctor looks back at me, "Do you know what happened?"

—What do I say?

Why am I even questioning it,
it's the truth, it's all true.
Sounds like bullshit, but it's true, nothing less.
Why do I think people won't believe us?
Oh yeah, stereotypes.
We look like we
fit the mold
of irresponsibility.

I scope myself out in the reflection of the lobby mirrors. I got an old military jacket on, one long strand of bleached blonde hair that streams down from my thick, wavy, brown locks, army green *Docs*, black and white nail polish that's all scratched up along my fingernails, *A Clockwork Orange* shirt and beside me, Cindy, who's wearing a *L7* shirt, torn jeans, bleached white and dyed black hair on one side, the other side shaved, a nose pierce, too many jelly bracelets, tobacco stained teeth, and the doctor is giving us both a serious look of disapproval. Munts is all mismatched because he peed his pants earlier and had changed into those green corduroys, a torn up *Cramps* shirt, and a third of his face is always cloaked by a long strand of dyed black, or green, or purple hair, while the rest of his head is completely shaved. Weird how you'll never really notice your friends until you look at them through a stranger's eyes. "It was an accident," I tell the doctor, "Kid tried to scare us with the knife, jumped on a table, and fell down."

"Is that true, young lady?" he asks Cindy.

"I wasn't there, but Tyler's an honor roll kid so, like, you can trust him," she tells him.

The doctor turns his attention back to me and lifts his pen light— CLICK — shines the light directly into my pupils, "And what is it that you're <u>on</u>, son?" The light makes me blink. "Hey, that's bright!" and I swat the prick's pen away, "I'm not on drugs, man, fuck, it was an accident, that's it. Kid fucked up. End of story."

The doctor sucks in his sphincter, clears his throat, and vilifies my use of the English language, "I'd prefer you kept that language outside. None of this is okay." And he waits for my reaction.

— *Fine. Be that way. You win.*

"Won't happen again," I say to the fucker.

"You two are free to go, I only need to talk with his brother," he concludes and straight up walks away. Cindy cups my shoulder; we're quiet, mellow, the moment needs nothing more than time. We don't leave quite yet. We're keeping an eye on the doctor as he has his discourse with the Munts. Seems civil enough. Munts is bummed out, feels guilty, worried, fearful of his parents' reaction. The doctor says something, must be good news, Munts lifts his head, cracks a smile, thanks the guy, and rejoins us, "Not going to die," he tells us with a smirk.

I've never been a fan of the smirk. I smirk all the time. Don't want people to be uncomfortable around me. They should think I'm okay enough. I can deal with whatever's going on. I don't notice when I smile, but I can totally tell when I smirk. A smirk is always carrying a load of thought with it. I smirk back at Munts. Cindy slides her hand down my arm, takes my hand; squeezes. I turn. She looks me right in the eye, "Ok, T, you want to know why I'm here?"

— *All ears.*

○　　　•　　　○

2:10am— We're outside the hospital. Cindy and I have perched ourselves on a cold, metal bench. The sky is exceptionally clear tonight. Munts, he's on a pay phone across the street. Keeps looking in our direction while he can't get his parents on the line. I guess they're still not home yet. Cindy's been silent ever since she told me she'd confess. I can't help but imagine her in the future, *her face worked, tired, exhausted. Twenty-Five. She's a waitress along the Castro. Still not dating, lives alone, takes a few classes at San Francisco State. Not getting too close to anyone anymore. Wonders why she's even content with being content as she patrons a few Lesbian Bars. She has a couple one-night stands, but really, she's not sure what she wants to be when she grows up and prefers to find out* *later and work today.* But now, in the present time she looks sad. Something's eating her up inside.

I have to break the silence, I have to wake her up, snap her out of it, and bring the *GoGo* back. "Let it out Cindy, just tell me everything," I pause to give her a moment and then she just lets it all out, crying, crying right into my arms, so sad, so hurt. I have a sudden dumb thought, *Oh G-d what if she's in love with me.* Dumb, dumb thought, worse than a *Horrible Thought,* and so poorly timed. Focus on your friend, she needs you, and she speaks, "Kelsey had a miscarriage."

—*Ouch. Bad. Bad for Kelsey. Bad for Davey?*

"Oh shit, how's Davey?" I ask her. She gives me the most, evil eye I have ever seen. "You're an asshole," she strikes.

o   •   o

2:14am— Dead silence. I want to take the last two minutes back, press rewind, and put in a different tape.

•   o   •

2:12am— TAKE 2: Roll camera, SPEED, roll sound, SOUND ROLLING, aaand ACTION! —Cindy and I chill under a tree on the lawn of the hospital. The lawn curves along the entire body of the building, leads to the *Petaluma Lake.* The entire sky is reflected in the man-made pool. Cindy seems uncomfortable. She doesn't really want to tell me what's going on. I smirk, crack my neck, and deliver the rewrite, "Just tell me what you want to tell me. No pressure."

"Davey's sister had a miscarriage," she says with bloodshot eyes, so sad, filled with empathy, "That's it, that's everything."

—*CUT!*

o   •   o

2:11am —

> *I stretch my back.*
> *Don't speak, it's okay,*
> *just look at the stars,*
> *they're bright.*
> *Cindy looks up,*
> *sees a shooting star.*
> *She's quiet, it worked;*
> *I've changed the past.*
> *Cindy seems calm,*
> *sad eyes,*
> *says,*

"I'm here for Kelsey; she had a miscarriage."

> *—You cannot rewrite the past.*

•

○   ○

2:15am— Every which way is a downward spiral of confusion, questions, strange anger, disappointment, discouragement, fear, anxiousness, concern, love, compassion, worry, dismay, concern, concern, and I honestly believe Davey must have it so fucking bad in the head right now. Straight into her eye, I'm not fooling around, I have to pierce into Cindy's soul, take control of the situation, take the film back from the *Executives*, write it my way, "Where's Davey <u>right now</u>?" Cindy pulls back, "Fuck you," she's pissed, "This isn't your story, Mr. Director. Kelsey's really sick. It's not Davey's fucking kid, so why you all about him?" and she shoves me.

•

○   ○

> *—Is she deaf?*
> *Which part of what I said meant,*
> *I did not care about Kelsey,*
> *or that I thought*
> *Davey was screwing his*
> *born-again sister on the weekends?*

None of it.

I so just wanted to watch a couple of movies with my buddy tonight. My parents are going to freak out about this. Complain about my irresponsible friends, again. My friends are fine. Typically irresponsible. Teenagers. They are not overtly irresponsible, but sometimes I might be overtly responsible. Can't relax, let it go, be free. Maybe they'll understand, but I haven't called them yet, so right now Mom's worried because it's so late and if they called Munts house they got no answer, just like him. I'm feeling the judgement. Judgement all around me. Every day, right now, from her eyes, makes me think of my parents, disappointment, judgement; don't judge me, don't judge me with faulty pretense. This gets to me. Unjust. Don't treat me unjustly. That's my ticking time-bomb. That I can't control. I will snap, and then get judged again. I can feel it. This gets my blood boiling. I feel it in my veins, like my white cells crystalize, needles burst into my bone, through my muscles, tear it all apart, rip and tear at the terrible world, worn and torn and terrible, but I can contain it, I've broken earlier, now I'm strong again, strong enough to fight myself from fighting myself. What did I say to Cindy, what did I insinuate with my well-chosen words, "Where's Davey right now?" aka "I do not want your story, Davey is one of my best friends in my small, *tiny ugly world*, so whatever you have to say means nothing to me because I can only accept Davey's story. Davey I know. Davey I trust. You, you are just a friend, not a brother, not a friend for life. You don't care about me. I know this. If I disappeared tomorrow it would not change Cindy's world, so don't judge me. So, chill bitch, and tell me where my buddy is, so then I can be there for him. So, "Please Cindy, where is Davey, and NO BULLSHIT!" —I *Tyler Tantrum*, slam my fist into the metal bench, suck my split knuckle, spit the blood out on the concrete.

Cindy's walked away from the bench, acting out, but she ain't got nowhere to go, but home. "Aren't visiting hours over, Belinda?" I jab her again and look to Munts for support, but he's finally got his Dad on the line, and throws

68

up a finger signaling me to hold on.

"I was going to the bathroom," Cindy starts, "I've been here since this afternoon and I keep drinking these generic sodas that make me have to pee, so, I came back in the ER to use the bathroom."

—What the fuck is she talking about?

She has more to say. I'll wait; let her say her shitty peace. "Well?" she asks, "Happy now?" but I'm not sure what I'm supposed to be happy about, "Now you know why I was here. Now you know why I was in the ER waiting room, where I found you crying like a baby over a flesh wound."

—Hey come on, that's not fair.

"You're pathetic," she judges me, "You don't care about anyone, but yourself." —AND SNAP— I stretch the constriction of my throat and bark at her, "Fuck you, Cindy. Go, Fuck, a Fag's Vagina! You suck! JUDGE ME?! I care, bitch. I care about my friends. Davey's my friend. That affects me. Fuck you," she doesn't fight back, too exhausted to deal with me drop kicking her with tone, "You go and cunt out on me for caring? What the fuck is wrong with you? UGH!"

—CUT!

•

•

•

•

•

chapter *SEVEN*

*M*unts and I find Davey along the exterior of the south wing of the hospital. He's squatting outside Kelsey's window, nursing a generic soda, and playing with the filter of his last cigarette as it burns out. I can smell the filter fumes. Munts had pulled me out of the clawing hands of psycho Cindy. She went after me for my petty outburst, but Munts got me away before she scratched my baby face. Davey sees us coming, he's not surprised, maybe deep inside he's appreciative, truly moved to have such good friends because, much like Cindy, tonight he's too close to crying, and his back is turned to us while he stares at the grass that leads to the lake. He keeps kicking the rubber soles of his boot into the grass.

○　　　•　　　○

We're standing right above him. He won't look at us, keeps his cool; guard up, walls, all sorts of walls. Instead he looks past us, up at the stars then down at their reflection in the lake, whispers, "Twinkle, Twinkle, little star, how the fuck you get away so far?" and then, "Munts, you got any weed?" as he digs his dead cigarette out into the soil of the grass, and violently flicks it toward the lake. Munts humors him,

"Yeah, dude, I got ya," and scrambles through his pants pockets, but I know he doesn't have any weed, I know it's scattered all over the bloody carpet in the living room. I know exactly what Munts is going to say, 'cause Munts hate's seeing people uncomfortable, and will do most anything to get a smile instead of a frown, *"I can call Mitch and get some."* He stops looking for the weed, bites his lip, thinks, and then says it, almost to the t, "I can call Mitch? Score a dime?"

Davey, jonesin' for intoxicants, turns sour as his brow lowers, his eyelids tight, "No, I don't want you to call Mitch." Davey switches to me, I'm startled, he's like a blonde mountain lion, scoping out the threat, "What's up, *Aquaman*? You here to <u>save</u> my sister?"

"Thought Jesus had that covered," I smirk, "Looks like he fucked that up, real bad." —BAM— Never saw it coming — Tumbled. How? What? "Ow!" I think that's grass in my mouth? It's brittle, moist, and kind of slushy. I don't dare close my mouth. Davey shoves my face deeper in it. I am NOT going to swallow, I can smell it now, dog shit pushing its way into my orifices; my arm twists, all happening because Davey the lion pounced on top of me, and we've rolled down the slope of grass. Someone did not find my joke funny this evening. He's pounding on me with his boney fists, skin-tight, like metal against my skull. Munts stays out of it. Steps up, but doesn't get involved, and I got my forearms covering my head to fend off the beat down, so the lion grabs ahold of my blonde streak, yanks my face out of the dog shit and he's about to bash me in the face, but throws me aside instead, gets up, covered in mud, doesn't bother to brush any of it off, "Don't be dick," he says and kicks me in the side, but I block it, and it bruises my arm, but at least he didn't blow out my spleen out like when *Stepanoff* got his beat down in the cemetery. Kid was hospitalized for like a week for that shit. Davey should know better. He used to say that shit was fucked, that you should never kick a friend in the gut. Guess I crossed a line tonight. *So be it.* Pirate radio sounds good, and may keep me away from anything social. Hide out, disappear, nah, not my style.

○　　　　　　　　　　　○

Davey digs his feet into the muddy slope one foot at a time, makes his way back up towards the hospital window, swears under his breath, "Goody two shoes swim team fag." I heard that, and roll over my muddy self, "I heard that, psycho." Davey slowly turns back. He's so fucking skinny, so white his skull glows in the moonlight, but what a bite on him. I thought I had a temper? Is he going to strike again? I'm ready, bring it on, want to kill your best friend, go ahead, your loss, but he's calm now, guess he got whatever it was out of his system for the time being, even though his hands are clenched, tight, boney fingers dug deep into his palms, reminds himself he's still alive, like TV, still feels something, not a dream. This is real. This is life. This is our show, live, not *Memorex*. If he had a knife he'd cut himself, but instead comes back down the slope. I flinch, but he lends me a hand up, "Get up. You look like shit? Smell like it too."

-
-
-
-
-
-
-
-
-
-
-
-
-
-
-

chapter EIGHT

 $\mathcal{W}$ e tell Davey the tale of the troll, the attack, the destruction, the surrealistic nature of it all. Munts insinuates that he might make a zine out of it. We've got our backs against the hospital wall staring at the mirrored lake. Davey and I admit our disagreement was petty, friends against friends, no more bullshit, we can handle each other's assholey-ness in the face of dog crap. We're both covered in mud, "You can get that stitched up in there," Davey says about the moonlight that reflects off my split lip, turns to Munts, "That story's royally fucked up, man," and back to me, "I guess *Speedo* here was a fucking Ocean God tonight. *Uranus* itch much?" I correct him, "*Neptune*."

"*Neptune*?" Davey asks back.

"Yeah. You called me *Uranus*."

"I don't get it?"

"*Uranus* is the *Greek god* of the sky."

"<u>Your</u> Anus shits itself," he replies.

"But *Pluto* bangs your anus."

"*Pluto's* a dog, dude," Davey says, real matter-of-factly, like he's correcting me this time.

"He's also a planet, and a god, but yes, *Pluto* is a dog, and yes Pluto's always behind Your-Anus," I state.

"I still don't get it," he says, confused.

74

"It's a play on words, man. Uranus. Your anus. Pluto? The planet after Uranus? Pluto. Get it?"

"Stupid, you gotta stop," Davey says, with a smile, he might be having a better time, at least a forgetful moment of shit-land.

Munts excuses himself, "Hey guys, I'm like, like going to go check on my brother." Munts is digging his knuckle into his stressed temple. Poor guy's worried about that kid. We both remember his shitty night, and this will lead us right back to thinking on Davey's shitty ass night.

"I'll catch up with you at school? Maybe they got the knife out," Munts says as he dig, dig, digs at that migraine. Davey and I cringe, ow, —*metal against the nerves, under your skin, pulled from the flesh, the thigh area too large to sedate; besides the boy's way too young to be pumped with morphine; oh the horror.*

"Go see your brother dude. Tell him I'll dub him some music to make him feel better," Davey offers Munts. They slap hands, grip each other's palms, cup their elbows, sentiments, and strength. Davey pulls Munts into a hug, "Be good, bro." Munts returns, "You too, man," gets up, turns to me, "Thanks for everything *Aquaman,* laters," and leaves. "Hey, let's not make *Aquaman* a thing, 'kay?" I say to Davey, who chuckles. "You get the best nicknames." I frown, "No, I don't." He cocks his head, "Kinda do." Now we're alone, reality check. Davey and I just got into it, wailed on each other, hard. Things are tense aren't they? Deep inside he might still have volcanic blood, just playing me with a poker face. I better play this cool, don't be a Dad to Davey. He's your friend, Tyler. You have no authority here.

o   •   o

I've known Davey since we were seven or eight. We met at an after-school summer program. It was a pottery class and a *Logo* computer class. In pottery, we would make oblong vases and ashtrays painted in blacks and blues. Our teacher was this universal hippie lady from *Cotati,* a small town just outside *Luma,* but compared to us, it's pretty tiny, one main road, and the countryside residential area. They got their own authentic music hall, the *Cotati Cabaret,* 21 and over,

Fishbone's played out there. Never played the *Phoenix* yet, what's up with that? *Tom Waits* lives out there as well. *Norman Greenbaum's* out there, used to work at *Jeromes' Good Dogs*, as a cook, a drunk cook, taken for a no residual ride for his ultra-hit *Spirit in the Sky*. Still wasted in *Cotati*. In a few years *Ron Howard* will use it in his *Apollo 13* space flick, and bammo, *Norman* will get some financial just deserts. Music industry is fucked up. Anyhow, our Hippie Teacher's teeth were yellow from all of the weed she puffed. At that age, we thought she chewed tobacco like a baseball player. We were so naïve, ha. Couple years later we figured it out. Learned all about weed. Kelsey and her friends used to have it around all the time. Not Kelsey specifically, but her friends did. Kelsey wasn't always a child of the *Lord*; she used to be cool as fuck. We'd go with her and her older friends up to the *Russian River* to dick around in the water, jump the bridge, inner-tube, watch them get high, spy on them as they sucked face on the rocks. Kelsey was always cool to us. Treated us as equals, sort of. Never let us smoke weed, but never made us leave. She saved me once up there too. I drowned. Got caught in the current, my shorts tangled up on the branches of a dead bush in the middle of the river. Pulled me under. I couldn't get up. Couldn't breathe. Kelsey was the only one who saw me. Swam over, had to rip off my shorts, pull me to safety, did the CPR. I was naked on that beach. Sand all up in my ass. Davey was really scared. Could have been his fault? But I took his dare. It was my fault. I took full responsibility. Davey felt guilty. Never dared me again. His sister got weird though. It really spooked her. Found God. Needed a scapegoat, needed a reason why bad things happened. She got lost when I got saved. I didn't see them again for the longest time. We weren't necessarily separated, but neither of our parents were going out of their way to plan play dates, besides I didn't even go to elementary school in *Petaluma*. I was bused to *Marin County* for grades One through Six, Private School.

I only had a few friends from *Petaluma* growing up. Most of them were on the swim team with me. They were Pauly, Pat, Scott, Darigen, Amy, Dan, etc. Davey and I started really hangin' again come *Petaluma Junior High* when

I was relocated to Public School. He seems to remember more as we sit and reminisce. He spits tales about when he came over to my place and Mom made us her specialty, cornflake chicken, and how we watched movies all night, how my parents actually checked up on us, but were cool about it. He recalls another time when he tagged along to a swim meet in *Napa*, and they let him be a Timer and hold the check-in cards when a competitor took to his or her lane. Says he dug clicking the stopwatch on and off, how they even let him be responsible for writing down the times, and that he had done a good job, that my Dad bought him two hotdogs with mustard and relish. How he had never had relish before and that's a major plot point for him. Thought it was cool that I was part of a team back then, and it seemed like I had a lot of friends, and how out of place he felt, that this was not something he could be a part of, not coordinated enough, not dedicated about anything, and that, that was the first time he had ever felt sad inside. Felt like he may never fit in. Born an outcast. Born feeling adopted. It was at that swim meet he had decided to be my best friend, but then I drowned and we lost touch, until Junior High. He had helped me meet new people, showed me the ropes of Public School, the pecking order of jocks, punks, hicks, skaters, girls, stuff like that. Says he still feels adopted. He's been saying that ever since I can remember. Davey's not adopted, just despises his family. Finds them fake. All of them. Blames Kelsey's moral transformation on his parents, not my accident. Figures they *Christ*-programmed her as a child. "Dude, your accident just opened a door for them to get her back in," and he gets up, peeks into her hospital room. I'm about to join him before he sits back down, saddened. Sad about the miscarriage, or still bummed out about losing his sister years ago?

Davey was born under a bad sign. He's never conformed. His own father calls him a bad sign, for no better reason than being a hyperactive kid, no other reason than having no interest in sports, cars, country music, and *Jesus*. All that adds up to Davey whole heartedly believing he must have been adopted. Davey is his own xenophobe.

"Summer was always excellent with you, man. You have

no idea how lame elementary school was," Davey finishes.

"You went to a swim meet with me?" I totally do not remember that.

"Really? Totally remember that day, like perfectly."

> —*Did he really go to a swim meet with me?*
> *I go to so many of them who could remember?*
> *Maybe he did?*
> *Can't believe it meant so much to him.*
> *What a deep kid he was.*
> *I still don't feel that deep,*
> *and my skull is always analyzing shit,*
> *but man, Davey's heavy.*

"We didn't need *Mini-Thins* back then; we were mini-thins; quick, speedy, tiny, little things," he says, "But it's the accident, that's probably why you don't remember shit," he reminds me.

"*Spirit in the Sky* brother," I say, "Never saw it, just a drifting darkness of nothingness, and no memory. My head hit that tree in the river so hard that I just disappeared. I guess it must've been before that, huh? The meet you went to?"

"Probably. Hey, you got any *Thins* on ya?" he asks.

"No, and dude it's already 3 in the morning," I stop, "Oh shit it's 3 in the fucking morning and I haven't called my Dad."

"You're busted, huh?" Davey knows I'm busted.

"Probably. You too? Not as bad as your sister though."

"Hell no, not even close," and we both chuckle about that.

"Should I call my Dad?" I ask him.

"T, I broke up with you for a reason, I don't want to influence you anymore, so don't ask me shit like that."

"Broke up with me? You better be gay blowing me before you use words like that. And I ain't gay," I say, keeping this civilized.

"Don't worry, I don't like the taste of chlorine," he jests.

"Dude," I stop the lameness, "Dude, I wanted to talk to you about that shit, man. I'm your friend, Davey, and I'm strong willed enough to make my own decisions without falling into your mindless hypnotism. You're no cult leader, just my friend." Davey's hurt. Even though he says he doesn't want me around anymore it's obvious he loves me. Needs me. Not butt-buddies, but more than just a friend, he needs me to be family. We are brothers. I continue, "So ball up and let me be your friend. Let me decide when I'm going to be there for you, or when I'm going to stab you in the back. This is what friendship is, man. Trust first and then you go and deal with it when that trusting friend fucks you in the ass. But I'm not going to fuck you over, so chill, 'kay?" but he has no response. He's listening. He's just not going to give me anything to work with. "Look dude," my monologue rolls on, "You get a raw deal man, but I love you. I've got your back, and when you screw up, then, and only then will I kick your ass to get you back up on your feet, or to stop you from sinking deeper in your own shit." Done. Said my peace. Fuck you, "Cool?"

Davey is silently impressed. "We cool? You gonna let me jerk you off now?" I laugh, he laughs, we do the palm slap, man hug, and together peek into Kelsey's hospital window. Kelsey's asleep in her darkness, a soul in that has tumbled into a terrible depression based on human biology. Our own reflections look back at us through her, and Davey says, "She tried to kill herself, T. It wasn't just a miscarriage." And Kelsey rolls over toward us and I can see her wrists covered in bandages, and even though her eyes are closed I can see how deeply sad and sorry she is.

chapter NINE

i'm heading downtown, hope to run into someone, anyone, well maybe not anyone, as I see Allison the talk-aholic; Allison, who's already got her arm up attempting to wave me to attention.

—FUCK.

I trip over a dog leash that chokes the miniature canine being walked by some child. "Aren't you afraid you'll get kid-swiped?" sometimes I am so inconsiderate as I suddenly recall *Polly Klaas*. "Sorry, didn't mean that," I apologize, but he flips me off and keeps walking. Allison laughs at me from across the street. "Don't trust him, kid, he's a total Pedophile," she yells, and really that doesn't make anything better, as conservative antique shoppers give me an evil eye, so now I have to flip her off and cut down the alley.

I've wandered the entire downtown, crossed the river behind the *Apple Box Gift Store*, walked along the river bank, crossed back over the draw bridge, past the vacant dilapidated warehouses, back through some residential streets, and as I'm coming up to the *Boys and Girls Club*, I ditch into the bushes, and now I'm standing at the gaping mouth of one of our bigger storm tunnels, a creek wide, 12 feet tall. There is a slight stream of water entering the void.

○　　　•　　　○

Prior to all of that I had cruised by *The Phoenix*, which is closed on Sundays, and no one was loitering so I checked all the halls of *Thrifty's RX*, and saw someone's Mom browsing the cold medicine—

"Hello," I make contact.

"Oh, hi. Tyler, right?" she asks.

"Yup. You sick?"

"Oh no, this is just a little something for my arthritis," this unrecognizable Mom lies as she puts like four packs of *Sudafed* in her purse.

—Is she stealing those?

"Ouch. Well, feel better and say hi to," but have no idea who came out of this thieving woman's womb, and then like a hammer to the head it comes to me as she asks, "You and Trish don't see much of each other anymore now, do you?"

—Oh, you're my ex's Mom.
Wow, you've changed.

That's how I know this woman; my junior high school girlfriend of two weeks. Mom's really let herself go. "Nah, We're in different cliques, ya know? She still doing ballet?"

"Well she's taking a little break," she tells me through her hallow, leather tight face with a smile of rotted teeth. This woman used to actually be really attractive. Now, now she looks starved, dehydrated, shriveled, basically mummified.

"Well it was nice seeing you again. Should I have Trish call you?" she says already stepping away.

"Oh, sure. Did you move?" I am so bored that I've actually tried to continue this conversation.

"No, we did not move. Have a nice day Tyler," and she walks away; and it all comes rushing back to me. I never actually went to her house with Trish; I had gone to the house with my buddies, to her Mom's parties, this lady's crazy ass parties. Trish and I had broken up by then; she dumped me, probably because of her psychotic upbringing.

Trish's Mom had the most raging parties.

I step into and through the *Thanksgiving* aisle. I spy with my little eye, paper turkeys, ceramic scenes of fabricated truths, *Native American* face paint, *Pilgrim* costumes, and because I despise *Thanksgiving* more than most holidays, I kick aside a bouquet of plastic squash, wave, to Trish's Mom, and head towards the automatic door. Leather face Mommy is buying gum.

> —*How 'bout paying for five packs of Sudafed you snuck into your purse?*

There's an underworld here in *Luma*, go figure, right? Small clans of speed-freaks hidden in refurbished chicken coops and dilapidated town houses. They're not kids, they're adults, some of them have children going to school with me, but I'm not up on all of it, and honestly didn't know Trish's Mom was a *Crystal Meth* cook in training.

I have this theory that every time something bad happens right before your eyes you open a passageway in your brain that makes you aware of more bad things. You start to notice stuff that's not so right, smells unkosher, a *Spidey-Sense* for the macabre, and even if you don't know what it means, or exactly what you're experiencing, you now notice it, when before that you never really caught on to the other six fucked up situations happening around you.

o   •   o

After *Thriftys* I made my way down the alley behind the parking lot, down the cement stairs that lead to *Putnam Park*. The park was empty, not even a family having a sandwich, no old ladies watching the fountain; nothing. Even more bored, I made my way to the river. Most of the stores are closed along this whole trek, save for the Antique shops— *Sundays, Sundays, Sundays* —7-*Eleven's* open, but I have no quarters, and it's overrun by junior high school rug rats, so I crossed to wander aimlessly through the *Old Mill Mall*.

o   •   o

Blah, Blah, bla— so here I am up by the *Boy's and Girl's Club*. I crossed the street, disappeared through the brush, crept down the muddy slope, and stopped here at the mouth of *Petaluma's* mighty storm tunnel. The walls are coated with punk-rock graffiti, nothing gangster, not yet, not so soon, few more years it'll be all *Hip-Hop.* I'm going in solo.

o   •   o

A year or two ago— maybe a few months ago —Davey was standing in front of Munts and I at this man-made hole under the city. It was Munts who reassured us, "Yeah been in there like a few times." I know Munts likes to embellish, but what's an adventure without doubt; we all stepped inside, Munts had brought a flashlight.

Fifty/sixty yards inside and the tunnel takes a long curve and the sunlight vanishes. If it wasn't for Munts' flashlight we'd be in pitch black. "It keeps going," Munts said. We continued along the side, the water flowing down the center of the tunnel as it widens, and slightly deepens a few inches.

"Snakes down here," Davey says trudging on.
I stop, "Really? You had to say that," I turned back to Munts who's been lighting our way,

"Flash the ground, I want to see what's down there," I insisted. There must've been a hole in my boot because my

foot felt wet—• • • *My brain shifts into the Present Tense*

The memory places me here and now
•

. . . .   •

•
·•—Munts tilts the flashlight down onto the sloppy, stream of a surface. Nothing. It's just a slow flow of muddy water that leads deeper into the tunnel. I'm scanning for life forms.

"Munts are there really snakes down here?"
"How the fuck would I know?" he replies.

—Thought you've been here before?

Davey is yards in front of us deep into the darkness.

"You've been here before," I complain to Munts.

"Just a couple times, never went this far," he admits.

"Dude we barely went anywhere," I'm stunned.

"I found something!" Davey yells, his voice echoing off the curved cement walls.

"Holy shit, echo's rad," I yell, "Right behind ya, nut wads!"

— nut wads – nut wads — nut.wads — wads — wads — ads — dsss — Sssssssss.

. . . .We catch up to Davey on the other side of the water flow. He's beside a smaller circular tunnel in the wall, about a foot higher than ground level. "What? Oh, That looks rad," says Munts as he slops right through the water, soaks his feet and leans into the hole with his flashlight, "Goes on for miles."

I tip toe through the stream, this shit has got to be gross, where is this runoff from anyway, smells funky down here, and I'm at the hole and I'm looking in, and Davey's looking in, and Munts is making the flashlight do light circles down the cement cavern of forever.

"Let's do it," Davey says taking the flashlight, pokes me in the belly, and climbs in. The tunnel is shorter than us, and we have to walk like spiders, our arms stretched out, hands pressed up against the upper curve, our feet making steps along the bottom curve, but the water level in here is at least six inches, so none of us want our feet to slip into that sickness. This is fucking super crazy, we better not get lost down here, and I turn back to see how far we've gone already. I'm the last in line. I can't see the opening we came in through. It's pitch black. Could be a couple yards, could be a football field away, can't tell. We've spidered along for a good few minutes, so we're deep, and I think this tunnel has curved around a couple of times already. "I see light!" Davey yells back to us— *Doesn't echo in this tunnel, not wide enough, I guess?* —I can see the light as well. Comes from above. Davey steps right into the light and now I've caught up to them, "It's a grate in the road," I tell him.

"No shit?" Davey says, "Where do you think we are?"

"I don't know? Few blocks from *McDowell Park*?" Munts guesses.

"Could be the park?" I can see some trees, I think?

"Nice," Davey says, and keeps going forward.

"Really? How far do you want to go?" I yell after him, but he's spider-running, and shit he's got the flashlight, so Munts and I have to spider after him, and soon enough the grate's light behind us is gone and we are back in the pitch-black darkness chasing the bouncing flashlight in the hand of the most irresponsible one of us all, Davey. I slip, one foot touches down in the water and that sucks and the guys are getting farther and farther away from me. I gotta keep going. I have to hustle. Munts the non-athlete is getting winded and suddenly everything goes dark, and we all stop, and no one speaks. I do my best to see something, anything. I can't see shit. I know Munts is right in front of me, I can hear him wheezing. Why can't I see him? I reach out and I touch his face. He screams and— SPLASH —He topples into the water and I'm freaked and try to help him up, but he's thrashing around, accidently kicks me, and finally gets up on his own. I still can't see a fucking thing, then suddenly there are strobe-light flickers and it's Davey making an attempt to light his Zippo. Flick, Spark, Flick. Nothing. Spark, Flick, Spark. It's terribly nerve racking, "STOP THAT!" I yell at the prick. He stops. "Holy shit," I'm taking a deep breath, "Okay, I can't see shit; what happened to the flashlight D-man?"

"I dropped it," he says quiet enough.

"I'm going to kill him," I tell Munts.

"Yeah, like now," Munts says, probably dripping wet.

"Ok, chill. Davey!" he doesn't answer, "Dude! Let's go back!"

"I don't know. What if it's faster this way?" he says, he's right beside me. Fuck, it is really dark in here.

"But we know this way is cool," I tell him, "We might even be able to get out at the grate?"

"Nah, let's go this way," Davey won't listen to reason.

"Hells no," Munts is over the adventure.

"Pussies," D complains as he puts a hand on Munts, "Ew, you're all wet."

"I know, asshole," he says and— LIGHT —suddenly the flashlight turns on right in Munts eyes, and I don't know if I am going to laugh or cry.

"Wow, you suck dude," I say and D-dick shines the light

right into my eyes like the doctor. I'm blinded, "Get it out of my face!" He lowers the light, and Munts lets out a "Holy shit!"

"What?" Davey asks.

"Look down," Munts says, freaked, massaging his temple. We all look down. The stream is pouring, from both directions, into a body sized diameter hole that goes straight down. "No way," I'm shocked." We all could have fallen into that shit, been teenage *Baby Jessicas*. How many holes have there been? Munts slipped a few yards back; he could have totally died, disappeared into the tunnel's anus forever, oh that is the most *Horrible Thought* ever. I stop that one from scribing itself out of my psyche.

"I don't think we should fuck around anymore," Davey says.

"Fuck you dude, you almost killed us!" I'm pissed.

"I fucking know that!" he yells back at me, Munts must be going deaf, "So let's just get the fuck out of here the way we came, and I'll point the flashlight down from now on," he ends calmly. Munts just says, "Yeah, let's just do that."

"No shit," I say, "But I'm holding the fucking flashlight this time," and I swipe it out of Davey's hand, lead us back, never actually see another hole in the ground. That was the only one.

•   •   •   • •• •   •   •   •

I really thought we were going to die that day.
—Lesson learned—
Don't let Davey lead the way with the only flashlight.

•   •   •   • • •   •   •   •

•

Today— I'm back at the tunnels alone. I've only gotten as far as the outside light will let me go. This place is too dangerous without a flashlight, a death wish. I hear voices. There are people down here. I wait it out. They aren't coming closer. Smell burning plastic. Might be some homeless guys. Probably smoking crack. I think I'm outy.

•

○   ○

Back home. Bored, staring out my bedroom window at the dairy trucks that consistently roll by my house up to the Dairy Factory a few blocks down the way. I'm still selfishly relieved that last night was both a Munts family accident, and a Davey shit show, instead of a Goodman disaster. I like my drama-less family. The sun melts oranges into purples across the surrounding hills. The *Phoenix Theater's* billboard was empty today. I try to remember who played this weekend; we didn't go to any shows. Probably *Greenday*. We hate *Greenday*.

chapter TEN

*C*hanukah   in   *Marin*   with   family—
—School
—Swim practice
—School, finals creeping up on us
—Head-on-collision, Allen Anderson, age 17; Rest In Peace.

·

○   ○

December means no more morning swim practice until
March. That means one more hour of sleep per day for me.
Winter Bliss.

Munts can't come out and play 'til after *Christmas* 'cause
he's grounded for almost killing his brother. We see each
other at school. He's been hooking up with Erin, but would
really benefit from a decline in probation so he can get past
kissy-kissy under the bleachers; they don't really fool
around under there; they usually suck tongues outside
Chinese & Donuts. Davey's been coming to school, no one
brings up his past absence, and no one brings up the rumors.
Cindy has been avoiding me, but she chilled on the devilish
glares when she does cross my path, so I just think she's the
kind of person that needs a lot of cooling down time.

Primus is playing the weekend after finals. I hear some

girl named Sheena from *Casa Grande* has been asking about the camera guy at all the *Phoenix* shows. I'm flattered, I think I know who she is, but I really don't, but my boy hormones are deeply interested in this mysterious Sheena. I'm guessing it's all rumor and pig fat.

I study for finals. I'm working the *Spanish* for a B, "Si senior, me hablo espanol." I really can't get a D. Dad's working longer hours for the holidays, Mom's reading a lot more, Munts wants to exchange presents for *Christmas*. Davey's been over a couple times. Tells his folks he's studying for finals with me. Like we're in the same *Honors* classes, not. We just listen to music, flip through back issues of *Maximum Rock n' Roll*, movies, shoot the shit about politics. "No way. *Clinton*? Maybe he's okay, but his *VP*? Fuck that. That muther-fucker sticks his dick in *Tipper Gore*. That bitch started the *PMRC*; no excuse, cunt's a censorship whore. Fuck the *Clinton Administration*," he says, on a loop, and I guess, well, fuck, how do you justify that *VP Al*? And your last name's *Gore*, embrace that shit. Cut your guts out, show us what's really inside.

Davey's done sewing up his leather liner with Mom's needlepoint kit. We're watching *A Clockwork Orange* and twenty minutes in and he's already getting up off the beanbag, his attention span dwindles quickly; the guy can't sit still. He's at my bookshelf scrolling through the titles. "You read all those, Red?" Davey asks.

"No. Come on, watch the movie," I don't like being distracted.

"I'm watching," he replies as he slides *Dalton Trumbo's Johnny Got His Gun* off the second shelf from the top, "Is this good?" Davey asks, flips through the pages, and waves it at me.

"The fucking best, borrow it. Come on sit down, you're making me nervous."

"You're always nervous," Davey starts as he turns back pocketing the paperback into his leather, walks right past the TV and over to the tape rack that he's been through a billion times, "You're high strung, dude, all wound up, kinda *Jewy*."

"Hey *Nazi-Punk*, fuck off."

"*Nazi* scum fuck-fuckers," he mumbles.

"Yeah, right? So don't say shit like that about being *Jewish*," I defend my heritage.

"Sorry, stupid joke," he apologizes.

"I know, I just want you to shut up so we can watch the fucking movie," I say as he flops back into the beanbag—slush.

"It's true, though, you're right. I hate *Nazi* fucks, and jokes like that are totally fucked up. I'm sorry," Davey continues, now pounding the beanbag.

"It's cool, dude, I'm really not offended."

"You should be."

"Nah, it's cool. Just stop that," I say about the annoying beanbag punches, "That shit is neurotic." *Malcom McDowell* and the girls are undressing in the hotel room. I pause the tape. Davey won't let it go, "Cool? It's not cool. It's never fucking cool. *Nazi* fucks are assholes and I'm sick of people thinking I'm one of them. I'm sorry."

"Grow your hair," I say...

—and shut up.

"I'm not a skinhead, dude," he says brushing his hands through his gelled up, inch long, spiked head of bleached, blonde hair.

"Dude, look where we live? This isn't the city. We're 45mins North, bro— chick-fuck *Petaluma*. People drive by this place. We don't even count as a suburb of the metropolis. You look like a skinhead to these farmers and, fuck, even the hippies think your style's questionable," he glares at me, "It's not you, dude, it's them. Grow your hair."

"Chicken shit conformist like your paaaaarents," sings the anti-shit. And I shut the fuck up.

-
-
-
-
-
-
-
-
-
-
-
-
-
-
-
-
-

chapter ELEVEN

*P*rimus *sucks! Primus sucks! Primus sucks!—* This sucks. Something's wrong with the *Phoenix* soundboard and 800 revved up hippie-funk-punk-metal-heads, hicks, chicks, and twits are all impatiently waiting for *Primus* to come on stage, and I've got the shits from eating burritos at a four table Mexican chop-shop where dropouts play *Skate Hockey* in the back lot. *Skate Hockey* is simply hockey with skateboards. A couple of *Luma-Skaters* claim they created it, but I know that's bullshit because it's not rocket science to combine the two sports, especially when no idiot in their right mind is going to be caught playing *Rollerblade Hockey*.

•
○   ○

I've made my way up the lobby stairs. I'm considering dropping off the *Cosby kids* in the boy's room, but when I get there, the place wreaks of piss and the door-less stalls are a fine deterrent from leaving *Rudy* in a bowl— I bump into Tom Gaffey as I step back from the scribbled-up door. "R-r-rats again?" Tom stutters.

"Rats? You got rats?" I ask

"In simpler terms, someone told me some jerks were

pissing all over the floor up here," Tom redefines, "Rats."

"Yeah it's pretty bad in there. *Claypool* ever going to play tonight?" I inquire.

"I'd hope so or I got a riot on my hands, even though the vacation time's nice when they close this place down. You're too young to remember the last time. Guy fucked a chicken on stage. That gave me a few months off, but more or less, I'm trapped; the kids need their music. *Claypool's* gonna play," he reassures me, clears his throat with a couple clack-clacks, Tom's charming and characteristic tick.

"Okay?"

"Told *Les* these kids don't care if he plays electric or with his ass-cheeks," spits Tom.

"What he say?" I ask.

"Fix the sound system, Tom," he answers.

"Really or was it more like," and with my best *Les Claypool* impersonation say, "Trout don't swim downstream, Gaffey. How 'bout a tug?" Tom laughs and says, "Nope, just fix the sound,"— clack-clack.

I shrug and us two comrades of the *Phoenix* go our separate ways. Tom tends to the sticky pee, and I am back at the stairs and still have to drop a load.

"Lord, have mercy! They smokin' asparagus!" Tom cackles as he rushes out of the bathroom, covering his nose with his shirt. He catches up to me weaving down the steps, "Jesus, Tyler, it's a fucking zoo in here sometimes,"— clack-clack — passes me, weaves through the acid-heads on the steps. Everyone who eats that shit always ends up sitting on the steps. I don't get it.

"You're the zoo keeper, buddy," I yell at him, but Tom just waves it off as he enters the salty sea of a crowd loitering around the lobby waiting for some *Frizzle Fry* for their frantic brain mush. You don't even realize how bad I gotta shit. My stomach bubbles, begs for relief, my anus so clenched, and Tom vanishes into the venue. Some hippie chick with the most dilated eyes looks up at me as I'm squiggle down the stairs. She asks, "Where have all the rainbows gone?" but I got no time to philosophize with Lucy-D, 'cause I know my bowels are going to flow a river of poo and no logs. I gotta go home.

—Run fucking home,
shit in the first floor bathroom,
rush back, and maybe, just maybe,
I'll just miss the first couple songs,
but I've seen Primus like twenty times here
so whatever, right?

I make a break for it, step over the rainbow sucker, and her boyfriend tells me to go the other way, as someone else grabs my ankle. I nearly stack, but get a firm grip on the railing, twist my foot out of the jerk's hand as they all laugh at me, and shit like this makes holding your diarrhea a hell of a lot harder. I've tightened my grip around my stomach, elbow my way to the front doors, gotta get out.

—Fuck, Primus really fills this place.

I use my back to push on the long, horizontal, door handle, open the door, cool air rushes inside the 85 degree, 98% humidity of the lobby, and I'm out, turn forward and— BAM— right into the blue eyed gems of this striking brown haired girl; her thick, wavy hair just falls over her bare shoulders revealed through her hand cut collar of a fading *Jane's Addiction Nothing's Shocking* shirt, and if it wasn't for the bubbling, intestinal shit-quake in my abdomen, I probably would have really screwed up and checked out her tits, but I didn't. "Where's your camera?" she asks.

I step to the side, away from the door that keeps opening and closing, people breaking out of the heat for a cigarette, the whole time keeping my eyes on her, "Oh, I don't get to film everything," I humbly reply as some long-haired dude rudely walks right between us.

"That's lame. Is it 'cause you suck?" she jokes.

"Noooo," I'm grinning.

—ah fuck,
I can't believe this sick-looking girl
is talking to me and all I can think
about is rushing the fuck home

to unboard this gravy train.

We drift to a slightly less trafficked area. "I don't suck," I continue, "Look, I don't want to be a dick, like, but, I kinda gotta go." She's not offended, and in fact says, "Uh, hate to break it to you buddy, but I'd have to <u>like</u> you, before I cared if you ran out of a conversation."

—Oh, I so fucked up

I try to mend it, "No, no, I didn't mean..." She interrupts me, "Go to your meeting, brown eyes, maybe I'll see you at *Denny's?*"

—Oh fuck, Denny's? I'm banned from Denny's.

The girl is giving me a second fucking chance here and I'm banned from *Denny's* because of Davey's dumb-ass, and I'm so gonna shit my pants if I keep talking to her.

"Davey and I got 86ed from *Denny's*. Maybe I'll see you at *Lyons?*" and I'm out, walk away, don't look back, slowly pick up the pace as I pass the ungodly amount of rocked out loiterers along the block. I glance back in hopes of cathcing another look at the girl through the crowd, and I do and she waves, turns away, heads back into the *Phoenix*, and I trip over Jimmy-the-Germ's legs that he's got sprawled out in the middle of the sidewalk.

"Watch it *Aqua-Toad*," Jimmy barks at me.

"Fuck off," and I run home and the shit-river's an insta-upside-down geyser as my naked ass cheeks hit the cold, plastic seat, *brrr*, and I say under my breath, "That girl was totally hitting on me. Must've been that Sheena chick. Damn, she's hot," and another hot stream drops.

Knock-knock on the bathroom door and my Dad asks, "You alright in there?" And I fart.

chapter ELEVEN & ^a_HALF_

i cruise back up the block to the _Phoenix,_ still on foot, my car's in the lot as always. Amazing how different the world looks when you no longer have a load of burrito sludge in your abdomen. I can see straight, and as I get closer, past _Swensens,_ I can hear the rumble of a sound system that's working. I pick up the pace as _Claypool_ hollers into the mic, _"We need new pornos!"_ and a crowd of 800 plus repeat after him, "We need new pornos!"

I'm at the doors, they're closed, locked, and some stoned kid right outside says, "Sold out, dude." I ignore him and press my face against the ticket booth window trying to see into the dark office. Light suddenly fills the small booth and I can just make out Gaffey lean his long torso inside in search for something under the counter. I start whapping on the glass to get his attention. He looks up and with no hesitation waves me in. I turn to the glass door and he's opening it for me, "Get in here; they went on like twenty minutes ago," clack-clack. I squeeze through the door, Tom slams it closed on some other kid who thought he could squeeze in behind me. "Where's your camera?" he inquires.

"What? You mean I could've shot _Primus_?" I'm flabbergasted.

"I'd say so. Well, next time. Have fun," and he leans back into the office.

I quickly make my way down the hall to the arena, cursing the gods-of-poo and Gaffey for not telling me earlier that I could've shot a *Primus* show. Fuck! Past the pool table, totally empty, through the black double doors, bursts of heat and human energy— into the theater hall, and it's packed; people fill the back aisles of worn, red, faux suede fabric theater seats. I'm trying to get to the main floor, can't see anything, and *"It's pudding time, children."*

I squeeze into the sea of sweat and eccentricity, my feet lifting above the floor from the mass of monsters. This place is so packed. I'm no longer walking, I'm floating amongst the waving body mass, using my upper arms, wade through the outer layer of the circling mosh pit, twenty to thirty people thick wondering— *where Sheena is; if that was even the Sheena girl who's been asking about me* —I break through, almost get swooped away by the mosh current, but plant my heels against the wooden floor, anchor them, my swimmer shoulders push back the layers of people behind me until this burly dude to my left hooks my arm and says, "I gotcha, kid. You wanna go up?"

—Up?
Aw shit, no, not really.
I just totally took the nastiest dump
and don't think I'm in any shape to crowd surf.

—but this 250lb bear with a *Faith No More* shirt has already got his other arm under my leg and this other kid to my right follows his lead and they lift me up, and I'm wiggling, try to break free, but the crowd's a behemoth of a mob and I have no control over the situation as someone pushes up on my spine and I'm Up, being tossed around by the 1,600 arms of this *Phoenix* behemoth. I am their throw toy.

Tumbling above the crowd, I can feel random hands push on my ass, sweaty heads of hair sweeping along my exposed back; exposed because my shirt has scrunched up against my neck. I'm choking to death and can't decide on using my hands to unleash the shirt or stop the crowd's elbows from digging into my ribs. I will say that the cool air above the crowd is refreshing amongst the putrid steam that rises from the evaporating sweat of this behemoth of rock.

o   •   o

I land stage-right, third row, 'cause the crowd's calmed down as *Lester* has a pow-wow with *Herb* and *Ler*. I plant my feet, squeezed in tight between *Shannon Ferguson* and *Neil Rosen*. "What's up, Goodman?" *Neil* asks. "Hey," I say through my pants of air from the tumultuous ride. They both shrug and *Neil* leans into me, asks, "You know our friend Ian?" I look past him and this Ian kid is standing right there, giant tall, young, flight jacket, with wrists that burst out from his sleeves, "What's up? Tyler," I introduce myself, "You need a bigger jacket."

"Orion," he corrects his friend, too quiet to even hear.

—Has this kid ever been to a show before?
Speak the fuck up.

"What?!" I yell at him.
A little louder Ian simply says, "My name's not Ian. It's Orion."

"Good to meet you Orion, you a senior?!"
"No, freshman."

—God he's tall.

"Cool! Guess you can see everything from up there?"
"Yeah," and smirks, but our new friendship is cut short, "We're *Primus*, and we suck!— One, two, three, four *—They call me Mr. Knowitall, I will not compromise. I will not be told what to do. I shall not step aside, HEY!"* — Bassline —and the crowd goes wild, a bopping wave of gyrating youth as *Claypool's* calloused fingertips pluck the thick metal coils of his electric bass, accompanied by the droned strum of *Ler's* handy guitar work creating a mist of sound around *Herb's* nonstop hard hitting, jazzy drum riffs that keep the audience afloat in time.

It's a great show; it's always a great show when *Primus* comes home to roost, "*Primus Suuuuucks!!*" I yell at the top of my lungs as the trio does a dramatic pause before continuing the jam.

o　　　　　•　　　　　o

Show's over. Hundreds of funk-punks beat with exhaustion, and stemming *Lysergically* laced blood cells, all filter out the side doors of the theater. Tom's right there directing traffic in the hopes to empty this place quickly and without casualties. "Safety first," he yells at some *Sebastopol* punks who are spitting on the crowd to get out. I'm standing out front by the ticket window scanning everyone's face in search of that girl.

—Maybe I should be waiting by the side doors,

—but I'm here now. I check my *Swatch*, a broken-styled design, big hand on the 12, little hand pointing down, no number 6, "Twelve Thirty?"

—What am I waiting for?
She didn't say meet me outside,
she suggested Denny's.
I shot that down,
suggested Lyons instead,
and now what T
?
Now,
you look desperate,
holding your dick
trying to catch this girl
before she goes to Denny's
because there is no way in hell,
no way, she's going to go
looking for me.

!WHAT THE FUCK!　　　•　　　*!I'M BLIND!*　　　•　　　*!CAN'T SEE!*

EVERYTHING'S GONE BLACK, WHAT THE FUCK?! I got my eyes open, do my best to see through the fingers that have wrapped around my face. Who the fuck? Say something? I thrash.

"Guess who, *Scorsese*?" a girl's voice.

—Cindy? Roussa? Sakina?

"Sarah Rennie?"
"Nope."

—Um, Jessika, Brooke?
I can see Victoria Webb walk by,
not her.
Who the fuck is this?
Devin? Jenny Staples? Grace Brown?
I know too many girls.
Who the fuck?

"*Samantha Fox*?" I jest.
"Try again," she says.

—Fuck!

That's it, no more games— I turn around. Sheena? If that's her name, is right there, her hair now a little less wavy from the heat of the concert. Dragon's breath of cold air escapes her tender lips as she suggests, "A bunch of us," she starts, but I can barely hear her over the outside chatter and the twinkle in her eye, "...are going out to *Elephant Rock*. Want to come?"

"I need to get gas," I say, accepting the invitation.

"You have a car?" she asks, takes a step closer, still don't know if she's that Sheena chick, can't ask, still hasn't told me, knows my name, I should know her, right? Even if she isn't her, I like this girl and she's coming on to me, so I'll continue to dodge the name game until I gotta ask, "I got a *Little Red Civic*; we call it Bruce," I say. She steps even closer, I can feel her body heat a few inches away; presses her hand on my chest, "You do not call it Bruce," she says with such disbelief. "No, I don't," I reply.

—This girl's really going for it.
See it in her eyes. Tigress.
Wants what she wants.
Good. I like that.

"Who's all going?" I ask.
"A few of my friends from *Casa*. You go to *Petaluma High*, right?"
"Yeah."

—Okay Casa, getting closer,
A little more info and I can safely assume
she is the Sheena.

"I thought you were a sophomore?" she says.
"No, I'm a junior," I correct her, and then I pry, "How do you know almost everything about me?"
"Don't ask a girl such questions," she schools me as she wraps her arm around my bicep, snuggles in close, walks us toward the parking garage, "I'm a senior," she informs me.
Okay, so now we're arm in arm, heading toward a group of people I do not know, and I still don't know her name. As we near the pack she gently releases my arm, but it's not a dis, as she takes my hand instead and walks us right up to her friends.
"Hey, Eddie, this is," she pauses, looks at me, "It's, Tyler, right?"

—Damn, she just beat me to the name game.

I'm hope this Eddie in leather, dark eye liner, short brown hair, gold studs in both ears, Anarchy tattoo between his thumb and index finger, says her name so I can breathe. I shake his hand.
"What's up, dude? You comin' with us?" Eddie barely inquires.
"Yeah man. Who's all driving?" I ask, but he doesn't answer, looks at her instead, and comments with a question, "He's cute, freshman?"

"Junior," I set that record straight, "You go to *Casa*?"

"Ha, Junior College dropout," he laughs, "I'm your elder."

"Okay, you guys dating?" I ask about Eddie and Sheena, *maybe*, as she gives him a huge hug and kiss on the lips.

"No kid, I'm gay, I just don't go announcing it to everyone," he declares, sniffles, wipes his nose with his sleeve and readdresses her, "You getting a ride with him, or you two want to come with us?"

—I do believe he just announced it to everyone,
but that's cool, means she's probably single.

She looks at me, shoots me a sweet, friendly grin, "Tyler here'll take me. He's got a *Little Red Civic*; calls it Bruce."

"No, I don't."

"Yes, he does."

—This is one of the best nights of my life.
This is the shit. All I have to do is
not ask her, her name, right?

"Alright, you want to follow us?" Gay Eddie asks me.

"Yeah that'll be cool, but I got to get some gas first," I tell him. He rolls his eyes, "You know how to get there?"

"Yup," she replies while bopping her body side-to-side.

"Be safe," Eddie urges the girl, kisses her on the cheek, turns to his cohort, "Let's roll," and they all file into the parking garage.

—Gay, huh?
That explains the two gold earrings.
Not a lot of gays in Luma.
I got no problem with gays,
they're just people, normal people;
it's just so rare to find 'em here.
I'm aware. My folks have gay friends.
I've got a gay friend in town; an older dude,
movie buff; name's Jeff, dubs VHS tapes for me.
Chill, beatnik, great taste, coffee-holic, never hits on me,
super normal, smokes a lot of weed, not a pansy, just normal.

Normal and gay.
Eddie's earrings are way flamboyant,
at least for a punk.
Very take-it-up-the-ass gay.
Maybe two studs means he's a taker?

Everybody wears some form of colors these days. *Crypts, Bloods, Jews* with their *Tzitzi, Neo-Nazi's* with their red suspenders and white laces. I don't fucking know. Two earrings, has to be code. The girl's telling me about Eddie's car as we head into the lot. "He drives an '84 *Volvo* he picked up in *Oakland* from a police auction. Got the little money-maker for $200. Safest car in the world." I think I heard her, maybe I zoned out.

"He dropped out of college, huh?" I ask.

"Guess so. Eddie and those guys are all from *Rohnert Park*. I met them last summer at the *Cotati Cabaret; Tom Waits* show," she says.

"*Tom Waits*? That's awesome," I say as we pass my car.

"Would that be your *Little Red Civic*?"

"Oh yeah, I zoned out there. *Tom Waits* show, at such a small venue, that must have been amazing," I say as we head back to my car. "You like *Tom Waits*, huh? What else? You like, um, *10,000 Maniacs*?"

"Not so much," and I unlock her side of the car, open the door, bow, take her fingers, and assist her into my carriage, "Would you be so kind to join me on a night on the town in the quaint and somewhat romantic city of *Cotati*?"

"How bout we go zone out on some giant rocks, and see where that leads us, junior," she's cocky, I like it, and she starts to giggle, kicks her legs up onto my dashboard, striped leggings, she pulls her skirt down over her knees, "I don't like them either. How 'bout *The The*?"

"Yeah, actually. Dig The The," I say, confident, yet worried I've just been tricked into admitting something not cool.

"Wow, nobody likes them. You're an original," and she pulls me down to her level, leans into my ear, "I like them too. Shhh," she giggles again as I make my way to the driver's side.

It's the *Violent Femmes, Hallowed Ground* that she's chosen to slide into my tape deck for the ride. The roads to *Elephant Rock* are long, dark as night, windy, and the shadows of the little hills out in the countryside towards *Bodega* are just mesmerizing to the tunes of the *Femmes*, and I have to make sure I don't go off into movie-land in my mind with this atmosphere and awesome little lady beside me; the roads are just too dangerous for daydreams at night.

"It's Sheena," she says under her breath, but really, it's just that the music is so loud.

"Excuse me?" I ask. I think I heard her right, but this is no time to get <u>this</u> wrong, especially after all the paranoid bullshit I've gone through over the past 45 minutes based on this name game in my brain.

"Sheena, my name's Sheena! You never asked," she says louder.

"I didn't have to," I say with confidence.

"Oh yeah, why's that?" she's so flirty.

"I knew you'd tell me."

"Oh, and how did you know that?"

"You kissed me first, remember?" I jest while I drift our drive across the single yellow line; have a little fun on the road. I glance over at Sheena. She's smiling at me. She liked my joke. I roll back into our lane, song changes. The girl leaps upright in her seat, cranks the volume, "*Country Death Song*! Best *Femmes* song ever!" she screams, kisses me on the cheek, and begins her sing along with *Gordon Gano*.

"*Violent Femmes* are from *Oakland*, right?" I ask over the music.

"What? Where do you get your information, dude?" she says, and continues singing, now right into my ear, "*We'll go out tonight, we'll go to the caverns, we'll go out tonight, we'll go to the caves...*" then the girl pops out of the passenger window. The foggy cold air washes against her. Her *Jane's Addiction* shirt presses against her well-shaped breasts, brushes the hair from her face, and screams the lines of the song into the Northern sky, as a black *Camaro* soars past my side at an ungodly speed, and as much as I enjoy Sheena acting out an *80's Teen Movie* in my car, I can't help the *Horrible Thought*— *in the rearview mirror, I watch as the Camaro swerves across the double yellow line*— *Horrible* — *BAM* —*head-on collision. The Camaro has ran right into the face of a mini-van, a fisherman on his way to work; takes this road five days a week, always curses the kids that drive too fast, too drunk, too stoned, sexing, being fuck ups. The Camaro somersaults over the van, the impact crushes both windshields, the fisherman's body presses up against the steering wheel and crushes his ribcage. His head snaps forward, back, forth, back, forward once more. His rib-bones puncture his lungs, blood splatters from his mouth against the dashboard, knees jam under the deck, the brake pedal bolts back, snaps his foot at the ankle, sideways. The fisherman's face gets sprayed with shards of glass, jabbing into his eyes, cutting apart his cheeks*— *Horrible Thoughts* —*The Camaro clears the van, but the teenage driver has no control as it continues to tumble over the ditch, down the slope, shakes his ragdoll body half-way out of the window, and finally lands upside down, the roof crushed, the driver cut in half, the junior high girls in the back seat, crushed to death. If only they hadn't begged him to drive faster because they were breaking curfew. If only they hadn't gone to the beach with a Senior. If only they all hadn't died*— *Horrible Thoughts.*

"Pull over!" Sheena yells snapping me out of my daymare, slides back into her seat, leans into my ear and whispers, "That's the rock," and I slow to a stop, check my rearview mirror, coast is clear. Looks good upfront as well, make a left, cross the line, roll into the *Elephant Rock* turnout on the other side of the road.

○   •   ○

The darkness of the night out here is a thick fog from the bay. The ghostly mist eases its way along the narrow valleys dug out by prehistoric rivers through these ancient hills, low on the ground, like a blanket on the grass. There are cows grazing down there, but it's night so I assume they are sleeping, standing up. You can see the sky clearly from the rocks. There is a partial moon. Sheena and I have nested inside a slight cave of one of the giant elephant shaped rocks. It's quite crisp and my teeth chatter, but my libido trudges on and bares the weather.

"You're shivering," she says, so kind, so soft; scoots closer.

"I'm cool," even if my balls have shrunk into my stomach.

"Don't be a tough guy."

"You're really beautiful, you know that?"

"Don't say shit like that."

"Why? It's true."

—Is she blushing?

Sheena acts bashful. I didn't expect that. Maybe I can tell it's an act. I play along. "Come on, you don't know how hot you are?" She shushes me, licks her lips, and presses them against mine. They're warm, wet, and we wrap our arms around each other as our tongues slide into each other's mouth. I can feel her tiny taste buds all along her luscious tongue. We're salivating. Hooking up is the shit. Her under tongue tastes so sweet. Her gums, sour. I'm so turned on. She's moaning. The vibrations of her larynx make my lips tingle. I consider *sliding my hand onto her thigh, up her dress. She's a senior, right?* She squeezes my package through my jeans.

—Oh, shit I'm going to blow if she does that again.

Before I cum too quick, before she grips me again, I make my move, slide my hand along her inner thigh, up to her groin, and firmly press my palm against her. She moans again, takes my hand, lifts it up, raises her skirt, and places my hand right under her panties.

—Am I going to get laid tonight?
So, fast, no dating?
Is this how true love happens?
Am I going to marry this girl some day?
Shit, I don't have a condom.

Sheena starts to gyrate into my palm, but I don't see a purse. A girl without a purse is not carrying a condom in her pocket. She is getting wetter and wetter— *I think she's having an orgasm* —and she twitches, shakes, and exhales. We sit up. Sheena's nuzzles into me. I'm her new favorite teddy bear, but I have to shift my dick 'cause my boxers are soaked in pre-dribble. I'm a little embarrassed about that. At least she doesn't notice, yet, and asks, "Are you a virgin?"

"Yeah," I say, under my breath.

"It's nothing to be ashamed of," she consults me, "We all start out that way."

"I'm not ashamed."

"Good, 'cause you won't be a virgin forever. Not guys like you," she says and kisses me again, but I stop her.

"What's that supposed to mean?"

"Don't be a dick, I'm complimenting you."

— Should I believe her?

"All I meant is that you got your shit together."

"I guess?"

"Girls like that. Real girls, that is."

"Real girls?" I ask, confused, am I being mocked? Babied? Is she trying to emasculate me?

"You're so cute. Yeah, *real girls*—not sluts, not attention whores, but <u>real girls</u>; girls with value," she tries to explain.

—I don't get it? Do I?
Think, T. Think on that.

"Hello? Earth to Tyler?"

"Sorry, I was just..." I start, but she takes my hand and begins to play with my fingers. I stop talking. I try to stop thinking. Everything is quiet. My heart races. We can just hear the faint sound of *Morrissey* coming from Eddie's *Volvo*, the doors ajar, laughter and the mumbled discussions from the cohort at the bottom of *Elephant Rock*. I'll be fine. I don't know this girl. I can't take things so personally. She's just more experienced than I first imagined. Relax, listen, and learn. Be her student. "Tyler," she hesitates, collects her courage, "Tyler," she repeats, and that's always a sign of bad things to come, "I don't think we should do this."

—I'm gonna play it cool, but she might be right.

"Do what?"
"This— you and me."

—Hm?
I can remedy this.
I can turn this around.
What would a movie do?

I lean in, go for the kiss, my kiss this time, don't fight it baby, this is love, you're mine, but Sheena pulls away, "No, don't do that." — Crash — Burn — I fucked up. My eyes sink back into my skull, my chest aches, hold my breath as the cave closes in on us, tighter and tighter. This is bullshit.
"Please understand," she begs.
"Understand what?" I am not very understanding.
"Agh, see, you're still a kid. I'm too old for you, you need to get hurt more before you can be with someone like me," she tries to explain herself, and yeah, maybe if I was a little more experienced like she says, I'd understand what she's talking about, but I'm not and I don't understand, and I'm suddenly hurt.

—Why?
Don't know.
Why do I care?
I do care, feel care.
Why's she doing this?
Is she a slut? Loose? Bad?

"I guess I'm hurt now Sheeeeena," I whine like a two-year-old.
"See, that's what I'm talking about. I like you, I really-really do, and maybe I'm the one being totally stupid here..."

—I can agree with that.

"...but I'm afraid I'm going to hurt you, and, shit, I don't want to be the first girl that hurts you."

—Which part of not hurting are you doing right now, bitch?

She's waiting on a response from me, again. I'm thinking. Have to think. This I don't like. This illogical bullshit I don't deal with well. Unjust. She was so confident all night, she knew how to do this, she brought the best out of me— *I thought she liked me?* —My gag reflex becomes inflamed, constricts. I'm choked up, but do my best to reason with her, "You're scared I get it. But this is me, the guy who's got it all together, right? I'm not going to mess this up. I won't treat you bad like the other guys," I say through chattering teeth, completely unaware that I totally just offended her.

"What's that supposed to mean?" she uses my own line against me.

—The scripts we could write together,
but what did I say that upset her?

"What do you know about the guys I've dated? You don't know shit, dude. You're making shit up in your mini-movie-making head. One night, not even four hours and you're all fucking judging me?" she says as she brushes the cave's dirt off her skirt, preparing to leave.

"I didn't mean it like that," I say, confused, trying desperately to get her back on my side, "I didn't mean to judge you."

"Look," she starts again as she gets up, but the mini-cave is too short so she's awkwardly bent over— uncomfortable — but she has a thought to finish, "I made a couple mistakes, okay, but I was a little girl and it's none of your business, 'kay?"

I'm listening. Calming myself down. Her disgust, anger, offence has leveled the playing field. She senses my new calm, lowers her tone, and takes the upper hand, once again.

"You're a really nice guy, but I'm a bit of a fuck up," she admits.

"Nah, come on, how bad could you be?"

"I'm not such a good person?" Sheena rephrases the same thing.

Her face has changed, kinda of like the two sides have shifted, diagonal. Sheena is really upset, and holds it all inside. How bad is she? I guess we can just be friends, but she doesn't think so, she's a wounded lamb that puts on a strong facade so people don't really get to know her and she keeps talking, "Look, tonight was really great, I've liked you for a long time, and really, I don't want you to think I'm a slut or anything."

"I don't," I reassure her, unaware that now, I too sound like a limp lamb.

"You're sweet, and I really wish we could do this. You and I, move in together after high school, take some courses at the JC."

—Whoa, hold the phone. Junior College?
Hells no. I'm going to real college.

Okay, now I realize she is not the right girl for me. She's simple, sweet, small town, not going to be my wife. And this, this realization gives the confidence to plant one last hard kiss on her, and we start going at it again, back on the ground, in the dust, my dick gets hard, she pulls me on top of her, spreads her legs, grabs my ass, and pushes me against her. We dry fuck for a few minutes and I cum my pants, full on this time. Felt great, but getting a little gross down there. Real sticky. I'm sure there's a stain.

o   •   o

Eddie sees us first as we make our way up the grassy bank that leads to the car turnout. Naturally, Sheena's fixing her hair and I've got my hands in my sticky pockets. Eddie calls out to us, "He gonna take you home?" lights his clove cigarette as his friends start to crowd into the Volvo, "Nah, I'll go with you."

"No, you don't have to do that, I'll take you," I butt-in.

"Don't be a gentleman," she tells me.

"I'm not."

"What then? You like me, you think if you drive me home..." and she stops herself.

"You love birds can fight about this tomorrow. Come on girl, I got ya," Eddie ends it for the night and makes his way to the driver's side. He doesn't get in, he waits, watches.

—Stay out of it Eddie.
Don't be a cock-blocker.

Sheena's uncomfortable with his eye on us. She takes my hand, leads me to the side.

"It really was a nice night," she's genuine. I think?

"I'm cool," yet I'm at a loss for words. I got no more fight in me. My pants are gross. Hard to think when I'm this sticky. Can we get this over with?

"You're going to break a ton of hearts, Tyler. Maybe we'll see each other at *Denny's* sometime?"

"I'm banned from *Denny's*," I remind her.

"Well *Petaluma's* pretty small, I'm sure we'll run into each other. Love ya, drive safe."

—You don't love me.

And with that Sheena was gone, poof, disappeared into Gay-Eddie's *Volvo* and for a second and a half, I was a little jealous of him, but he's playing for the other team and I can't help but lie to myself thinking maybe she does likes me? So, I make my way to my *Little Red Civic* and cruise home through the fog, alone— in silence.

•

•

•

•

chapter TWELVE

i want to call Munts. I want to call Davey, maybe I should call Cindy? No, Cindy hates me right now. I want to kiss and tell, but that's rude. I'll distract myself with homework instead.

1. History Essay
2. Jerk off
3. Science Hypothesis
4. Winter reading for AP English. I chose _Hubert Selby Jr.'s No Exit to Brooklyn_. My English teacher, _Mr. Liroff_, the only truly laid back, liberal, _Family Ties_ of a teacher is a great sport. Always does his best to bring a little more to the table than the status quo, and yet, even _Liroff_ had to get _Selby's_ book approved by the Principal. "I can't get fired, Tyler. It's not like you're asking to read _The Wind in the Willows_," he laid out for me as he flipped through the softcover, "You're talking about alcohol, rape, homosexuality, and whatever else that could get me fired from that book."
5. Call Munts to tell him how I almost fucked Sheena Ellison.
6. Jerk off again.
7. Write a short story
8. Jerk off again.

MINI THINS

•

•

•

•

•

•

•

•

•

•

•
•
•
·
·
·
·

chapter THIRTEEN

$d$avey's been complaining for the last twenty minutes, "…a cornucopia of exploding dick-heads behind my eyes. You have to cut the fire in sixteen different ways in order to get anything done. It's like digging up quicksand, man, I just don't care anymore,"—but before I can get a word in edge wise, he keeps on going, "She's just such a cunt, man. I don't know how many times I fucking came through for her. Did her deals for her? I was all there, man, I was a good brother."

"You're still her brother," I interject just to hear my own voice.

"Dude, I was the one who got her the cash for that abortion bullshit. So much bullshit for her and how's she repay me? Invites me to Church this Sunday. CHURCH!"

"What the fuck are you talking about?"

"Never mind," Davey totally changes the subject, "*Mr. Bungle's* gonna play in March."

"You hate *Bungle*, and no never mind, dip-shit, you tell me what you were just talking about. You got Kelsey an abortion? When? I thought she had a miscarriage."

"Don't be all smart now, *Speedo*."

"HEY!" I squawk.

"Just don't be a dick. I told you what's up, I'm done, I just needed to vent, dude," classic D.

"Whatever, but I still don't get the *Bungle* thing. You hate *Bungle*, why you want to go see them?" I ask.

"Ugh, smoke some pot dude. You like *Bungle*, that's why, 'cause you fucking love that funk shit, so I thought you'd like to know, that's it," Davey puts me in my place.

"No shit, and you're an asshole," I reply.

"All wet for you."

"Gay."

"Pooping out your name, like Sheeeeeeeena."

"Vanilla Cream Enema," I say, forcing dribble spit out my lip and down my chin.

"She ain't gonna marry you."

"I know."

"You're such a pussy. You are so in love with her."

"Fuck off," and I wipe my chin clean.

"Fuck yourself off, T. She likes you, and She-na, don't fuck nobody she likes. Yer outta luck. Move on. Find a different chick. Sheena's broken goods."

•

•

•

•

•

•

•

chapter FOURTEEN

$t$omorrow   happened
today, and yesterday was a *Vegas Convention* of bullshit and
expectations. I saw Sheena after school, after swim practice,
lied to my parents, said I was going to the big library by the
other swim center, the summer swim center, said I had a
paper on the *Revolutionary War, France*, I don't lie to my
parents, except when I lie to my parents, and we met at the
gas station at *Lakeville* and *Casa Grande Road*. She had gotten
us a pack of *Mini-Thins*, then went straight back to her
house. She cut my hair— I'm screwed.

o   •   o

Like a demi-goth-hippie-sprite, Sheena came scampering up
to my car before I could even get out. She's popping open
the passenger door and sliding in, gets right up into my face,
"I got some *Thiiins*," and plops into the seat, "It was four
bucks, you owe me two."
    "Okay, sure," I guess?
    "Let's hang out at my place. My parents went to *Bingo*,"
she fibs.
    "Really?" I ask.
    "No, my parents don't play *Bingo*; they went bowling, or

fuckin'— something lame. Make a u-turn, go out *Lakeville*," are the directions as she raises the *Mini-Thin* package to her mouth, bites down on the aluminum wrapping. I can feel the tingly, tin-tin feel of metal in my own mouth. She tears it, "Go." I shrug, turn the car on, putt-putt *Little Red Civic*, and roll out of the spot.

Sheena lives on a small farmhouse just off *Cougar Mountain Road*. It's fucking far for *Petaluma* standards and takes a good fifteen minutes of deep country road to get there. She's already popped the pills, without water, and has been going through my tapes as *LIVE 105* plays out their *Modern Rock* over the radio, half of *Losing My Religion*, all of *Stone Roses' Fool's Gold, Tom's Diner by Suzanne Vega w/DNA*, a round of commercials, *Liiiiiiive ONE-O-FIIIIIIIIIVE*, *Mens Warehouse*, some random *Marin County* Car Dealership, the new exhibit at the *De Young*, *CAPE FEAR* coming out in theaters.

"You want to see that?" I ask.

"*Taxi Driver* guy? Sure, why not," but she's not paying attention, she's consumed with my tapes, trying to read the handwritten label for *Butthole Surfers' PCPPEP*. The commercials end, *Liiiiive 105*, and *Teen Spirit* starts to play. I'm quick to push in whatever cassette I had in the jaws of the tape-deck, instantly silencing *Nirvana*, and we're joined by *Camper Van Beethoven* and— EJECT —I have to stop that shit right away because that's just embarrassing; being caught listening to *College Rock*, acoustic shit, all because I was goo-goo happy to meet up with Sheena and got gay-happy listening to that shit, and I'm begging the universe that she didn't just notice that *Blip-Vert* of sound. Should have just listened to *The The*...That we have in common.

"Oh, dude I think your tape deck just almost ate *Camper*, man," she says.

"Huh?" I'm astonished at her fine-tuned hearing.

"Hold on," and she pulls the cassette out to examine the destruction of the spooled tape, "Dude you could've totally lost this tape, man. It's okay though. Can I try it again?" she asks.

"Try what?"

"Hello, earth to Tyler," she commands my attention,

"Ground control to Major Twat; *Camper Van Beethoven*? Can I put the tape back in?"

"Yeah, it's cool, you like them?"

"I like music ya' know? Oh, my head's tingling, touch it," Sheena takes my hand and brushes my fingers through her locks, rubs my fingers against her scalp, makes my hand open and close like a spider. "AHHH!" she hollers, rushing my hand away, her body shivers all over, her lungs giggle, spooks me, makes me swerve.

"*Mini-Thins* so craaaazzzy!" Sheena exclaims, "I love 'em. Man, tingly, ha-ha, tingly on da head. TURN HERE! LEFT!"

I cut right across the yellow line and onto *Cougar Mountain Road*. Out of my peripheral vision, I catch the headlights illuminate the street sign.

"*Cougar Mountain*, really?" I ask.

"Yeah, no man's land. Oooooooh, scared?" she asks, "Right up there, third driveway."

I pull onto her gravel driveway, stop at the gate. House is about another 30-40 yards ahead. Sheena hops out. She's got worn jeans on, and her little ass peeks through the break under the cheek. Sheena's cool. She unlocks the gate, waves me through.

—Tomorrow happened Today.

o　　　•　　　o

The house is cold, 60 degrees, feels like 30. Whole place has hardwood floors and stained wooden walls. Got that cabin feel. I like it. "I wear a sweatshirt like most of the time," she tells me as we enter. The front doors, a monstrosity of carved redwood, bear faces, deer, trees, logs, etc, open with a thud, and each step is a thick clop against the floor, furnished like a farm house, handcrafted rocking chair, embroidered pillow casings, a loveseat for a couch placed beside the bunny eared 15 inch *Zenith* TV on a tree-trunk stool, drapes by Mom, three wolf heads above the fireplace— killed by Dad —and against the wall a *K-Mart* baby pen for a piggy that I see snoozing on a pillow with the word and images of bacon crafted in needle-point.

"That's Skag. I made my Dad let him live inside," Sheena explains.

"Why?" I ask with honest curiosity.

"I was like eight or something. You wanna a beer?" Sheena offers, as she passes the redwood dining table, swings open the kitchen door.

"No. Your house is crazy. Your Dad a hunter or something?"

"Got my first rifle when I was six. That middle wolf's my first kill," she says pointing him out. "Really?" I'm surprised. She rolls her eyes. "No. God you're gullible. Sure you don't want a beer?" I shake my head, she lets the door go, disappears into the kitchen. The door swings back and forth, thud, swoop, thud, swoop, thud.

I've squatted down beside Skag's pigpen. What does Skag mean? Weird fucking name, Sheena's a little weird when I think about it. Skag looks weird. Something is different about this baby pig, but maybe it's cause he's asleep. I move in closer, quietly. Do pigs bite? They eat shit, so I definitely don't want to get licked by this monster— not *kosher*, even though I eat the bacon. I think I'm noticing what's different about this little sin-of-a-meal. His features look developed, but that's a bit mature for a baby pig— *Wait? Didn't she say she was eight when she got him?* —His eyes are closed and he's so wrinkled, raisin wrinkled, and, I think the thing might be retarded.

"Here," Sheena taps my shoulder and offers me three *Mini-Thins* and a *Pepsi*, "You didn't take any yet."

I swipe the pills and drink, pop one at a time, sip, pop, sip, pop; sip. Sheena rolls right back into the story of the Skag, "And so, like this embryo-like mini-piggy was born last in his litter, and I was there, 'cause it was time I learned about the birds and the bees. Duh, I knew plenty even though I was little, but Daddy's girl don't need Daddy knowing dat," Sheena flops onto the couch. She's so fucking sexy. I've totally forgotten she went bitch nuts on me at *Elephant Rock*. Takes a sip of her beer, stretches, continues, "Skag looked like a little piece of poop when he was born. Tiny, tiny little poop pebble. Pops almost stepped on the little guy, but I saw him move. It was alive. You were alive, right Skag?"

Skag opens his eye, blinks the crud from his blinkers, and snorts. I could be watching my hot girlfriend lay out on her couch, sipping a cold beer, leaning it against her waist with the neck of the bottle positioned right between her breasts, but I'm not, I'm looking at the Skag wobbling to my side of the pig pen. He moves slowly with his mouth hung open. He's definitely retarded.

"I saw him, kinda squiggling on the ground, and he made this squeak sound, so I scooped that little piggy up and ran him to safety. Washed him off in the kitchen sink. Saved that piece of bacon from becoming baby backs— Let's cut your hair."

—Huh?

"You know how it feels soooo good when someone runs their fingers through your hair when you're on the *Thins*?" Sheena squats beside me, places one hand on my knee as she runs her other fingers through my hair. The *Thins* have kicked in and the microscopic goose bumps along my scalp scatter and spread from her fingernails, "Yeah," I answer.

"Well, I bet clippers feel super crazy," she theorizes.

—My dick is so hard.
The wolf is aware.
Looks at me.
Stares.

"Well, what do you say?"
"What, cut my hair?"
"Yeah," she says, sweet and innocent.
"Sure."
"Great!" leaps to her feet, grabs my hand, pulls me up the stairs, "I'm gonna cut your hair! I gonna shave your balls!" I follow her down a hall of framed family portraits. Looks like Sheena's got brothers. Mom's hefty, Dad's heftier, and man was she an awkward pre-teen. "Come on," and yanks me into the bathroom, pulls the tennis ball light cord, illuminates the bathroom. It's an average sized shit spot,

with a standing sink, a pull-string enamel poop box, and a bull-hoofed bathtub decorated with horns for the hot and cold handles.

She scoots me toward the shitter so she can rustle through a milk crate under the sink. She's looking for the clippers amongst hair-curlers, brushes, hairdryers, a dildo, but that's probably just an electric curling iron, and she finds it. It's vintage, '80s, "Turn around," Sheena instructs me, with a hand on my shoulder. I hear her plug in the razor, a loud— CLACK —from the head turning on, and immediately turns it right off, "Fuck. Some psycho left it on," Sheena explains.

"Don't cut my hair," I announce.
"Shut up."

— CLACK —

. ..VVVVVVvvvvvvvvvVVvvvvvvvvvVVVVV.. .

My eyes are closed, I'm focused, a total sucker. The vibrating sounds jet along the nerves behind my eyes, yet her theory has failed, *Mini-Thins* really do not enhance this experience at all, but if asked I will lie, hate to disappoint. And tomorrow happened today, and she turns the razor off.

"What happened?" I panic.

"Chill pill. We forgot music," and she rests the electric shaver beside the sink, and steps out of the bathroom, *but her hand brushes against the cord as she leaves. The razor shifts, slips toward the edge of the sink. My peripheral vision is just wide enough to see the faucet drip and my hair shavings that have plugged up the drain. The razor falls, clacks ON— Fuck, I reach into the sink, to save the clippers— Stupid —My fingers latch themselves to the plastic, magnetized by the surge of electricity of the machine, scorch my palm, fry my nervous system, end my short-lived life— Horrible Thought.*

•

o   o

Sheena comes back in, sees the razor balancing on the side of the sink, unplugs it, "Dude that's like totally dangerous." I think I know that. "You're the barber," I say, but she grabs my head, turns it around, "Barber-ess. Sit still." I can hear the music start crawling out of her room, down the hall, the tunes from her double-decker ghetto box, a triple-dub of *Siouxsie and the Banshees' Peek-a-Boo*— CLACK! —The razor pops back on as her hand straddles my head, and she's back to work.

—I'm over thinking this does she or doesn't she like me thing.
Not to sound like a girl or something, but the obvious metaphor is
every strand of hair is a stupid daisy petal.
But why do I care if she likes me,
I still don't know how much I like her.
And maybe that's it, maybe that's what sex is all about;
levels, tiers, different kinds of attractions and emotional needs.
So, it's not like I want her forever, this I know,
I can do better,
but to think she wouldn't want to be with me,
at least for a little while,
that hurts my ego.

The bathroom's linoleum floor is weird, lots of glitter, poorly distributed, clumpy— "Done!" THUD the razor turns off.

o   •   o

There is a reflection in the mirror. We're supposed to be looking at my hair. I'm looking into the future— *Sheena's there, but I'm not beside her. She's smiling, then she's crying, now she's thirty, thirty and pregnant again. Her mind creates an apparition, a reflection of me. Her future is reflecting upon her past, me, in the mirror, sixteen, her new pal, a nice guy she can mentor; keep him nice, let him get the fuck out, have a future.*
She'll wonder what I'm up too. Is he famous yet? Married? Divorced? Probably lives in LA. I bet he's happy. Happier than me. That makes me happy. I didn't ruin his life. I stayed away. Didn't take his virginity. I was a good person for once. I really loved him. Maybe my kids'll find love like that. I'll tell them to do it, plunge in, runaway with a Tyle like guy. Let him or her bring out the best in you. And she's crying, and her husband comes

home, sees her in the bathroom, masturbating, pregnant, masturbating to my reflection in the mirror, and he will beat her again, and he'll threaten to leave her with the kids, and he'll leave her on this very linoleum floor because they still live with her parents, and I'll feel bad about Sheena. Watching her from the mirror, alone, on the bathroom floor, bruised, broken, hung from the noose of hope for a better life for her future children, and I'll raise my head, look at my own reflections and—

> *—Holy fuck she gave me a Travis Bickle Mohawk.
> My Dad's going to cut my balls off.*

•

○   ○

"Did Kelsey really get an abortion?"

"I don't know," I say as I obsess over the line of hair on my skull.

"Yes, you do. Everybody says you're Davey's best friend."

"Do they?" I found a few long hairs just above my ear; I pull one out, cringe, "You missed a spot."

"Let me see," and she's rough as she grabs my head and shifts it sideways, "Yeah, hold on—" With one hand pressed on my head, she plugs in the razor back in— CRACK, buzzzz —"OW!" she's nipped my ear, blood, a bad one. "Oh shit, so sorry. Here!" with the razor still screaming in her hand she reaches and spins down the toilet roll, scoops up the slack, rip, and hands me the strip. "Put that on your ear," she says— THUD —the razor turns off. Sheena's pulled the plug this time. Drops the robot-rat on the counter and she's gone. Down the hall. Probably her room? The music has stopped, maybe the tape jammed?

> *—Man, my ear bleeds a lot.*

I toss the red clump of toilet paper in the crapper and grab a few more squares.

•

○   ○

I creep my head into her bedroom. She's on the floor respooling the tape with a #2 pencil, in her bra. Her shirt is draped on the bed and there is a little bloodstain on it. I jam the toilet paper behind my ear. I want access to both of my hands. When I look up, she's standing, looking right at me, removes her bra, her breasts look nice, bigger than my palm, her nipples cold, hard, I wonder how long I have lingered looking at them, my pupils lined up with her cute, tiny little clits of flesh on the smooth curve of— and I look up, and she's closer, and her hands are sliding along my cheeks, around my head. I feel the blotted TP fall, and she's looking me right in the eye, licks her lips like the first time, and our mouths press against each other, and my cold hands touch her very smooth and naked back— "AH!" she yelps jumping back, giggling, "Your hands are cold."

"Sorry."

"Do you want to have sex?" she asks.

"Really?" is my stupid reaction.

"Yeah, really," she says pushing into me a little more.

"Do you have a condom?" I ask, because—

> —I certainly don't
> or do I? Hmmmmm?
> — — — — — — — — — — —?
> Shit, can't remember?

"Shit," she says, steps back, goes for her shirt.

"I'm sorry, I really didn't..." I start as she puts her shirt back on.

"It's okay. Really, I shouldn't have even brought it up."

"Let's relax, sit down," I offer, but she's already got the brick layers working on the foundations of those walls.

"I didn't, like, want to have sex with you," she starts.

"What?"

"Like, dude, I was like totally serious about us just being friends and stuff. I got carried away. I'm sorry, I'm impulsive sometimes," she apologies, but I'm not so sure what she is saying.

> —Is she saying I deserve better, again?
> Carried away? No way. By what? A winged horse?

I'm not that hot, what's to get carried away with?
If you like me, then like me.

"What if I did have a condom?" I ask, wondering if I should check my fucking wallet.

"I don't know, what if this, what if that; you don't, end of story. Fate saved us from being stupid teenagers and ruining a good thing," she says.

"What a load of crap, Sheena! You buy that crap from *Sixteen Candles*? That's raw bullshit. Ruin a good thing? So, you just fuck assholes," I'm crass, but I've had it with her games.

"So, you do believe me. We shouldn't do this?" she says, cowering to my anger, my disappointment in her, my loathing, and now I see it in her eyes, how suddenly she <u>really</u> wants to have sex with me, needs it, like a punishment, like before it was almost what she was supposed to do, now it's what she has to do, and she's unzipping my pants and pulls out my dick and sucks on my erection. I say to myself, *"This is not a lesson. This is not the way to get a girl, something is wrong with Sheena, I think she's been abused,"* and I can't cum, and she stops after five minutes. "You didn't like it?" she assumes.

"No, I did. I did."

"But you didn't cum."

"Am I supposed too?"

"Uh, yeah?"

"I felt like I might, but then it went away."

"But you were still hard?"

"Felt good."

"Okay, I guess?" lets it go, gets up off her knees.

"I'm gonna go freshen up," she excuses herself and I'm left standing there with my half-hard chubby sticking out of my zipper hole and not sure if she's going to try again, or do something else maybe? Probably not. I put it back in my pants, zip up, and make my way out of her room. I do check my wallet though, just in case, nope, no condom. *So be it.* I peek my head into the bathroom. She's reapplying a light shade of lipstick.

"I should probably get going."

"Did you have fun?"

"I did."

"You like your hair?" she inquires, giving it a good pet.

"No. But that's 'cause Dad's gonna fucking yell at me about it. And that will have no end. So, no, I don't like my fucking haircut."

"And you didn't cum, so what did you like about tonight, Mister?" she asks.

"Maybe I'll see you at *Denny's* sometime."

"I'm banned from *Denny's*," she says; smirks.

o   •   o

I rub one out into a paper towel in my room that is illuminated by the light of *Basic Instinct* on my TV. *Sharon Stone* breaks chunks off of a block of ice— I gotta pee.

-
-
-
-
-
-
-
-
-
-
-
-
-
-
-
-
-

chapter FIFTEEN

i'm   on   my   sad-horse.

"Cheer the fuck up man, it's a real drag," constitutes Davey as he crushes his half empty juice box and tosses it at a passing dog, "Too many strays around. Where do they come from?"

"Little *Mexico*," interjects Munts.

"That's racist dude," I protect the immigrants.

"I'm not being racist, that's where all the crack dogs come from. *Brown Power* breeds puppy love," Munts gets racist.

"Okay, that's fucked up," now Davey's even offended. *Brown Power* is the *Latino Petaluma* gang, truth is, they're fucking loco. They have this thing for beating down on punks for no reason with baseball bats. It's pure evil, unjustified, like *Nazis*, but *Cholos*. Sometimes I think it's because they want to beat on the white jocks, but fear the retribution would be too genocidal.

"What should I do, call her?" I ask.

"We're back to that?" Munts droops in pain.

"Sheena's a slut, *Speedo*," Davey starts in, "the sooner you accept that, the sooner you'll get laid. Drop the whole relationship crap, it's the '90s, brother, wear a rubber, and fuck that girl."

I'm really not sure what to say to that. Davey's usually not that crass about this stuff. I'm kind of just staring at him, trying to read why he's so uppity about this point, why he's got to cut her down like that, demean my intentions. "You got a tissue?" he asks.

"No, what's up dude?" I ask.

"What?" Davey.

"What's up, man? Why be like that?" Me.

"I don't know what you're talking about," D.

"Sheena— Why you such an asshole about her?" Me.

"Because you're acting like a freshman, get some balls," Davey gets up, sniffles, rubs his nose on his sleeve, sniffles again, "Allergies. What?"

"Hey, man, just sit down."

"I gotta go," Davey adjusts his leather, "*Conspiracy* at the *Phoenix*, Friday."

"You need us to buy you a ticket?"

"Fuck off," and this testy version of Davey leaves clearing the view of the river. Some old creeper rows his metal motorboat up the river, against the current. "Row, row, row your boat, gently up the stream," I sing.

"Well, I got laid," Munts tells me.

"Merrily, merrily, Munts' life is but a dream. Really?" I ask.

"Yeah, couple days ago, Monday night."

"Where?"

"Erin's."

"No way. Her own bed?"

"Her stairwell."

"No!"

"Totally. Her Dad goes to the neighbors for Monday Night Football," Munts paints me a picture of words, "She calls me up at like four-thirty or something. My mom's home early from work, answers the phone, talks to Erin for like twenty minutes, the fucking phone cord is way tangled by the time Mom's all handing me the receiver, mouthing how sweet Erin is, and that I should sex her as soon as possible because she ain't sticking around. Dude, my Mom says this."

"You're Mom's special."

"My Mom is amazing," Munts continues, "Anyway, dude, I gotta dangle the phone, like, to untangle the shit, and get it to reach all the way to the bathroom. Dude, first thing she says to me is that she feels funny, starts this heavy breathing, total 1-900 shit, and asks if I'd come over when her Dad leaves."

"Okay, I get it," I try to stop him. I don't need the details. Jocks share details. It's gay.

"No, no wait— So, I go over there, right? And all the lights are off except her bedroom window; upstairs," and I drift into his dream—•—*Munts approaches the door, notices the TV flicker from the neighbor's window. The football game is on the big screen. Coast is clear. Munts rings the doorbell. It doesn't work. He looks up at Erin's lit window. Her silhouette steps into frame. Removes her shirt, her bra. Munts knocks, the door opens. Erin has left it open for him to enter on his own accord. He slips inside, closes the door, locks it tight, all the locks, knob, dead-bolt, and the chain.*

The house is dark. The light from the neighbor's TV is just strong enough to cast a stream of flicker through the window along Erin's stairwell. Munts takes the steps one at a time, checks his pocket for the condom, step, step— His lady appears at the top. She is completely naked under her pink plastic sunglasses. She has the beautiful form of a young horse. She is Munts the Stallion's filly. He reaches the top step, turns to his filly, mounts her from behind, and the front door is being unlocked from the outside— Thunk — Thunk — BAM— the door gets caught on the chain-link. Munts pauses his thrusts. Turns his head. He sees the door partially ajar. It slams shut. Re-opens— BAM! —caught against the chain-link again and again. The stallion removes himself from inside his prey. Erin the filly peeks around the side of her taker, and watches the door. Silence. Nothing moves. Munts stands guard, takes a deep breath and the door bursts open tearing the chain out of the wooden frame, the door thrown off its hinges, and in the doorway, the filly's father, a Bull with strong horns spread along his brow. His nose steams. His hooves stomp. He is revved up. He will attack. This is his child. He will destroy the horse that has mounted his filly before she's grown into a mare.

o   •   o

"That's pretty much it," Munts finishes, "I bet next time I'll last a little longer."

"Did you give her an orgasm?"

"I think so. Said it hurt at first, so I went slow. But really, I kinda came too quick."

"Did you try again?"

"Says I can try again Monday."

"Good for you, Munts. At least one of us isn't a total loser."

"Call Sheena. Don't listen to Davey, he's just jealous," Munts comforts me.

"Why? Does he like her?"

"No. I don't think so? I think he's just…"

—Well?

"I don't know? She's your girlfriend, not his. Call her."

"Yeah, but she's not my girlfriend either."

"Have you asked her?"

"To be my girlfriend?"

"Yeah."

"No."

"So, ask her."

"I don't know."

"What's to know, dude, it's all you talk about."

"Not really."

"You're full of shit."

—Probably.

"It's something to consider I guess."

"Dude, you're weird," Munts psychoanalyzes me.

"I'm not rushing into anything," I rephrase my trepidations.

"Whatever," Munts can really care less, "Let's go to *Thriftys*."

"Why?" I ask.

"Rubbers," he says, "She only had one. Left over from Junior High. Sex Ed."

—Smirk.

chapter SIXTEEN

*L*ounging in a *Phoenix* theater seat, solo, just me in this row that is particularly rocky. I sway. The rest of the seats sway with me. Me and the ghosts of *Luma's* past. The foundation of the *Phoenix*, below my *Docs*, a plot of land broken in 1870. The doors of the *Hill Opera House* opened thirty-five years later. Burnt nearly to a crisp by 1925, rejuvenated into a movie house by 1935. The *California Movie Theater* boasted a 16mm screen, two stories tall, balcony seating. In '57 another fire wrecked the place and was rebuilt into the *Showcase Theater* where a young *Jeff Dorenfeld* put on their first live concert, and *Tom Gaffey*, as a young man, gets a gig working the place, leaves his post, returns in '82. All those ghosts of an audience past sway impatiently along with me as we await the next ensemble to perform.

The *Conspiracy* is checking their mics. They have a good turnout of about two to three hundred people. *Hoodlum Empire's* headlining, that helps. Davey didn't say they were playing. Davey's pals with *Rob Rock*. I dig it. They're really tight. And *Rob's* lyrics, too witty to tell. He might be a genius. THUMP! THUMP! THUMP! *Dimitri Katzoff*, the *Jewish-Negro* drummer is whappin' toms, symbols, kicks on the bass drum. *Josh Staples*, the bassist, begs him to knock it off. *Dave Young's* late— he's been fucking up with *Mike*

Mullens at the *Brady-House*. Heard *Madrone* has dropped out and moved to New York and now *Lincoln Barr's* their *John Frusciante*, and *McLaughin* is right at the side of the curtain pounding the last third of a forty before he joins the *Marines*. Should be a good show.

My seat thrusts forward, Erin's pushed up against the back of it. She's giggling. Munts climbs around her. I'm not jazzed about videotaping the show tonight. I'm still taking a ride on my Sheena sad horse. "Sit down already," I'm cranky. "Hemorrhoids Goodman?" Munts asks and sits, Erin beside him, backwards, on the rim of the seat, my row, and she won't stop making it rock. She's gone purple and red with her hair tonight, wore her *Ska* attire, plaid skirt, white tee, suspenders; Munts looks the same as usual, but now he sports a friendship bracelet that twists around his wrist. Erin transfers a couple black jelly bracelets from her wrist to his, and I think I'm totally going to puke until Davey drops into the aisle seat beside me. "Sheena's here," he says to me, "Great, thanks," I reply.

"What, don't you want to talk to her?" he asks.

"I'm over it," I say, only to be slapped on the back of the head. I turn to see Sheena's walking away from us.

"Oh, you fucked up dude," Davey laughs.

—Shit!

I plop the camera into Davey's lap, "Watch this," and crawl over his lanky legs, stumble, stack onto the aisle rug, scrape up my palm, and chase after Sheena.

      o   •   o

In the lobby, I'm just barely able to make out Sheena on the curb with Eddie. Eddie shoots me a very disappointed look of, "oh no you didn't." She sees me bee-lining the doors. Her mascara is smeared, she's crying, I'm an asshole. I punch down on the door bar, the chill of air slides in, and Sheena's already got Eddie by the hand, pulling him away from the theatre, and like a big-mouthed-asshole from a *John Cusack* movie, I run into the street, "Sheena! SHEENA!" —take a breath— "SHEEENAA!" but she's gone, across the street, down the alley between *Thriftys* and the parking lot, and I'm not stupid enough to run after her.

> *—I don't get it, well not all of it.*

She wasn't supposed to hear that. No one is. I don't know, maybe she really liked me? Maybe she didn't think I'd like her? But once she had me, knew it was possible, her fake confidence got the best of her. Collapsed. Fell for me. If she had just kept it going. Didn't get all weird, well, then we'd probably be an item.

> *—I didn't want to hurt her feelings like that.*
> *She wasn't supposed to hear that. I was venting.*
> *Feels like we broke up, Secretly together.*
> *I treated her like an asshole, went back on my word,*
> *Just like the rest of them, a prick in us all.*

Two skaters take to blows on the sidewalk. An elbow to a nose and it gets bloody. A couple other skaters collect the loose boards. Can't let people get to weapons. That gets dangerous. And Tom comes limping out of the glass doors, wielding his broom of intimidation, "Girls, break it up," he clucks at the skater bros taking each other's beat downs. I have nothing better to do than go back in, slump down beside good old D, be pissed, pout about it, "Thanks, Davey."

"Dude I didn't do anything," D.

"Fuck," Me.

"Sorry man," D.

"I fucked up," Me.

"You didn't know she was there. I, well, I thought you liked her, that's why I brought her over, thought I'd..." Davey stops, not sure if he's getting through to me, but what I'm waiting for, is the proverbial, *I'm sorry, bro,* and sure, he's saying more than that, those are just words, status quo, but I'm too pissed to hear any of that, I'd rather judge and blame him instead of anything rational, "Thought you'd what?"

"Thought I'd make it up to you for saying that crap about

her," he apologizes.

"Ah man, I suck. I didn't want her to know that shit."

"I know, bro. You want me to talk to her?"

"What are you going to say? Sorry, Tyler didn't mean it, he's not over it," I say, "What's that going to accomplish?"

"Get you laid?"

We both laugh.

"Don't talk to her," I plead.

"Nah, fuck it, I'm going to talk to her," Davey gets up, drops the camera in my lap.

"Dude?" I plead.

"No way, done deal, I'm coming through, besides..." Davey points to the stage. *Dimitri* counts off and *The Conspiracy* bursts out into song without *Dave Young*, and my D's out, down the hall and gone. "I think he's really going to talk to her," I tell Munts, but he can't hear me, and Erin drags her man out to dance, climbing over the seats; so cute together. I was such an asshole—

> *—oh look, there's Dave Young,*
> *just in time.*
> *His mic isn't working,*
> *the band plays on.*
> *Dave's confused,*
> *yeah, try that mic instead, dude.*

o • o

What I don't know, but came to believe was that Davey ran out of that show with all the intention in the world to stand up for my honor. To help mend a childish plot line. That was Davey. There was the proof Davey had a soul. Bright. Loyal. Admirable in his rebellion. Some souls, like some bodies, are born blind. Davey wasn't blind. Davey wore blinders. Black rimmed, purple-lensed blinders to anyone he knew too well. Family. Faux adopted. I wasn't his brother. I'm an only child. As much as we both knew Davey adopted me, his self-inflicted trauma could only say I was the culprit. Kidnapped his friendship when we re-met that lunch hour in seventh grade— it was his duty to guide the new kid —Distracted by his bleak premonition of a shittier future, Davey, post freshman year, feels like if he knows you for too long, you become the past, and the past, history is the seed of the festering rot to come. Tonight, he set out to fix shit. Hunt my doe down. She was by the redwoods across from *The Plaza Theater*. Found her with Gay Eddie, a stranger to the D.

I wasn't there. I should have been there. I can only imagine what could have transpired between the meeting of such minds.

○　　　•　　　○

Davey probably opened with, "He's really sorry."
"No, he's not," Sheena's not happy.
"No, really, he is. Tyler's a good guy."
"No shit," sarcastic, cat, purr, "I told you I'm cool."
"You really liked him, huh?"
"Maybe I did," purr.
"He's too young for you," Eddie butts in.
"Tyler likes you. He's just introspective," D.
"Over thinks shit?" Sh.
"Book smart," D.
"Book smart? Well you know me, I like 'em dumb."
"Yeah, he thinks too much. Makes things up in his head," is what Davey thinks of me.
"That true?" Eddie steps in.
"Oh, Davey this Eddie," Sheena gets distracted. Saved from thinking.
"Dave," he likes to be called with strangers, new people, out-of-towners, potential-ists, and disbanded enablers.
"Dave, so her boyfriend's delusional?" Eddie wants to know about me.
"Don't be a fag," Sheena slurs to Eddie's use of the word, "He is not my boyfriend."
"He's all creative. Tyler exaggerates things to make a story, but not like, in a bad way. He's not a liar," Davey's verbal essay on Tyler Goodman, "Come on Sheena, you've been around him." She's barely listening, but Eddie's all ears so Dave explains it to him, "Splatter. Always connecting dots, splattered info, like a shattered windshield." Eddie

nods, "Right on," he says, and Davey drops the last part back on the girl, "If you tap Tyler the wrong way— chchcchchch — shattered, scatters the info in his brain, like a web, and he can't help it." Sheena knows. She gets it. Sheena ain't ignet. Sheena's bright. Sheena can totally comprehend the abstract, compartmentalizes it into the modern lexicon, keeps it simple. She gets it.

"Why?" Eddie asks.

"Why what?"

"Why's it matter?"

"Because he's my friend?"

"So, he's delusional," she's barely trying to comprehend.

"He's just built that way. Like you. Like me. We're built backwards. You normal?"

"I'm gay," Eddie announces to Dave.

"He's not delusional," Davey wants Sheena to believe, "Believe me."

—If she believes,
then he can move on,
he can get to know this stranger.

"I'm not a slut."

"He doesn't think that."

"Really?"

"Hey Dave?" Eddie did not get the attention he desired.

"Huh?" D.

"You do Acid?" Eddie.

"Sometimes, not so much anymore," Davey answers.

"You want to sell some Acid?" Eddie asks.

"Why?"

"Money?"

"How much?"

"Let's go to *Santa Rosa*, Prince David."

"Davey's not gay," Sheena clarifies any vague conclusions.

"I know. Still pretty. Don't worry. I'm not coming on to you. Straight boys in high school, nuh-uh, that's drama. This is all about business, not pleasure," Eddie turns to Sheena, "I can control my lustful emotions, unlike the love birds of *Elephant Rock*," and she kicks him in the shin, and it hurts, and he drops his cigarette, and Sheena finally smiled, but Davey didn't laugh.

"That's cool," Davey says. "How much money?"

"We'll see," Eddie says hopping on one foot, rubs his shin.

"Stop acting," Sheena requests. Eddie stops.

"I'm parked by *Apple Box*," Eddie lights another cigarette, offers one to Dave.

"You coming?" Davey asked Sheena as he took the smoke, and Sheena said, "Sure," and they moseyed across the Blvd, alongside the *Old Mill*, piled into Eddie's car, and drove the fifteen minutes up *101 North* to the heart of *Santa Rosa, California*, the big little city of *Sonoma County*. They have the indoor mall, and the city is a whoppin' five streets in diameter; twenty-five full blocks of stationary stores, one record shop, tailors, bakeries, trinket store fronts, clothing, coffee shops, book stores, and western wear.

o • o

And there I was in the *Phoenix*, barely videotaping *The Conspiracy*, and in my skull, on a loop— *Sheena hates me, Sheena loves me, Sheena wants to castrate me.*

o • o

They've cruised through the empty, subpar-urban, *Santa Rosa* streets and Eddie's pulled over and parked a few blocks out. "I'll wait here," Sheena wanted to be alone. Davey, Dave, followed Edward's lead, across the block, around the corner, through a waist high white picket gate, and up to the steps of some two-story apartment building, four units in all, pressed the buzzer— BZZZ —and Davey stood by, offered Eddie a menthol. "Yeah, cool. Smoke those every once in a while." He pocketed it for later.

"Yeah?" came out of the intercom.

"It's Eddie."

"Yeah, come up,"— BZZZZZZ —and Eddie opened the gate, let Davey go in first, adjusted his balls, sniffled, followed him in, and changed Davey's world forever.

•

o   o

The Conspiracy's set has come to an end. Munts and Erin want to skip *Hoodlum Empire* to screw somewhere. I'm in no mood for the show anymore either and cock-block my buddy by walking out with them both. *Rob Rock* of *Hoodlum* will go missing a year later or less. Poof. Vanish into the æther, lost along the future *superhighway*, sadly labeled a missing person, dead or alive, no one will ever know. Tragic. A soulful poetic drifter who will drift into oblivion without leaving a message in a bottle.

It's unanimous; we decide to go to Lyons for some coffee and French fries. My pal can fuck his girlfriend tomorrow. Tonight I need love, companionship, attention, s?

> —*I wonder if Davey ever found Sheena?*
> *Maybe they disappeared into the fray?*

•

o   o

He could do this. Davey could live in an apartment like this one. *Santa Rosa's* better than *Luma*. This would do. A two-bedroom spot, furnished with folding chairs, a plywood tabletop propped up by milk crates. The entertainment center is a 12inch TV with bunny ears atop a *VCR* atop a stool. There's a cassette rack for fifty tapes in the corner. Ten tapes in total are randomly displayed throughout the skyscraper styled case. The remaining hundred loose tapes and cases have been dumped out onto the stained beige carpet, and shifted through beside a generic *Radio Shack* dual cassette ghetto box. The kitchen was bare. Davey sat by the table, started to read, skim the band names, and doodles that overlapped each other on the slab of wood. Carvings, drawings, writings, scribbles, claws, broken glass, and stabs; history. A history lesson Davey can swallow. People have been here before.

Eddie's still by the door, steps into the kitchen with the guy, a white male, 26ish years old, razor shaved head, with a solid, black circle tattooed on the back of his skull. Eddie waits as the guy goes to the back bedroom, returns, leads

Eddie to the living area. "Hey," the guy welcomed Davey with an elbow tap to the arm. Davey wondered if this guy was gay like Eddie. Could be? Doesn't come off gay. But could be. It really didn't matter. Davey's no bigot. Davey'd punch a bigot in the throat before it got another word out. No, Davey wasn't eyeballing a stereotype, or making assumptions, he was just analyzing, like me, but not people, instead he started hypothesizing about all the money that he could make selling *LSD*. The tattooed punk told Eddie to sit and wait. So, he plopped down beside his new buddy, his new comrade, his assistant, business partner, and asked "You got a pen?" Davey pulled out a white-paint pen from his leather and handed it to Eddie. The tattooed punk shuffled through the pile of tapes, ejected something, put something else in, "He's on the phone," he informed the boys, pressed play, went to the pisser. *DYS* plays out. "Why do they listen to *straight-edge*?" Davey whispered to Eddie who shook the pen— rat-tat-tat-tat-tat-tat-tat —dabbed the tip against the wood, pressed, firm, again and again, "These guys are actually *straight-edge*. They just sell stuff," Eddie told him, scooted him over, "But shut up about it. Draw something." Davey's good with that. Made sense. Free enterprise. Eddie drew a dick, suckling on its own balls. Two other *straight-edge* punks came out from the back. "No more *Oakland*," the leader told Eddie, "They got a place in the city now," then tossed him the merchandise.

·

o   o

Sheena was staring out the window of Eddie's car. Just looking at the pavement. Streetlight, dark—

—*Wondered if Tyler was truly sorry.*
—*Maybe he was scared, just like her.*
—*And she'd go on to think about,*
—*"What if Tyler hadn't have said that tonight?"*
—*Maybe, if they were both older?*

That's a pipedream. She's tangled up in stupidity, rushing life, flies, time, scorpions, memories, dreams, loneliness, rape culture, body shame, incest, vomit, Christianity, social norms, anti-hate, love, lost love, hate, boredom, extreme boredom, sex with losers, rape culture, condiments, mustard, ketchup, relish, big cities, sadness, & dying momentum—• •   •   •   •   •

... .

.

.   .   .   .• —and then Eddie and Dave got back in the car.

•

○   ○

I've had, like, three cups of coffee, ate a plate of fries, and think about a scoop of chocolate ice cream, as I sweep my hand along my head, "Oh shit, I have a fucking Mohawk."

•   •

○

—"WHAT IS THAT?" Dad was pissed. Bitched me out for a good twenty minutes, gave up, concluded in broken grammer, me & my friends, "Losers, all of you," and I promised I would shave it in a week, told him, "Look, dude, in a week the shit'll grow out." I was trying to explain that I didn't want to look like a skinhead, "give it a week. In a week, I can use an extension and have a buzz so I'm not called a *Nazi* at school, alright?"

"Well, it's fucking ugly, and you look like an idiot," and Daddio scampered away, and I guess he got over it 'cause he doesn't say anything, and—

•

○   ○

—Oh fuck, there's Davey and Sheena, and great they've brought their gal pal Eddie to *Lyons*. Davey and the dropout head our way.

—Where's Sheena going?
She's not even looking at us.

141

I don't even know those guys, Meathead Jocks, probably listen to *G n' R,* East Side farmers, I don't know any of them. Sheena seems to know them, they're real happy to see her, the guy with the buzz-cut-mullet points over to a table of some of my own acquaintances, and hassles Sheena about being one the freaks now. She flirtatiously swats his insult away, giggles, points to our table, tells the clan of dumb-somethings some joke that makes them cockle, because meatheads don't cackle; their dicks are too big (small) for that. They cockle. Fuck 'em. Eat hay. "So, what's up, Daaavey?" I say to stop myself from caring.

"Davey?" Davey questions me, "Since when do you ever call me that?"

"Huh?"

"Sheena ain't gonna talk to you man. Not tonight. Skooch over," he pushes me deeper into the booth, "Eddie, this is Munts, Munts, Eddie, Eddie, Erin, and, what's your name again? Oh, that's *Speedo.*"

"What?" I'm so offended.

"Just kidding," he says, "Tyler. He's my best bud. Known each other since forever," he tells Eddie.

"Yeah, we know each other," Eddie says, "How you be?" he asks me.

"Better," says the sad horse jockey; me, as Munts eyeballs Eddie, jealous, or shall we say, scoping him out to see if he should be threatened by this swave Edward who might scam on Munts little lady. Davey senses it. We all do. Erin thinks it's adorable.

"Don't worry, he's cool, Munts. He won't hit on your girl, he's a homo, pitchin' for the other team," Davey says in raw form. He's all hyped up— *Mini-Thins,* but he's not sharing, sniffles, blows his nose in a napkin, Eddie leans into the table.

"See, Eddie here, he's a beauty queen dropout," I join in on the cut downs of the night.

"Hey kid, cool it?" Eddie warns me.

"Kid?" I butt in, "You're not a fucking grandpa."

"What?"

"We don't like to be called kids, fag," I snap, go too far. Eddie's lunges to strangle me, knocks over hot coffee and waters, everyone freaks to avoid getting wet, burned. I'm up— I'm cursing him out, my rage about Sheena, delivered towards her buddy that rubs me the wrong way, his arrogance, his grandstanding, his constant announcements about being gay, "Fucking muther-fucker. Bring it on!" Eddie's about to get up, but Davey puts the hand out, steps in, the referee. Everyone in *Lyons* have got eyes on me, everyone but the girl. Sheena's currently jamming her tongue down the throat of the Mullet head, and I'm out, I'm just fucking out. Eddie the dropout darts his boot under my legs to trip me, but I'm aware, stomp down, try to crack his ankle, but he pulls back and shoots me that, that guy'll fight dirty don't fuck around with him, look; and he's fucking right—

—there is no fair in fighting,
there is only getting out alive,
and I plan to get out alive,
kicking and screaming.

I'll rip your fucking ball sack right off if I have to. Shove my hand down your pants, grab them testicles of organic tubing, twist 'em tight, yank them right the fuck off. I'm little. I'm a small guy, Jewish, well aware of hate, ready to strike like the Mossad; cunning like a fox, as quick as Bambi in a fire. "Go ahead, make my day."— A Horrible Thought I'm ready to execute.

o   o

Whap!— I slam open the glass doors of *Lyons*, exit and head for the parking lot.

—I can just drive home.
Fuck those guys. Fuck this place.
Fuck this whole chicken-shit of a town.

And I'm at my car, digging out my keys, ah fuck, Munts and Erin, I'm <u>their</u> ride; all this *Tyler Tantrum* bullshit is for naught, I can't strand my friends. Not those two. They ain't done nothing wrong. It's too far of a walk, right? How far? Thirty minutes? I find my keys.

> —*No way, Testy Tyler,*
> *the walks more like an hour,*
> *maybe longer for Erin?*
> *Fuck, do the right thing?*

"Fine," I say aloud to myself, leave my keys in my pocket, look back toward the restaurant's windows. I can see my friends at their table. They're all talking, laughing. At me? Honestly, if I just relax and think it over, they're probably not laughing at me, and I shouldn't have called Eddie a fag. I shouldn't call anyone that. Have to lose that word. Rip it from my vernacular.

I guess Eddie's kinda cool? My joke went too far. But I did have a point. We don't like being called kids. It's demeaning. Calling him a slur was me trying to prove a point, an example that he kind of did the same thing, I wasn't calling him a *fag* per se, I was making a mutherfucking point. But I guess, kids have not been as persecuted as the gays. My mistake. I, out of any of my friends, should know better. He gets it, right? He's smart enough unless he dropped out 'cause he's dumb as nails; highly unlikely, I think he's just rebellious like Davey.

> —*I don't trust Eddie.*
> *Why?*
> *Don't know.*
> *But you just justified him.*
> *Yeah, well, that's emotional.*
> *Trust first Tyler. Do it. Be better.*

I've waited in the parking lot for about thirty minutes now. Munts is cool and he's getting Erin out as fast as he can. It's not as cold as usual, but the fog's creeping, and the *Kenilworth Park* playground across the street is being swallowed up by the air's smoky water. I gotta get up, my legs have fallen asleep. A curb's good for fifteen, twenty minutes, but once you've zoned out and crossed that twenty-one-minute mark—

—Fuck they're buckling, get a grip,
use the light pole for balance.
Okay, I'm young, I'm invincible,
I can get through this.
I feel something again,
my balls, pins and needles;
pins and needles in my balls!

I gotta shake this unwanted acupuncture away. I'm doing the jig as Erin scampers out of *Lyons*, bursts into laughter at the sight of me. She falls to the ground, for no reason, and starts rolling around on the pavement, mocking me. My balls will not drop, sucked up in my intestines, and Munts' girlfriend is getting trucker's oil all over herself. "You're both idiots," Munts brings to our attention as he steps out of the restaurant. "My balls fell asleep," I explain, and I think it's easing away, warming up, blood stream, blood flow to my man sacks, and Erin's cross-legged in the middle of the lot, "Do it again," she commands an encore of my dance.

"No," I say.
"Again!" She squawks.
"No!"
"Yes!"
"NO!"
"YES!"
"NO!!"
"Yep...," and Munts cups her mouth, yet she blabbers through. Munts takes his hand off her mouth, "HELP!" Erin yells, "CENSORSHIP! CENSORSHIP!" Munts tries again. Fail. She scrambles away, her nylons shredded, "*Nazi*-Fuck! Speech killllaaaaaa!"
"Are you done?" Munts asks.
She hisses at us both, "Speech killlaaaaasssssssss!"
"Oh Jeez," Munts exhales, "See what you started?"
Davey and Eddie approach us, "T," Davey calls my attention.
"Dee," I pronounce, "Weirdo, what up?"
"Let's make a movie?" he requests of me, words mangled

between the chewing his tongue.

"Uh, sure. We always do that."

"Cool. Cool. It'll be cool to hang again for a sec."

"Do you have a day planned for this outing, fag," and then I cup my mouth, that one slipped, lesson not learned. I blame my balls. Don't make eye contact with Eddie. Probably wants to kick my ass for sure now. "That one was justified," he says to me, "Calling me a fag, in *Lyons*, here in this town? Come on, man, that'll just get me a beat down."

"Nah, come on," and I get this look from everyone. Really T? You hit your head? "Hicks out number liberals twenty-five to one up here," Davey says. "I get it. I get it," I wasn't thinking, "Sorry. I'm an asshole, I'm just..." Eddie steps up to me, "Shut up. Come here," walks me over to some cars to have a man to boy talky-talk.

"Sheena's not going to be your girlfriend, bro," he lectures me, but I'm really out of my emotional skull, a super brat tonight, *"People worry, what are they worried about today,"* I sing ever so obnoxiously.

"Why are you such a wiseass? People like you, but you're such a wiseass," he criticizes me, justly, much ado about everything lately, and I'm trying to pay attention, but Munts is ready to go, Erin's spinning herself dizzy, and Davey's digging into his flight jacket?

> —*Dude, you don't own no flight jacket.*
> *He gives us monthly reminders about that.*

"I gotta get some money. Fucking need a flight," D.

"No, we're not lending you fifty bucks. Figure it out," Us.

Guess he figured it out? But what's he doing? Why's he got keys in his other hand?

> —*You don't drive,*
> *and when have your parents*
> *ever locked their door?*

Davey looks back at me, gives me a chin tilt of acknowledgement, and turns away all sneaky like. I'm not listening to Eddie ramble on about the pretentiously dry, repetitive, and obvious, "...dichotomy of rebellion and anarchy," but he steps into my spy eye on the D.

"We cool, kid?" Eddie asks.

—I need to go to bed.

"You'll figure it out," he tells me, but I don't know what "it" is in reference too, as he waves over Davey who marches over like a good little soldier. What the fuck, dude? Why you suddenly Eddie's bitch? If you kiss him, I will fucking puke. Davey's steps up to us, "We going?" Eddie takes his keys back from Davey, "Yeah," then volunteers a few last words, "She likes you, but like just— she ain't? She ain't all there up there, ya know? Daddy issues," and he keeps going with his hand on my shoulder, "Can't shit where you screw. You, little man, you're her toilet, not her bedroom. Go get laid, her advice, not mine," Eddie turns to Davey, "Let's do it."

"Where you going?" I pry at 1am on this Saturday night.

"*Sausalito*," he actually answers me.

"Why?"

"Drugs," Davey says.

"Really, dude?" Eddie rather he not joke like that.

"Eddie's gonna get me a job at *Gillman*," Davey lies.

"That's in *Oakland*," I remind him, but I'm too tired to debate this obvious point.

"Yeah, yeah, but the guy I gotta meet to get the job is in *Marin*. So, we're just gonna do that, 'kay Dad?"

— Very funny.

"Oh, the movie. I'll figure that out. Call you tomorrow morning, we'll figure it out," Davey goes on and on, as Eddie heads to his car.

—I wish Munts had his own car.

"He's probably right," Davey says.

"About what?"

"About Sheena. I talked to her," he finally tells me.

"When?"

"In the car. We all went up to *Santa Rosa*," he says as he rubs his eyes, his bloodshot eyes. His pupil nearly trembles, he sniffles, I'm not retarded, and I think I know what's up.

"She said," he starts up again, only to be interrupted by whistlin' Eddie. Davey flips him off, "Drop her, dude," grips my hand with reassurance, "I'm out, drop her." And Davey's out, off to Eddie's car. I don't get why Davey's all into Eddie, and not sure what Mr. Eddie really wants out of my friend.

"Take Erin home, please," Munts is right beside me. Erin's cross-legged in the middle of the parking lot. She pantomimes exhaustion, "You kiss that lunatic?" I ask Munts. He shrugs, picks his nose, inquires about the boys, "They're going to *Gillman* this late?"

"*Sausalito*."

"Who the fuck lives in *Sausalito*?"

"Some guy that's gonna get him a job at the *Gillman*? Something like that," Munts is as much as a disbeliever as I, "Dude, I don't know, he's a liar," and I end it there.

"Whoa, taco fire. Chill," Munts sounds as tired as me.

"I know. Hey drama-rama!" I yell at his girlfriend sprawled out dead on the pavement, "Get up, we're leaving."

"I do not listen to *Dramarama*. I listen to *Soundgarden*," she corrects me.

"Dude, that's even worse," I tell Munts.

"She's a chick, man."

—He said it, not me.

○   •   ○

We pile into the *Little Red Civic*. Erin wears a shit-eating grin, glares right at me. "Can I help you?" I ask the freak. "No. Just being plastic," she answers. Munts waves me off, ignore her, and I start the car, turn, check my rear, the window's fogged up, "Can you wipe that for me?" and Erin obeys, revealing Sheena through the glass as she exits the diner, lights a *clove*, doesn't look my way. *NIN - Pretty Hate Machine*, CHA CHA CHA CHA, starts to roll out of the car speakers, well timed. Yeah, "*God Money*," and I peal out, right past her. She knows

my car. I see her in the rearview; she's watching me—
"WATCH OUT!" Munts yells— I hit the brakes, spinout past
the double yellow line, force a big rig milk truck to swerve, I
accelerate since I didn't stall this time, peal out again, lose
control, spin, slide, and we're back on the right side of the
road heading towards the sidewalk, the Library, and I hit
those brakes so fucking hard we jerk forward, and —BAM—
right into a fucking bus stop bench. No hesitation, I'm
reversing, rolling the wheel right, peel off for a third time,
drive away, shaking, adrenaline, angry at myself, spooked,
and embarrassed. I can feel the fire as the blood rushes to my
cheeks, and my brain scolds myself all the way to Erin's
house.

> *— You think about girls too much.*
> *You meet them. You obsess over them.*
> *Think about driving, not girls. No, not girls, Sheena.*
> *Why do I like Sheena so much? She kissed that douche-bag.*
> *What the fuck? Must be my fault. I blew it.*
> *Munts' got it down,*
> *Davey's a fag,*
> *and me,*
> *that's easy,*
> *I'm an asshole.*

•

o   o

8am, Dad woke me up. Dragged me out front. We're on the
curb; I think he believes me.
   "Like the whole fucking football team, I fucking swear," I
tell him as he massages the damage on my car, "They took a
bat to it," and I pantomime the attack, bam, bam, bam. We
are not going to repair it.
   "Stop being such a smart-ass and they won't bother you."
   "Yeah right, Pops," I smirk.
   "Like that. You do that and I want to smack you."
   "Are you done?"
   "You're grounded."
   "No, I'm not. Want me to pay for it?"
   "You don't have a job," he says like I'm a deadbeat.

"I could get one."
"I doubt it."

—Typical.

•

•

•

•

•

•

•

•

•

•

•
•
•
•
•
•
•

chapter SEVENTEEN

*i*t's 7:30, Monday night, and I'm not all so eager to go back downstairs to have dinner with the folks. I can't stop thinking about that douche bag's tongue twirlin' around inside Sheena's mouth; I'm jealous as fuck. I don't know why I'm so fucking jealous, but I just am. Fuck her. Fuck her, fuck this hick infested town, and fuck Davey for shovin' blow up his nose. Why the fuck is he doing cocaine anyhow? Who does cocaine in *Petaluma*? Who can even afford it here? Stick with the *Mini-Thins*, Dave, coke's for *Marin* Count-ies, *Lucas* babies, hoity-toity yuppie *BMW* driving—

"Tyler! Dinner!" Dad yells from downstairs.

"Not hungry!" I yell back.

I can hear his footsteps.

—I'm not getting out of this, am I?

My bedroom door swings open and Dad steps right in.

"Whoa, Dad! What if I was masturbating or something?" I defend my privacy.

"Then you'd be the loser I thought you were," he answers.

"Ha, ha."

"Dinner's ready, and you're eating. Come," he demands.

"I'm eating in front of the TV, then."

"Good we can watch the game."

"Ah fuck, fine, I'll eat at the table," I compromise.

"You never want to do things with me," Dad huffs and puffs. I drag myself off the floor. "That's crap, I do plenty with you. I just don't watch knuckleheads run into each other and not bleed." He pushes open the kitchen door for me, "You watched them beat up your car up, though?"

—Very funny Dad.

The phone rings.

Dad and I enter the kitchen as Mom puts the receiver to her side, "It's for you, a Sheena?"

"Oh," I am surprised, take the phone from my Mom, but Mom has a ground rule all of a sudden, "After dinner," she says. I put the receiver to my ear.

"Uh hey, I can't really talk. Well, not right now."

"You're blowing me off again, really?" Sheena says.

"No," says me.

Mom's blood-red fingernail flags me. Her silent insignia. Cut it off.

"Look, I gotta eat dinner. I'll call you in an hour."

"Sure, whatever," Sheena clicks off.

"Thanks, Mom," I strike, bitter, always feeling like I'm a bitch to everyone else's agenda. People don't realize how selfish they really are. Same people that complain about selfish attitudes are generally those who unconsciously act as if their agenda is yours. Guilt.

"If she really likes you, she'll talk to you later. Let's eat," Mom has no compromise.

o   •   o

The dinner conversation tonight amounts to silence, no words, just chewin'— *Who's mad at who? Who, who, who?* — and under my breath, my lips, my tongue, take my honest thoughts and direct them to a song I've loved a million times again, *"Who fucked who? Who screwed who? Who took who, man? Who fucked who?"* - NoMeansNo

"Tyler?" Mom's curious.

"Oh, just singing something," I tell her. She wants to know more. Not mad, curious. Maybe I've cleared some air, "A *NoMeansNo* song," I take a bite of the lemon chicken, "Just had me thinking."—rrRRRINGGgg—the phone. Mom gives me the scornful eye. Has peace been broken once agai—rrRRRINGGgg—I shift, begin to move, someone's got to answer it, scrape my chair along the linoleum.

"Let the answering machine get it," she insists, I freeze, Dad looks toward the phone—rrRRRINGGgg—We all...

...wait...—rrRRRI—CLICK—Beeee*eeee*eeeeeP!!

"Hello, you have reached the Goodman residence, please leave your name, number, and message at the sound of the tone and someone will get back to you at our earliest convenience," my prerecorded voice reels out through the mini-mono speaker of the machine. I wrote that garbage. Dad forced an executive decision after he heard my original message that sampled *American Woman* by *The Guess Who* and me saying a simple, "Don't make us guess."

o   •   o

"Tyler, it's Munts— You there? Tyler? Pick up braugh, pick up da fucking phone!"

— BEEP —
The answering machine clicks off.

"Don't your friends have families?" Dad asks.
"No, they killed them all," I tell the prick.
"You have a real attitude lately," he barks tossing his napkin over his plate.
"Don't start," starring Mom the pacifist.
"He's been a little prick this year," Dad, the antagonist,

says.

"Fuck off," says I the *Rebel Without a Cause*.

"Tyler, apologize," insists the diplomat.

"Fuck that, he started it," I say packing the pipe-bomb under the table.

"Don't talk to your mother that way," Bark, Bark, the guard dog is foaming at the mouth.

"*Senores y senoras, Nosotoros tenemos mas influencia con sus hijos que tu tiene. Juanas Adiccion*," I quote Stop as I wire the bomb.

"Tyler, don't start up again!" misreads the Diplomat, infuriating the President, confusing the Cause— "Fuck that, I didn't do anything," reads the protestor's picket-sign, held high, marching on the establishment, trudging on, insisting his voice is heard, for all, justice, justified, reasonable or not, a fight against the Status Quo; the fight against Family Dinners! A noble cause. RISE! RISE UP!—

I slam my palm on the table, nick the bell of my spoon, sending it into the air, past Mom— flip-flip, fl-stab, right into the dry wall.

"You're a real asshole, you know that?" Dad hollers at me, "Leave the table."

"Bullshit I didn't do anything!" and suddenly the protester wants to play, rather not be shunned, cave, never excommunicated. And there lies the power of the State; that's how they rounded up the *Jews*. The Diplomat tosses her own fork into her ceramic plate, gets up, gives into the War, leaves it up to those who started the fire, no more water, nothing to put it out, *Congress* breaks for the day, doesn't filibuster, bows out to the *Senate*, "I'm not hungry anymore," Mom says.

"Mom," I plead for reconciliation, something, anything that doesn't instigate a *Government Shut Down*, but she exits the kitchen; leaves the table.

"Great, now you pissed her off," Dad blames me.

"I didn't do anything."

"No, you never do anything, you're perfect," he mocks me.

"Come on?"

"No, don't come on. You have a real attitude lately and we're both sick of it."

"Whatever, I do what I'm supposed to. Grades, swimming, what the fuck," and I get up, "How about Spanish? You're flunking Spanish and speaking it like an asshole right here at the table," he has to find a weakness, "You're all out of excuses, Tyler."

"Cabron," and I leave, and I don't call Sheena back, and I figure I'll just see Munts at school tomorrow and now…

○   •   ○

…I'm in my bed and I can hear my parental units through the drywall of our adjacent bedrooms. They gossip about me. Pillow talk about my, "fucked-up friends." They always do this. First time I noticed was when I was in *Junior High*. Their *Tyler the Terrible* conversations have grown more frequent this year. I can hear everything they say and Mom actually sounds more upset with me than Dad is, and their door opens, immediately followed by mine and Dad's *Fruit of the Looms* walk in, right up to me, "Apologize to your Mother," his underwear demands to my face, "You know the rule." I push his waist away, gross, grab my sweatpants from the floor, put 'em on under my comforter, get up, "Yeah," and walk past him to fulfill the obligation of law; never go to bed angry.

•   ○   •

I kiss Mom on the forehead, "I'm sorry, Mom, it's just that that girl that called broke up with me for some farmer."

"You can't let these girls get you so upset that you fight with your father," she advises me.

"Yeah, sorry Dad," I apologize to him too. Mom's kind of right, "but you shouldn't be so mean about my friends."

"Go to bed, you have practice in the morning," he pokes.

—*Where's my apology?*

The Senate recesses itself to the bed, to cuddle the Congress while the impoverished shuffle along home, to the projects, the rooms built by their masters, for their people, living off welfare, government assistance until they can get up on their feet; when they turn 18. "Goodnight," I say and leave.

·

·

·

·

·

·

·

·

·

·

·
·
·
·
·
·

chapter EIGHTEEN

my lunch is best spent off campus today, buried in my *Yellow Submarine* yellow, waterproof, *SONY Walkman* listening to the *Pixies Wave of Mutilation, Pump up the Volume slow version*. I'm solo at *Chinese & Donuts*, with a plate of chow mien and a chocolate old fashioned. This place is not as vacant as I anticipated. Tabitha's here with fuck buddy Jimmy-the-Germ and some other royally punk, white-trash, kids I generally don't shoot the shit with much, excommunicated *Phoenix* kids, rowdy, the worst of the worst, banned from the concert hall, banned from the diners, banned from the *7-11s*; it's almost admirable. Jimmy's cult is younger than me, freshman, baby face, self-tattooed, riddled in acne, wandering eyes, minimal vocabulary, vast knowledge of their own invented slang, and they're pissing off the Asian lady who works the counter; a widow, the sole owner, no children, probably *Chinese*. "You kids go now, too loud, make mess of my store," she yaps from behind the donut display. Jimmy farts, Tabitha laughs and one of the freshmen spits on the ground, "No more! You go!" she yells even louder. I'm just watching. I'm an observer. Collect crap to write about later. The chow mien sucks, already ate my donut.

Jimmy gets up first. "What up," he says to me, takes Tabitha by the wrist. She's lining her lips, "Hey!" but he's in his own world, and tugs her out of the booth. "You're such a dick," she squawks as they head to the door, out of the shop, only after Jimmy gives the trashcan a good kick, toppling it to the ground— DING-A-LING, A-LING-DING —rings the metal bell on the door handle as they exit. The shop owner comes around the counter to clean it all up. I'm thinking it's time for me to go as well.

"You no like your food, you no need to come here either," she scolds me. Dry ass noodles and a cheap amount of chocolate spread distributed on oil-fried dough? What's not to like? I pay, don't I? She is still staring at me.

"What? I don't hang out with those guys," I say.

"You leave too. No more you people, you eat lunch somewhere else," she's madder than usual, bends down, and begins to scoop up the crap with her bare hands.

"You cook with those dirty hands too, bitch?"
She waves me away. I get up, scoop up my plate and drop it in the trash.

"See, I got manners," I tritely pronounce.

"Eh," she's a bitch and I leave with a shove on the door triggering the bell once again— DING-A-LING,
A-LONG,
DONG,
WONGGGGGGGGGGGGG

.　　.　　.　　.　o　　　　　•　　　　o　.　　.　　.　　.

The parking lot outside *Chinese & Donuts* is totally empty and I'm just there. The glaze of nothingness coats my eyes, as I stare out beyond the emptiness of the air, straight down at the cracks in the asphalt, thoughtless, my headphones cradled around my neck. I've forgotten about the music, what I ate for lunch, them; I've forgotten about everything—
"What up?" Munts interrupts my vacant abstraction; I look up from the black tar. He's right there, in front of me.

"Whoa, I must have zoned out."

"I called you last night," Munts reminds me.

"Yeah, I know, parents were giving me shit about the phone," I explain, "What'd ya want?"

"Davey's got *Crystal*, shit-load of *Crystal*," Munts tells me with a twinkle in his eye.

"*Crystal*?" I ask.

"Yeah, *Crystal Meth* dude," taps his nose, "Got a bunch of it from that gay guy."

"Okay, so?"

"So, you want some?"

"Why would I want that shit?"

"Uh, you do *Mini-Thins* like all the time?"

"I thought you said *Meth's* trashy. That it rots your teeth and turns you into a criminal."

"That's only when you smoke it," Munts is making shit up, "Don't worry, I don't have any, yet. No. Tomorrow. I gotta get some Dad cash first."

"Your Dad's going to give you money to buy drugs? That's pretty retarded man," I don't believe him.

"What? No, I tell him it's for dogfood and he—"

"Whatever. You shouldn't do it," I lecture my pal. He'll do whatever he wants, but I figure better to say something then go to another funeral, "Was that what he was snorting at *Lyon's* the other night?"

"Probably. Really, you don't want to try it?" he tries again.

"No," I'm adamant about that.

"*Mini-Thins*, speed, what's the difference?" he doesn't understand my hypocrisy.

"I don't know," and neither do I.

"You sure don't," Munts might be disappointed in me. Not sure.

> *—You don't need me to do drugs.*
> *You do plenty on your own,*
> *w/ our friends.*
> *Why me?*
> *Now?*
> *Don't ask.*

Munts hears something. There's a tune quietly amplified from my headphones. "*Concrete Blonde*?" he judges my taste.

"*Leonard Cohen*," I correct him. Munts can't believe that, pulls the headphones up to ear, "That's *Concrete Blonde*."

"It's a *Leonard Cohen* cover," I specifically clear the air as he drops the headphones back around my neck, "Besides, if you don't like 'em how come you recognize them?"

"Just because I know what balls look like doesn't mean I'll tea-bag ya; Erin likes them."

"Balls?" we are so obnoxious, "Hey, how's Davey got money to buy drugs?" I ask.

"Nah man, he's sellin' them," he answers.

"That's fucking stupid. Where is he?"

"He's at school," Munts replies as if I'm some sort of 'tard.

"Now I know you're full of shit."

"No, really. He's here, got a mission, move his *Meth*."

"Oh, sorry, I thought he was here for extra credit," I am so disappointed in my friends.

"Yer being lame again," he says, "I'm getting some, gonna try that shit," Munts needs a new fix.

"Your life," I sound just like my Dad.

"All the pot's making me tired," he tries to justify his new interest in hard drugs, "Davey says I can fuck for like an hour without cumming on *Meth*."

—Do what you want.

"Whatever," I crack my back.

"Why you so uptight today?"

"Tired of the *90210* stuff. *Petaluma* TV drama, *94952*."

"What are you talking about? Nothing's happening. Shit's as boring as ever."

"Never mind," I end the conversation and we head back to school, mute, solemn, "I can't wait till I turn eighteen," says I.

"Why, so you can vote?"

—Yeah, so I can vote.

I punch Munts in the shoulder. He farts, I burp, the day is actually, really fucking boring.

o   •   o

Out front of the school's east entrance, Davey picks at his tooth with a rusted safety pin, "Hey," I call over, "What up T?" he acknowledges us as we step onto the curb.

"Nothing," I tell him the truth.

"Munts tell you what I gots?" he brags.

"Yeah, I told him," Munts elbows my gut, "He don't want any—being superior about it." Davey rolls his blue eyes. I don't want to look at him, I'm losing respect for this guy, I'm just not into it, peddling drugs, bragging on it.

"Why you gotta judge me all the time, man?" this guy knows me too well.

"I'm not, I just don't want any part of that shit," I'm snide about it.

"Fine, but you don't have to be a dick," he strikes back, "Not all of us have rich mommies and daddies."

"My parents are not rich," and it really bugs me that people always think that, "My Dad is a salesman at *Macys*. What part of that reads, rich?"

"They act rich," he clarifies. Munts nods in agreement.

"Dude, that's so inane."

"Whatever," he doesn't want to go down this rabbit hole.

"My parents are not rich, you're fucked if you think that. My Dad works his ass off, so does my Mom," I'm getting flush in their defense, "Maybe if <u>your</u> Mom got a job you'd be better off."

"My Mom's incapable of anything," D says, "So, you want some *Glass* or what?"

—Wow, like I thought we already cleared that up?

"No."

"I'm gonna get some," Munts places his pre-order.

"Cool," Davey's stoked on that.

"You guys sound like losers," I had to say it, I just had too.

"You sound like your Dad, dude," Davey insults me, and so I push on him, "Fuck you, bro!" He gets up in my face, "You fucking pushing me now?!" and shoves me back. "You pushing me? *Speedo's* pushing on me?"

"I'm sick of this," I'm beyond flush. "Remember when I made you eat dog shit the other night," Davey reminds me, Munts steps between us, "Whoa, what the fuck? Can you guys just chill for once?" I step back, "I'm just not into it, man. I'm not into trashy drugs and assholes like Eddie, that's all," I say my peace, trembling from sporadic nerves; anxious, afraid Davey might be on the *Crystal Meth* right now. One day I will be less naïve about the things I know nothing about. As for now, I will continue to assume the worst and cling on to the *Horrible Thoughts* like *Linus van Pelt* and his *baby-blue blanket*.

"Eddie ain't an asshole; you're being an asshole," Davey defends his new friend.

"I'm sorry," breathe Tyler, you are being an asshole.

—Leave it be. Not your life.
You are not your Brother's Keeper.
You are an only child for a reason, embrace it.

"I'm just in a shitty mood," I continue, "Sorry for pushin' on you. Sorry, sorry, sorry," and here it comes, a tall glass of sarcasm with a twist of lemon, "Happy dick?" and now I gotta pee. "It's cool," he rolls it off like nothing, knows me too well, "It's that Sheena shit, huh? I get it man, you always get crazy when it comes to girls."

—Now who sounds like my Pops?
But Davey I believe.
Dads don't know.
Dad's safe-guarding.
Dads don't know nothing
about the Nineties; the now.

Munts still stands between us. He's the referee. The scales of balance. If D and I really wanted to go at it, Munts would never be able to hold it off. We'd destroy him to destroy us.

"Yeah, whatever, I don't want to be late to class," says me.

"Still friends?" Davey the puppy dog.

"Yeah, what do you think?" I say, half-heartedly.

"Cool, cool," he responds as I start to walk off, "Hey man, we hang out this weekend 'kay?"

"Sure, call me later," I acknowledge the request as I shuffle away, kinda hoping he doesn't end up calling me, which would be typical, but you never know; guys got a new mission. And when shit seems strained, weird, janky, or tested, Davey's the guy that will try to over bond to stay current, stay in the family, the family of strangers and friends. Loyalty, true and false, never wants to let down a friend, never wants to be alone, needs acceptance, seeks it in his peers, seeks it in strangers, figures soon enough they'll all be *too far gone* like him or hopefully farther. Sometimes the guy's an optimist, a romantic, fanatical in fantasy, but it's a beard; Davey's petrified— I go to class.

·

·

·

·

·

·

·

·

·

·

·

·
·
·
·
·
·

chapter NINETEEN

*S*wim practice sucks this week. We're in training for a meet this weekend up in *Ukiah*. That means lots of sprints for everybody. Lots, and lots of long distance for me, shoved over in the end lane where the wake of my teammates crash against me, roll me up against the wall, and forces me to run my hand along the tiled gutter, *ugh*, stroke-stroke.

I'm growing out of the whole athlete thing. I just want to hang out with my friends after school. I want to have a normal life. Skip class. Ditch my homework. Hang out in *Putnam Park*, smoke cigarettes, drink coffee, scan tapes at the *Music Coupe*, graffiti up some walls, learn to skate, hookup with girls I don't care about, stop hating on Davey for his free spirited time. I want to get home too late for dinner, break shit in the streets, you know, do some normal shit for once, not train for a swim meet that I could care less about anymore. I complete my *1500*; stop short a few yards from the wall. "Tyler, all the way!" the coach hollers from across the pool. Pathetic. I roll my eyes. My goggles are all fogged up, can't see him in detail, drop my head and flop out three more strokes to the gutter, rip off my cap, and pop myself out of the pool. "Done!" I yell. The coach doesn't respond, ignores me. He rarely gets attitude from any of us. I'm the rebel. I'm also the fastest, so he's gotta deal, and dealing means ignoring. I don't blame him. Fuck it's cold. Fucking *February*.

○　　　　　•　　　　　○

The locker-room is filled with steam as us boys take our showers in our *Speedos*. Team-sport jocks always call us homos for showering in our suits, but really isn't it gayer to shower naked with your teammates? Not judging back, just saying, ya know? I'll never understand the contradictions that touch down in a pig-skin's puny brain.

I twist my shower nozzle closed and scamper over to my locker. Pauly's already half-dressed, pulls a cassette from his locker, and hands it to me, "What's this?" I ask without a glance.

"*OU818*, finally dubbed it for you, ahhh-yeaaaah," he says, draping a *Danzig* shirt over his head.

"Yeah, right-on man, thanks," I'm stoked as I survey the photocopied *Mr. Bungle* demo cover.

"They're gonna play the *Phoenix* again," Pauly informs me.

"I know. I'm totally going."

"Cool. Heard you hooked up with an eastside girl," he drops, snooping for some locker room talk.

"Not really; she dumped me," I tell him, finish padding myself dry and twist the locker combo.

"Yeah? But you hooked up, that's good," he congratulates me as he drops his black *Converse* to the floor— Plap, Plap.

"I guess, still didn't get laid," I confess.

"I didn't ask that, buddy. I was just looking for a name."

"Why?"

"Common courtesy?"

"You're so common," I respond.

"As common as they come. *Ride the Lightning* brother. She'll be back. *Jew* peckers are a hard thing to come by out in these parts."

"Ha, ha. Not my fault you ain't clipped," I jest.

"Don't look at my dick. Later, I'm out," and my musical mentor is gone, leaving me alone in the chilly locker-room, half naked with my towel around my waist, and I hadn't finished the locker combo and have to start all over.

o   •   o

Tomorrow's the meet, Saturday morning, rise and shine at 5am, up to *Ukiah* by 6, in the pool for warm-ups by 6:30, first event's at 7:30, sprint events, and I'm gonna have to wait until around 9:30ish for the *100 Breast*, then another two hours for my *1500* while everyone else eats dogs, shoot the shit, and listen to the *Beastie Boys* in their pup-tents. Even swimming kills my hangout time with other swimmers. I am so over this garbage. Maybe I should invite Davey, he can time the swimmers and sell 'em tweak before they take off on the blocks, fuck-face, retarded, idiot.

> *—So why was Pauly asking about Sheena?*
> *Common Courtesy my ass, what's he looking for?*
> *He knew I hooked up with her, knew she was eastside, so?*
> *Did he date her? Sleep with her? Something, right?*
> *If he did he wouldn't tell me. He's too cool to do that.*
> *He'd let it sink under the bridge, burrow into the mud.*

SMACK!— I punch the metal locker with my fist. I've scratched my knuckles against the sharp, metal, vent flaps. I suck my knuckle blood until I'm interrupted by the coach, "Tyler put some pants on, I want to go home," he yells, his words echoing through the empty locker-room.

"Yeah, I'm on it, it, it, i-t," I reply.

"Hurry up, up, up, uh-ppp," he commands as he lingers by the door to get me to hustle.

I dress quick, probably will get sick walking home with wet hair, fuck it, if I wake up sick tomorrow and can't go to the meet I'll be a happy camper. Fever of 110, sweats, chills, near death, yeah that'll teach the Coach for rushing my ass. "And hey, stop punching things," he says to me as I pass him by.

> *—Yeah, right.*

o   •   o

I don't wake up sick, I'm in perfect health, and now Dad's on me about getting my bag together so we can hit the road. I wonder if Pauly smokes pot? Probably. Does he smoke at meets? Did he smoke the night he banged my Ex? She's not my Ex. She's barely my past. Maybe I'll smoke some weed today? Maybe I'll just take a shit in the pool? Maybe I'll just fucking not give a crap and when the starter gun goes off I'll do nothing, don't dive in; just step off the block, flip off the timers, flash 'em my *Jew-shroom*, quit, go home, but I won't 'cause I'm *Tyler Goodman* and I am a good boy— *blech*.

•

○   ○

I've slept in the back seat the whole way to *Ukiah*. Maybe Mom and Dad were talking in the front, but I don't hear nothing when I slumber. I'm waking up now, can feel the car slow down as it pulls off the freeway. We must be in town. If I open my eyes the pre-meet lecture's going to ooze out of Papa Couch's mouth. I keep 'em closed. The car stops, and then pulls forward. Yup, we're definitely not on the freeway anymore. I feel Dad push on my shoulder, "We're almost there." I open my eyes, yawn, and lackadaisically sit up. I can see the *Ukiah* swim center in the near distance and the lecture begins, "Wake up, I want you in that warm-up pool right away, no dawdling this time," and he ends it there. His lectures about swimming are getting old even for him.

A massive amount of steam rises off the pool. It is friggin' colder than a witch's tit this far north, colder than *Petaluma*, how is that possible? Warm-ups started like fifteen minutes ago and that means we were late. Dad was late. That's why it was a shortened psyche-up speech. Keep on my good side and I won't call him out on his own mistakes.

—Ah, family.

Pauly steps up beside me, spits in his goggles, wipes the saliva around the lens, straps 'em on his head, "Ready kid?"

"Did you date Sheena?" I ask, snap my goggles on, and get an honest answer, "Who's that?"

"Nevermind," and with that we both leap into the pool,

feet first, straight down into the 76-degree water. Chills shriek up our spines all the way down 12 feet to the bottom. I barely get there, my toes scraping against the floor, no push up, I have to kick, and our warm has begun.

—My other friends could never deal with this shit.
Totally not disciplined enough.
Maybe swimming's a good thing?
Maybe I shouldn't be such an asshole
about all this swim-swim stuff?
Maybe I should shut up,
stop talking to myself
like I'm a psycho?
I gotta piss.
So be it.
Piss.

o   •   o

Pauly's in the first event. Sucks to be Pauly. He says it's great to be him, "I get to get it over with, sit and shit for the rest of the day." Lucky fuck. He gives me a high-five and joins his heat by the blocks, "Tear those losers a new asshole," I yell to him, *"Kill 'em all!"* Pauly adjusts his balls and steps up on the block.

"*100-yard Freestyle*, swimmers take your marks," calls out the announcer, "Get set—" I yell, *"RUN TO THE HILLS!"*

— BANG —

The starting gun sounds off and Pauly is quick off the blocks, a quarter of a second faster than the others, even though he's in lane six; lanes three, four, and five are saved for the faster swimmers. Pauly's doing his best, sprinting forward an arm's length ahead of the others, "Go PAULY! GO! GO! GOOOO!" and on the fourth lap, lane 3, 4, and 5 get the upper hand and, yup, Pauly comes in fourth again, but he don't care, he's there for the fun of it, not the competition. Pauly's the one guy on the team with the right

170

attitude. Coach pats his back, "Good run, you'll be in the finals." Pauly shrugs and turns his attention to me. "Tyler's gonna get us a win, that's all that matters," Pauly tells him and hoofs it back to our tents.

—*Great,*
thanks a lot for that,
way to be a Team Player.

Now the Coach zeroes in on me, "I want you off the blocks quick like Pauly, but don't burn it out like him. Be smart about it. I want you to let those guys get a little ahead of you. Let 'em get cocky. Let them burn out. Then take 'em on the last two laps. You're the kid with all the stamina, don't get anxious."

I smirk, "When's my race?" Coach checks his watch, "About two hours. Go rest up," and I am outta there, but Coach has a footnote for me, "Hey, Tyler, rest. I don't want you running around chatting up all the girls."

—*I'm gonna ignore that.*

This place looks like a campground for *Europeans*. Tents everywhere, guys wandering freely in their *Speedos*, community, chatter, hotdogs, candy, and yet the girls are covered in their one piece racing swimsuits; that is not very *European*. All our Moms sit beside their kid's tents in their unfolded lounge chairs, hidden under their *Ray-Bans*, engulfed in their chosen novels, forced to scold the chlorine soaked swimmers who drip onto their pages all-the-while begging these Mommies, "What's to eat?"

—*I wonder what Davey's doing?*
Probably Crystal Meth.
Probably with Munts.
3-way with Eddie?
Is that cool?
Meth?
Is that what I'd rather be doing?

Meth?
I don't know anymore,
Too Far Gone?
I'm burnt from staying clean all throughout high school.
I gotta cut loose, lose the reigns of responsibility.
Scrub the assignments, have fun, sleep less.
Crack-Cocaine?
Forget my future?
Be a killer? Be a bomber?
Town-hall gunman on PCP?
Forget who my real friends are?
Beat Davey to the punch,
set myself off into the fray,
run it down, off the highway,
get Too Far Gone first, win, take no
prisoners, save for myself, locked out of hell.

"But now we're old and bitter from growing up too fast
In a world that doesn't wait while you're living in the past.
- The Conspiracy

•
o   o

I've passed out in my tent. The outside world sounds like a muted concert with earplugs jammed in my head, but it's the scratchy sound of the tent zipper that snaps me out of dazed moment of tranquility. Dad's stuck his head in my tent, "You're up in twenty, wake up," he insists, "Take a little walk. Wake up."

"What lane am I in?" I ask.

"Four, you're always in lane 4," and he pinches my calf.

"Hey! I'm up, I'm up," I say kicking at him, "Get out."

Dad's head disappears back outside. He's left the zipper wide open. The sun glares right into my eyes. Bright outside, super-bright, I don't want to go.

•
o   o

My heat is all hopping around their lane timers, snapping

their arms into shape, stretching, spitting in their goggles. I'm cool. I'm not making a scene. The heat finishes their *100 Breast*. Tap, Tap, Tap, and lane 8 is way behind, still cruising in.

> —*Come on already.*
> *Now I'm impatient.*
> *I want to go, go*
> *and get out.*

Lane 8 finally finishes. Takes his time to crawl out of the pool. He's on the heavy side. Can't just pop onto the deck, has to prop himself up first, lean onto the deck; roll out. He could use a few more hours a day on that hamster wheel. I crack my neck, spit my goggles clear, and approach my starting block. All the other swimmers check me out, the guy with a Mohawk. Nobody likes the guy in lane 4. Want to fight? Want to beat my time? Bring it on. I shake out my arms. This time it's only me making the scene, lane 4, stretch the back, and clench my triceps. Spooked now guys? I could care less. I swim for me, not to beat you. I don't even know you. Lane 5 steps onto his block first. He's an eager beaver. I'll be a cock, step up last, after all the others. Coach doesn't like the showboating. I find it entertaining. Gotta enjoy myself somehow. The announcer does his thing, "*100 yards Breast-stroke*, swimmers take your marks." With synchronicity we all step to the end of our blocks, scratch our soles on the sandy grip tape, curl our toes over the edge, bend our backs, let our arms fall forward, dangle our fingers just along the block. I'm alone up here. Me. This is my time.

> —This me against myself—

Do well and the team gets a win, a bonus for the end game, the bigger picture that's obscured with notoriety, donations, standing, stuff that means more to their future than mine. Do well for yourself and in return you've done well for the team, it's kind of like life—

> —*I guess?*

— BANG —

The gun goes off, and without a moment's thought I soar into the air, gracefully enter the water, solid, sweep the water with both hands, strong, behind me, glide without extinguishing breath, then a powerful frog kick with another full sweep of the arms, burst to the surface take the first breath and go for it; hard, real intense, ignoring the Coach's instructions completely. Did I even here the Starter say, "Get set,"—don't think.

"GOOoo!

Go!

GOOoo!

Go! "

I can hear the crowd every time my head breaks the surface. I'm not looking, but I can feel I've already gotten a body length ahead of everyone else. I'm channeling some inner desire. My hands cut into the water like a killer. Slice, pull, slice, pull, tear the guts, ripe the insides, kill the man, all the men; ruin the world, ruin the purity, kill the water, and as fast as it all had begun the four laps of 25 yards each have vanished, lost in the tapestry of time as my palms smack against the gutter. I turn; look back at the late-comers, swimmers who are all still a couple strokes from the wall. I've killed it. Destroyed this event. Coach is right here, at the edge of my lane, looking down on me. "You over did it. Not what you were supposed to do. Out," he says, tempered even as he lends me a hand, pulls me up out of the water, hands me the towel, "What was my time?"

"Too fast for finals," he starts in as I wrap myself up in my towel. "With a time like that, by the end of the day, you are only going to slow down. Next time, listen, that's why I'm the coach."

"Sorry."

"Get dry, you have a *1500* you need to do at lunch," and he walks away.

"Whoops," I say to myself, laugh. Dad's been waiting for me. I hope he's not pissed too.

"Don't listen to the coach, you did awesome. Best time yet," Dad pats my towel along my back, "I'm proud of you. You had those other lanes by two body lengths the whole time. Epic son. Go relax in your tent. Read a book or something. No girls."

—Really?

I have to admit. It feels good to have a Pop who'll get impressed, proud of his son; really does wonders for the soul. I guess that's why I still swim. Make's Dad feel good.

—Is that lame?

chapter TWENTY

a *"Chapter 20 bankruptcy" is the* *practice of filing for a Chapter 13 bankruptcy immediately after completing a Chapter 7 case. A Chapter 20 bankruptcy can allow debtors to discharge their unsecured debts through a Chapter 7 and then file for Chapter 13 to catch up on mortgage payments or pay off non-dischargeable priority debts. But despite its benefits, a Chapter 20 also has many drawbacks and can be subject to bad faith filing objections. Read on to learn more about whether Chapter 20 bankruptcy can work for you.*

.ₛₛ$$$ • $$$ₛₛ.

I'm solo, just chillin' in a booth at *Denny's* tonight. They let me in. Think they forgot about the ban? Maybe figure me for okay? Saturday night and Munts is somewhere with his dick in Erin, the *Phoenix's* got a *Greenday* show so I'm not going to that shit, and Sheena's probably twistin' tongues with the Mullet-Man, and I've ordered a coffee, but the waitress is stuck tending to some old couple who can't decide if they want *Keylime Pie* or *Sundaes*, so I doodle on the paper place-matt with my *VHS* camera beside me, just as lonely and bored as I am and then Davey walks in. "They lifted the ban," he tells me, "Eddie got it done, sold the cook some...sorry, you don't want to hear about that," sniff, snort, and he slides into the booth, "What up?"

"*Greenday's* in *Luma*," I warn him.

"Oh my gaaawd *Greenday* sucks so bad," faux gags, picks out a menu, and starts flipping through the laminated pages, "Just came from there. Got 86'd for kicking in *Dirnt's* amp."

"No way, really?" I ask, highly impressed.

"No, but I heard The-Germ did," Davey fictionalizes again.

"Nice," I say, wanting to believe.

"Dude, you got your camera?" he asks.

I lift it from the seat, "Yeah, why?"

"Oh dude, awesome, let's go make that movie!"

"Now?"

"Great let's go."

Davey leans over the table, swipes up the camera and fiddles with it trying to figure out how one holds the thing.

"You put your hand there," I tell him, point out the holster, and slide out of the booth. He gets his hand in, presses his eye against the viewfinder, but can't find the Record button. "God you're dumb," I tease and press the red button for him. "Oh, cool, thanks," and we head out.

"What do you want to shoot?" I ask as we head through the glass door.

"I don't know, yer the storyteller, dude, I just made a promise to Eddie we'd make something tonight," he explains as I halt right outside the doors, the air is cold as usual.

"Eddie?" I ask.

Davey turns the camera on me, still rolling.

"Yeah, man, Eddie and Sheeeena. They want to make the movie, come on," he says as he zooms into my not so enamored face.

"I don't get it, dude, I don't want to make a movie with them, they hate me," I say. Davey drops the camera by his side, still taping, burning tape, and burning battery power.

"Don't be a vagina, bro, they don't hate you."

"Oh really?"

"Dude, just help me out with this," he pleads, "Just be a friend for once," so pitiful.

"What's that supposed to mean? And turn that off, you're burning out the battery and wasting tape." He pulls the camera up to his face in search of the record button. I press the red button again, "You're really pitiful. You know that?"

"Can't we just rewind and tape over this shit?" he asks.

"Shut up. Why are we making a movie with them?" I ask in an attempt to get back on topic. Davey gets closer and explains, "I owe him."

"Owe him what?" I ask.

"I owe him money," he says, "Come on, just do this for me."

"What do you owe him money for?" I ask before I put three and six together and figure Davey fucked up the whole *Crystal Meth* deal like he fucks everything else up. "Okay fine, but how does making a movie pay him back?"

"It just does. Now come on, you can sit in the back with your girl."

> *—I'm not comfortable with Eddie driving.*
> *Safe Volvo, unsafe drug addict.*
> *Sheena's waving at me.*
> *Here we go, again.*

o • o

"Hey," I say to Sheena as I scoot into the back, but before she has a chance to respond, Eddie's already turned back to me, slaps me on the shoulder, smiles, and speaks, "What up Tye-Tye? You gonna make me famous?"

"I thought you were above that shit."

"Haha, fag, no. I'm rearin' to shake up the system, kid," he says.

> *—Oh, he can say fag, but not me?*
> *And the Kid shit again. What a fuck, this guy.*

I so don't like Eddie. Not warming up to it. Tried? Not too hard. I'm even starting to think he acts gay because it makes him different. That he just does whatever is considered *Anti-Establishment*. I guess that would explain Davey's love affair with him, but come on, is this all an act?

"What do you want to make?" I ask, for D, for the peace.

"I don't know? Davers here says you're the brainiac, that all that reading actually does you good, so give us a good idea," says the poser in the drivers seat. Davey snorts a bump of *Crystal*, and Eddie revs his ancient yuppie transit and pulls out of the *Denny's* lot. Sheena turns toward me, or was she always looking at me? I don't know, but now she speaks, "How you doin'?"

"I'm okay, you?"

"Cool. I called you," she reminds me.

> —*How long ago was that?*
> *Last week? Yesterday?*
> *Two weeks back?*
> *Last month?*
> *Fuck, it's already mid-February.*
> *I guess I never called her back,*
> *followed Dad's advice,*
> *"Get over the girl whose playing games with you."*

She touches my hand, "Everything cool?" That makes me uncomfortable, so I scratch my nose and simply tell her, "Yeah, I've kinda been really busy." Eddie leans over to D, "Young love," and they both cackle. So obnoxious, yet all in all it breaks up the awkward moment.

"Let's have Eddie all down and out, like he's coming down from a *Crystal* binge and all itchy in the arms," is D's pitch.

"Then what?" I inquire, digging for actual content.

"I don't know, then what?"

A moment of thought, silence, brief, until Sheena chimes in, "Maybe I find him and try to talk him out of getting more drugs?"

"LAME!" Eddie yells, "Less drugs is LAME! I think I should find a bag of more drugs."

"And then like you do a bunch of them thinking you need to catch up on what you've missed, and like, Sheena shows up and they are actually her drugs, and she's all pissed you found them," Davey adds.

"Really?" Sheena says, obviously finding the idea as lame as I do, but I'm too creative to stop the jam session and I step up, "But Eddie's already done so much that he's going nutszoid and blood gushes out of his nose and ears, and he's turning into some crazed lunatic?"

"Yeah! YEAH!" Eddie yells and makes a hard U-Turn

throwing Sheena right into me. She looks up into my eyes. I can tell she's actually is *In Love* with me; girls sure have a funny way of showing it, sucking face with Mullet-Mush, not my idea of a well thought out fishing lure, but those eyes right there, those eyes don't lie.

"We need *Ketchup, Heinz*," Eddie insists, "So, do I get to rape her?"

"FUCK NO, ASSHOLE!" Sheena yells pushing on his seat.

"Yeah, no way, she should totally twist things around and start feeding you more drugs, turning you into her bitch," I interject, saving Sheena's honor.

"Eh, okay, but I'm still the star, right?" he asks as we cruise toward *Lucky's Grocery*.

"Yeah man, Eddie's gotta be the main guy," Davey protects his agenda, his debt.

"You're so into yourself Edward," Sheena complains, and I laugh.

"Ha, Ha," Eddie's sarcastic giggle, "Davey owes me money, that's what this is about, remember?"

> —*Way to kill the creative vibe, dude.*
> *Sounding pretty Hollywood to me.*

And the car goes silent until Eddie blasts *Gang Green's Alcohol* from his stereo. "We need beer too," Eddie amends the night's events.

"Hell's yeah," Davey agrees, but I'm wondering who'll flip the budget for the ketchup and the beer.

o　　　•　　　o

Sheena and I wait in the car in *Lucky's* oversized empty-ish lot; Eddie's outside the car smoking, also waiting for Davey who has gone inside to get the goods.

"They're never going to sell him beer, they know him, they know he's underage," I tell Sheena.

"These guys are idiots; don't you know that by now?"

"I guess. Maybe I'm just making conversation?"

"Conversation, huh? How come you didn't call me back then?" she asks. I'm uncomfortable. Hot. Cold. Hot. Warm.

Absent. Cold. Burning. I remember our night at *Elephant Rock* and this makes my dick move in my pants, "I don't know, maybe—"

"Maybe what?" she asks.

> *—Man, I don't want to get hurt again, but she's,*
> *she's being so cool. I have to play this cool.*
> *I like Sheena. Ted, Just admit it.*
> *Come clean with yourself.*
> *Don't be a baby.*
> *The girl likes older guys.*
> *Be that older guy. Be a dick.*

"Maybe I'm an asshole?" I project.

"You're not an asshole, you're the least ass-holey person in this chicken-shit of a town."

"Thanks?"

"It's okay you didn't call me back," she says as her fingers wrap between mine, "I get it, I hurt you."

"Uh, maybe, but I hurt you too, didn't I?"

"Not really," she starts, but the front door opens and Eddie jumps in, in a hurry, slides the key into the ignition, starts the car, and pops open the passenger seat. We, Sheena and I, turn around; out the back window we see Davey hustling towards the car with his shirt filled with shit. He stole stuff. Davey actually thieved out again. Man, this kid is so fucked up.

D gets in and before he can close the door Eddie peels out, flips a bitch, and drives toward the lady cashier who has chased Davey out of the store. We make a hard right, just miss her, and speed out of the lot.

"Dude, you could have hit her!" I yell.

"Ah, calm down kid, just spookin'," he justifies, "Davey ain't the only thief in town. Big business institutions are always sucking the—"

"I'm not a thief, dude," Davey tries to defend his actions.

"You're a thief bro, it's cool. Chill," Eddie says.

"I want to go home," Sheena suggests, and I hope her words are heard, 'cause so do I.

"Girls," Eddie says.

"That's rude," she complains.

"Panties in a twist?" Eddie and the D bust up laughing, "Let's go make a movie! WOO-HOO!" And we speed down the dark boulevard towards the *Old Grain Mill*. Sheena leans her head on my shoulder. We are both Eddie's prisoners now. Davey, like new clockwork, takes another bump of *Crystal* and offers a key full under Eddie's nose so he can snort one as he drives, and I finally realize I left my *Little Red Civic* all alone at the *Denny's* parking lot, ah fuck it, I'll get it after we shoot this stupid movie. "We gotta get you a bullet," Eddie tells Davey. Naïvely I ask, "A gun?" Eddie does not respond to me, he responds to Davey, "How straight is this guy?"

○   •   ○

Eddie is a terrible actor, he just doesn't have it in him, he's dry, and then he's too loud, and his crazy comes off more like an eight-year-old temper tantrum, but he's so high he thinks he's doing a fantastic job. What's strangely annoying is that Eddie keeps looking for something. Shoots looks left, looks right. *Nothing's there bro, chill, paranoid much?* For Davey's sake, I play along with it all. As for Sheena, she's got some talent, but I can tell she's not all into it, always asking me what she should say next, do, where to look, if we're done yet. Davey's the star, he's great on camera, and great at improve. He's just a natural and this brings us closer again. D and I are getting our groove back, and Edward's taken notice, "We done? We get enough for you two *lovebirds* to edit my movie?"

"Lovebirds?" I ask.

"You two are making Sheena jealous over here," he says pushing on Sheena, she is not amused, "You all might as well be gayer than me. Butt-boys much?" Davey and I look at each other acknowledging Eddie's an idiot, "Yeah, we got enough," I say in the hopes we have freed Davey's debt.

"You sure?" D asks, playing it safe; has to make sure Eddie feels his intent to feed the deed.

I can always shoot more, if I'm into it, and I'm kinda always into making movies, "Yeah, I think so, unless Sheena wants to do one more scene? Maybe lay Eddie on the tracks, seduce him to lie down and then we dub some train footage," the art is running away with me, "Tomorrow we could film a blood-filled balloon on the tracks and wait for a train?"

"I'm totally into that," she says. Ah, a date, score. The power of film.

"I'm not into it, sounds lame," Eddie shuts us down as he wipes the ketchup off his face with an oily rag he's pulled from his trunk.

"We have to have an ending, right now we have no ending," I hate faulty storylines.

"*To be continued,* dude," Eddie says throwing the rag on the ground and slams his trunk closed. I look toward Davey, I really do not want to continue this, please Davey, do not agree to continue this. Today, fine. Tomorrow with just Sheena and I is perfect, but a full-blown Holly-wouldn't continuation, fuck no.

"Yeah, that's cool, maybe we make a part two next weekend," Davey tells Eddie.

"I can't, I gotta do college apps next weekend," I lie.

"You're applying to college?" Sheena inquires.

"Yeah, *Cal Arts, NYU, UCLA*, a couple others too," I elaborate the fib.

"College is for yuppies," Eddie chimes in, "Let's go, I want to go home," and climbs into his car. Davey, Sheena, and I are still outside.

"Don't listen to him, you do your thing, we can film some other time," Davey tells me.

"Thanks, man. I kinda appreciate that."

"Don't make a scene, let's go," he says and makes his way to the passenger side.

"Where's *Cal Arts*?" Sheena asks.

"*Los Angeles.*"

"So, you'll still be close?"

"Yeah, if I get in."

"That's good, I want you to be close," she says, kisses me on the cheek, and heads to the backseat.

—Man, I think she does really like me.

Maybe I'm about to have a real girlfriend for once.

I head to my side of the backseat, happy, confident, accomplished. Davey's debt may have just paid me forward. Thanks Eddie, ya fag.

○   •   ○

Eddie pulls into the *Denny's* lot, right up to my car, "You want me to take you home?" I ask Sheena, but Davey interrupts, "Actually, dude, can you take me home?"

—Are you cock-blocking me?

"Eddie's heading to Santa Rosa. Totally out of the way."
"Sheena?" I ask.
"Eddie, you really going straight home?" she asks.
"Why? What do you want to do?"
"I don't know, but I don't want to go home yet," she says.

—My brain starts to spin.
What the hell is going on here?
Why ask him to hangout, why not me?
What the fuck, what did Davey just do to me?

And he then says the craziest thing out of his mouth yet, ever, "I really gotta get home, man. My folks are really on my ass for staying out all the time."
"Well, that's noble bullshit. Why the sudden lameness, *Davey Jones*?" Eddie criticizes the D's pussyfooting crap.
"Look, dude. If I want to start working at *Gillman* I better show them some fake-out respect, ya know?" None of us are buying it, "Maybe if I show up before 3am, stick around all weekend, clean the yard and shit, Pop's won't be such an ass about it all," Davey's half-baked confession.

—Dude, we know the Gillman gig's a lie.

"Alright, you do what you gotta do," Eddie lets him off the hook, "Yeah, Sheena let's go to *Cotati*. I got some pals who'll still be up doin' nothing; we can go there."

"Sounds cool," and then she turns to my attention, "I had a nice time, sorry for, well you know, call me," and she kisses me, slowly, and Eddie the prick reaches over, pops my door open, shoves me out, "Later, *Romeo*." Davey pulls a fiver out of his pocket, hands it to Eddie, follows me out, as Sheena climbs into the front seat and they drive away. I turn towards Davey, "I'm totally confused."

"Ha-ha, isn't everyone?" he says.

"I meant the money you just gave him."

"Oh, gas, bro," he informs me, "Can't let people just drive you around all the time without pitching in."

— You have got to be kidding me.

o   •   o

I drive Davey west into the countryside. Hope he's got another fiver in his pocket for my tank. He won't. The moon's just bright enough to illuminate the wooden fences and collapsed chicken coops along the country roads. We're listening to *Johnny Cash*, typical *Folsom Prison Blues*, and a happy Davey actually taps his foot on my dashboard, "You know, *Johnny Cash* is the only *Country* I can stand," he tells me, "Something 'bout him, probably 'cause he did a lot of *heroin*, something like that. Dark and dirty lyrics."

"Not really, I think most of his stuff is pretty basic. He's no *David Allan Coe*."

"You're right," he agrees, "This song's always cool, though. You think he really killed a guy?"

"Probably," but what do I know. We're teens, we'll believe anything sung in a song.

"You lied to Eddie, didn't you?" Davey asks.

"What about?"

"Uh, college applications?"

"I don't know why I said that. I just needed an out, ya know?"

"We're Juniors. Juniors don't apply to college," he tells me like a boss.

"How the fuck would you know?"

"I just know shit."

"Lame," I say.

"Lame, ha ha, now you sound like Eddie," and he laughs at me.

"Oh, that sucks, guess I can't say *lame* anymore."

"Next time come up with a better lie, one that doesn't jeopardize my shit."

"Sorry, but what's he gonna care? Not like he listens to me anyway."

"Eddie's got connections, man, he can really set me up," he defends his new mentor.

"Connections? To what, *crack*?"

"Look I'm not all unappreciative of your help. I really needed you tonight," wipes his nose, "I was all stressin' out. Thought you might be hanging at the Munts' house tonight and I hate going to Munts' house. His parents freak me out, too cool, makes me uneasy. Parents should be hard-asses, like yours who make rules and shit. "

"Your folks got all sorts of rules," I say in an attempt not to be singled-out.

"My parents are not like yours. Your Pop wants you to succeed at shit. My Dad? My Dad only cared about keeping his baby-girl a virgin and his adopted son under his thumb."

"You're not adopted."

"Whatever," he says, ejects *Johnny Cash*, "No more *Country*. And stop arguing with me all the time."

Honestly, I don't know what Davey's trying to get at. The drugs have him communicating in a circle, "You addicted to that *Meth* stuff now?" I ask.

"Okay, now that is lame," he says, "No. You don't get addicted to *Crystal Meth* unless you do it every day, all day. I don't do it all day."

"You're doing it every day?" now I'm concerned.

"Oh, now you're hearing things. Don't worry 'bout me, LOOK OUT!" he yells and I swerve around the dumb-ass cow standing in the road. "Holy fuck," I'm spooked, that was close.

"Ha, ha, you almost killed us," Davey says, "Don't do that shit, I don't want to die yet, I want to die later."

"I don't want to die at all," I say.

"Too bad dude, we all die, and we all die alone," he says.

•

•

•

•

•

•

•

•

•

•

•
•
•
•
:
:
•

chapter TWENTY-1

i call Sheena the next morning, 11am, figure Eddie got her home pretty late, probably sleeping in, won't ask her folks to wake her, just leave a message, yeah that'll be playing it cool, *that's the ticket*. The phone's ringing, ringing, rin—"Hello," her mom answers.

"Hey, is Sheena home?"

"She's not home yet."

"Oh, well do you know when she'll be back?"

"My daughter? You want to know when my daughter plans to come home?"

"Pretty much."

"You don't know Sheena very well, do you?"

—Sucked my shroom-head, she sure knows me.

"Maybe tonight, she's got school tomorrow. What about you? Do you have school tomorrow or are you another one of her drop-out friends?"

"Yeah, I'm still in school, *Petaluma High*," I tell her.

"Fantastic, do you have a name?" she asks.

"Tyler. Tell her Tyler called."

"Okay Tyler."

I don't have anything left to say.

"Is that all?" she inquires.

"Yeah that's it sorry, I thought..."

"Well, you're a polite one, I must not have met you Mr.

Tyler. Call back tonight or something," she says and the phone hangs up on me.

> —*She never went home last night?*
> *Why? And with Eddie?*
> *What's everyone see in that guy?*

Dad walks into the kitchen. "Who are you calling?"

"No one."

"One of your little pecker-head friends?" he asks, "Probably that girl again."

"No, just...nevermind," I say, but then I need some advice, "Hey, Dad?"

"Yeah," he sticks his head into the refrigerator.

"Nothing, I got shit to do," I take it back.

"You swear too much. Read a dictionary or something," he scolds me, "Fuck, there is never anything to eat in here."

o • o

Three days, two tests, a book report, swim practice, three lunches. Davey actually shows up at school, and yet still no call back from Sheena. I catch the D after school; he's sitting in the courtyard for some reason.

"What are you doing?" I ask.

"Waiting for the KKKs," he says.

"Really, why?" I ask.

"We're gonna hang downtown," he tells me fidgeting with his earing that looks infected, "What with you? Don't you have *Speedo* practice or something?"

"Yeah, man, but yeah."

There is a lull in conversation. Dining with the Davey three lunches in a row, has really strained our tongues, "You talk with Eddie lately?" I ask.

"No, I have <u>not</u> heard from <u>Sheena</u>."

"Hey, I wasn't—"

"Yes, you were. Go swim, she'll call you, maybe."

"What's that supposed to mean?" I'm touchy about his grumpy attitude.

"I don't know, I'm not her friend, she doesn't call me," he

reminds me.

"Yeah, but Eddie, you talk to Eddie, maybe—"

"You want me to ask Eddie if Sheena's asked about you?"

"Yeah, I guess, something like that."

"Not gonna happen," he says, "Wait for it, or call her again, show some perseverance."

"Nice word," I compliment his vocab.

"Go fuck yourself," says the grump.

"Can't."

"Dick too small?"

"Ass too tight," I say and he laughs, "Catch you later." I start to walk off.

"Hey!" he yells to get my attention.

"What?"

"Five bucks?" he begs.

"Really?"

"Come on, I'll get you back next week, promise," he begs some more.

"Next week?" I ask.

"Yeah, next week, after the weekend," he negotiates.

"No."

"You suck," the grumpy punk whines.

"Them's the breaks man. Really, I don't got no money."

"That's cool," he says looking over his shoulder for the girls, "Hey, do me this then?"

"What?" I'm so annoyed.

"You got any blank tapes?" he asks.

—That's random.

"A couple at home, why?" I'm curious.

"I just need one, man," he states, "That's what the five bucks are for."

"Come on, what for?"

"Kelsey's birthday, Thursday. Thought I'd be a nice brother, make her a mixed tape or something."

"Oh, well, okay, but you're not fucking with me, right?"

"Swear on my own grave."

"You're not dead yet."

•

○   ○

Swim practice was boring as shit again. I call the girl right when I get home, "Sheena, please?"

"Sheena's out with her boyfriend, try later, but not past ten," her Mom informs me, rocks my world, no room for an explanation, I've been humbled, tricked, let down, turned into an infidel, "Bye now," she says and hangs right up and there I am, alone in my kitchen, stone cold, obliterated by facts, distraught, speechless with the receiver in my hand as the disconnect signal loops and loops and loops.

—Did she say "Boyfriend?"

•

•

•

•

•

•

•

•

•
•
•
.
.
:
:

chapter TWENTY-2

i throw Davey against the fence beside the baseball field—

"BOYFRIEND?!"

—and I'm up in his skin tight, pasty white face, "You didn't tell me she had a boyfriend!" I yell, overreacting, not mad at Davey, mad at myself, mad that my Dad was right, again.

"Wow, chill, tiger," Davey says as he protects himself by crossing his boney arms in the poofy flight jacket his buttbuddy Eddie gave him. I step back before I punch him.

"Who's got a boyfriend?" Munts asks from behind me. Davey dusts himself off like I got him dirty, roughed him up.

> *—You ain't seen nothing yet toothpick.*
> *Say something else,*
> *say something really stupid,*
> *then you'll get it.*
> *Then you'll see*
> *the wrath of a true Tyler-Tantrum.*

"Yo, earth to Tyler?" Munts tries to get my attention.
"What?" I snap at him.
"Who's got a boyfriend?"

"Sheena! Sheena's got a fucking boyfriend!"

"No, she doesn't," Davey answers and I swing the fuck around, push him back against the fence.

"How the fuck would you know, David? Huh? Thought you weren't friends with that bitch," I interrogate him using his proper name; he hates that name.

"I just know things man, that girl *does* *not* have a boyfriend...Right?"

"No. Wrong! Wrong fucker," spittle spraying into David's face, "Her Mom said she has a boyfriend."

"No way, that's fucked, and she kissed you?" Munts chimes in.

"Hey, could you chill on the jacket?" Davey asks. I release my grip. I'm so confused.

"That bitch lied to me. And what the fuck was all that shit she said about me staying close for college bullshit. Huh?"

—Huh?

Davey's shaking. I've really spooked him. Does his best to crack a joke, "I don't think you're cut out for a long-distance relationship man."

"Long Distance? She just lives on the other side of town!"

"I mean college."

"Are you graduating early?" Munts is so confused.

"SHE HAS A FUCKING BOYFRIEND!" I scream at the top of my lungs.

"Dude, you're acting like a pansy over a chick you haven't even slept with," Davey rationalizes.

"AHHGH!" I growl. I'm so frustrated and grab his collar this time, "I want you to find out who <u>he</u> is." Davey looks confused, "Why me?"

"Because you know her!"

"I told you, she and I ain't friends." My brow tightens, like an arrow, irrational dealing with insanity, angry, unreasonable, fed up, hurt, disgusted. What can I do? Surrender to the teenage bullshit I'm trapped in? Surrender to the small mindedness of this Ex-Chicken Capital of the World, "You are the only person I know that knows her, and you owe me," I insist of my friend, Mr. Loyalty.

"I don't owe you," Davey acts offended, and I lose it. "AHAHHAHAHAHHGH! YES, YOU FUCKING DO!"

— Tyler top blown.

"I DO EVERYTHING FOR YOU!" now I'm shaking, "EVERY FUCKING THING IN THE MUTHER-FUCKING WORLD!!!"

—Now what? Knees wobble. Heart racing.

"He's kinda got a point," Munts donates his two cents.
"Hey, stay out of it," Davey scolds him, throws his arm around my shoulder, "Look Tye, calm down, I'm just kidding." I'm still mad as Davey goes into kiss-ass mode, "You're absolutely right. I owe you, but I owe you way more than this, so I tell you what I'm gonna do."
"What? What are you gonna do?" I'm testy, a disbeliever. Munts laughs. "What's so funny?"
"Nothing," Munts says, chuckles.
"Look, my brother," Davey starts in.
"What?" I'm so over it.
"Jeez, look. I'm gonna get a name. I'll find out who he is and if she really likes you or not," he says, "For real this time, promise. 'Kay?"
"Don't welch this," I don't want hollow promises from him anymore.
"When do I ever?" Davey bluffs as he lights a cigarette. Even Munts doesn't believe Davey about that. Dude welches all the time. A Davey past-time. Something you can depend on when it comes to him.

—Why is he my best-friend?

"But?" I start.
"Yeah man?" he asks.
"Don't tell her I asked you," I beg.
"My word of honor," he says, *and I pray it's true,* and he shakes his head, "You're neurotic."
"You calling me a *Jew*?" I joke.

"Not calling you a *Buddist*."

•

•

•

•

•

•

•

•

•

•

•

•

•

•

•

chapter TWENTY-3

*t*hursday, no Davey at school. Night, no Davey at home. Friday, no Davey at school. It's final period; *Algebra 2* for me and a *Pop Quiz* that I can't focus on. The formulas jiggle on the paper, spell out the doom of my irrelevant sexual endeavors; remind me I have nothing, but small-town experiences to offer the world, while I desire big city adventures. I am no mathematician, and Davey has not delivered; Davey hasn't even stopped by to pick up the precious blank tape that I have naïvely kept in my shoulder bag for the last two days, ready, waiting to be handed over, a future mixed tape for his sister's birthday— a birthday that happened yesterday —So that means he hasn't even followed through for *her*, and the bell tolls, and I have three unanswered questions left.

—I'm getting a D on this for sure.
And why? Why?
Because I let myself get distracted over a girl again,
the same fucking girl.

Timing plays a scripted trick on me as I exit the classroom. Davey pops out from behind the door. "What's the happenings?" he inquires with a shit-eating grin he bought in *Marin County*, and a playful swipe at my balls.

"Grow a pair," I say, and walk. He walks with me.

"Still pissed, huh?"

"You think?" and I don't even want to look at him as he cups his mouth and whispers into my ear, "I got a surprise for you."

"So do I; fuck off," and then we're interrupted by some douche bag right behind us, "*SPEEDO!*" and the vaginally moldy douche shoves me into some cheerleader who turns around and slaps me. King Doyle, the doucheist-bag of them all is the one who's pushed me. Walks by us huffing and puffing and blows his load in his shorts, probably. "You're a dick," Davey calls him out. King Doyle stops, turns back, "You wanna go faggot?"

"I don't fuck football players," Davey jests.

"You hitting on me?" he says puffing out his chest, adjusting his balls.

"What's wrong, you gettin' wood about it?" and that's, that, chase is on, and we speed out of that hallway like no tomorrow, down the street, past the school's car shop, past the baseball field, and we're in the clear. Doyle didn't even follow us out the doors. We're laughing. My chest hurts from running, as always. Davey's panting 'cause he's a teen-smoker and there, across the street, waiting for us, is Sheena sprawled out on the hood of Eddie's *Volvo*. Eddie sees us first, tosses his cigarette butt, and Davey slaps my back, "Happy Birthday, *Speedo*."

"What's she doing here?" I ask.

"She's your Birthday present," he says.

"It's not my birthday, why's she here?" I ask.

"We gonna stand here gawkin' at your princess-poo-poo, or are you gonna go over there and give her a big aquatic smooch?" Davey takes a step off the curb and starts across the street. I'm a little slow to go, but I figure, why not? Why not get to the bottom of all this? Why not find out why she's a two-timing twit. I cross.

Sheena turns toward me, looks me straight in the eye, slides off the hood, steps up, cups my face, plants one on me, and I push back. "No way, what's up with that?" I say, pissed. Everyone starts to laugh, even Sheena.

"What's so fucking funny?" I start, but they just burst back into more laughter.

"Shut up! What's so fucking funny?"
She cups my face again, "Calm down, sexy," but I swipe her hands away.

"No, don't do that shit, I want to know what's going on," I'm infuriated, "Why you kissing me?"

"Oh dude, you have no fucking idea," Davey says through a chuckle, "Breathe buddy."

"No, I don't. Why don't you all fucking tell me," I verbally harass this crew of nitwits.

"Heard you tried to call me," Sheena says all cute and flattered.

"Yeah, I did; a bunch, but excuse me for interrupting you and your boyfriend."

Eddie loses it, makes a scene, laughs his ass off, falls on the hood of his car, grabs his gut, and can't helping talking through his gasps of gay air, "Oh that's priceless. Priceless," he giggles and Sheena's just standing there with some shit-eating grin on her face.

—Inside joke much, fuckers?

Eddie pants and Davey's cuts his laughter 'cause he knows me too well. This is overkill. "Chill Eddie," D warns him.

"Cut the shit, I want to know what's so fucking funny," I snap at Sheena. Davey approaches me, "Okay, okay, calm down T, I'll tell you."

"Tell me what?"

—I am so over this shit.

"Eddie's Sheena's *boyfriend,*" Davey explains.
Eddie bursts back into laughter, spitting his cigarette to the floor. I shoot him an evil eye. Davey, with his index finger, slices his throat at Eddie to cut it.

"What the fuck?" I question everything.

—I'm not following.

Sheena gently pushes Davey aside and walks me to the corner.

"That's what I tell my folks," she starts.

"Tell them what?" Me.

"That Eddie's my boyfriend."

"I don't get it."

—Can you just communicate clearly for once?

"I can't tell my parents Eddie's a fudge-packer," she tries to explain.

"HEY!" Eddie yells offended.

"Chill!" she snaps at him. This is no time for Ed-wart's feelings.

"What are you talking about?"
I'm just not listening, not listening well at least.

"I like you, that's what matters, everything else is bullshit, 'kay?"

"I don't know."

"What don't you know," she asks with actual compassion.

"Black Girl, Black Girl, don't lie to me, tell me where did you sleep last night?" I sing into her face.

—I'm a bonafide brat.
Duly noted.

"Don't pull that shit with me, Tyler, I'm being real with you," she straightens me out. Davey and Eddie have stopped laughing. They watch us. Probably making bets on and against us?

"Bullshit," I'm going to speak my mind for once, "I call you, I call you again. And then, for no reason, without any f'n warning your Mom tells me you're out with your boyfriend," she's taking the abuse, "I call again, still not around, you don't call me back. Now you show up after school like everything is all dandy flowers, like I've been waiting for you, like I'm a baby puppy dog, and you call that being real with me? You're fucked up," I bite with words, and I bite too hard, and she slaps me.

"You're an asshole, I'm outta here," Sheena snaps and

walks off towards Ed-fuck's car, "Eddie, take me home."
Eddie shrugs at me and unlocks his car, "No, wait," I beg
her.

"What? How do you want to cut me down now," she's
mad.

"I didn't, I don't want to," I start.

> —but, but, but I don't know what to say.
> I don't know, if I want to be with her,
> or if I just want her to
> disappear.

Sheena waits for me to finish my inner-thought, everyone
does; always do. "Well?" she asks, but here comes Jimmy-
the-Germ in a rush, "Dave!"—We all turn as Jimmy makes
his way to the curb. He doesn't look right, something's
wrong, his face is cold, white, his brow all crumbled up, he's
rubbing his messed-up hair, he's stopped at the curb, stares
right at Davey, says nothing, maybe he's tweaked-out.
Whole town's tweaking these days it seems. "What dude?"
Davey asks, with no response from Jimmy, so again he asks
firmly, "What!?"

My eyes are on Sheena. I can care less about Davey's
drama right now. Today is my day. But her face has
changed, she's not as interested in our fight as I am, she
seems worried, like she can read the fear in The Germ's face.

"Your sister, man," Jimmy starts.

"What about her?" Davey asks with very little patience.

"She's dead, dude," and the earth trembles, the sidewalks
crack, open, and Davey loses his footing and the burley hand
of the devil reaches from the volcanic core of hell, grabs him
by the balls and pulls him...

...down.

.

.

.

.

.

.

.

.

.

.

.

.

.

.

chapter TWENTY-4

*t*here   is   a   first   for
everything, right? I'm at my first funeral.

○   •   ○

At first, I judged him. Thought the sunglasses were callous. Told him not to be a dick. Apologized for swearing, but begged him not to wear them. So, he took them off. Showed me the shiner his Dad had given him. "I get it," I told Davey, and he put them back on.

I watch the ceremony expressionless, bereaved of my own petty psyche, as they lower Kelsey's casket into the earth. And now I've heard my first *Eulogy*. I'm beside my pal amongst the crowd. His Pops had popped him in the eye when Davey had accused his Dad of killing his sister. I don't think he's crying, I think I'm trying not to cry. Their Mom can't stop weeping. The family and friends collected around the grave all so bummed. This is where it ends. The casket stops abruptly, thud, the straps lock and shake. Two *Latino* workers step up, release the bands, crank them back into their spools, and step away from the grave. D's Dad escorts his wife away, muttering to himself, "*Spics*, they should give those jobs to *Christians*. What are we paying for? Their thousands of kids under the border? America's gone to hell." She doesn't want to leave. He forces her arm, "You can come back tomorrow." She pulls away from him and walks on her own. Does she blame him as well? I'll never know, but D's Dad looks back at his only son, a look of blame. Up is down, down is sideways, and the blame game is still afoot. As these piece-of-shit despondent parents leave the burial of their *'virginal Christian daughter,'* everybody else takes a moment to say their goodbyes, as Davey gently sings to himself, *"Pictures of You," by The Cure.* Any other day, and I might have called him a wiener for that tune. Today is not that day. "She used my Dad's razor blades," he tells me, "Did it in the bath."

"Dude, that's fucked up, I'm sorry."

"You know what her note said?"

"Dude, you don't have to tell me."

"Left it under my pillow. Said— You're right D, Dad's an asshole."

chapter TWENTY-5

$t$onight?

!MISTER,

FUCKING *BUNGLE*,

AWE SHIT!

"Holy fuck, there's a fucking line around the block!" I whap Munts on the back, knock the wind out of him. "Chill dude," he tells me through gasps as we exit the parking structure and start across the street. There ain't no one in the front of the line that we know and *Tom's* not letting us slip in on this one, so we're gonna have to pay and wait. "*So be it,*" I say, but Munts smacks me this time, "Stop saying that, it's lame," so we make our way back down the line of funk-freaks covered in plaid, with mal-funk-tioned hair shaved around their skulls, while their top locks, head-banger long, drape over their tie-dyed torn tees, drenched clean with a mix of *Patchouli* oils, *Emerald Triangle* trims, ripped up blue jeans, *Docs, Converse*, all tripping balls, all mouthing off about shit. These are all the crazies who reside North of the Gate, who've driven in from *Sebastopol, Windsor, Tamales, Sonoma, Nerdy Novato,* along with *East Napa Nuggets,* green eyed

Guernville hippy kids, *Point Reyes* boat bait, and fucking *Ukiah* kids. "*Edan!*" Munts calls out to a dude down the line, by the bus stop. *Petaluma Market's* closing up shop, and the lights are shutting down. "What up Munts," Edan greets my bud, and introduces himself to me. This guy's got a grown out crew cut, a plaid button up, and solid blue jeans. His friends are more stylized in their choice of attire.

"Edan what?" I ask, because I have nothing better to say.

"*Gillen*, we're from *Redwood Valley*," he tells me, proud, like I care. "Cool, cool," I say as Munts pulls me into the line. A few people yell at us, call us cutters, but I flip em' the bird and they give up since we get into a conversation with these cats who have obviously held our place in line, not. Edan introduces his pals.

"Adam, Munts, Munts, Adam; and this is Nick," and Nick interrupts him, "Thirteen. Nick 13."—

—Okay, whatever.

"I'm *Davey*," says the gothic-guy with hand ironed, *Joan Jett* black hair, wearing a pair of ass tight acid washed B&W jeans, with a motorcycle jacket covered in *East Bay* band patches and pins, and I turn, "Did you just say, Davey?"

"Yeah brother, *Davey Havok*," he tells me like it means something.

"You all have last names?" I ask and Munts kicks me, "Why be a dick, dude?" and I apologize to *Mr. Havok* and the line starts to move, finally.

○　　　•　　　○

The place is packed, sweat-packed. The *Phoenix* is on fire. Show hasn't even started and we're slipping around the lobby amongst the sweaty sardines when this straggly haired lumberjack with a crack pipe smile beside me spits some random info my way, "Dude," smacks his toothless lips, "Can you believe they were gonna have *Primus* open. That would have been impossible," I concur, push Munts past the dude's armpit stench, "HEY WATCH IT!" some tattooed-sleeved truck-clucker in a *Megadeath* cut off yells after I've stepped on her foot and grace her tit. I've lost Munts.

—How'd that happen, he was right here?
Bungle better start already.
Hot as fuck in here.
Cramped.
I'm going in.

•

○   ○

Wall to wall. This hall is at maximum capacity. Squeeze. Squeeze. The balcony way up there seems empty enough. The lights drop— *oh shit* —a huge rush forward towards the stage, but we can't go more than a couple steps and the crowd's force rolls back, and we've lost yardage, and we gain a step or two, then another loss. I'm pretty certain we're back where we began, and yet there is another sudden push forward because the masked musicians have stepped onto the stage, I presume, but I can't see nothing, my face is pressed against some fat dude's back, and I'm forced to wrap my arms around him to help me slide around this beast of blubber when *Scummy* chops down, one strong, solid guitar strum, a sound off to *Quote Unquote* (a.k.a. *Travolta*) and it all begins, the crowd shifts, from the center, an outward spiral, a pit, a reverse whirlpool of people in the heart of a thousand heads. We rotate, the shit goes off, everyone begins to BOUNCE, BOUNCE, BOUNCE, as master *Vlad* soaks his slutty microphone with spit, *"All behold the spectacle, A fleshy limbless rectangle, Sitting on a pedestal, So Nasal handicap able!"* We're a mass of bobble-heads, ragdolls, doped up drop-ins, head massaged, and soul-washed by the facially disabled band. A bombastic, catastrophic conglomeration of cross-style harmony, accompanied by an upbeat-unpop-sterilized dichotomy of musical devotion, with a buttery butt spread fertilized by the lyrical stylings of this *Vlad* soon to be revealed as the *Mike Patton*.

Our bodies are the balls of a bouncy castle and the girls and guys alike are getting their hair caught on people's zippers, stabbed by safety pins that have popped off of leather jackets, elbows jabbed in our guts, knees colliding with jean pressed testis and tweeker twats, with tits sweating through their tight whites, and smoke, so much pot smoke, and some chick just squeezed my *"MACARONI!!!!"* yells the audience, and I'm out, burst through the mass of this *North Bay* lunacy, through the black doors, past the pool room, into the lobby; not empty— and I'm crawling over the Lucy's lined along the staircase to the balcony, and one of these Acid-heads grabs ahold of my shirt, her pupils so wide I might fall in, and asks me, "Have you seen my baby? I lost my baby."

"You brought a baby to a *Bungle* show?" I'm stunned.

"Wha?" she asks, confused, high. I push her aside to make my way to the balcony when I see this dirty old *Cabbage Patch Kid* lost in the patterned red carpet. The doll has its eye on me. I pick it up. Someone put a cigarette out on its cheek. I scrape the scorched, black, melted plastic doll, and turn to the Lucy. "My baby, you found my baby!" and I'm out, to the balcony, back to the show, up high, free of adversity, and I believe I can now watch & hear the show in peace.

•

o   o

The balcony's crowded. Couldn't tell from down below. It had looked empty. I was wrong. It's not totally full, probably just a quarter full, guess that's not all that crowded, but the shit is dark. I skooch through the third row, nobody's got booze or drink, and I step on someone's toe, my ass in their face, I turn, it's some dude. He shifts away from my buttocks, pushes me along, and continues to watch the show.

I make my way along the row 'til I get to three empty seats. I feel like the Lucys sweat got all up in me and maybe I'm tripping on their *LSD*, but it's just dark, and I'm a victim of wishful thinking. Rather be dosed than dose myself. At least that I can explain to my Pop's with a lot less retribution. Everybody's smoking up here. Not supposed to be. I'm not telling. I kinda want a cigarette tonight— Kinda —*Patton's* climbed to the top of a massive amp. Is he gonna jump? I hope he jumps. Probably piss in his shoe. Yup, there he goes.

Drink it buddy, ew gross, right down the hatch. *Spruance* takes his guitar solo, he's fucking around with us, *5150'*ed out, all *Eddie Van Halen* in the wrong key, its fucking great, I dig it, *Patton* wipes his mouth, and someone taps me on the shoulder, I turn—

"Want some?" says a brunette, shoulder length, wavy, chubby cheeks, cute, greenish-blue eyes, her lips formed, lowers her sunglasses, the joint in her fingers is reflected in the metallic shine of the lenses. I'm on the receiving end. I see myself, clearly, through the fog, amongst the haze of her offering.

"Sure," and I accept the joint. This is not peer pressure. *DARE* was not designed to deter this. This is getting high with a hot girl at a *Bungle* show. This is appropriate teenage behavior. Done. I inhale, first into my mouth, then down the hatch, into my lungs, and I remember what my pals always say, "Hold it, hold it," so I hold it, and hold it, and count, 3, 4, 5, 6, exhale— be cool, don't cough —turn back to the girl and hand it to her, cough, just a little one, clear my throat, cough again, raspy feeling, itchy throat, cough again, and again, can't stop, gotta catch my breath, cough, breathe, cough. Breathe. Breathe. Slow. Better. Okay, I think, and she suggests I take another, so I do, won't cough, I swear, and hold it in, maybe not, let it out, yeah, easy, smooth, don't, COUGH, horn section, COUGH, horn section, COUGH, Patton lifts his mask, pukes on stage, continues singing, and I have saliva dribble all over my chin. I wipe it clean, so embarrassed, don't look at her, breathe, breathe. She plants her blue leather *Doc* against the back of my seat, takes the joint from my hand, and says, "You don't smoke much. It's cute." The metal turns to ska, which turns to funk, to silence, to punk, to a waltz, and back to metal. Awe shit.

o   •   o

My seat rocks forward, the girl crawls over, "Carrie," she introduces herself as she slides into position, "Trevor," I tell her incorrectly; stoned, first time, stoned.

"Nice to meet you Trevor," she says.

"Tyler!" I say louder over the music.

"Oh, sorry, Tyler," she says, then reintroduces herself, "I'm Carrie!"

—Like Carrie the movie,
or Carrie the book?

"Hi Carrie."
"Did you get high?" she asks.
"Yeah, totally...really high!"
"First time?"
"Yeah, every weekend!"
"You get high every weekend?" she asks. I can't tell if she's impressed. She hits the joint again, blows it gently into my face, "I'm not a pothead. Allison's a pothead," she tells me, but she's gotta speak up, I can barely hear her.
"Who's Allison?"
"My friend. She left this jay up here with me," she says into my ear, waving the joint, offering it back to me, "Can I sit with you?"
"May I?" I correct her.
"Excuse me," she says, "May I sit with you, Trevor?"
"With me, or beside me?" I ask.
"With you," she says, cute, flirty. She knows she's calling the shots. "Did you say you're name was Carrie?"
"Yeah, like the movie."
"It was a book first ya know?"
"Duh," she says, and she figures I don't want the second hit, so tokes it herself. "Okay, I'll have another," and I take the joint, hit it twice, don't cough, smaller sips. I had watched her. Did as she had done.

The couple in front of us gets up, gives us space, moves down a few seats, which reveals the front row's clear as well. I grab Carrie's hand, climb us over the seat, unfold one for her, catch my hand under her ass, squeeze it out, smile, smirk; good smirk.

—I want to fuck this girl.
Shit, I mean, I like this girl.

o   •   o

The view is incredible as we lean against the brass railing, looking out upon the guts of the *Phoenix Theater*, packed beyond capacity, overflowing onto the stage, *Mr. Bungle* at the helm with their circus of music and masks, months before *Patton's* unmasking of his naked face while sporting loyalty on a t-shirt as he front-mans *Faith No More* on *Mtv*, but for now they are masked, they are still the shadows of their sound, a phantasmagorical circus frenzy of metal and stretched hide. In the back of *Spruance's* mind, a library of information connecting dots that span the universe calling for *VALIS* to organize the musical notation to propagate a clan of *Secret Chiefs*.

Carrie presses against me, my arm slides off the bar, she turns to me, opens her mouth, sucks upon my face, sucking tongues, salivating, hot, as the air vibrates with the bass, with my arms wrapped around her slim waist, my palm on her shoulder, holding her in my place, latched. I pull closer, her moderately sized breasts press against me, no judgement, bigger than Sheena's, my dick's solid, touch her neck, smooth along my fingers, down her revealed décolletage, the low-cut shirt, smooth, over the shoulder, along her side, under the short cut of loose worn cotton, her lower back so smooth. Carrie. Carrie is awesome. Carrie and I are hooking up to *Mr. Bungle* live, at the *Phoenix*, stoned — there is no worse a thought than the snowball of a real moment dissected by a series of *Horrible Thoughts*. This is not one of those timeless tales.

> —*This is basic.*
> *I don't know this girl.*
> *Never saw her before.*
> *She is not Petaluma 90210.*
> *She's Melrose Place. She ain't ruined yet.*
> *Never dated anyone I know.*
> *This I can smell.*
> *She smells nothing like Sheena.*
> *Looks at me different. Looks at me. Smiles.*
> *Carrie's cute as shit.*
> *I like Carrie.*

Carrie is liking me.
Carrie, Carrie, fuck me Carrie.
Please.
Love always, Tyler,
better known as Trevor the fleeting,
aka, show's over?
Muther fucker...now what?

o   •   o

Outside the *Phoenix*, an hour and a half later, I might have missed the encore, a re-rendition of *Quote, Unquote*, might have missed the second set, with my hand up Carrie's shirt, and now we're out by the *Swensens*, making out again, this time in the fresh night air. Tomorrow might smell like cow shit, but tonight reeks of chocolate and punk piss. The bulk of the out-of-towner trash are gone, drove themselves off into the night via their chariots, their *El Camino's*, their smoky soccer mom's *Dodge Caravans*, brother's hand me down *Chevy Trucks*, aged *Audis* covered in stickers, tan *Hyundais*, a few scooters, one or two of them actual *Vespas*, from *Santa Rosa*; Davey used to want a *Vespa*, until he hated *Ska*. A small trickle of funky sweat, scum-fucks still exit the venue in search of their own way home, by foot or by swallow, whichever way the wind turns, around, and around. We stop kissing for a moment, "Those guys are fucked up," I point out the stragglers.

She pecks my lips, "I'm giving you my number now," she announces as a notepad materializes from her canvas thread side-bag, butterfly print, art-deco, turquoise, and black, with owls in its wings, "You got a curfew?" she asks as she scribbles her digits between the blue lines, "*Casa* or *Petaluma*?"

"I go to *Petaluma*," I answer, "What time is it?"

"Let me check," she says, slides her number into my pocket, checks her black and white *SWATCH* watch, answers, "One, fourteen-ish."

"Oh, two, two thirty," I answer about my curfew.

"No, look," she shows me her watch; it's all wonky, weird, extra hands, real *Swatch-y*.

211

"I can't read that, besides," but she cuts me off.

"See, it's one, something. Ignore these hands. See. Small hand on the one."

"No, I meant my curfew," I say, "Two, two thirty. Then I pumpkin out."

"Oh my god I was joking. You really have a curfew?"

"I'm only a junior," just to be clear.

○   •   ○

Smells a bit rank under the train tracks, riverside, behind the *Old Steamer Mill* mall, clothing, hair salon, and souvenir sort of stuff kind-of-place. Trains haven't rolled these tracks in some zillion years. The wooden bridge walkway's rotting. It's safer under the tracks than on them. Carrie wanted to sit here. That's cool. Now I inquire, "So, what school you at? *Luma*, land of the *Trojans*, or *Casa Grande*, east side, track home princess?"

"Whatever dude, you know Westside's *Prince Albert* central. *Victorian* homes for everyone. East side is not breeding princesses," she schools a native, "I'm from *Hercules*, originally, then when I was," counts on her fingers, 1, 2, 3, 4, 5, "six we moved to *Frisco*; East of *Geary*. That was my favorite. Now Daddy's got us out here. Quainter life he claims."

"Okay, but do you go to *Petaluma High*, or *Casa High*?"

"Well," with hesitation, accompanied by a generalized question, "What if I said I went to *Kenilworth*?" I need a second take; speed, roll sound, scene a billion, take 2apple bananas, Charlie, and Action:

"What if I told you I went to *Kenilworth*," she grimaces.

"Are you telling me I made out with a Junior-High girl?" but before she can answer, "That would be illegal."

"Oh my god, are you eighteen?" she says, startled.

"No, seventeen."

"Whatever, then it's not illegal. Even if I was in Junior High," she says wiggling those eyebrows.

"So, it's not true?" I need transparency.

"No! Oh, you're gullible. I'm not a child. HA," she laughs, I watch her and I await an explanation, hoping she's willing to communicate better than Sheena. "I got held back," she says, "Went to *Kenilworth* when I first got here, last year, as an eighth grader."

> *—The thoughts want to creep in.*
> *Every word a trigger.*
> *Held back; she's a scam,*
> *gonna drag you down,*
> *you'll end up in jail,*
> *Horrible Thought*
> *or*
> *Horrible Truth?*
>
> *Eighth grade, how long ago was that?*
> *Three years? Two and a half?*
> *I feel like an adult compared to who I was back then.*
> *She's too young for me. I fucked up.*
> *I just almost fucked down.*

"Had to do eighth grade two and a half times if you want to be specific. That shit is hard on a girl's social development. I told my Dad he's lucky I didn't grow up a total slut. Oh, I'm fifteen, if that wasn't clear. You can totally touch my tits again, but only because I like you. If I didn't like you I would have lied and said I was twelve to freak you out."

> *—I'm confused.*

"Relax, I go to *Luma* like you dude. You just never notice me. Do I talk too much?"

"No, it's cool, I like it," I say, happy she's not a pre-teen.

"Okay, so when I was five I went to a private school in *Hercules* for first grade, a year early actually. I was super smart," and I interrupt her, "Me too," then I let her continue, "In *San Fran* I went to another private school and stayed ahead. Can you say Yuppie-Scum? But the school went up to the sixth grade and the Junior High's in the district all started at sixth grade, which made it some cluster fuck, blah, blah, and Mom home-schooled me, until *Petaluma*, Westside, by the bowling alley, you know that posh point before the freeway, all condos, I live there, but *Petaluma High* had an issue with my home-schooling garbage and I don't know something, something happened..."

—I gonna kiss this girl again.

"...and I don't know why, but *Kenilworth Middle School* took me, and I was like two years older than everybody. Now, I'm a freshman. Oldest freshman with a 4.0 ever. I've seen you around, I've always had a crush on you," she finishes.

"Are you a stalker?" I ask.

"No, but does it matter? You obviously like kissing me," she says.

"You are very cute."

"Thanks," she says with a breeze, the rank of the river tickling our senses, a seductive aroma, a sense of calm, a touch, warmth, two personalities, similarities, oddities, and we stop kissing, she smiles at me, ends our evening, in the morning, the AM, "Come on, you can call me tomorrow. Maybe we'll shoot the shit. Take a walk?"

"I believe yes," I say.

"Believe. Believe young Tyler Goodman."

o　　　•　　　o

I walked Carrie back to the *Phoenix*. Allison, her friend and cohort of the night was getting high with some skaters. The place is closed down. Dark. Cops give up around 3 am around the *Phoenix*. Whole town is closed down by now. I meet Allison. She's cool. We'll all be friends. Kiss Carrie goodnight. Watch her walk away with her friend. Allison drives a *VW Bug*. That's cool. I've broken curfew. "New girlfriend Dad," is what I got going for me. Yawn, girls are gone. I'll go home. I turn and *there he is, creeped in when I let my guard down, thought it was smooth sailing home, no care in the world, four blocks and then bed, but no, there's Davey, crossed-eyed, bowlegged, freaked out about a drug deal gone wrong, where he had shoved a balloon of Heroin up his ass, Heroin that Eddie gave him to drop off at the Gillman in the back, by the dumpster, but when he pulled it out it leaked—about a third stayed in his asshole, while another third sprayed out on the blacktop, leaving an approximate final third cupped in Davey's boney hands between his legs. The other guy ran for it, left D-man alone, and now Davey's back in town and he's sure he's overdosing in his anus, grabbing my shirt, spitting in my face, crying, begging, pleading,* "*You HAVE TO HIDE ME!*" But none of that is true, nothing happened, no Davey tonight, just a *Horrible Thought* trying to ruin a perfectly Harmonious Memory, in which has been captured in the fine purchase of this clever *Bungle* shirt I now wear upon my back, the shirt I almost forgot to get. Well done, T-man. To home with you.

•

•

•

•

•

•

•

•

•

chapter TWENTY-6

*t*here's   a   blinding normalcy to the days, the air, the way people move from class to class, through lunch, past Carrie and me, lip locked, exhibitionists, ditch last period, hoof up the slope of *English* street, trek the dusty path up to the last mound of hill, to the *Great Oak*. A massive tree with braches as thick as an elephant's leg, and roots that have dug in and out of the compact soil. The second branch up, a tree nearly all to itself, reaches out and up, a perch for punks, that when challenged, can hold five to six of us. We respect the *Great Oak*. This *Great Oak* has out lived those whitey had chased out of these hills. And Carrie and I, we're comparing life notes, favorite cartoons of the '80s, dreading the impending twenty-first century, now less than a decade away, but what could be worse, the end of the '90s or the oncoming *Oughts*? I kiss her. We go at it for a minute or so. It's getting really heated, but she stops me, "Tomorrow," Carrie says, cool, not testy; nobody has crossed a line.

—But why tomorrow?
She on the rag?

No rubber?

○   •   ○

—TOMORROW—

We're on an elephant root of the *Great Oak*, making-out, and I go for it again, slip my finger under her panty line. This time Carrie melts into me, around me, pushes my finger inside of her. She's so wet. Wet, smooth, like an oyster, slippery, wetter, moan beautiful Carrie, moan, and she stops me—

"I don't want to cum," she tells me; warns me.
"Why?"
"Yeah, it'll be too messy."
"Blur," I say.
"What is?" she asks.
"The scene going out of focus."

chapter TWENTY-7

...*C*arrie's eyes are soft, her breath, in the silence of the hills, smooth along my ears. We're playing with each other's fingers, warm, soft, and she's kissing me and we're pressing against each other, her fingers release my hands, her back is cool, my fingertips caress her lower spine, fog has shielded us from the exterior, drops of dew streak the slope of my *Little Red Civic's* hatchback. She's removing my shirt and I don't remember when she unzipped me, took my dick in her hand. We switch places, and I'm there, I'm all there for this girl, with this chick who I thought was twelve, this chick who got me high before she hit on me, not Sheena, someone who fell from nowhere, someone right there behind me at a *Bungle* show. I didn't know you then, I know you more now. Wet, wetter, she's doesn't resist, pushes into the break of my fingers, her eyes glistening, looks right at me, into me, "I'm ready," she breathes, and, "Yes," she gives consent, and I get the condom from my pants. She's humming, touching herself, her eyes are closed, and we are in sync. I'm warm as I close in on her. She takes me, guides me in, slow, more, two fingers, a little more, she eases her fingers off, I get closer, kiss her neck, she gyrates, I follow, she likes it, I take the lead, we make love for minutes or so, and she whispers, "You have a rubber on, you can cum when you want." He had forgotten. He wasn't sure. Was playing it safe, inoffensive, respectful, but now she's wrapped his fingers into her hair, pulling it back, thrust, that's what she's telling him. He understands. And thrust, tug, "Ahhh," she liked it, and thrust, tug, "Ah. Faster, not hard," and faster, and again, and they go for gold and the *Little Red Civic's* rocking the quake of '88, and it's over and its comedy, and love, and humor, and laughter, and friends, and copasetic, and a little bit dirty, and totally kinda of kinky—

—Hot as fuck in here.

I pop up the hatch. Steam swooshes out. *Sonoma Mountains.* No light. Moonlight. Can't really see shit. Deer. Cold. I step out, naked, feels nice. The town doesn't look so dead at night from up here. Twinkle, twinkle little big rigs, and reds and blues, someone's broken the law down there, off *Old Adobe Rd.* Get him. Get that drunk, redneck, rifle toting, milkmaid, bastard. Sex makes me feel superior. My dick takes a piss. I let it do what it's got to do. "Oh, that's cute," Carrie says, watching my tinkle twinkle. "Gold, Madame. Pure *California* gold," and I shake, and she tosses me my drawers, boxers, stripped— "You're hot."

—Drive home,
kiss her goodnight,
&
don't doubt tomorrows,
for nevermore.

chapter TWENTY-8

$m$unt's has to travel all the way across campus to meet me for lunch. Everybody and nobody and everybody passes by, "Hello," and the "Hey yups," with a couple, "Not gonna happens," and, "No ideas," and there's Cindy, "What's up, Cindy?" and I didn't mean to make contact, but she took the bait, or did I? She's headed right towards me, "You gotta talk to Davey," she points me down, but continues on, passes me, through the doors, into the halls, no turning back. I got the message. She sent it well.

> —*Okay, so I have no fucking idea.*
> *I haven't talked to Davey since I met Carrie.*
> *Not my brother's keeper. Just a friend. Ask Eddie.*

Munts was spotted draining his pizza grease by the cafeteria. "You got a burger too?" I ask him as I pick into his take away paper bag. "Got cheese on it. You can't eat it, not kosher," he says and knees me in the thigh. "What'd I miss Muntsy?" He takes a bite, slurps the loose cheese, chews, talks, and chews, "I don't know, man, why? Where you been? Oh, no more peperoni today."

"What do you mean where I been?"

"Carrie, huh?" swallows, "Can she move things with her mind?" he asks.

"No."

"Really? You telling me you don't get a hard-on when she looks at you?"

"Dude?" I'm offended. Talk about my girl with respect. I feel different about Carrie. Carrie's a girl of value.

"You had sex with Carrie," Munts doesn't ask, he states a fact.

"How the fuck did you know that?"

"Your monkey eye," he points to my pupils.

"What the fuck?" I swat his finger away.

"The virgin monkey eye looks right into you when you give it any sort of attention, like a puppy dog. Your monkey eye's gone, gone ape shit. You got laid. No mo' baby monkey eye."

"Alright, I'll accept that," I say, wear it proud; no matter how Neanderthalic it sounds.

"You gotta talk to D. Cindy's all cranky about it, says Brad's all pissed off, and some guy Koop, Kepper?" Munts is confusing himself, "I don't know?" getting nervous, drills his index finger into his temple, "Don't piss your pants over it Muntsy," I warn him. "Not funny," he's sensitive, "You know I got a problem," so I tap him on the shoulder. "No, you don't. It's all in your head. Tell me the story," but he's waiting for something, another sign, gesture, "Really, all up here," and I tap my head, "Tell me the rest." Munts takes a deep breath, walks in a little circle, shakes off the piss perspective, stops, snaps his elbows back, and pounces back into the tale, "Lots of people are talking. Things about Kelsey, Davey, maybe Sheena, but, I don't know, just stuff. That's it really. Oh, and Trish's Mom needs to find him."

—Is that it, really?
Nearly pissed your pants for that, Munts? No way.

"People are talking."

—I ain't hearing nuthin' about it?
and I know everything.
I'm like a robo-fly memorizing everyone's false starts.

"That's it really."

—That is a lie.

"Oh, and Trish's Mom needs to find him."

*"It's been said before,
but I'll repeat it.*

*Don't you feel like,
you've been cheated?*

*It's been shoved down your throats,
you eat it.*

*They say it's true, you believe it.
Small parts isolated and destroyed." - NoMeansNo*

"I think he stole some *Crystal*," Munts finishes his thought, "Want a bite *King Kong*?" offers me his cheeseburger, I smirk, no thanks, he takes a bite, chews and talks, "It's pretty much fucked."
    "Like a lamprey squiggling up yer Poppie's anus?" I ask.
    "Ew," Munts spits out his half-eaten bite, "I'm eating."
    "Don't lie to me," I clarify my passive aggressive revenge.
    "I didn't lie to you," he's defensive.

*—Hiding something?
Have you spoken your peace?*

"What?" he spats out for a reaction out of me, something beyond my glare of thoughts, *Horrible Thoughts*, a thought of *Carrie and Davey, no, why that?*
    "Tyler!"
    "Sorry," my feet touch back down on the concrete.
    "When did I lie to you?"
    "When you said, *that's it really*."
    "I don't remember," and he shakes his head, thinks I'm crazy, takes another bite.
    "That wasn't it. You had more to say," I over explain

myself.

"Dude, I told you everything I know. There <u>isn't</u> any more to say. I'm not lying," he's gotten frustrated with me. This is the point. Right here, where everybody cracks on me. When I overthink, think yards beyond the words, the words they say, they hear. Not the syntax. Hear it all and you wouldn't be hurt. I am not calling you a liar, you just happened to lie when you said the sentence, "That's it really," and then followed that up with a line about my buddy stealing drugs. So, no, that wasn't it, that was not the whole story, and stop looking at me like I'm over-reacting; I'm not. I'm chill. I got laid. I'm good. Smooth. Butter. Happy. Bell tolls. Fuck lunch. Back to school. "You gonna finish that?" I ask Munts about the remainder of his cow patty. "All yours," he hands it to me, I scarf the unkosher meal down, puke it up twenty-minutes later, in the hall, miss the bathroom; guess who gets to skip swim practice today?

○　　　　　•　　　　　○

Mom's not even home when I get there. She knows I puked. Nurse made me call her before releasing me. Got out of school, got out of practice, got home early, not even sick, cafeteria food has a funny way of making a man's day. We're good. Now I can dick around. Call around, see if I can't track that piece of shit Davey the Dunce down.

—Where in the World is Davey San Diego?
I'm gonna have to call Sheena.
Oh, fuck I can't call Sheena,
I got a girlfriend, now.
This is an emergency.
I gotta call her.
Gotta find Eddie. Find Eddie, find Davey.
No other choice. Gotta call Sheena.
Call Sheena find Eddie.
I'm forgetting something? Something?
Whatever, call Sexy Sheena. Sheena, call Sheena.
Carrie. I forgot to tell Carrie I went home sick. Tomorrow.

"Okay," I exhale, pick up the colon phone, dial, tap, tap the neon green buttons, slide, click, slide-click, the plastic buttons scrape in and out of their casing, slide-click, faster, click, clack, beep, bop, booop. She better be home. A man answers, robotic like voice, "Yell-ooo."

"Is Sheena home?" I ask.

"Yeah. Who's call-ling?" he asks, and I figure it out, it's a voice box; Sheena's Dad got fucked up hunting, in the line of fire—

> —I remember; she told me that, crazy.
> Shotgun pellets riddled his neck,
> Trached him up, Vocal Boxed,
> Gun love, Veteran,
> NRA guerrilla;
> Votes often.

"What's your na-ame, son?" the robotic larynx asks again.

"Uh, Sheena?"

"You got a gi-rllls na-ame?"

"No, I'm looking for Sheena— *is this guy deaf too?* —I'm Tyler. Tell her Tyler's calling."

"You got a ner-vous little pecker, don't ya?" and suddenly, silence, all I can hear is the wheeze in his chest. He must have the receiver pressed up against him. Wheeze, whooze, wheeze, whooze, shuffling— I wait. I wait. —I hear him un-cup the receiver, and he speaks, "It's a boy. Nervous pecker."

"Daddy!" Sheena yells, they laugh, he slaps his baby-girl's bottom, "You sure grown up Pep-per," sounds off the fatherly robo-voice.

"What up?!" Sheena's yells into the phone, "*Speedo,* I have one question. Can I *Nair* your balls for swim practice?"

"Hey, whoa, slow down Charlie," I can't have that. She's funny. I got one, "No, not my balls. Anus hair. Diggle-berries slow me down."

"Okay, I'm hanging up now," and she hangs up. Phone re-rings, I answer it, "Hello?"

"Did you cry?"

> —Patronizing twat.

"Never," I lie.

224

"Did she blow you first, or just missionary?"

—WHAT?

"How did you know that?"

"No shit, Tyler Good-dude got laid?!" she starts laughing, "I'm sorry, man. I didn't know, I swear. *(giggle)* I was fucking with you," she pauses, what's she thinking about, she thinking about us, herself, me, her Dad, "So no shit, for real cowboy, you lost it? Whole thing? Rubber *Trojan*, penile penetration and all? Who was it? Was it that rich chick everyone sees you with? Did you slip a pinky in the poop shoot?"

"Yes. No. No, I didn't slip a pinky, come on."

"Oh, next time," she says and then drifts. I can hear her breathing; she's lowered the receiver towards her neck.

—She had a really nice neck.
I remember her neck.
Her throat.
Is she doing her nails?
Purple?

"Hey, have you seen D-man?" I ask her.

"Yeah, he's with Eddie," she's back, "Running around the city with gay-guys."

"What are they doing?" I'm not real clear on the meaning.

"You know," and she whispers, "The *Santa Rosa* acid thing."

"I heard it was something else," I'm trying to compare stories. Connect the dots.

—Connect Four.
Black blocks Red.
Red wins Diagonal.
Polygamy. Polyamorous.
Three's a Crowd.
What's Davey doing?
Exactly?

"What I saw. My eyes don't lie to me."

"What'd you see?"

"The sheet of Acid they got, duh. Hey, you gonna go to Kelsey's unveiling?"

"Unveiling?"

"Kelsey's gravestone? Remember?"

"Oh because it was so sudden, huh? I forgot," shame latches onto my tailbone, buggers into me, fisted into humility, up my vertebrae, searing along the back of my neck to ruin my hearing. Shame gives sight to the blind, but may silence all sound, and fester, to corrode your self-esteem, deplete your ego; shame.

"Yeah."

"I gotta a question," I say, with trepidation, concern I may be mis-interpreted.

"Hit me," she's game.

"What did you mean by running with gay-guys? Davey's not gay is he?"

"Fuck if I know. I never tried with him. You're his best bud, you should know," she implies, subtlety, but an implication. "I don't know," I tell her, "Never asked. He's had girls though."

"So?"

"So, you don't know and were just joking?"

"About what?"

"The city."

"Jeez, calm down *double-O-seven*. They sell the stuff at clubs and bars. Gay guys go to both, like all the time, so, uh duh?"

"Kids in Junior High used to make fun of him for coming off effeminate," I tell her and tell her more, "Paisley. That's what they called him. Cause he wore a paisley shirt to first day. His Mom made him wear it. Combed his hair with gel and decorated him in that stupid paisley button up. And he was the only kid, guy, with an earring. I told him that never helped, but Davey's ahead of his time, a real psychic, of shit."

"Tyler?"

"Yeah?"

"I'm glad you got laid. You sound, laid, laid back. Ha, I never thought of that before...Whoa, cool."

"She got me stoned the first night I met her."

"Rewind, getting laid, not it. You got stoned. Thank God! I knew you sounded totally different. Sexier. Smoke more pot. Better for you than fucking virgins."

"She wasn't a virgin."

"Isn't she younger than you?"

—Somebody has been studying.
Stalk much Sheena?

"Freshman."

"Whoa, really?" Sheena sounds judgmental, "How old was she when her cherry got popped?"

"I didn't ask."

"You better ask," she seeds my puny, undeveloped, male mind.

"Why?"

"I'd want to know. 'Specially if her ex is still around, ya know, at school?"

•

ONE

○   HOUR LATER   ○
•

Mom called, interrupted Sheena and I. Call waiting cut it short. Good, 'cause I had bigger fish to fry. I want to know who's dick got in first. Davey drugs and gay thugs could wait. Do I know this de-virginizer? Is he a friend? Have I shaken his hand?

Mom's meeting Dad for dinner in *Larkspur*. She knows I'm not really sick. "Order a pizza. There's ten dollars on our dresser," she told me, and I did, and as I wait for delivery, I can get to the bottom of who deflowered my beautiful princess Carrie. She answers her own phone line, rich kids, "Hey Testicle."

"Please, don't call me that," I scold her right off the bat.

"Well you are testie," batting her eyes through the receiver.

—I'm no fool.

"So, like who exactly was the other guy?" I ask.

"You don't know him," she says.
"Does he go to our school?" Me.
"No," Carrie.
"*Casa Grande*?" The Prosecutor.
"No, it was before high school," The Witness.
"When you were in junior high?" The Prosecutor.
"I object," The Defendant.
"Over-ruled," Judge and Jury.
"Seventh grade, but I was held back remember?"
"Oh, I guess that's true. So, you were like, thirteen?"
"Fourteen. Well, almost fourteen. Does it bother you?"
"No. I guess it's cool I don't know him."
"He's from *Marin*, you don't know him."
"*Marin*?"
"Yeah, he lives in like this really nice house, and his parents and mine are really good friends. It happened at this *Christmas* party. You know how *Christmas Parties* can get," Carrie volunteers information.
"No, I'm *Jewish*," and I'm snide.
"Yeah, that's right, you have *Dreidel* parties."
"Do you always go there for Xmas?"
"Every few years."
"Really?"
"My Dad and his Dad were roommates in college."

—*Oh, I smell a potential shit storm coming this December.*

"How many times have you had sex with Mr. Christmas?"
She laughs, "Jealous of *Christopher Cringle* are ya?"
"That his name?" I ask like a child.
"No dude, *Jew*-miss much?" she says all snarky.
"No. Just want to know about my girlfriend."
"Well it's not polite to ask. What if a girl asked you how many times we've done it?"
"I wouldn't tell her, and it doesn't matter because I'm not talking to other girls, I'm talking to my only girlfriend."
"Come on, you don't think you'll ever be with another girl, *Romeo*?"
"Do you think that?" I ask.
"Uh, sure."

"Sorry, didn't realize you were just passing through."

"You're being unreasonable. Why are you even thinking about it?"

"Cause it matters. Sheena got me thinking, and fuck I asked, and now I know; *Santa Clause* fucked my girlfriend. *Jack Frost* fucked you first. Ho, ho, ho."

"Who's Sheena?" she asks, straight, no fluff, nothing else matters. I fucked up.

"No one."

"Oh. Well fuck you Tyler. And to think I liked you, like really liked you," she's gotten mad.

"You're over-reacting, I didn't do anything with her. I'm a virgin," I miss-speak.

"Not anymore you're not. Now you're experienced, just like me. Oh, wait, excuse me, not experienced, whorish. You're whorish just like me now Tyler; good for you," she is really offended, and I have been misunderstood, completely—

—*That's not what I'm saying! Why's your brain go twist my words, about this, tonight, about us? I'm being clear and simple. Not algebra. This is not a column in our Biology book. This is my dick in your vagina, real world, rubber or not, real world. You got AIDS? I didn't have AIDS. Did he have AIDS? Did he give it to you? Are you a carrier? Maybe that time I went in a little, to see how it feels, to be naked? Did I get sick then? What about later? Remember? I was gentleman. I had asked, you said never, I said I like to try, you were nervous, I figured we'd like it. You were bashful. Said okay. I asked again, you said it was okay. I knew you were nervous. And, and you liked it. You giggled. Wiped my mouth with your shirt. "Did I taste okay?" and I didn't know what to say, it was, so different, unique, like a fruit, wet, fruit tart, meat, form, I tasted it again. I loved you. Loved you Carrie. Did Misses Claus squirt a naughty not nice present down my throat while the mice were asleep? Huh? "Merry Christmas, Kike," breathe Tyler, breathe, you don't have to kill her. Fuck you, Carrie. Fuck your childish shit. Everything's just an experience to you. Moments to do. It's pathetic. Sustains nothing. That's what matters to me, my life, my health. I'm a fucking baby. I have my entire life ahead of me. And you want to keep this shit a secret, tied* up in your little leather pouch stowed away, hidden in the back of your closet. Yeah, like I'm supposed to trust you now? Trust him? No, I'm gonna slice him up. Wait 'till Christmas Eve, under the armpits, then along his lower back, you in the thigh to stop you from kicking me. I have to rub his open armpit with my finger to stop him from thrashing at me. He cringes, the paper-thin cut, can't really move his arm up or down, stings— his nipple, and that even hurts me, can't bring myself to split the second one, maybe his cheek, anti-climatic, can't re-write, trudge forward, GET DOWN! and I gotta fist you in the face cause you keep trying to fuck my mojo, a jab to his gut, ooh that was good, different, stab it again, again, and again, fuck he's heavy, wants me to save him, begging me, looking at me as if I'm not his assailant, "He's crazy," he tells me. You're cumming too. I don't think Chris Cringle's gonna make it. I've laid him out beside us. You're so warm. I missed you. We haven't fucked like that since the Hatchback. Never thought killing your ex would make you cum so hard. I have to lick you clean, bite your pussy lips, tear them off for your crimes, spit them on his lifeless face, fist him, pull his intestines out his ass, dress you in them, piss in your mouth, shit on his cock, puke into your cunt. I love you. I forgive you. You were young. He probably raped you. Men are assholes. No, don't pull it out. No. Leave it in. Yes, I'm wearing a condom. Two. You can't be too careful these days, not now, not in the Nineties baby-girl, not in a poop hole. Maybe I'll piss off my condom in there. You like that cunt? Did he piss on you at Christmas? Oh, shhh, no, I was careful, I cleaned and jellied you up first. Who knew boy blood would be good lube. Now if it was me who gave some seventh grader HIV, who down the line gave the AIDS to her new boyfriend, and he cut my dick off so he could ass rape his ex-girlfriend, I'd watch myself bleed out. Might even suck a dick before I die. I could lift my severed cock, suckle it like you did. It won't be able to cum so I won't have to worry about being gay or anything before I croaked, but I wouldn't cry like a baby like he is— — — — — —Wow, never thought I'd do that before I was eighteen. I think they came off in you. Both rubbers, same time. Was it like a water balloon in there? Oh, shit it's coming back out. I gotta sip on that. Yellow, golden urine, blood, hers and his, dripping out of your bleached white, cunt waxed, salty, suburban shithole, yum— — — — — — —Kiss me baby, kiss me, and tell me,

I'm a god."

"Tyler, you there."
"What?" I'm stern.
"Are you mad at me for having other boyfriends?"

—I am not responding to stupidity.

"He didn't mean anything, I was just a kid."
"I'm cool."
"Tyler?"
"Huh?"
"I think we should break up," she says, "But I want you to know, I really did like you." She hangs up the phone, I think? I'm not paying attention. Feel like I walked away, left the receiver on the counter. I didn't, it's in my hand. I put it back in its cradle, miss, it crashes on the floor, cracks, I've walked away, biting my tongue, I don't want to make it bleed, that'll hurt tomorrow, bite your lip, fuck it, shit sucks, break your finger, come on, errrr —CRACK— FUCK THAT HURTS! Fuck. Better tell Dad I got it lodged in the car door. Fuck it hurts, but I feel better, can't remember what, what was I doing, I was angry, about something, angry, infuriated, about what? About a bitch in cunts clothing, go to hell, curse a nun, disrobe a priest, burn the steeple, shoot a congressman, sawed off shot gun, *Aries*, *Mars*, isolated, revolting cock, infuriated. Kill your parents, dose your teachers, rape your newborn, die laughing, fuck the moon, and shit on the earth.

○   •   ○

Before bed I have a final, clear, and rational thought.

—Sheena is either a genius, evil,
or in love with me, to set me up like that.

chapter TWENTY-9

*C*arrie's avoided me like the plague for the past few days. Munts has been all sucky-face with Erin, and when I need him most, Munts the born-again romantic goes off and decides a five month Anniversary is more important than my breakup, what a guy, although, he's still considerate to the core, "What happened to your hand?" he asks when I finally catch up with the 4'9" artist.

"Jammed it up," I lie, showing him the splint that holds my index finger in place, "You ever do that? Hurts, man, hurts like— fucking Carrie's a cunt."

"Whoa, take a valium," Munts is nervous, seen me on edge too many times by now. He's stepped back, covered his head with his hoody. My puppy dog eyes plead with him, "Don't judge me," I'm defensive. "No, judgement, man, but that shit's nuts. You gotta chill out," he tries to comfort me. I'm in no place for it, "I'm chill."

"No you're not."

"*So b*—" but he cuts me off with a finger.

o　　　•　　　o

The unveiling was nice, I guess? Davey's Mom cried, his Dad didn't. I had gotten here before Davey. He came late, mid-way through. Strolled up in his purple sunglasses yet again. No shiner this time, just attitude. His clothes look unkempt, worn for days, maybe a week. I can feel him staring at me from across the grave.

> —Davey's a shell of himself.
> His flesh, firm cheesecake
> and if you touch him,
> you'll sink into his sour fluff.
> If you leave him in the sun he will melt,
> and dribble his self into the gutter.
> Blackened by soot and oil,
> Davey's mollified, curdled essence
> will slide through the storm grate,
> downstream, along the sewer,
> and out to sea.
> The waters will divorce the clumps of his self
> into miniscule bits of fermented cheese,
> to be fed upon by the fish and crustaceans,
> only to be pooped out,
> dropped to the ocean floor,
> left to fester in the death that is never-ending.

They served a lot of cheesecake after the ceremony; Davey didn't eat any of it. Davey's no cannibal.

○　　　　　•　　　　　○

We walk along the outside the cemetery hall. Davey needs a smoke, lights his, and offers me one.

"No, thanks. Can I talk to you?" I ask him.

"Let's go to *Denny's*," Davey suggests.

"Yeah man, let's do that," I'm happy to see a somewhat sound and reasonable friend today.

"What'd ya do to your hand?"

I don't tell him. Don't want to make this about me. I am not here. You need this time, not me. My heartbreak is petty.

○　　　•　　　○

Little Red Civic ride, 2 miles, 7 minutes, near silence, he asked about Carrie, I said we broke up, he said I could do better, I said, she liked *Bungle*, "How'd you hurt your finger?"

"I don't know."

"Carrie?"

"No."

"Liar."

○　　　•　　　○

"Cup of coffee," I place my order with the new *Denny's* waitress. Pretty. Twenties. Maybe I should ask her out?

"Can I get some fries?" Davey asks.

"Yeah, I'm buying," and I tell the hot new waitress, "And some fries." She has a life sign tattoo below her ear. *PKD* would have seen that as a sign. I'm not that spiritual, yet.

"Totally forgot to eat this morning," Davey defends his order.

"You don't have to do that, I got ya, on me buddy," I remind him.

"The city's a very different place than *Luma*, man."

"Yeah? Hold on," I want to ask the lovely waitress something, anything, "Um, do you have pie?"

"*Marin's* like totally weird," Davey says ignoring me.

"We got cherry, apple," she has to check, looks down the aisle at the rotating pie rack.

"Cherry," I flirt, Davey touches my splint, "Ow, dude?"

"You got a nasty temper, Tyler," he tells me. The waitress has walked away.

"Thanks," snide, in reference to his cock-blocking performance.

"Your life," and he leans forward, "Fuck her, Carrie's stuck up. Can't date rich chicks."

"You dealing drugs?" I'm straightforward.

"I got some *Mini-Thins*, want some?" he changes the subject, sort of, and proceeds to pull the packet of *ephedrine* out of his flight jacket's inner pocket, tears it open with his teeth, pours out the six tablets, slides two over to me with the tip of a spoon, "Down the hatch," and he pops his four with a crisp iced water chaser.

"You're spending a lot of time with Eddie," I say, pop the pills, check out the waitress.

"Eddie's a fag. I'm in it for the money."

"You're a legend," and I'm so sardonic, my hair already tingles. ` .` .` . "I do my best," says the D.

—been a while since I popped a few Thins.

Sexy brings us our coffee. "I was wrong, all out of Cherry." Davey doesn't believe her. Looks back at the rack, "You sure?" he insinuates, she smirks, walks away. "Why you gotta do that? I like that girl," I tell him. "Her?" and he checks her, "You can't go all the way with Sheena, and you think that one will go out with you?" sips his coffee, winces, too dark, "You better break your whole hand, you ain't right," and he shuffles through the mini-creamers.

—They're all the same, genius.
Pick one already. Back to business.

"You're no fucking legend D. Why's Munts saying you stole drugs from Trish's Mom?"

"You know Cindy, she's all up in everybody's business."

"I didn't ask you about Cindy."

"Munts? Come on. I know Cindy told you to talk to me," sniff, "So, talk to me. What do you want to know? Is Trish still hot? Smoking."

"I'm not interested in Trish," I tell him, remind him, move the story along.

"You're a good person," he says, earnest, like he is comparing himself.

"How so?"

"You just are. It's your nature," he pokes my finger again, stings, "That's why you hurt yourself."

"That's not why," but victims will always lie to themselves to protect their ego.

"You put people first. They don't see that about you, but I do. I know you like a brother. You rather hurt yourself instead of ruining them," he's looking me right in the eye, he wants me to know this, he needs me to listen, "I admire that about you T." My finger throbs. Maybe I shouldn't do uppers until it heals? "You should come with us sometime; to the city," he suggests.

"I go to the city," I'm not isolated here in *Luma*.

"I mean on one of our runs. Bet Eddie'll let you film it," and he turns around, "Where the fuck are the fries. Hey!" he yells toward the waitress behind the counter. She scolds the chef, she turns back signals Davey it'll be another minute, "Lame," and he turns back towards me, "Maybe I'll join the *Marines*?"

"You're full of shit."

"Don't talk to Cindy," Davey's scattered chatter is all over the place, "She could have helped Kelsey," and starts patting his pockets down, "I swear I had another pack," looks up to me, "We'll hit *7-11* after."

"Outta smokes?"

"*Thins.*"

"So, where's Eddie?" I ask.

-

-

-

-

-

-

-

-

-

-

-

-

-

-

chapter 30-ONE

*M*unts, Erin, and I have cruised down to the city three weekends in a row. Each time we go, Master Dad and I have an unessential argument about the drive, even though he said that when I turned seventeen and a half we could. He's just a tormentor. He gives in soon enough, gives me my keys back— And I'll chug 30 mph in a 25 residential zone —Takes forever to cross town. Stop sign,

...and go,

chug, chug, chug— Stop sign...

...and go, chug, chug, chug.

Stop sign, don't roll, there's a cop. Wait. Wait. Go? Go? Come on Copper what are you waiting for, go please. Come on! Ok, I'm going to go. Slowly, don't stall, "Bye," don't look back, just once, he went left, bye, bye, and I pick up Erin first. She smells like *Strawberry Bubbalicious*, because she's chewing some, blowing a bubble, pop, and then she has all sorts of questions about Carrie and me. "No, I don't talk to Sheena." What would she have to do with Carrie? Why's every girl think it's because of Sheena? Whatever, "Maybe we've spoken a couple times, but it's always about Davey, it's no big deal," and Munts gets in the back seat, "I got brownies!" In his hand is a quarter pound *Ziplock* bag with three brownies. He hands 'em to Erin. She opens it. I get a chocolate whiff of marijuana and she offers me one. I decline. Shrug, takes one for herself, returns the rest back to Munts who decides to school his darling, "Tyler ain't gonna eat those. Designated driver," kiss, kiss, "Fasten up," and it's 65 - 70 mph up the 101 till *Novato;* Highway Patrol doesn't start to care until you're in *Novato*— 55 mph signs zip past my window —*Lucas Valley, San Rafael*— Past *Frank Lloyd Wright's Marin County Civic Center,* up and over the hill, chug, chug, Little Red, *Corte Madera, Larkspur, Tunnels, the Golden Gate,* and my *Red Civic* is a perfect match of red paint. "Remember when we used to call you Red?" Munts asks from the back over the *Circle Jerks* blasting through the stereo. "No," I say as my mind wanders watching *a stranger as he crosses the bridge, across traffic forcing us all to swerve. We're going to die. Crazy pants makes it across and jumps over the railing, falls, falls, falls some more, and snaps his neck on impact, paralyzed, still alive, can't swim, swallows water, drowns. Traffic has stopped. We all need a moment. A moment— Horrible Thought.*

Erin is civilized enough to give me a buck out of the $5 needed for the toll.

○　　•　　○

Parking sucks. Parking in *North Beach*, sucks even worse. Parking in *North Beach*, in a stick shift, with your stoned friends, god awful, "Go up there," Munts points.

"No. Flat ground only, no hills," this is my rule.

"Pussy, park up there," Munts taps me on the shoulder, points. He's anxious, edible stoned, wants out of the car. The Munts needs to move around when he's this baked. The Munts doesn't want to pee his pants in front of his girlfriend. Nobody wants that. "Please Tyler, just park the fucking car." I cut left throwing Munts against the door, "Come on man, not funny," he's testy, and we head up a hill. There are three vacant spots— quick, clutch, break, emergency break, car slides, oh god, stops, fuck I hate you Munts. I claim the spot with my blinker. No one's coming, this is good. Now back in, roll, clutch down, don't stall; count of three...

—One. Breathe.
Two, fuck I'm scared,

"...and THREE!" I yell, unlock the emergency rod, release the break petal, slide, ROLL, slam the break, we don't even rock forward from the stop, the car wants to go downhill, I hate you Munts. "Come on T," Munts says, encouraging, but oozing with fear. Pump it. That's right. Dad said you have to pump it if you need to roll back. *Pump it, pump it up, good, pump it real good,* and it's working and its bumpy. Just a few more pumps and we're golden, "STOP!" Erin yells from the back. She's watching out the back window. "You're really close," she warns me. I breathe. I'm gonna have to push on the gas.

Double step— pop, pop —Clutch, accelerate— No delay.

Not a second, not a moment, no nano seconds— nothing, just make it happen. Goodman, you have no choice. Go! Clutch, Accelerator, POP, POP, and we leap forward, and I cut it and we're straight enough, SLAM the break HARD, pull the emergency bar, we're in. Breathe. Rotate the wheels out toward the street.

•

o   o

You can see the whole city from up here. Twinkle, twinkle dotted hills. Munts drains the lizard against a wall, sideways waterfall, so romantic, "Ever been to *North Beach*?" I ask Erin. "Nope," she says. "Like strip clubs?" I ask. "Too young to go," she says. "Garlic?" I ask. "Sometimes," she says.
"How about vintage postcards?"
"Love 'em."
"Italian men?"
"Can we go?" Munts interrupts our conversation.
"Thought you just did?" I jest. No one laughs. We walk. "We're off *Chestnut*," I tell myself aloud as we turn the

corner, onto *Columbus*, behind us glows the *Big Al's* giant tommy-gun sign, and the *Condor*. "What time is it?" Munts asks. "9:30," I blurt out over the sirens. "Let's hit up *City Lights*," says he and the light turns green and he pulls Erin into the cross walk. *City Lights* is directly across from us. I watch them get to the other side. I wait. I want to watch them. Poetry. I find it poetic to watch, record, exploit. I watch my friends, so in love, so nonchalant about it all, and me, across the asphalt divide, alone, incapable of letting things go, carpe diem, I cannot. Maybe someone in *City Lights* will help me release myself from myself —and I find the kids meandering the fine art aisle, Erin and Munts flipping through a *Fluxus* manifesto of sorts. I weave on by, ignore them, invisible, a stranger, lost in the city, transported into the bindings of *Science Fiction*. A feminine ghost of a future's past waltzes by me. She is indecisive. She has auburn highlights along her wavy, brown locks that reach the middle of her back. Purple nail polish. As our shoulders brush in the tight aisle, she parts a strand of her beauty around a single ear speckled in a hundred studs. Is she deaf? Maybe? She has a hearing aid of sorts. This aberration is the most beautiful dream I have yet to have.

—She's heard me.
Through my skull, she is telepathic.
If I had been any more vocal,
She may have never heard a thing.
But I am a silent killer,
as faint as a single thought.

And she's run from my fondness, around the aisle. I will cut her off at the path as sharp as a knife along her throat. Death to us all. For the sake of love. Burn the night, kill the hype. They are playing *Public Enemy* over the speakers. Not what you'd expect from the *Beatnik* hub of the *Gold Coast*. "You always have the hottest girlfriends," Munts has told me in the past, when Erin wasn't a thought. I can't help it. It's what the eye is willing to spy. I am my own *Miniature Secret Camera*. Might be my curse. Might be my naïvety. I am the fool. A fool in love again as I turn the corner and see her deaf green eyes. Her nose is simple, her lips proportionate, and she's passing by once again. She looked inside of me. She wondered, "Is he blind?" My heart is blind I tell her with my mind. She grins. Blushes. Bashful, passes by. Will I have her? Will she be back, meet me beside a *Scarlet Letter*? Why would I leave her like that— Naked along the corner, muddied in the gutter, raped, pillaged— nevermore. I am not as vile as *Edgar Allen Poe*, am I? Leave the stranger. Lose her amongst fiction and fantasy, with my tail between my legs, alone, dribbling cum upon the bathroom floor of *Allen Ginsberg's* home away from home. They are out of toilet paper. My naturally aborted chances of reproduction can only be swept, spread thin by the use of my pathetic rubber soles. Was it worth it? Public masturbation? Had too. Overwhelmed by her deaf beauty. I've never felt so desperate.

·

o   o

Munts asks me if he should get the book. I don't know. I don't want to touch it. I think I got some semen on my hands. I wipe my pant leg, take the book, turn to a black and white, silver plated photograph of a fat fuck shoving his fist up a cow's ass, while a farmer's daughter jerks him off into a bucket. "I relate to the jerk off," I tell him, laughing to myself, laughing, and wondering if that girl might still be outside, smoking, killing time, inconspicuous, maybe she's a tourist, needs some friends to show her around, "Coffee," Erin insists and we exit, the Auburn Beauty of City Lights is nowhere to be found. Fuck it, I will find her. It is my destiny. I feel sad.

·

o   o

We're waiting in line at the *Steps of Rome*. The line extends out the door. We're outside. "What's so great about this place?" I ask Erin. "Everybody gets cappuccino in the city, and everybody, cultured people like ourselves have that cappuccino at the *Steps of Rome*, capiche?" and Munts shoves her forward, "Move," the line's moved, major. It was a huge party of like seven people that was ahead of us. We're past the counter, nothing fancy, just cappuccinos, Munts isn't even having one, and that party of millions has taken up the remaining indoor tables, so we gotta stand with our ceramic monster cups, on the sidewalk, and Munts is ready to make a move on. "Done?" he asks his little lady, she holds up a finger, downs the rest. I still have half a cup. We're leaving.

o   •   o

—Breathe. You can do this T—

I have to pull out of the evil spot on the hill. I'm using the *Chrysler* behind us for leverage. "Better to be against it then slam against it, right?" Munts doesn't want a stick shift when he grows up. "Where to?" I ask. "*The Haight*," Munts calls out to the crew, "Dead ahead, across the concrete oceans, take care to the under toe, beware the waves, skyscraper high, and swarming with ships and pirates alike, mate."

"What?" Erin asks.

"Nothing," I say and spin my tires and pop out of the spot, "*The Haight*, right?"

"Yeah, *Haight*! So High!" Erin yells in my ear, and so we drive, and we drive, and it's not all that far, but it's not close and we get there and we park, easy parking, flat ground, and we're laughing, and joking as we turn the corner, step onto the *LSD* laced sidewalk of the *Hippy Underground*, but the *Haight's* a bust. Place is all closed up at night, nobody around, no one but bums. Bums scattered everywhere.

Squatters.
Squatters with pitbulls.
Squatters with Bums.
Bums with Squatters.
Dealing drugs.
Drug dealings.
Handicaps with signs for handouts.
Beggars, begging for drugs and booze.
Loose change.
Couple quarters for a cheeseburger.
Golden Arches by the *Golden Gate*.

Now that's the glory of *Hippy Culture* 20 years gone a long time ago. Man, that girl at *City Lights* was beautiful. We figure there's nowhere else to go but *Pier 49, Fisherman's Wharf*.

○ • ○

The *Wharf* blocks, unlike the *Haight*, are still packed with tourists. So much giggling, unstoppable flash photography, chatter, bump me here, bump into me there. Fat people take walk breaks in the middle of the sidewalk, grainy vegans killing trees with "Don't kill a cow pamphlets," polo sweaters, old ladies on the town, midgets with rainbow umbrellas in drag, candy corn, candy apples, *PG-13* nightlife chaos, dancing mimes, *420* and "*I lost my heart in San Francisco to my wife's brother's abs and moved to Polk street*," iron-on shirts for sale. I pull Munts out of the shop, "It's just so obnoxious," I tell him. "I wanna make shirts," he tells me.

Ripley's Believe It or Not beckons for us to enter, but none of us have the money for that— cross the trolley tracks, onto *Pier 49*, past the arcade —Robotic sounds of lightning, thunder, and zap-guns, fade as you get further out on the docks, replaced by the barks of sea lions slutting it up under the moonlight, *sittin' on the dock of the bay*— Aarch, Aarch, Aarch —*watching the tide, roll away*— Aarch, Aarch, Aarch. Munts has his arms around Erin, kisses her neck. I'm happy for Munts. I'm alone. Is that *Alcatraz*? I'm not sure, I wonder if that beauty from the bookstore is going to meet us here. *I did invite her didn't eye? I learned sign language for her. Gave up my apprenticeship to life to be with her, like her, gauged out my eyes, learned to read braille, learned how to feel music, think nothing. "I felt you in the bookstore," I'd say as she joins me along the wooden railing.*

"But I'm illiterate," she's suspicious, but how would I have known.

"You don't need to read to love," I whisper into her ear. She cannot hear me. I am a fool— Aarch, Aarch, Aarch *—I have forgotten about the seals.*

o   •   o

Erin's shivering. "Ready?" Munts asks me. Sure, not like I'm doing anything. And I look for my lost love one last time as we walk back through the *Pier*, all the way to the car, at each stop light, along the red *Golden Gate*. I figure I'll stop seeking her out once we've crossed the bay. A girl like that isn't going to find me past *Marin*.

We're driving home, back to *Petaluma*, back home, a hometown that I'm always just passing through. Munts and Erin have fallen asleep in the back, left me alone with *Mazzy Star* on *LIVE 105*, and it's foggy. I'm only willing to drive 25 in a fog like this. The city was cool. And I think about the illiterate, deaf girl from the bookstore, and then I'm thinking about Sheena, and I don't know why, and even so it's all for not, I still get a little wood, and it makes my heart hurt, and I'm sick and tired of feeling like a pansy all the time. Sensitive. Emotional. Conscious. Aware. Naïve. I'm not doing it anymore. Next time, I don't care. Next time...

o   •   o

"Hey Munts, wake up," I call to the back. He grumbles, wipes the drool from his chin, "You're home." He leans back to go back to sleep. "Home, Munts! Home!" and he snaps to attention. "Ho, fuck. I think I fell asleep," he tells me. "Get out," I want him to leave, I want to go home, I still have to take his kissy face girlfriend home, "Goodnight," and he's dawdling, kissing his girlfriend, night-night, and goodbye-bye, and yum-yums, and call me, and miss you, and blow jobs, and anal sex before bed, and milk and cookies, and cock-holding, and jet-fueled poppers with hot wax, and "Good, Night!" I yell to stop this romantic shit that's killing my dreamtime. "Testy Tyler," Munts says as he gets out. Yeah, well you know what my high point was tonight, stoner? I jerked off in the *City Lights* toilet, yeah for me.

o   •   o

"Sad about Carrie?" Erin asks on our way to her place.

"Worried about Davey," I lie, but once it comes out, yeah, I am kinda really worried about Davey. I've neglected him over a girl, over sex. I've wasted my time. Got laid, but feel empty, emptier.

"So is Munts," Erin says.

"Empty?" I ask.

"Uh, no? He's worried about Davey," she corrects me.

"Oh," and at some point, between then and now I dropped her off at her house, thought about what would happen if I hooked up with my friend's girl. I don't want that, but I thought about it. Toyed with the story. Got a hard-on as she took her time getting out of the car. I checked her out. Not my type, but if she wanted me too, I might have. No I wouldn't. I'm not like that. *Horrible Thoughts.* I don't think Erin noticed. If she did, I'd deny it. All of it. All the nothing that didn't happen. All the *Horrible Thoughts* I had in that car that I am still not willing to admit. I'm sorry Munts, I didn't mean to do those things to your girlfriend in my head without your permission. I tried not to think about it, but it just kept writing, and writing, and I'm falling asleep, on my pillow, in my bed, still in high school, still a clean bill of health, no criminal record, and not an adulterer.

●   ●

❗

•

:HOT IN THE CITY, NIGHT TWO:

Same routine, but this time Daddio gets to complain about the teeny-weeny scratch I got on my back-bumper. "Why are you even looking?"

"Because I have to make sure you don't kill yourself."

"That is so extreme."

"Your mom and I don't have to let you drive your no-good friends to the city. Why don't they have a car they can scratch up?"

"I didn't scratch it all up."

"What's that?" he says pointing out the faint tear of paint.

"Jesus, you're so annoying," but that pisses him off, stomps his foot. He is forty-six years old and he stomps his foot when he doesn't get his way. Hm? Wonder where I get my Tyler Tantrums from?

We're both in the street, outside of our home, everyone knows us in the neighborhood, and he's yelling at me again, making a scene, so angry about nothing, nothing that compares to the last time when I lied about the Baseball Jocks busting my balls, my windshield, but here we are again, and I'm patiently listening, squeezing my splinted hand— *Old man take a look at my life, I'm a lot like you were* — and yet, he lets me go, gives me back the keys, and I pick up Erin, then Munts, and this time we plan to meet Davey in the city. Davey and Eddie. They said to find them at some *DV8* club, southeast of *Market*, under the freeway?

○   •   ○

"Is that a freeway," I ask the Munts. "Yeah, I think so," he says, but he didn't even look up. He's doing his other job, he's protecting his princess from the seedy underground, under the *101*, warehouse district, empty area of *San Fran*, and my body collides into a parking meter and Erin laughs, "Dumbass." The *DV8's* stashed around a corner, and the drug-o-holic, butt buddies are out front puffing on their cancer sticks. I'm honestly impressed by their actual attendance. Eddie speaks first, "Place is a bust. Let's go to a play instead."

—A play?
This place is a bust?
There's a line around the block? What gives?

"Looks happening to me?" I like staying on target. What's shifty eyed, Davey Crocodile have to say about it, "Well?" I ask him.

"Nah, can't get in tonight, 21 and over. No guest list," stop looking at me, says his demeanor, look left, look right, chew gum, smoke cigarettes, let's walk, walk where? Walk that way? Where's your car? Parked over there? Okay we'll meet you there. Where? "Fuck, just follow us," Eddie finally instructs. "You know where you're going," I ask. "Stop asking," Davey punches me in the arm.

Do you think they're tweaking, aren't they always tweaking, I gotta pee, you always have to pee, what if you had to shit, "I don't shit I'm a girl," Erin says and we pull into the side alley parking lot of some warehouse spot, behind Eddie's *Volvo*.

○   •   ○

Exorcist: The Musical, and now it all makes sense. By far the best play any of us have ever seen, replaced *Dorenfeld's* transcribed, *"Heather's the Play"* last year at the *Phoenix* which reigned supreme, until tonight. Weeks later and we're all still laughing about it. From start to finish it was one big Drag Queen pile up of Dramodey. My comrades had all packed into Eddie's car in the lot before the show. They took their turns snorting broken glass up their nostrils. They always cringe when it burns the open flesh on the inner side of the cartilage. Davey always wiping his drippy snot drops with his flannel. Eddie carries a handkerchief, and Erin doesn't like it, made her teary eyed, but Munts convinced her to do another, and she'll be jacked up for the rest of the trip, and I opted out 'cause I'm a pussy with a Dad that'll kill me if I even cough on my car.

From there we cruised to some random Donut Shop, had some tasty treats, and it was back to *Luma*, "Munts?" I have a question. "What up?" Turn right, down his cul-de-sac, stop at his driveway, and yank the emergency, "I expected to get in more trouble than that tonight. Didn't you?"

"Next time we'll get hookers," he says.

"You can't even afford *Jolt*," Erin squawks.

•

—:THIRD CITY JAUNT:—

trip,   *up and back again,*   *third night,*   *backwards,*   *and in*

r e v e r s e : e s r e v e r

multiplied x / x four

$$C_{20}H_{25}N_3O$$

divide by 1 + 2

fractioned

in xis

eno

i

am here forever   *now & again*   *be4 the dream*

•

.   ...(((o-[_*_]-o)))...   .

We're standing in line at the *DV8*; Eddie has gotten us on some list this time. Supposedly, if you're on the list then your age won't matter, but that's Eddie logic, and that's always up for interpretation, and guess what? They're not even here, and Munts pulls something out of his pocket, "Don't get all weird," he preps me, "but maybe I brought us all something," opens his fist, shows Erin & me a dime-bag containing three paper-thin, mini-*Chicklet* sized, hard-candy squares. Closer and I see each piece is embossed with a plus sign. The beveled crossing lines go from edge to edge, and the border's beveled as well—

—*Like a square waffle. Yeah that's what it looks like.*

"What is it?" I ask. "Window paned *LSD Gel*," Munts says. "That's *acid*?" Erin takes the bag. Inspects it. Holds it up to the streetlight. Munts takes the baggy back, "Whoa!" Munts calls party foul, "Don't do that." The line moves forward. "Here," and he opens the mini-baggy, and I could use some *Mini-Thins* about now, already yawning. The line moves again. "Okay, quick. Take this," and he scoots a single four square into my palm, "In your mouth, put it in." Dab. "Yeah, now just leave it there, it'll dissolve on your tongue," he's whispering, hands cupped around the other tabs, "I, stull fell et un my tung," I mumble.

"Shush. Leave it there. Here," and he turns to Erin. "I don't want whole one," she's scared. "We'll split it," Munts compromises. "Is that cool? You're not disappointed?" The line moves. "No," and he opens his hand and starts to scoot out another single flake of hardened gelatin. Two tabs slip out. "Shit," Munts isn't sure what to do. "I'll take a whole one," she says, "No, you don't have—" but it's too late, she's licked her finger, dabbed a square, stuck it to her tongue, and there's one left for the Munts. "You think Davey'll be pissed we took it all?" I ask him before he drops his own *Lucy* for the night. "Davey's the one who gave it to me," he explains. The line moves, we're a few people away from the door. Munts looks left, looks right, looks fucking suspicious as all hell, raises his eyebrows at me, and finally drops his *acid*. I'm waiting. Watching him. Impatient already. Is it going to happen now? The line moves— "Tyler Goodman plus two," I tell the doorman. "She with you?" he asks us, "Yeah," he looks at her, looks back at me, "She's too young," and he lets her in first, takes me aside, "Nothing, no charge, you're in for free," he tells me, right in the eye. The aquarium of a club is bright, almost a white blue, a white blue muddied the moment they submerge my tender fleshless hands into their tropical salt water tank.

*

I think the squares started to hit us when the ginger raver by the stairs lead us to the exterior terrace of the *DV8*, opened his fist, and showed me an animated pentagram on his palm, but Munts assured me it was some strobing, "Just a black light trick, dude. Give it time."

*   *   *

We're standing under the short palms by the lamp heaters

out back on the patio. Munts keeps blinking. "How long's it been?" he asks me, "I don't— Since we got in?"

Erin sneaks up on me, "What?" she asks. Now I'm blinking, "You snuck up on me." She blinks, "I've been here the whole time," —Tug, tug— Munts is pulling on my shirt, "What?" —stop blinking, stare, stare at his eyes— "How long has it been?" Double vision. Blink Tyler; slowly, blink, eye?

> — Check your watch, that's what I should do.
> I wonder if they're telling themselves what I'm doing?
> Third person. Second fiddle.
> Ty-mester fester, bo-did.
> What am I thinking?

Munts tugs on my arm again.

"Um? An hour? Wow, really?" I can't believe it's been that long already. Munts nods, "What?" I ask. He's looking at his palm, "It's cool," and that's pretty much it, time was said. Time. Issue- Blank / Drifted / ing, the Parallax. The parallax? What is that thought? What's Munts thinking about? Erin's got a dirty fingernail, I guess? Things are stretchy, shift, I'm confused, gotta giggle, whoa queasy, it passes, Erin stops looking at her fingernail. Did you get it out? I ask her without words. She doesn't understand me. Never will. "Wanna go inside?" Munts asks, takes the lead, "Come on," and he takes Erin's hand, and we follow him back up the metal stairwell to the terrace. I don't remember this stairwell. I remember that guy though. The Palm Devil sees me, opens his hand to me, again, and now and forever more, reveals his eight-hundredth eye, blood shot, singular, hemorrhaging from the laceration in his palm, an opened dilated pupil that peers into both of my soul circles, simultaneously, singular, singularity, a chemically induced psychedelic experience, extract, redesigned, a work of technology, a drug— technology itself —tonight my friends and I are cyborgs, technological, chemically imbalanced a change in our perspective. How can the entire world slant left? Need a *V8* in the *DV8*.

* * * * *

Step up, going down, Munts catches me, "Watch your step, man." I missed that one. The last one. Where's the Devil? I'm looking around too much. "You're ginger friend went that way," Munts yells over the techno I hadn't had noticed a moment ago. Things are weird. I feel funny. Smiling. Things are comical. "You're funny," I tell Munts. He shakes his head, pushes me through the open doorway, back into the club, behind Erin, and I forgot what I was saying?

There's techno everywhere. I joke to myself that it looks like little Techno's are bouncing around on the walls. I don't see that. I feel it. Think it. *Acid's* not as visual as everyone likes to...exaggerate? Is that what they do? Probably? How do those little Techno's defy gravity like that, so cute?

"Whatcha looking at?" Munts asks me.

"I was just pretending," I holler into his ear.

—Crazy loud at the edge of the dance floor.

"Pretending or hallucinating?" he asks.

"Pretending! I'm not hallucinating, duh?" I correct him. He shakes his head again. "What?"

"Nothing. Let's dance."

* * * * * * *

Erin dances with herself. I'm gonna call her *Billy Idol*. She's into it. Oh, Munts is with her. She's not by herself. I am. Dance? Alone? I'm *Billy Goat Idol* —you can feel the music — musical breath against your body — lots of girls — dancing with each other — and other guys — Too many thoughts. I can't stop saying my thoughts out-loud in my head. *Acid* is a headache. I thought it'd be different. Head hurts. "You need some water," Munts suggests. How'd he know? "Go get some. Over there," he tells me directing me towards the bar.

* * * * * * *

"Can I get a water?" I yell over the fog-horn, whistle blasts, "Water!" The bartender's turned his back on me. He heard me, right? What now? Do I pay him? A tip? Here he comes. Fucking headache—SKOoOT! SKOoOT!—Hand him a dollar. Do I have one?

—Why is he waving at me?

"What?"
"Water's on the house," he tells me.
"House music, right?"

— I get ya, cool.
Thanks for the water.

Turn, sip, Munts is over there dancing in place. My head feels better. That was fast. Sip. This glass is really cold. I don't think I need anymore. One more sip. Look-in-g-lass, sip. Beautiful in there. An artic wonderland. Sexy. Finish it. Dance. Join your friends. Dance. Close your eyes. Dance. Move your feet. Cliché. Song. Colored lights and solid prisms design gradient projections along my inner eye— my third eye —Open sir, a wondrous visionary, open the third eye. Instead I blink and blink again. Both eyes. My third eye still lies dormant, buried by the growth of my skull, so young, defenseless, a closed perspective, still cut off from the influential world. Crack the skull. Open, like an egg that has fallen and broken his crown. Crack the skull. Blink. Both our eyes. Strobe/ Strobe. S t r o b e. E b o r t s. Strobe/ Strobe. eyes Me, you, Erin, Munts, him, her, us, them, dance, blink, dizzzZY

*   *   * Munts dances in place *   *   *

...Mesmerized by his reflection reflected along the transparent cement floor. Down there he is privy to the inside world. "Skinless dancers," he explains to me. He can see through their translucent leather, our translucent casing. Munts can see our veins, our entire nervous systems, bone, brain, energy, an *Alex Grey* painting animated in motion, a radiant deconstruction of pulsating, lust mucus, oozing from our sex into a psychedelic wonderment that produces a molecular, polymorphic, diagnostic that is complete and ready to lose it's sight amongst the monotony of monotheism, and I open my eyes.

. . * * * ***** * * * . .

I have left my worldly ties behind.

* * . . . * * *****

*

Atop a two-story padded column, inches from the ceiling, I know there is a pond of humanity below me. I sway. Gyrate with the fat of the warehouse pole. The club wafts to the current of dance below. Eternal stars. There is metal in me now. The chemicals. Metallic micro-robots, non-programmed, omnipresent in absence, chaotic in calculation, designed to wreak havoc on all that one has left to believe, and even though it cannot be proven, it is not inconceivable within the grips of the biological transmigration of *Lysergic Acid Diethylamide*— reds, greens, purples, blues, scorpions, slices, damages, slings, sluts, thieves, amazing —Fireflies along the open ceiling. I could climb this pole to the heavens. *"Darling come here, fuck me up the~"* and I'm yanked from reality, down the cylinder escalator that lead to *Hashem* and the orgy of Deities upon his MT. Olympus, yanked below by the iron fist of authority; a large, oversized *African American* in a black and white lettered shirt. *Bouncy Castles in the Sand*? And I see Munts has also been pulled from the ladder by his own *Bouncer Castlely Guard*, but I'm not fooled, it is apparent that Munts has gotten busted by a *DV8* Bouncer. "Where is it?" I ask the big guy. He doesn't answer. "The Castle?" He shakes his head at me. I point to his chest. "The Castle? Where is the Bouncy C—" Munts saves me, "He's with me, sorry," and pulls me away, "Why are you picking a fight with a Bouncer?" but that was like ten seconds ago, old news, "Where's Erin?" I ask him, he doesn't know, won't admit it, but leads me all the way up and down, backwards, inside and out, and all over the fucking club until we find her in the black-light chill-out room.

Some guy, rolling on X, is trying to get his arms around her. "How come we didn't look in here before?" but Munts has ignored my question as he's headed straight to his maiden. "Go get her tiger." Hope he gets the girl. He deserves it. Munts is a good guy. I'm a good guy. Girls should know that. They don't. Think I'm fragile. Why's Erin freaking out? Munts pushes the guy. Are they fighting? I can't tell. Everything's moving.

...Ey e S c A n ' T   F o L k Us...

Looks like the boys are swinging blows. Maybe not? Erin's freaking out. Getting over there is difficult. Don't want to lose my balance. That could be dangerous. How far down is it? Looks far. No, wait, its not, I'm on the ground, good, I gotta get over there, "You okay?" I get to Munts in a quick three to four steps. The *X-man* seems to have backed off. He's not leaving, just hovering, helicoptering, but steering clear of our personal space. Erin's begun to cry. Don't cry Erin. "Why's she crying?" I ask Munts. It really hurts me to see her cry. I'm getting a hard-on. I want to help her.

—Munts, I want to help your girlfriend.

Erin looks up at us. Her tears are freezing along her face. I didn't realize she was in a beanbag. Where are we? We were squatting? When did we stand up?

"You left me alone!" she yells at Munts and falls into his knees, wraps her self around his legs, weeps into his *Sears*, brand jeans. Maybe I should get a nurse? *Red Cross*? She won't stop crying. Tripping so hard she can't stop crying—all the while I'm having trouble staying focused on her post-traumatic dilemma.

—If only everything would stop bending out of shape,
    hold its form, refrain from spontaneous creation? —

* * * * * * * * * .

—Okay, I'm done. Can I stop this Acid now?
Munts? Can't hear me. Munts? Hey!—

* * * * * * * *
*

"Munts!   Munts!"
Scratch the record, chill-out, ambient trip-hop, space-garage.
"Maybe we should go?" I suggest to my friend.

*   *   *

Palm check. One Mississippi, Two Mississippi, Five Missis...
"I don't know man, I'm tripping pretty hard," he looks
around, concerned, deciphering a code, "I've never tripped
this hard before," he admits. Munts' eyes are spun, we've
lost our guru. We're on our own, uncharted waters, no light,
too much light, the strobe, sirens, a naked couple on a couch
behind Munts, in the corner, fuck, sex, two bodies, a blurred
existence, might as well be wet clay, where one body
becomes the other's mass. Where casual encounters become
heresy. Where I am left a voyeur to watch their suburban
future swallow them up in the jaws of the couch, gone,
digested, recycled, casings, to be filled with horse hair & pig
ear & cow marrow. Never stop crying, Erin. Flood the earth.

Crie out your ShinY DiamondS
CarriE
ME
A
WAY
*

We're at a payphone somewhere in the club— near the
restrooms. I smell urine. I try to avoid it, but the stench is
strong. "Is there another phone?" I ask some girl in a leather
mask as she walks by. Fuck it. I gotta make this call. The

quarter is not cooperating with me in the least. The fans of the club keep blowing the 25cent piece around like a flag— *How does it do that? Go in the slot,* but it won't. "I can't do it," I tell Munts. "Told you," he retells me, "Law of *LSD* physics. It is physically impossible to call your parents while tripping. It just goes against nature, against instinct. *Acid* ain't gonna let you do something that stupid."

But Goodman's been brainwashed with discipline.
This good man has been born with a name to live up too.
Goodman knows,
                    Tyler's
                        gotta
                            call
                                his,
                                    F
                                     a
                                      t
                                      h

                                    e

                            r .   .   .   .   .

                                                                .

                            Focus, Goodman, focus.
                            What would Tyler do?
                        Another quarter, that'll work.
                    This one's just a dud. Happens.
                            Remember 7-11?
                        Always had a couple of
                            duds trying to re-up
                                on Mario Brothers.
                    I can't find the other quarter.
                My hand's lost in the lint of my pocket.
            Get through this & you're tossing the splint.
                Munts face shifts when I move left.
                    Gotta look at something else.
                        Check all my pockets.

Stop / Think?
Spe-
Ak

. . . .

.

.

. . . . . ."I, —I can't drive us home right now," I say aloud,
using my voice again so my guru, our *Shaman*, so young, too
young to know, who is my rapist, my— eyes roll back into
*my head, B.li.n*K— I'm awake, back to reality, nope —Munts
has vanished. Everything's gone, black. No stars. No air.
Nothing. Only me sinking in this dilated Abyss.

—I don't understand.
I can hear the music, the chatter.
Feel the sweat, smell the fog machines —

Trembling.
—Trembling Tyler—
afraid to open his eyes.
What if I'm lost?

Left in the club on my owN
TrusT
—} _*_ {—
and when i do open my eyes
2
my surprise
munts also struggles
inserting the
quarter
in
to
the
phone
.

.
9-1-1

I'm waiting—He knows what to do next—I don't know shit

you know

.   .   *   *   *   *   .* .   *   *   .   .

"You're right dude, we need to call your Dad to pick us up,"
he decides.

—easier said than done—

*   *   .   .   *   *   *   *

*

"This *acid's* way too strong," Munts is really starting to
perspire, "I just called nine, one, one," and now he's rubbing
his temple. Poor kid's got it bad, real bad. I feel for him. I feel
good, myself. Suddenly? I'm empowered by watching
Munts-the-experienced squirm under his subconscious.
Normally a miss call to the Police would send me— *row, row,*
rowing my boat quickly down a paranoid stream, full of delusional
rapids, back-wood hillbillies with sawed-off peckers and itches they
can't even find to scratch —but now, here, in the sky with
diamonds, nah, it ain't no thing, all part of the great flow of
the cosmos, "*don't worry be happy, 9-1-1s a joke in my town,*" I
sing to my deliverer, but he's gotta pee and leaves me with
Erin, oh shit, Erin, thought we lost her for a minute. And
look who's back, if it isn't the Persian Piper with a hard-on
for *Xstacy*, and he's right up on her, like magic, hypnotism.
She starts talking with him again, drifts to the side, away
from me. Munts is missing it. Munts is taking a pee while
this Persian Perv is persuading Erin away from us to dream
of genie. There is something gross about this guy. He's
stroking her arm with his finger, touching his crotch with
the other. Gross. She's listening to him. Grosser. He has a
spell on her. Where's Munts? Man, I don't want Erin to fall
for that guy. Hurry up Munts, and I hear in my head, "*There*
is no love here. Pretty is a wire framed lie," and I believe I hear
Erin say, backwards, in the distance, belonging to a memoir,
"*A little before midnight,*" and the guy turns into a pillar of
salt, and with a single gust of wind from Erin's lips, his
particles blow off into oblivion, and I need to know, "How
long's this stuff last?" and Munts is back, sadly informing me

of the answer to my question, "Twelve Hours, why what time is it?" and out of the blue, like a long-lost letter, returned to sender, and left for shred, Erin says what I predicted she would, "A little before midnight."

"Ah man, we've only been tripping for like 2 hours," Munts is blown away, "We haven't even *peaked yet, Al.*"

"Oh, we're fucked," Erin says.

"Speak for yourself, I feel excellent," and I smirk, and it feels good, and I want to cum, "Stop that," Munts takes the soggy napkin out of my hand, "You look crazy." I lean into the bar, crack my back, want to go swimming, feel great, gotta dance, wish I could fuck— That girl right there, beautiful, but Munts pulls me back, "Where you going *Romeo*?" His eyes keep moving, "To talk to that girl," I tell him. "That's a mannequin," he yells into my ear, remembering he has my dirty wet napkin in his hand, throws it on the ground, shakes his fingers dry, looks up, I'm moving in on the girl.

*   * * _*   _* * *   *

*

The club gets bigger every time I complete a circle. I'm dancing. Every so often one of those loops makes the place gets smaller, compact, but I get around that real quick. Hop instead of dance, don't talk to strangers, don't touch the girls who don't want to be touched, don't tell everyone how high you are, unless they tell you first, and I'm just around the bend,

    past the bathrooms,
        highs-of-nine,
            cloudy eight-balls,
                    easy-7s,
                        9s-of-kitten-
                            tails &
                 "What are you doing here?"
        —I bump into *Carrie*
      She's ecstatic to see me,
    in the flesh,
right here,

in the *DV8*, by the loudspeaker, tripping balls, and I say, "I'm sorry, I'm tripping really hard. Do I know you?"
  "What?" she can't hear me?
I step in, closer, place my hand along her waist, a naked waist, baby-T, iron-on rainbow pop, her skin is softer than I remember, and she's got her belly pierced, I like it, it's cute, "Are you my girlfriend, Carrie?" She giggles, her flirty hands on my chest, playful neon fingernails, "Yes, but I'm not your girlfriend, I'm your wife, right?" she says with a question.

Is she on something too?
I feel sober now, yup.
Must have come,
Down, runn-
in
*

*

*

. * * * *   * * . . .

* *Carrie's kissing me. When did that happen? Start? Mmm* *

*   * * .   . * *   *

*

*

*

i stop
her eyes are twisted
smiling
but it comes with a twitch
Perspective, so enhanced
I can read her perfectly now
Happy, but should she be?
She's at a tug-of-war with her body
a fleshy corporation
trade marked for the reproduction industry

against hate
love

"What are you on?"
I ask, I fall back, deaf, Love/Letters, echo, dig in, victim.

Love.
Everything'
s scatte
red
.

L o v e
o n—
LSD.

I don't like,

Sobriet —
— y.

I want— to hallucinate— —
mathematics   —the odds   —again
I rather not have options —
Roll the die, dice, Dayenu!

I $ n 't EVERYTHING 2+2= $ a l E ?

———$ r i g h T $^{+}$ N$o$thin g = ^{4}A price $———

— — — — — — — — —And a K i $ $ balancing — for $ a l e ?

L o v e—
L o v e—

. L   o   v   e ~ * .

.

.

.

.

.·. . L . . . oƲ. ·. ·. . ..e . . . . .We took Some eX-Tastyyy

she giꝶgles

—after~Slippiℵg~her~TOngue~Out

of

my

mouth.   .   .   .

.   .   .   .   .   .

.   .   .   .   .   .
.
.
.   .

.   .   .   .

.

.

.   .   .

.

.

.

.   .   .   ."Who's we?"
                                                                                                            I ask.............
"I don't know," she giggles, licks her lips, "You're adorable,"
snuggles into my chest, giggles, plays with my nipple,
"Cute," and for a moment I forget that she's there. I'm
watching Sheena dance by one of the columns. She sways,
smooth, lovely, like a mermaid underwater, in the teal
turquoise light rays that breakthrough the surface of the sea.
I love her. She's my mistress. The sea. I love the sea. I think
I'll walk this woman into a stream, lose her to the current, so
I may jack off upon a rock, fire my seamen downstream,
oppose the pink salmon, against the tide, into . .   .   .

. . . . • — — —*the* ₘₒ*u*t*h*s

of plankton-succulant / aquatic-colored / African-blue / acrobatic-vestibules / siren-sexy school of
MERMAID. *eYe*s

. . * . * * *   * * . * . .

*   * . .   . * * *

*

8ₑ𝒼ₐTɪ𝓋ℯ.ID~ɑrɪv𝐸ₘₒNₑ.Zₑᵣₒ08
.0.
...yₒuₐᵣℯNOGₒₒDₘₐₙ ...

*   * * .   . * * *

*

Here I am a mystic, the myth, a raging hard-on,
a rage turned on, inner, agro-transgressive

carnal:lanrac

So large in my pants— she touches him, can't believe how big I've gotten in her Mermaid eyes covered in a mist of a dance floor. In my inner ear, Carrie whispers, "I don't remember it being this big," and he cums, returns to my face, kisses on me; Carrie, whispering in my ear, we are not indiscrete, we are in the middle of it all, against one of the columns. Sheena's vanished, probably into the mouths of Mullets. I will find my Shiny Dancer another day, "Oh hi, who are you?" I ask this girl kissing on my neck. I can't see her behind her long, brunette hair, at least I think it's brown, but it's dark, spun in lights, and I remember, I took *LSD*; me.

eye for got

Wow, how strange. It all seems so comfortably strange, to forget, "What did I say?" I ask the girl, "I can't hear myself." She says nothing, nibbles my earlobe, I ask her this, "What's your name?" because I'm not sure if her name's Carrie, or

Janette, or something, maybe Yasmin? Her face is so close I can't see her, is she speaking? "What?" I yell into her ear. She shifts my head, puts her lips back against my ear, "I'm not always a slut."

"Okay!" I yell back.

"L o v e m e?"—.

ˑ—"What?" I didn't hear that.

Say it again. And again Carrie. Remind me—

—who are you?

She's looking around. I don't know. Is she? Mine? Does it matter? I don't even have a hard-on anymore. Things don't feel so sexy on *LSD*. I'm over it. "I'm over it!" I yell, "Over it!"

*

Take note, thinking about sex is sexy. Sheena. Dancing, way over there, with Claiborne, that half-*Jewish* raver kid from school. "Kyle!" I yell over to him. He ignores me. He's rolling. And he's trying to roll with my woman, well the woman-child I traded in for a Sea Lion from the docks of *Pier 49*. I wish she'd come back. If Sheena came back then I might want to have sex with this girl. What am I? Kyle has no face? Where'd his face go? He's invisible. Shenna's alone again, swimming in the fog of *San Francisco*. She was so beautiful. Warm. Warm around my penis, getting harder, warm, feels so good. Wow, Sheena's really dancing, in the dark, in silhouette, naked, I can see her nipples, so sweet, tempting. I want to like them, yeah right there, on the tip, yeah baby, right there, on the tip, lick it, lick it Carrie, oh I think you're going to make me cum. "You going to swallow it," I ask the girl who is giving me head on the dance floor, "Um, hm," vibrates along my staff. I clench her hair, don't explode, instead my children ooze out, long, drippy, easy, sexy, into her mouth, down her chin, dribbling onto her baby-t, and she stands up, confused, leaving my dick hanging out of my zipper, confused, wiping her mouth, eyes twisted, I don't know this girl. This Carrie looks different to me. She's changed so much since we broke up. I discretely place myself back in my pants. I don't think anyone has noticed us. Kyle appears, "You have no where left to go. Death in state. Move on. Move out of Dodge," and he replaces his face with a mask and vanishes, forever. The girl, not Carrie, is still beside me. I don't even know where I am.

"You don't like me, do you?" she says, TiMiD, shy.

"I don't want to remember!"

—! i.YELL.*OVer*THEBLASTINGMUSiCK!—

&
under the
conversation between

IiD & EgO

...COmPeTyler w/ MY.SELF...Vs...R...e..f...l...e.....c....tion

my
(THIRD)
o n EYE *o n*

•

•.|.•

I

AM

"Don't tell on me!"
"I can't hear you!"
"You!" she's crying, "You hate my face!"
"I don't even recognize you!" I just miss you, you, Me"
Where's she going? Can we just walk away from people? Is this what people do? Forget, like it never even happened? Is that what I'm going to do? Hurts my feelings. I am sad
—Sadness is me. Cruel, cruel worlD—

.Low. sad. love. ME.

My HAND Has Taken A HOLD
of My H&
WON'T let GO
NO FREEdumb NO

* * * . . * * *

*

...I'm on the floor, Indian style, tugging at my hand, but I can't get it to let go of myself. Tug. TUG. I have to sort this out. We'll never get out of here, unless? Ugh, can't... ...remember. My hand is too distracted. Have to figure stuff out. Don't have time. Focus on the hands. Compressed between two of the massive speakers, my fingers finally release their grip and pantomime a puppet show, mimic my past relationships, mock me, a loop, again and again, hello, goodbyes, hello, good, bye-byes. I should chew them off. Start at the wrists. Bite into them. Ravenous. Salivation swashes along my gums. Let it drip on your lap. Eat the hand, bite the wrist that beats you, and Munts grabs me, swats my hand away before I chomp

down.

"WHAT ARE YOU DOING?" he yells at me. I look up, Munts looks spooked, must have seen a ghost, "I think I'm coming down," I tell him. Munts is drifting away into the fog. I wish he'd come back...

...Munts floats back to me

Erin is rubbing my shoulders. She's nice. I'm kinda tense. Munts has an announcement, "Look they're closing in like," and POP, POP, POP, the fluorescents of the club turn on. There is no music. When did the music stop? Where are we? Ew, everyone looks like shit. Haggard. "Where'd Carrie go?" I ask Munts. "Don't know, didn't see her," he says getting out of the way of some ravers. "We need to go," he says and offers me his hand. I'm up. Standing... .

. ...head rush

Never stand up again, "Now what?" Munts adorns a face of

disappointment. His number one student has gone astray, "You are not coming down, bro," he says.

"I feel fine."

—I try to talk to myself again,
but the lights, so bright,

I'm not here anymore. *Lost in a mindfulset.*

Munts pats my back, sends me onward, with the crowd, exiting, all of us, them, me, out the mouths of the *DV8* doors—COLD—freezing—SWEATING—hordes of raver zombies, disorganized, unglued, too glued, drooling, lost, hungry, brains, eggs, brains, drugs on brains, green eggs, and spam—

         *   *   *   *   *   *   *   *

                 *

Down the street, around the corner, I'm with Erin and Munts, and Munts is with Erin and...

...San Francisco? How'd-y get here?

Glisten. The windows of the morning night hover high. The moon reflects the stars against the sun. Brighter. Igniting. So beautiful with white light, flickering around these massive bug lights bursting from the earth in this dark blue, gradient of deep purple, "*In da garden of Eden, baby,*" I sing and step closer towards the lights, where there are more, closer, quicker. So many. Giant fireflies. Souls. The souls I have attracted. *Zip around me.* Around. Warm, CALI...for...NIHLISTs...

...Outside the club I'm not sure why Munts is picking me up out of some puddle. I don't care that I'm wet. Probably washed some sweat off. I'm slow to ask, "Where'd we park?"

Munts grabs me, again, I remember. "Dude! You need to stop moving," he yells at me— *I'm okay, I'm okay* —"I just pulled you out of the parking lot and now you want to run into the street?" Erin's petting my arm. "You okay Tyler?

You tripping too hard?"

Using the corners of my eyes I check, yeah I'm okay, not tripping too hard, and I nod to Tyler. No. Munts. Yes. Not, tripping too hard. "It'll be okay," he says, but I don't understand why. "We can walk it off. No one's driving home yet," and I believe him. The inner brow raised, his ears stretch down. I mimic him. I want to empathize. What's it like to worry about a friend who isn't in trouble? Trouble

.

—wow—

|

I take in the fresh *San Francisco* air, the fog, even under the under pass, take it in Goodman, and then take that walk. "Yeah, the car. Where'd we park that? Time to go home," and they follow me to my car, down a road, down a path of blinders, my mind focused on the tunnel of light and the smears along the peripheral perimeter of my existence. There is no trying. You can't read the signs. You can't recognize the sidewalks, the poles, trees, trees so thick they move, slow like a sloth, thick like an elephant, and I feel as if I follow their roots then I may get closer to my destiny, which is? The *Little Red Civic*, "Right here," and I step up to it. "Nice, nice, and no you're not driving, but good on the memory," Munts pats me on the back, taps his nose. "*Jew* joke. I get it. Ha-ha," and I make sure I have my car keys, dig into the pocket, nope, other pock— "What are you doing?" Munts is worried as shit. "I'm looking for my keys," and he flips his arms in the air, "Oh my GOD! Erin talk to him. PLEASE!"—"Chill. I just wanted to know I had 'em," and I jiggle them, slide them back in my pocket. My pocket... ... .

*   *   * .   . * *   *

When you stop moving, you, tend to drift off. The cement has time to move. The grains. Cement is made of billions of grains of sand. Static. Molten static. Beveled, embossed. A face in the sidewalk. I don't want to lose it. The impression is cryptic. There is nothing like it. There is no image, just a face. Eyes, a brow, strong wide nose, empty eye sockets, the brow widens, the mouth like long bricks of hard, malleable, flesh cement— Me —and there goes Munts again, trying to save my life from stepping into the street again, "I'm not, don't worry," I tell him, but it's not him. Erin's the one pushing me into the street. "We've had the walk sign, like forever. Go," and we cross to *Washington Square Park* where there is grass. Green grass. And I'm stoked for some nature, and really don't care about it once I'm there.   Urban grass? Disappointment. Not suggested on psychedelic drugs. This is what I take from that stupid park, and we move along, like a current down the stream. Yeah it is like that now, now that we're free, outside, no borders. The walk is an ever flow, the trip is smooth no matter how boring the grass seems to have become. "Get over the grass dude," Munts complains. I keep bringing it up. I'm surprised that's all. "I know, you've said that too," he jabs me in the ribs. "Ooo, hey. How long does that part last?" I ask, disappointed; this new universe may drift away too soon.

"Two/three hours, but the last two hours are pretty close to normal. We're in hour five."

"How long walking been we do?" Erin can't talk write no mo', rite?

"No, we took it five hours ago," Munts clarifies, "This one's still gonna be pretty weird," and we wait. We wait for a sign.

—What now Munts?—

"Bet you could drive in an hour," and that's it, done deal, we walk. And walk. And walk, "My jaw fucking hurts," I start complaining as we circle back and pass *Macy's* window displays. "That's the *Strychnine*," Munts has got his jaw rub on as well. Erin? Erin's distracted. Zoned in on some diamond jewelry in the small window box. From a distance they already remind me of the star windows from, the parking lot? Nah. That was the outer-inner space. These diamonds are not as amazing. I'm up close now. My nose pressed against the glass. I can feel the oils from my pores as they make the glass slippery, but the diamonds, they barely glow. My visuals are losing their luster. What a strange name for a diamond? And then I say it aloud, "What kind of name is *Paolo*?"

"Hey, I was having a really good hallucination," Erin pushes me aside, walks on. "Sorry," I apologize. She's fine. She'll kiss Munts and Munts will make it all better. I look back at the name. "*Paolo*? Weird, someone made that shit up," and I spit on the window. No reason, no rhyme, but I did. Instinctual. Something under my gut, spit on the name. Spit on the establishment so pretentious to shove the money of the gods in the face of downtrodden, for love of country. "Well fuck you!" and I flip off the window. Feels good. Feels right. The friends think I'm a freak, I believe I am an artist—okay, key's in the ignition, roll down window. Crank. Crank. Crank. That's enough. Close your eyes. You got this. Open them and all will be fine. Why are Munts and Erin are waiting on the sidewalk? Do I have to roll down their window to talk to them? No, I can open the door, duh? I lean over, unlock the door, they open it, Erin gets in the back, Munts takes the passenger seat, genuine, real, puts his hand on my shoulder and straight up asks, "You okay to drive?" I cock the rearview mirror, catch Erin in the reflection, ask her, "I kissed Carrie tonight?"

Munts answers, "Carrie wasn't there, bro. You kissed some stranger."

—Now who's lying—

"Don't fuck with me, I'm not that high anymore," I tell him. He just rolls his eyes. Are we all dead and alive now, again?

*　　*　　*　　　　　　　　*　*　*

"You sure you're cool to drive?" Munts asked in the past.

—Ugh mental trip—headY—

"Yeah, stuffs not really moving, but maybe? I thought we were cool. Everything seemed solid again. You thought so, right Erin?"

"I was sleeping," she remembers, "But before we crossed the bridge? I was high as a fairy-farm."

"You scared me Tyler. I've been scared since we pulled out. Almost hit the bus."

     *   *   *   *

"Dude that bus was double parked," is how I remember it, but now I can't talk, I gotta focus, we're coming to the tunnel, other side of the tunnel, fog, forever…and I close my eyes, open them the next morning, and remember the head-trip from home to the city in reverse, upside down, remixed, remastered, and full of holes…

     *   *

                 …hours, minutes, seconds of holes. If at any time twenty seconds felt like a lifetime, in the *DV8*, on the street, and now, I cannot remember most of the dreams of the night, and it feels like a thousand lifetimes that I can never get back. Or have I been, yet again, reincarnated a few times over? What a fleeting moment life is when eternity can never be stopped. Where's Kyle going to move to? He should go to Australia. Then Kansas. Ohigho

                      *

Munts just says, "Take it slow."
"I keep thinking about my future," I admit.
"You worry about that stuff, huh?"
"All the time," hurts me.
"Why? Shit'll happen when it happens," says the Acid King in my passenger seat, doodling on the moisture on the window.
"That's what I worry about. That shit that happens that ruins everything."

—I don't know why I'm being so open with my buddy.
        We never talk like this. Not Munts and I, but it's nice.

"You're trippin' son. Just keeps your eyes on the road," and he starts to flip through the radio stations and it's annoying

as fuck, and Erin has passed out in the back, and I gotta keep
my eyes on the road, not fuck up, can't just let shit happen... .

*   *

"Go home, call me tomorrow," Munts hops out, "Drive
safe," slams the door, and I drive home, perplexed about
Carrie. Maybe it really wasn't her?
I don't remember.
Did Sheena fuck Kyle?
Maybe that's a good thing. Probably means it wasn't her.
But who was she & do I have to get tested?
HIV? San Francisco? Me? Straight?
What have I done tonight?
Will I do it, again?
With Who?
Me or
You
*

.

.

.

.

.

.

MINI THINS

•

•

•

•

•

•

•

•

•

•

•

•

•
•
•
•
•

275

chapter 30-TWO

*g*ood   morning   Goodman.
"Window-paned? That's the same stuff Davey's got," Sheena
knows, leans back on her couch, probably got Skags between
her legs with her fingers rolling over the hills of the
mongoloid midget's fatty pig wrinkles. She'll lick her first
two fingers, salivate on them, "Tyler," slide them between a
flabby Skag wrinkle, "I wanted you," but I'm not tripping
anymore, I cannot see everything anymore. My head just
hurts, and the *Advil* has not done the trick. "You've taken it
before?" I ask her.

"Yeah, I'm experienced, but that stuff's serious. You like?"

"It was only one hit," I tell her, lean the receiver on my
shoulder, pop the fridge, grab a *Pepsi*, pop the can, and for
the first time, figure out why they call it *Pop*. Makes that
sound when you open it. Genius, I am not. Fizzy drink.
Pepsi. Pop. Coke, cocaine.   L.   S.   D.

"Well I've only taken two hits at a time at the most," she
tells me. I sip. The bubbles tickle my upper lip. I shaved this
morning. Not all that into shaving. I use an electric three-

circled ring thingy. Rather have a beard. I'm a baby. It's happening, slowly— still too young —I feel naked, vulnerable all of the time, not mentally, but physically. I am facially defenseless. "So, you've taken *more* than that?"

"More? Lots of times," she shifts on the couch, "Skags, come here. Su-iee. Su-iee, but never took more than two at the same time. You're a daredevil *Speedo*."

"One," I remind her, sip.

"No, you took 4," info Munts did not make me privy of last night in line, or yet, or probably ever.

"Window panned," I say aloud, two words, not one name. Alert. Now aware. Dumbfuck; one single slang word can define a lifetime. I ate four.

—Three more than one.

"You're so stupid," she is not talking to her pig, "Each little window is a tab of pure *Acid*, more or less. Little windows. Looks window panned. That's like not just style. You're probably still tripping. Drink some orange juice."

I look at my palm; it is not moving.

?

US

< What is? >

Thought in motioN

?   o—[— * —]—o   ?

Who hunts cattlE

YOU

ask

?

"Crows," I say, get faint, need to lie down, switch rooms.
"Tyler?"
"Hold on."
Phone down. Cord pulls it, slides, grab it before it stacks, prop it in a drawer— TV room, pick up phone, put on couch, back to kitchen —Get some cookies. No cookies. How about

ice-cream? Just a bite? Dad's so weird. A banana? Ugh. Hang up phone— / —back in the TV room, I flop on that couch, and flop hard, phone flings to the carpet, safe. I reel it in, head pounding, jaw still locked up, "Dad took my keys away. Oh, and I hooked up with Carrie again," I spew.

"That happens," Sheena says.

"Yeah, but I did it on acid. Is that supposed to happen?"

"She tripped with you guys?"

"Yeah, not really. Bumped into her there, kinda weird. She was on X."

"Rolling. She's a slut, don't take it personally."

"Um, okay?"

"I mean, she is pretty young, and you know she sleeps with guys."

"One guy."

"Two. You were number two, for all you know. Girls lie about that stuff. She was on X huh?"

"Yeah."

"And you saw her, and hooked up. Pretty typical. Who gave her the X?"

"My head hurts," I complain.

"Tyler, who took her home? Who banged her on the dance floor?"

—What's on TV?

Click the remote, TV zap-snaps on. Always makes my back skip when it does that. Screen's too bright. I turn it off. Click. Beeuww, and it implodes into a bright spec of a pixel and pops off.

"So you two back together?" Sheena chimes back in.

—Just Say No—

o   •   o

Now I'm in Goodman Jail
Hard time
Man the fields
wash the beets

School
Swim practice
No car weekends
No weekdays
No video camera
School
Extra credit assignments to keep me busy
Swim practice & Swim meets
No Movie Saturdays
No *NoMeansNo* at the *Phoenix*
I want to Cry
Just say No
forever
now
?
S
C
H
O
O
L
E
D
.
.
.

.

.

Munts and I are outside the *Phoenix*. Sunday. Closed. "Heard Tom's gotta drive a cab on Sundays now," Munts says. Nobody is around. What happened while I was in jail? Where'd everybody go? Grew up. Left town. Had babies? "You been good?" I ask Munts. "Alright. Fighting with Erin."

chapter 30-*THREE*

 t om has posted the new Summer schedule. Hand written on loose-leaf paper from a spiral notebook. He didn't bother to tear it from the perforation. Nope. Ripped it right out of the coil.

PHOENIX THEATER SUMMER LINE-UP:

JULY:
FRI- Greenday, NOFX, Kid Skool *(Not Going)*
SAT- DOE, BluChunks, Lung Butter *(Going)*

FRI- Fifteen, Neurosis, No Use For A Name *(Not Going. Davey'll go)*
SAT- Sonoma Garage Band Fest. 1pm – 1am *(bands to be announced)*

"Wanna start a band?"
Munts takes a moment to think on it,
"What we call it?"
"K-coke & the Banshk—"
"No. No band," he cuts me off.
"Bad name?"

FRI- Primus, DOE, BluChunks *(Going)*
SAT- Conspiracy, NonComposMentis, Dark War Baby *(Going)*

FRI- Disposable Heroes of HipHoprisy, Shark Bait *(Going)*
SAT- Movie Night *(don't know which yet)*

Munts palms my back, "You okay there Tyler?"

"Yes."
"You want to go to this show, *Speedo*?"
He underlines the next listing with his pinky.
"Yes."
"You wish you were there right now?"
"Yes."
"You want to lick Carrie's butthole?"
"No."
"What if it was the only way to go to the show?"
"French lick her."
"You are one sad muther fucker."

AUGUST:
FRI- Victims Family & Steel Pole Bathtub *(God cares about Petaluma)*

SAT- Social Distortion *(Consider it)*

FRI- Fugazi *(Going)*
SAT- Skankin' Pickle, Hoodlum Empire, Conspiracy *(Going)*

"Dude, when the fuck is Fishbone going to play?"
"We should have gone to Lollapalooza 3."
"Shut up."

FRI- Melvins *(Going)*
SAT- Body Count, DRI, My Mom *(Ice-T in Luma? Going)*

FRI- Faith No More, Dwarves, *(Skip)*
SAT- Mr. T Experience, Jawbreaker, Wynona Riders *(We'll See)*

SEPTEMBER:
Back to School, Twits! HAHAHHAHAHA, love Tom.

"Yeah, man, summertime rolls," I say.
"We gonna take more *Acid*?" he asks.

•

o   o

We get coffee at the *Apple Box*. Nobody's around. "What are we missing?" Munts shrugs. We hoof it to *Walnut Park*. "Why there?" I haven't been there since I was kid. "No one nowhere, might as well try new things," Munts' wild rational, so I follow him. We stop at *7-11*. "No, no more *Mini-Thins*," the attendant scolds us, "You go buy drugs somewhere else."

"Chill, chill, man. No biggie," we tell him as we exit, "Okay what the fuck was that?" Munts doesn't know. I don't know. And look there's Jimmy-the-Germ as we turn the corner. The Germ might know, "Hey, why they aren't selling *Thins* anymore?"

"You fags still do that?" He's into bigger and better things, "Lame."

"Hey," I yell after him.

"What?"

"See Davey?"

"Not being a loser and buying *Thins* no more," he slams us with his middle finger and leaves. We decide to skip the park and head back downtown, which is a whole whoppin' three blocks away, but a lot can happen in this small town by the river. At the bus stop, the city bus stop, we find, not waiting for a bus, but loitering on the bench, my first ex,

lovely little Trish.~*Thrifty* flashback.

> —*You're Mom's fucked up now. Wonder how Trish's been, it's be like, forever?*

"What up, Trish?"

o   •   o

She's got a new boyfriend. "Sasha," he says, thick accent, male *Russian* exchange student. Tall. Reaches his hand out, he's slouching, doesn't need to lean forward to reach me. Munts doesn't want to look at him. I shake. "Good to meet you Sasha," fucker squeezes my hand, my finger's still tender, hurts like all hell, I can only smirk to hide a grimace.

"No shit, Tyler Good-lame," Trish hops up on the back of the bench. She still wears stripped stockings and black *Docs*. Trish had full vampire goth-punk potential, but she grew up living around the hay in a supped-up chicken coop, so that *Mad Max* lifestyle has saved her from being totally lame. She was a cuter when she was twelve. Maybe she's not all that hot? Maybe all the other girls in town just got prettier. Yeah, I think that's it. She's still cute though, "You got taller, funnier looking," she says about me and taps Sasha. He offers her a *Clove* cigarette. Munts has turned his back on us. What's up with Munts? Trish takes the stick, Sasha lights it, offers me one, "No, I'm cool."

"Where are you from?" Sasha asks me.

"Uh, we're from here," I answer.

"You remind me of someone," he tells me.

"You two a new item?"

"No," Trish says.

"I like red hair. Everywhere. Casey," he says.

"Sasha has a crush on *Casey Bundock*," Trish fills us in, "You know Casey."

—I don't know Casey.
Maybe I know her?

I yawn. A big one, no end. "Sorry," I apologize for my gaping mouth, "I don't think I know her." Another one's coming on. Hold it in, fist against your mouth. Don't do it twice, don't, YAWN, shake it off, "Hey can I ask you something?"

"No, Davey did not steal from my Mom," she says, "And yes, you do know her."

"Oh, well, cool, that's cool," I say, no yawn, tap Munts. He shrugs at me, "So Davey didn't do it?"

"You know Casey because you tricked her into letting you hang out with her 'cause *Tawd* had a camera," she's offended by lack of memory.

"Red head? Freckles?"— *oh yeah, I know Casey* —"I did not trick her. I tricked, Tracy. And *Tawd* did not have a camera. *Madrone* had one. And you were in that stupid movie too."

"And I dumped you over it," and she bends down, whispers into the *Russian's* ear. He perks up, he's a fucking giant, "Oh you *Speedo* boy. I too wear *Speedo*." Munts laughs.

"You're not on the team?" I protest and shut Munts up, "Stop laughing."

"Dude, let's go," my buddy says through his shattered comedy, but I need a moment.

"You even go to *Luma*?" I ask the *Socialist*.

"He's at *St. Vincents*."

"I not *Catholic*. They think be *Russian*, I *Catholic*. I not."

"Then why the man bikini? I know my reason, my Dad

makes me wear mine." Munts explodes. Kid's going to piss in his pants if I don't stop saying retarded stuff.

> —*I just don't like the Russian.*
> *Are there even Black Russians?*
> *My thoughts are acid-cracked.*
> *Shoot me now.*
> *Acid's trying to call me home.*
> *I need to get smart again.*
> *I guess I could get more from Davey?*
> *But? Thinking. Thinking. Think Tyler, think.*

Munts tugs on my sleeve. I'm not done. Hold on Munts.

"Okay, Davey's cool. Everybody else is just making shit up? That it Trish?"

"He's your friend," Trish can be so condescending.

"Your Mom. I saw her," I tell her, accidentally casting a threat.

"He stole it <u>FOR</u> her, ok? From her goddamn fuck face of boyfriend," she snaps, Sasha puts a calming hand on her knee. I see it you, macho communication block from *Siberia*.

"Is he after Davey or something?" I ask.

"Mom dumped that *Nazi*," she says, "Besides, she paid Davey to steal from him, so you don't have to get all shitty about it."

"Why the crack-head do that?" I cross the line for real answers.

"Judge much?" Trish is going to shut down. That's what she does. Lights off. Drops off, into Trish. Can't pull her out. She'll sit there. Stare at the lining of her eyes. How does she do it? I've always asked myself. Not where does she go, or if she'll come back, but how she disappears without going anywhere?— *How does that happen? How can she become invisible to herself? Like Kyle. Magicians.* —Munts takes my arm, "Let's go," I tug away, "No, I want to know about this shit," I'm angry, loud, rash, confused by my own rationalizing— *Davey must have owed her big money. No. She paid him. Was Davey fucking Trish's Mom?* —Sasha stands up. This guy is gonna get in the fucking balls— *Probably a rapist. His Gran-Daddy killed Jews. Locked them up at least. Did he help*

Davey? No, that doesn't add up at all —to protect Trish— *I never trusted Trish's Mom. Liked her, trusted her I do not, never. Why'd she pay Davey? He wouldn't really sleep with her. I can believe it* —I step away from the big guy. Munts gotta pee by now. I calm down. Ask nicely, "What do you mean your Mom paid Davey to steal from her boyfriend?"

"Look, my Mom doesn't talk to me about it. Ask Davey."

"I can never find him anymore," and according to Sasha of Cock Mountain this conversation is over. I'm not stepping up to this. Munts is not going to have my back today. This is not our fight. No one's really. "Tell your Mom to stop fucking up Davey's life," and that does it, Sasha goes for it, I see the thick short fingers of his massive arm reach for my face. I duck, swing, hope to connect, but my fist slams against his belt buckle, a thick metal embroidered oval, rips up my knuckles of my good hand. Run!

○ • ○

Did Munts follow me? Did Sasha chase after me? Will he find me? Look, look back <<<<<<<<<<<<<<<<<<<< "My Mom's fucked up, why is my Mom so fucked up, Tye?" Trish and I were in Junior High, on the giant cement blocks in the courtyard. We've been an item for a couple months. I am getting to know her well. I've seen her shut down a number of times now. I can count it off, three, eight, ten, six, five, four, three, two, me, alone, Trish has vanished into her Super-Ego. When we first met, she had told me I looked stupid in my jean jacket. Told her I was retarded.

Now, two months later and she's the visible, invisible girl. Her Mom hasn't been home in a week. She's not out of food or nothing, but none-the-less, her home feels vacant with no vacancy. Her Dad had been someone her Mom didn't know in Houston. I always used to joke, "Maybe he was a Moon-Cricket from Alabama," but Trish is totally not black.

"You all up in your head," she had complained on the movie set where she broke my heart, in front of my friends, on camera. We argued about being eighth-graders. "I'm too busy, too much homework, too much swim practice." She didn't care. She wanted a boyfriend, not a friend who she could be a girlfriend with. Now I was taking up her time making a movie? "You wanted to make a

movie?" I reminded her, trying to get the mini-show back on the road. "Fuck your self on camera," she had said, stormed out, back to her vacant home. Her mother was gone for a week or two. Back with a habit, back with a new dick. Magicians.

—After we broke up—

Her Mom invited me, Davey, and a few other Phoenix kids to a couple of her chicken coop parties. There was cocaine, booze, naked girls in the hot tub, maybe heroin, but I didn't see it. Trish's Mom just opened the door and let us in. Never even spoke to us to the whole time. Figure she'd keep her distance and let us boys be boys. I was suspect, but who cared. Her Mom's friends talked to us. They did drugs in front of us, gave my friends beer, got them stoned, whisky in their colas, but no hanky-panky. For some reason they all always drew that line in the sand. The redline that was so flirty to walk, so sexy to tickle, toy, and wade with, with the naked ladies in the hot tub, outside the remodeled chicken coop, out in the country, under the stars, with AC-DC blaring from the stereo, and metal motor hogs pulling up to join the fun. We were freshman young, and Trish was never there, and we had a fucking blast and yet thought, as cool as Mama Trish was, it must suck to have her as an actual Mom.

•

o   o

Munts calls me, "You're an idiot." I don't know what he's referring too. "Trish? Why you gotta be like that? You know it sucks to be her," he clears up his vague insult. "Davey's the idiot, not me," I tell him. "Duh? But leave her out of it."

"Fine," and the conversation ends.

Here I am. Bored of waiting.
Small town. Big Dreams.
No patience. Lack.
Find a pace.
Breathe
Fool
Me
0

Summer. Summer. One more year. One. Time. Slip. Forward. Pause. Psychedelia. New. Life. New. Friends. New.

·

·

·

·

·

·

·

·

·

·

·

·

·

·

chapter 30-FOUR

*d*ays take forever. "Have any of you talked to Davey?" I've asked everyone I know. Three weeks in and people are answering even before I ask— they've all heard the rumors of my new paranoia, my obsession, my friend folly— "You gay for Davey, bro?" Jimmy-the-Germ gets in my face in the bathroom. "That's very football-ish of you Jimbo."

"I ain't no jock," says the greasy punk.

"Where's Davey?" I ask as I step to the urinal, but decide Jimmy's being creepy and even though they've taken the doors off all the stalls last year, I figure it's more private than whipping it out while The Germ hovers with the *Crystal Meth* sniffles.

"You still buy—" *don't ask that question Tye.* He asks, "You gotta any Thins."

"No." Phft—Sizzle, sudden smell of sulfur. Germ's lighting matches. "Cool. Well where's Davey?" he now asks me. Shake again. "That's what I asked you."

"Yeah, (*PHFT—Sizzle, sulfur*) So like where is he?" he asks again.

"I don't know. Hey? (*Shake again, Zip up*) Do you ever buy off him anymore?"

"No," he says, startling me, he's right there, standing in the stall's empty doorway. I leap back, no room to have done that, lose my balance, fall, and reach out for support, but my hand dives into the bowl. I hadn't flushed, after or prior. My hands drowning in my pee, who knows what else, I didn't check, could be poop, my hands in there, Jimmy's right there, leaning against the stall frame, "Don't ask me that," he warns me. I draw my hand out of the toilet covered in melted TP. Wet. Gross. "Gimme a hand?" I ask, offering my smelly digits for rescue. "Go fuck yourself. I don't have to buy off him. I sell for him now," he tells me even after scolding me for asking in the first place. Kid's fucked up.

"So, where is he?"

"Don't know."

"Why ask me about it then?"

"You asked me."

"No. I came in here to pee."

"That's gay."

"Do you even know what that word means?"

"Fag."

"Football-ish Jimmy. You're changing. Getting old."

"Homo."

"Racist white-ness, can't repress it Jimmy, let it flow."

"I do like *Judas Priest*."

"Really? You know he's a total fag, right?"

"I just don't want my friends turning gay," he says, still standing in the doorway.

"You're fucked up. Move to Ohio."

"Davey ain't gay, is he?" and he waits for my answer.

○　　　•　　　○

The whole school has a bent demeanor about itself this week. Everyone's on edge. Almost turning into an *Over the Edge* of high schoolers. Guess it's more dramatic with JR kids. Fuck it, *"This fucked up world's taken my best friends and turned them into total strangers,"* says *The Conspiracy*. Predicted by Davey even before I drowned. Where are you bro? Humming your Anthem side-saddled in a Volvo? Y e s?

○　　　•　　　○

Finals? Probably.

SATs? ACTs?
zCIAz
zCRAZIEz
sEYEs
W
?
.

o   o

CALL HER

o   .   o

Sheena answers her phone, "What up?"
   "Am I overreacting?"
   "Yeah, probably. No one's seen him, huh?"
   "Someone saw Eddie's car at *Denny's* couple days ago."
   "Good, drop it. They're staying off the rumor radio."
   "On the radar. Everybody knows what he's doing."
   "Oh, my god, chill, it's only a little *Acid* and a mini-bit 'o *Crystal*. No one cares."

—This is not helping—

   "They ain't working for *Tony Montana*. *Crystal* is not *cocaine*. No one cares about Eddie, or Davey," she embellishes the absent of fact.
   "You know, right? You met the guy Davey works for?"
   "Huh?"
   "You've been to that apartment in *Santa Rosa*, right?
   "Yeah. Met him that night."
   "They're chill guys, right?"
   "I think Davey's super chill. You just got get over Eddie."
   "Fuck Eddie," and don't change the subject, "What were they like?"
   "Who?"
   "Their bosses," what is she so confused about?
   "I don't know. I was in the car dude. We've already been

over this."

"You just said you met him? Did he come outside?"

"No, I said I met Davey that night," she can't believe I don't understand her. I need a transcript. I swear I asked her if she met their boss at the apartment that night.

"No, dude. I said I met Davey that night we went to the apartment. I never met those other guys."

—I could tear my face off.
This conversation is so fucked.
Sheena don't know shit. What the fuck?

"Let's play a game," she breaks the silence.
"I'm not in the mood."
"Let's see how long until you break," she continues.
"Oh, I'm about to fucking break."
"Don't be crazy."
"I'm not crazy."
"Seven days. No calls. No calls to me."
"That's stupid."
"And if you don't call, you get a surprise."
"Now who's acting crazy?"
"On your marks."
"Dumb."
"Get set."
"Why's everyone getting sporty around me today?"

She doesn't answer. Silence. I know what's next, a gunshot. And I dive off the block, full speed ahead, laps upon laps upon laps.

"Go!"

"Sheena?"

Sheena hangs up the phone.

"No shit."

And it's back to cruise control, leave it be, forget about it, listen to more *Naked City*, lyrics bring you down, make you think about stuff— I don't want to think about stuff —I want to do my homework, swim, and wait for summer. No more girls, no more Davey, no more drugs; just Tyler Goodman o

n

CRUISE CONTROL~~~~~~~~~~~~~~~~~~~~~~~~~~~~~~~~~*

•SCHOOL's

OUT FOR

• SUMMER – (Dear Self. Find another tab of Acid) •
.   .   .

That was uneventful; especially for a kid who had lowered his expectations to a basic drool for the last two months of school. No fires. No psycho-traumas. No sex, no violence. None of that crossed my track. I drifted through the halls. Let those idiots shoot themselves; let them get ulcers from caffeine tablets, and aneurysms about *Senior Prom*, and *Junior Prom*. How desperate for attention is a Junior Prom? Wait another year to wear that crap, impatient pussies that fuck jock peckers. Didn't faze me, I drifted on by. Cruise Control right through Finals. Whole school was going bat-shit crazy in the head for nothing. 80%+ are going straight to the *JC* if not *Mommy and Me* classes. No stress needed folks. *Petaluma's* not going to flunk you outta staying in town. These local *Pop-Trend Setters* just have nothing better to do. Stress spices the watered-down *Kool Aid* bowl. I figured at least six *Horrible Thoughts* would leave a lasting apparition in my eyes, but I got out too easy, we all got out too easy; Davey even got out too easy, showed up for the last week of school. He had a pass from his parents, *The Kesley Excuse*. Out of the blue, like nothing happened, like he was never M.I.A. Davey's been back at home, coming to school, getting along with the folks, seeing a Therapist — / — that he lies to. Lies and stories. Fabrications and complaints. Davey doesn't see a therapist. The therapist sees Davey, blindly out.

•

We're having a cup of coffee at *Denny's*, Saturday Night, 1am; memories.

"Remember when we got banned," I want Davey to relate,

be his old self, this new one's got me reevaluating everything I've ever believed.

"First Saturday I've been in old *Luma* in a while," he says, blows on his coffee.

"And?"

"It's like a vacation. Lame," he says, pours a creamer, "Needed the break though."

"Why? The real job so hard?"

"Hanging with Eddie every weekend <u>is</u> like a real job after a while," he says sips his coffee, spits it out onto the booth.

"Dude, they just started letting us come back here."

"Don't drink it. It ain't right," and he's waving over the hot waitress, but she ignores us.

"Eddie's annoying, huh?"

"You have no idea," waves at her again, she still ignores us, "It's all just too *Glamour Punk* for my taste," and Davey breaks into a fine impersonation of the Eddie, "*Lou Reed, NYC* is real, trust me. *Cisco's* no place for anyone with a dick. Gays are like taffy here. They bend with the wind, bend over for a four-leaf clover, in a hippy-bonnet."

"What's a hippy-bonnet?"

"Like a gangster's do-rag, but tie-dyed."

"You made that up," I try the coffee, "Tastes fine to me?"

"That's what he talks about, all the time, he's like perma-pressed to the *New York* scene he knows nothing about."

"He should move."

"How about you? You okay? You get A's, college boy?"

"I did alright. B+ in *Algebra 2*, but I'm cool. Did you steal from Trish's Mom's Boyfriend?" and Davey smiles.

—Well?—
stop grinning, say something
my thoughts are still
front and center
diethylamide
acid
lys
er
g
ic

The waitress walks right by us. Davey doesn't bother with her, just keeps grinning at me, then simply without a visible motive asks me, "You like *Nazis*?"

"What the fuck kind of question is that?"

"I stole from a *Nazi*. I feel justified in that," he tells me and sips his coffee, spits it back into the cup, "So gross."

"Hey, *Nazis*? What the fuck, hello, explain yourself," I'm confused.

"Linda's boyfriend, ex-boyfriend, he was fuck. Found a *Swastika* patch sewed onto the inside of his flight jacket; real fucking *Redneck-Neo-Nazi* from *Sebastopol*."

"No fucking way?"

"Totally, sewed right inside, like he flashes it like a badge or something— super creepy fucked up."

"Where's he from?"

"*Sebastopol*, dude pay attention."

"Just checking."

"They're everywhere now. Like white fleas. Doing marches in *Oakland* and shit."

"No way."

"You need to get out more. Skinheads everywhere. Watch your back, if you know what I mean," he pushes his coffee aside as not to be tempted again.

"Why because of my mushroom top?"

"No, 'cause of your *Jew* nose," he laughs, I smirk, he continues his story, "So, Eddie and I are, like, getting some shit for the ride back to *Marin*, like, at that grocery? I forgot its name already—"

"*Luckys*?"

"Yeah, there and I see Trish's Mom—"

"Linda?"

"Yeah Linda, Trish's Mom."

"You said that."

"Shut up. Look, your no sex Ex's Mom, L I N D A, was stocking up on some booze, and I wanted her to buy me some, right? And she tells me about the *Hitler Adolph American* sleeping in her bed, right?"

"Okay?"

"Oh," he pauses, the waitress is passing again, "Hey. HEY!" she turns, strikes with the look of murder, and "Did you just hey me?"

"This coffee sucks," he complains.

—   *Come on maN*   —
— *that's my future wife* —

"I don't drink coffee," she says. Her sarcasm is just so sexy coming from those lips.

"I'm not paying for it," Davey's a dick.

"Get over your prepubescent self," she walks away.

"That was kinda hot," I tell him.

"She's a lesbian," he says, "Buys from Eddie. All tweaked out. They went to high school together."

"Oh."

"Still want to marry her?"

"Absolutely," I'm so crushing on her. Davey takes my coffee and sips, "Yours sucks too. So, whatever, Linda was all freaked out about her boyfriend, but didn't know what to do about it?" He dumps a pound of sugar into my coffee. Tries it. "Better. So, I went to her Coop one night, hung with them. Took a hot-tub, gave him a *Xanax* that I got from the Ed, waited for the *Fascist* to pass out, stole his keys, then went through his truck. Dude had like half an ounce of *Meth* in there. She gave me, like, *(he has to think about it)*, half for my good deed. I gave that half to Eddie and he swapped that for some *MDA*. Now that shit sells fast."

"So, you stole drugs from a *Nazi*, and flipped it? They call that *Blood Money*, genius."

"No, I'm *Robin Hood* in the *Swastika Forest*," Davey slides back in his seat, and now that he's stopped talking he can get back to gnawing at his tongue.

"How long were they together?"

"Month or so," he says, waves at my wife-to-be, but she flips him off. I look over my shoulder. She's complaining about Davey to some trucker at the counter, looks up, and smiles at me. *Really? Hi baby-doll.* "Hey!" Davey needs my attention. "What?" I turn back. "I was talking to you," he commands.

"And are you in trouble?" that's what I want to talk about if we're gonna talk, "Like is this guy looking for you or something?"

"Nah, he got busted in San Rafael, the bowling alley—started some fight, called the cleaning lady a *Spic*, got *86'd*, pulled a knife, called the security guard *MLK* then stabbed him, oh, and pissed on the cops from the roof of his truck. That part I can support."

"Sounds like your kinda guy."

"Very funny. I'm cool, all cool," he assures me, and with two fingers parts the blinds of the booth's window.

.—{*Waiting 4 someonE*}—.

"You're different Tye. That *Acid* changed you. Your eyes look different," and yet he's not even looking at me, still peeking out the blinds, "Kinda spooky," and he turns back to me, "Like zeroed in. You're too smart for *LSD*. Nobody needs you getting any more brilliant."

"You sure?"

"Smartest guy I know. Now that you've dosed—" he looks over at the waitress, smiles this time, looks back at me, "...I'm afraid you can read my mind," he says in all seriousness.

"Just deductive reasoning, friend."

"Well stop it. It's intimidating."

"Why's that D, pray-tell?"

"Not *Midnight Mass*."

"*Baruch Hashem*."

"Amen?"

*

"*So be it.*"

●

Whoa, today's Sunday, no school tomorrow, "Hey Old Man, no swim practice tomorrow. Right?"

"Yeah, you're on a two-week break," he says, angry about it, disappointed, nonsensical, but my life gives him a purpose, and now a strain of paranoia about my drugging. He means well, I know this. Just wish he'd accept that he's done bred a good man, balanced enough, equitable, always ready to make him proud, and I do, and he knows it, and he is proud. It's just that, for some reason, he thinks the world will trip me up, not me, the world. I got this Pops. I'm not going to drown in the wet cement of urban development. You won't lose your only son. Not today. He walks into my room, "You and your loser friends going to go to the city to do *heroin* this week?"

"*LSD*," I correct him.

"I know what it was," he smirks, "You have two weeks; that's two weekends. You can go to the city on Sundays through Thursdays. No more weekends. You do stupid things on the weekend."

"Sundays are weekends. Literally."

"Don't be a smart ass."

"My brain's up here," and I point to my noggin. He shakes his head, "Your brain's in your dick, you can't fool me."

•

!

!   I call Davey   !
"Yeah, I can go tonight, buuuddy."
"*Pauly Shore*? You suck cock."
"Suck the *weeeeeeeeeassle*."
He hangs up on me.
I grab my keys.
Later Dad.
Drugs
to
deal

!

o   o   o

I got Davey riding shotgun, and an anxious Eddie in the back, not so much anxious, but stoked, super interested, high on his supply, ecstatic that I'm chauffeuring them, "Vacation, like a limo back here, even got an ashtray in the middle," he claps the metal ashtray open and closed, "Tee Pee, you ever been to *Marin*?"

"Yeah, duh?"

"Fuckers are rich up there," he tells us something everybody knows, "Rich kids and Hangers."

"*Hangers*?" I don't know this term. Don't care, raise the volume on the *Dead Kennedys* screeching in competition with the metallic twaddle of the engine as we chug our way down the *101* toward *Marin*, past *San Rafael*. I'm still waiting for the *Meth Mogul* to tell me the exit. We're nearing the tunnel, and out of nowhere Eddie leans forward and says, "You missed it."

"Missed what?"

"The exit, it was back there," now he tells me. I turn to D, "He never told me where to get off."

"You forgot to tell him," Davey repeats like a fucking parrot.

"You're in the front."

—And they do this every weekend?—

—and we gotta get off at *Alexander Ave*. All green. The fog keeps these hills green all year. *Muir Woods*. Tall fucking trees up there. Went to sleepaway camp around here. Well a one night camping trip. I was like eight. Sucked. They didn't have tents. We slept in sleeping bags on the ground. Woke up covered in dew. Soaked. I flip a bitch and get us to the other side of the *101*, head back North, through the tunnel, exit at *Rodeo Ave* and into the little rich town by the bay, *Sausalito*. "I thought *Rodeo Drive* was only in *Beverly Hills*?"

"*Rodeo* just means Shit-Eater's Ave," Eddie fictionalizes, "Every town's got one."

"That's not true," Davey says, "*Petaluma* don't."

"Thanks for clearing that up man," I'm grateful, not.

"Don't want people to make fun of ya. Thank me later."

"Take this to the water," Eddie says, "Then, um, right?"

"Left," Davey corrects him.

"We'll see," Eddie doesn't believe him, or himself.

o

As we wait at the last light, I watch the bay still as can be. It was not a straight route. We turned left and right and up and down all through the *Sausalito* hills to get to the main strip. This place brings back memories— *   *   * —I remember getting ice cream here with my parents after seeing *Star Trek IV: The Voyage Home* at the massive theater in *Corte Madera*. "You think I like movies because I was born near that movie theater?" I asked Mom.

"I don't think so. I think it's because we took you there to see *Star Wars*."

"We've seen all the big ones there," Dad says, "Tyler?"

"Ya?" and Dad told us about some *San Fran Chronicle* article he read about *Star Trek IV*, about how they never actually filmed the Institute scenes in *Sausalito* like they said in the film. He continued his own op-ed on the article that revealed to him that all filmmaking was a lie, and that you should only believe what you read in Newspapers, not books, and never film. "That's so random, Dad," I said catching a chocolate drip from the bottom of the cone. "They filmed it at the *Monterey Bay Aquarium*, just said it was here," he wants me to learn about my career goals. "You've never taken me to that Aquarium." He takes my cone, takes a bite from the scoop, and with a mouthful continues to antagonize me like a pretend older brother, "You're not worthy. Get a job and you can go." Mom slaps him on the arm, "Ben!"

Dad gives my cone back. "Don't listen to him, he's just picking on you. We can go next weekend."

o

I must be growing up. Keep getting caught up in reflection. Eighteen's right around the corner. I can feel it. Smell the vote. Make a difference. Graduate next year. Move away. "You guys know the Mohawk punk on the bus in *Star Trek Voyage Home*?"

"The one about the whales?" Eddie says with the intonation of actual interest.

"Yeah," I'm impressed. Eddie might have a soul, yet.

"Never saw it," Davey adds.

"Well, you know *Brooke*?" I ask D.

"*Brooke Vermillion*?"

"Yeah. She knows him. Her Dad works at *ILM*," I tell them, "Her Pops made that that *Nien Nunb Japanese* looking alien," I geek out. Neither of them have any idea who that is, "Flew the *Millennium Falcon* with *Lando* at the end of *Jedi*."

"No. What about the punk in *Star Trek*," Eddie asks.

"Oh, nothing. He ended up animating *RoboCop* 2, *Kirk Thatcher*," I tell him.

"Never heard of him, but *RoboCop's* badass. I want to move to *Detroit*," Davey says.

"You would," I say, naïve to the untainted culture of *Detroit Motor City*— The light finally turns green, "Left," says Ed —Click the turn signal, roll out into the intersection. Click, click, click, click, and just as I start my turn, he corrects himself, "No, right!"

"*Right said Fred*," I joke and switch the clicker to make the hard turn from the half left into a full right. We cruise pass the overpriced boutiques, "Right again," and now we're back up in the hills filled with houses, houses surrounded by trees, hidden in the woods, the woods by the bay, the woods of the rich and the prep-ified.

These roads are crazy narrow, windy, and I have no idea where I'm going, so I take it slow. "Grandma, can we get there already?" Eddie's got to share an opinion I can live without. He leans forward again, "Up that way." I have to shift down to make it up these hills. "Your car sucks, next time we take the *Volvo*," another unnecessary complaint, "You're gonna make a left soon." At least he's paying attention this time. "There! Left," nearly too late, and I have to squeeze around the bend of a road knot, where you could go left, or straight, or right, or stop and give up, but Eddie said left, so we've gone left, and now, finally, I guess we're there as he has me pull into a gravel driveway that leads to a *Redwood* home with magnificent, huge, two story high windows of golden light, and Eddie taps my shoulder, "Park by the *Blackman's Weiner*." I pretend he didn't say that and pull beside the black *BMW*. Here we are. The drug den of *Sausalito*? I think Sheena's wrong. These guys might be working for the *Nor. Cal Scarface*.

○   •   ○

The gravel goes crunch, crunch, crunch, as we step out, and dickhead has to give me instructions, "Don't be yourself in there."

"What's that supposed to mean?" but Eddie walks away from me.

"What the fuck?"

"He means don't get weird 'cause their gay," Davey tells me, does another bump from his bullet, "But..."

"I'm not prejudice, dude."

"Yeah, cool. I know that, you know that. Eddie's just sensitive," he says, sniff, blows his nose in the flannel he has wrapped around his waist, and as I start to walk, he palms my shoulder, stops me, has something else to tell me, a warning, "But hey, don't accept any drinks unless it still got its cap on."

"What? Why would they poison me?"

"Cute, T. Very cute," he steps away, wants to catch up to Eddie.

"What's cute?" I ask. He stops, turns back, shakes his head at my naïvety, and comes back, crunch, crunch, crunch, "Rape you. Not poison you, rape you," he clarifies, "You want to get raped by a rich dude in *Marin*?"

"No."

"Then don't accept their drinks."

"That's fucked, you know, that, right?"

"Hey, I know they want to fuck me and Eddie. That I know. And that's enough of a reason for me to keep my guard up," and he peeks out from under his purple sunglasses.

"I'm not worried 'bout it," I respond plain and simple.

"You're fresh meat, *Speedo*. Just watch that *Jewish* little tushie," which he slaps and walks off, crunch, crunch, crunch.

○   •   ○

The front door is coated in stainless steel, finished with the spiraling of a wire brush. There is no handle and no keyhole.

"How do you open the door?" I ask.

"Push dude," Davey rolls his eyes.

"But there's no keyhole," but they have no answer to that, yet Eddie whacks me in the shoulder, "Be cool, okay?" and presses the diamond doorbell which triggers a series of jingle-bells. "That's," but Davey cups my mouth. "Dude, you really gotta keep it to yourself," and the door swings open, inward, opened by a short-haired, bleached blonde, fifties-something yuppie in a well fit *Armani* shirt, his three top buttons open, which allows his grey chest hair to flirt with the air and in his hand, a glass of white wine. He taps the bell of the glass with his silver pinky ring. He is Mike.

"Eddie, a Sunday run? I love it," Mike announces, wraps his arm around Ed's shoulder, gives him a squeeze, a smooch on the cheek and leads him in, "How prosperous you've become." I lean into Davey's ear, "Are they, doing it— OUCH!" D's pinched my bicep, "Shut up," pushes me inside.

○   •   ○

This house is apparently all about the *view*, designed for you to look out of, not to be looked upon. The back of the home is a series of reflection-free windows that peers out through a frame of *Muir* and *Redwoods* over the bay. Surrounding the home is a redwood deck. I don't see an exit to the deck, but none-the-less I love it. I could squat in a place like this.

The art collection is minimal, yet terribly gay glamorous; three large paintings/photos. First I spy a B&W of *Marlene Dietrich* cuddled in a fur around her neck, sporting a matching barrette. The photo is twice my height and framed in that same wire brushed steel as the front door. Across from her is an abstract, probably oil, flesh colored— looks like a vagina —but probably an anus, and I turn; between me and the third piece of art stands yet another guy. This man is entirely more flamboyant than Mike. He's a brunette with red highlights, powdered face, eyeliner, shows off his *Iggy Pop* physique through an aquamarine bathrobe, with tight yellow leather pants. He twirls his pearl necklace.

Smiles at me, smirks, comes closer, and reaches out his perfectly manicured hand with baby-blue painted fingernails. This flamer takes my hand, drops his necklace, cups my palm with a light touch, "I'm Kaye, short for Kayne. You're new," he slurs as he looks me over, caressing my hand, "Cute too. *Italian*?"

"*Jewish.*"

"Snip, snipped, mmm. You came with my babies?" and he waves his fingers at Eddie.

"I'm just their ride," and I take my hand back, thank you.

"Bet you're a wonderful driver," and now I feel his sneaky hand on my lower back, creeping up my shirt, "Like the view?" I step away as he smiles at my nerves. "Adorable," he says, does a little spin and faces his babies, my friends. But Eddie and Mike aren't around, must have gone to another room. Davey's already made himself at home on the single, white, leather, lounge chair with its back to the massive windows, "Hi Kaye," Davey says.

"Hi Daaavey," Kaye repeats, "Need a drink?"

"No, I'm straight," he refuses.

Kaye turns to me, "He ain't all that straight." I look at Davey. Davey snaps at Kaye, "Fuck off."

"Woof, woof," Kaye jests and looks back at me. He double taps his nose to insinuate Davey has a problem. "Yeah, totally," I agree and make nice with the Kaye. He steps right back up to me, squeezes my cheek, "You are a doll!"

"He's not your type either," Davey protects me. Music comes over the speakers, a *Marvin Gaye* tune, *Sunny*.

"Who's not his type?" Mike says as he escorts Eddie back into the room. The Ed's got three beers and Mike's got a cocktail. Mike goes right up to Kaye and kisses his lover on the cheek, hands him the drink, but Kaye has a question, "You're not drinking?" Mike raises his other glass, "I have my wine." Kaye turns to me, says over Mike's shoulder, real catty, "Sundays used to be our nights," then to Mike, "Wine does not make Sundays very special."

—Wow these two sure are characters—
I can see the attraction of this gig
these guys are funny

Eddie hands Davey a bottle of suds. It's unopened so I guess its safe? Davey uses his lighter to pop the top, slugs a quarter of it, "Thirsty, for a guy who didn't want a drink," Kaye the cat purrs at the D. "I just like beer," my buddy says as Eddie offers me one of the bottles, "Designated driver remember?" Eddie rolls his eyes, "Whatever," walks away, puts my bottle on the coffee table in front of Davey, "You get two," and steps up to the windows that face the bay, "I want to move to *Oakland*," he says, and everyone ignores him.

"How long have you two been together?" I ask the homeowners.

"Two years, almost three," Mike responds as he takes a seat on the arm of the couch beside Kaye, "You have a girlfriend?"

"Not right now," I answer, nervous, Davey's got an eye on me, swigs his beer. He's worried I'm going to say something stupid, "Recently divorced," is what I tell them. Davey shakes his head in embarrassment.

"Well, honey, there's more than just ladies to fancy on," Kaye slurs, pats his Mikey on the crotch, winks at me. Mike moves Kaye's hand, "Have some class."

"Yeah, well I'm straight," I say, only to have Davey go stink eye and Eddie turns his back on *Oakland* to better manage the situation.

"Nobodies straight," Eddie chimes in, "Everybody's got a little gay in them, right?" he asks Davey. "Guess so?" Davey answers, uncomfortable, now avoiding my eye contact.

—What am I missing here? Davey gay now?—
Pretending to be gay? What's up, bro?

"Well, you'll get on just fine," Mike says to me, turns to Davey, "Right?"

"Yeah man, Tommy gets a lot of play," Davey says to him.

—Tommy?—

Eddie finishes his beer, sets it on the table, and blurts out, "I can't do next weekend."

"Ah, how come? Of course, you can," Mike's a boss.

"No, I really can't, not next week," Eddie looks skittish, fidgety about the topic. I haven't seen him look vulnerable before. I like it. Like seeing Eddie squirm for once. I grin.

"Eddie," Mike pauses, closes his eyes, takes a breath, "What's so important that you have to ditch your responsibilities?" All eyes on Ed. Mike leans over to D, "What about you?" Eddie looks nervous. I thought this was all casual. No big deal. Eddie sure looks like this is a big deal and this Mike guy is not going to let him out of it, is he?

"I'm still in," Davey is so polite to Mike.

—Is Davey gay with Mike?—

Eddie steps back in to the conversation, "No, just me."*— Is this why I'm here?* —Mike turns his attention to me, "How 'bout you? You have a car. Davey's gonna need a ride, 'specially since Edward here has pending business next week," and with that snide attack, Mike gets up, leaves, to the kitchen. Eddie tries to explain himself to Kaye, "I really can't come next week. Next two weeks, actually." Ed's got the shakes. So vulnerable. Guess Eddie is their bitch?

"What's wrong, baby-doll?" Kaye asks so sweet.

"Uh," Eddie looks to Davey for support. "Tell him," D says. Ed confesses, "My Dad had a stroke."

—Is that true? Davey? That is why I'm here, huh?—

And suddenly, thoughtless, without a plan, I open my mouth, "I can drive Davey."

—What am I doing?—
Take it back.

"No dude, you don't have to do that," Davey manipulates me with lip service.

"Why? I did it tonight," I speak out again.

—Someone cut my tongue—

Davey looks at Eddie. Suckered me. Both of them. I know they set me up. Whatever. I'm my own person. I make my own choices, I guess? Maybe this way I can me keep an eye on Davey, keep him outta trouble like he says I do, maybe get a chance to talk him out of all this stupid shit. "Not just here kid," Eddie explains, "There are two other stops."

"No biggie," I'm a tough-guy, complacent, hope I'm doing what my friend needs.

"First the City, then *Santa Rosa*," Eddie warns me.

"Yeah, I get it," I say, notice Kaye is really eyeballing me now that he might get to see me again, "Yum, I like this idea." Davey leans forward slaps Kaye on the knee, "That's not gonna help."

"Oh, Dee," Kaye looks up at me, "Don't mind him, thinks everyone's a homophobe."

"Tommy, don't fuck with us. Don't make promises you can't keep," Eddie threatens me using this new nickname no one had made me privy too before starting this *Yellow Brick Road* down *Drugstore Cowboy* adventure. Mike returns with two paper lunch bags, "Who's making promises?" he asks as he steps up to Ed, slaps the paper bags into his bitch's chest. E-dunce takes the bags. "I'm disappointed in you," Mike says, eye to eye, balls to balls.

"I'm sorry," Eddie apologizes, but he's not, I think Eddie's lying about it all.

"His Dad's dying," Kaye informs his lover.

"That true?" Mike asks Ed.

"Yeah."

"A real tragedy," Mike is not happy.

"Shakespearian," Kaye the *Johnny Carson* sidekick accents from the couch.

—Hey Dad, I got that job you think I need—

o   •   o

—and we're back in the car, and we're quiet, and I don't know why I'm such a pushover, but here I am, here we are, and I'm backing out of this graveled driveway, crunch, crunch, crunch, "*San Francisco*?" I ask.

"Yeah, *Castro*," Eddie says, and Davey pops the *Dead Kennedys* back into the cassette player and it's a *Holiday in Cambodia* to the bridge.

"I still don't understand what you guys are doing," I tell my passengers.

"We make trades," Davey tells me.

"What's that mean?" and I hit the turn signal, right— Click, click, click —We're waiting for two families with a belly full of *Mels Diner*, to cross the street so we can keep on moving. Eddie leans forward, "*Santa Rosa*, gives us *Acid*, we bring Mike a few sheets of that and in return he gives us these," Eddie opens one of the paper bags, holds it between Davey and me. There has to be like 200, 300 pills of *Ecstasy* in there. "We bring these to the *Castro*, and the *Castro* gives us the *Glass* that we take that back to *Santa Rosa*."

"And what do you get out of all that?" I ask as I pull forward to turn, slam the breaks. The fat kid in an *A's* baseball cap has lost the hat in a gust of wind and ran in front of the *Little Red Civic* to catch it. I almost killed him. Davey rolls down his window, "Fat fuck!" and I pull away. "That was mean," I criticize D's new inconsiderate nature. He can care less, waves me off, and Eddie continues to explain the responsibilities of the job, "We get paid later. We get paid in Money Order from some construction company up in *Walnut Creek*. Really just that simple. Your car gonna make these hills, kid?"

"It's cool," I say as I switch gears, down, to second, chugged-y, chug, chug, chug. Eddie has an addendum to the job at hand, "We don't get busted. The only guy whoever gets caught is the peddler, the street thug; besides, these fags are selling to their fag brothers, and naturally, other butt-boys," he knocks on Davey's head, "Knock on wood, the whole game's protected by fairies and fairies are good luck. Rub one out," and he pets my head, rufflin' my hair that has finally gotten some length back since the Mohawk debacle of yester-year.

—Hey, wait, Sheena never gave me my surprise! —

The *Little Red Civic* rolls its front tires just up and over the lip of a hill. They all have Stop Signs. It's evil. No reason for it. Four way stops. Could just have a two way stop and make the cars that cross the hill on flatter lands stop, but no, some genius thought this was a more civilized design. A *Lexus* pulls up behind me. I check it in the back window. "Fucker's close," I say aloud. Eddie checks. "Crazy close," he adds, "You'll make it, but next time," and he leans in, "Stop before the lip, hold that brake on the 80-degree slope, and when he pulls up, pop it." I look at him. Eddie's got the evil of evil's grin, "Let it roll, smash him, shove him down the hill, teach him a fucking lesson."

"Rear-end fault," I join in the fun.

"*Rice-A-Roni, the San Francisco treat*," okay, Eddie's funny. We laugh. Friends? Fuck it, why not? Davey interjects, "Gimme a bag," and Eddie hands Davey one of the baggies. He peaks in. "I'm gonna take one."

"Davey don't like these guys," Eddie informs me as Davey pops a tab of *e*— "Is it better than *Acid*?" I ask.

"Totally different," Eddie answers for him. Davey's quiet. He's just gonna wait for it to kick in.

"Do you feel it?"

"No," Eddie answers again, "Takes like 30 before you start rolling."

"You have to take thirty of them to get high?"

"Just drive," Davey's annoyed by my naïvety.

We continue up the next slope of hell. That fucking *Lexus* is going to do it again. "Roll it kid," Eddie whispers in my ear. I check the rearview mirror. I can't see through the reflection of city lights in the *Lexus'* windshield. What if he's a gangster? What if he's following us? Could be? Wants to jack the drugs. Davey'll do something stupid. I believe Eddie and I are charming enough to weasel our way out of a confrontation, but not Davey, especially Davey on drugs. I squint, bite my bottom lip, pop the clutch and leap forward over the lip, hit the brake, pop the clutch, pound the accelerator, peel out, and get up and over the next tamer hill, with Eddie laughing in the back, "He's still way back there."

"Is he following us?" I ask.

"No, turning left. I think you spooked that *Palo Alto* computer nerd."

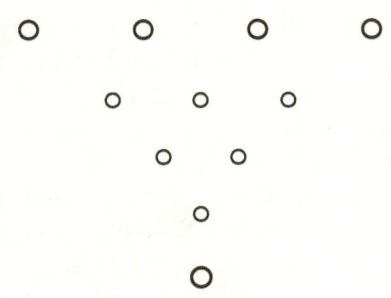

:THE CASTRO:

Sunday night, the foot traffic is lite. A few male-on-male couples are out for a last glass of weekend wine, a school professor's still out on a hunt for luck before the work week begins. I don't see one girl around. None. Place is like an army base without the uniforms, and that's where I'm wrong, there are a few men in uniform. We're at a light as usual, and lone and behold, another *Mid-Western* family's crossing the street. This clan has come to the *Castro* to see the gays in action. Probably don't see much of this in *Missouri*. The Dad pulls his youngest son in close as they pass a couple of Beefcakes. Davey does it again, jets half his body out of the window, yells at the family, "NAMBLA! NAMBLA! NAMBLA!" I pull him back in. "Dude, what the fuck?" Eddie even scolds him, "Yeah man, you know that'll get us beat out here." Davey laughs, "You guys got lame." I cross the intersection pass *The Castro Theatre*. That place looks mighty from the outside. I've heard it's awesome in there. Been closed for a couple years. Looks reopened.

Eddie instructs me well, finally, "Turn left at the light. Then two blocks, and take the hill on the right."

"Thanks," I am grateful.

"So, polite," Davey mocks me.

"Why you hate these guys?" I ask him.

"You'll see," he says, leans his head against his now rolled up window. I don't get it. Maybe he's bummed Eddie's quitting? Doesn't trust me? Thinks I'm soft. I'm not soft, bro. I got your back, you'll see, I'm up for the task.

It's another big hill, one of the kinds that has steps molded into the sidewalk. All the houses look like they lean to the left from the car, and here we go, all the way up to the center of this psychotic slope in first gear. "Why'd people build shit here?" I ask, no one knows and we just find a spot to park. Luckily, the parking is all diagonal, no parallel bullshit on this pyramid. We score a spot just down from the top, a dead end, and an entrance to a small park. In a flash, Davey's out of the car. I take a moment to read the parking sign from behind my windshield. As Eddie squeezes out I ask, "Can we park here?"

"Yeah, no one gonna care," he says holding the door for me. I reread the sign. *No Weekends 8am – 6pm*. I don't know what time it is. It's not dark, but it's summer. "What time is it?"

"Just come on," Eddie wants to get a move on. I get out, and he lets the door slam closed from the mighty gravity of the hill.

Eddie leads us down a few of the steps of the hill to a two story, typical *Arts & Crafts* style *San Francisco* home that's been divided into a couple apartments. The house steps have been painted in rainbows. "Second floor," he says, but before he takes a step up, he needs me to understand, and understand good, "You keep cool like the other place, 'kay?"

"Yeah, yeah, I'm cool," I say, "You cool?" I ask Davey. "He's fine. Just watch it up there, I'm serious."

.   . .:NEW WORLDS:. .   .
.ORDER ON.
.A HILL.

. .
.

Right above the front door is a stained-glass window, rainbow. There are so many rainbows around here. Whole *Castro* is filled with rainbows. "Guess they like rainbows," I elbow Davey. Not funny. My cohorts are really taking this one seriously. Eddie is about to knock when the door just opens. Guess they were anticipating our arrival?

I'm expecting another yuppie-couple, but we've traded down, that is not who has answered the door. A massive Beefcake of a man has replaced my gentle assumption. Takes me a second to process him, as he and Eddie greet each other with a thud, thud, patting of a hug, no words. I scan this man. Take it all in. Observe, collect as much visual information as I can in a short time.

The guy's huge. He's at least a half a foot taller than Trish's *Russian* bodyguard. He'd got straight-razor shaved skull. Not the most attractive head. The thing's spotted in indentations, pot marks, not pretty. In his ears, two golden studded earrings. His beefed-out chest busts out of his unbuttoned, small, black leather vest. His arms are massive and carry a single solid, metal studded, leather bracelet on his left wrist. Around his bounty of biceps are matching tattoos; two solid black bars of ink that wrap all the way around the middle of the monstrous muscles. He's a glorified *Tom of Finland* replica in the flesh, with steel toe *Docs*, blue laces, and fists full of diamond rings set in stainless steel bands. He doesn't hug Davey, just a hand shake, then before letting go of his hand, looks at me, doesn't know me, and Davey vouches, "He's cool, was our ride tonight." The giant has words, words expressed through some sort of *European* accent, "You just tell us first next time." Davey takes his hand back, "Yeah, Eddie's bad," blames the D. The big guy says to me, "Americans, no loyalty. Too Independent," and gestures for me to enter his home; the door   closes   behind   me...

o   o

I'm looking at the gayest place I have ever been. The big guy's taken a spot beside me. Got an eye on me. I can feel those pupils examine my face; memorizing it? I could suggest investing in a *Polaroid*, but Eddie would castrate me. "Paolo," the *P-Tom of Finland* introduces himself to me, "Welcome to our home," squeezes my shoulder, firm; power.

—He's so stronG—

"Tommy," I introduce my(fake)self. Davey's proud, nods at me. "Sit," Paolo releases my shoulder, and I step, gently, one foot at a time, with care, towards the...

...Breathe, Tommy, breathE...

...but now I'm nervous. I can't just sit down. I think I'll check out the window, that's not suspicious, right? But that's where I'm headed, gotta follow through, make it look natural, find a way out if this goes bad. No one seems to care— *Paolo? Why do I know that name?* —Davey and Eddie have already made themselves at home on the couch, a long baby-blue leather, glazed, that could comfortably fit 4-men, maybe six—

—if their all fucking each other in a knot...

ouwoo(grimace)ewwz
THE THOUGHT GIVES ME THE HEEBIE-JEEBIES
I don't want to see that 6+9=DiX TwixeDDDDD

o   o

—They can do it, just don't want to see it—

x •—{–^–}—• x

Culture shock and muscle mass has left an impression on my shoulder. The window's surrounded by velvet black lite prints of Muscle Men illuminated by the string of purple *Christmas* black-lights. The window's open. I take a peek outside. The neighbor's wall's like a two-person alley away. I could almost touch it with a broomstick. What's down below? That's some drop. The garages go underground on the hills. They're the basements of *Frisco*. The slope the homes are built upon adds a whole story to the lower ends of the houses. Earthquakes that rumble & tumble. Paolo, diamonds from *Macys*. His rings. Diamonds. Paolo. That's it.

o   *—Head rush. Close your eyes. Better. Open 'em—*   o

There's a cement wall that separates the aligned properties.

They could have left it open. At least that way you could actually walk straight through to the back of the property. With that wall in the middle even *Kate Moss* would have trouble squeezing through. Useless. Waste of cement. I pull my head back in and deduct that, that is not a worthy escape route.

—Wonder if a I guy that big goes down with a knee to the balls? —
Maybe? Not sure. Still don't want to find out.

Paolo swipes Davey's feet off the glass coffee table. I've never seen anything like it. Looks like perfectly cut ice cube from the heart of a glacier. Must have cost a fortune. The table is a solid foot thick slab of aquamarine, clear glass, resting, balanced, on a massive, purple, squared gem. "No manners," he complains again. Davey smirks and digs into the cheese plate. Beside the plate of cheese and crackers stands an open bottle of wine and a set of five wine glasses. "I let it breathe," Paolo tells me with another hand on my shoulder.

—It's really intimidatinG —

"Sit," he tells me again, this time steering me toward a matching baby-blue lounge chair. I obey. I can't place his accent. *European* that's for sure. Not *Russian,* maybe *Yugoslavian?* I wouldn't know. I am however very fascinated by this table. This whole apartment is one big lair for a Gay-Evil Villain in the latest *James (Castro) Bond* film. "Gay James," I say under my breath. Davey shoots me a look. Sorry.

—Where are the cats? —
All great Bond Villains have a cat?

I see no sign of pet life, not even a fish, and Paolo pours Davey a glass of wine, "Make yourself comfortable. Gary's still showering," then pours Eddie a glass, and politely offers me one, "I don't drink; designated driver." Eddie raises his glass, Davey raises a cracker, no cheese, not risking the wine, "To Tommy-Gun," Eddie cheers. I smirk and Paolo walks off.

—We just wait? —

The TV's on, local news, muted. I read the *Closed Captioning*— "Two more hate crimes off *North Polk*. Tension grows between community and police. *Mayor Jordan*, today, held a press conference to insure the public, "We are not, and will not, turn a blind eye on this terrible trend."

"That shit's crazy," I say aloud.

"What?" Eddie asks.

"Never mind," I don't really want to talk about it, not here, what if I say something stupid? Davey sips his wine. I'm confused. Both of these guys are breaking their own rules or maybe I'm just an idiot and believed their bullshit? Davey notices me watching him, puts the glass down, sits back, crosses his arms, and watches the tube. A *Trix* commercial, "*Silly Rabbit, Trix are for Kids,*" reads the captions.

Eddie shoves a nudie centerfold in front of D's face. The cover reads *MENten* and the cover photo is of a midget sitting on a weight lifter in a *Speedo*. He's benching two other naked midgets whose dicks have been obscured by their small thighs. Davey swats the magazine away, "Come on man!" Eddie laughs, shows me. The Centerfold is worse, way worse, a 20 manned, midget orgy, in a train circle, around three weight lifters who spray the naked, ass-fucking, mini-men with *Golden Showers*.

"Now that's entertainment," I jest, hear something, look towards the kitchen, "Someone's coming." Eddie drops the magazine, closes it, lays it on the table, and turns back. This new guy is way easier on the eyes, the nerves. He's more like Mike. Over fifty, 5'6ish, works out, shirtless, chest covered in grey hair, blue jeans, grey eyebrows, dyed black hair, very different from his counterpart Paolo. Prefer he'd put on a shirt, but not my house. He approaches me first. At a closer look, I can see his entire left arm has been burned; totally scarred up— *Don't stare* —Flip flops, no socks, he's offering me his deformed hand, burned worse than his arm, unreal, melted skin pulled tight along the bones of his fingers, hairless. I can't be rude. I have to shake his hand. Feels strange. He has a soft grip, as if he has just given you his hand to hold. The skin feels lifeless. Nerves shot, but it affects my skin as well. Feels as if I have no sensation as in my own skin— *creepy*.

"Good to meet you," Gary introduces himself. He's got an *English* accent, maybe *Australian*? All in all, it's his striking blue eyes that ease my insides. This guy can see into my soul. Ice blue attentive portals. Notices my existence. I feel important, to him. No, he makes me feel important.

"Yeah, totally," then out of curiosity I have to ask, "Where you from?" and I release his hand. "*South Africa*," he says and rubs the back of my neck, "Polite young man. You two could learn from him. Cares to be friendly," he tells the ding-dong boys on the couch. Eddie speaks up first, "He's our ride."

"I heard about your father. About you quitting," Gary lets go of my neck, soft— *Did he just flirt with me?*

"You're not mad, right?" Eddie asks. "Awe, Eddie," Gary scooches Davey over, takes a seat in between them, throws an arm around the backrest of the couch, "Family first, Edward. Family first."

"Yeah, well maybe I could be back in a couple weeks?" Eddie's like a puppy for this Gary. If it's not Mike, then Gary's definitely fucking Eddie.

"Shhh," Gary pets Eddie's face, Paolo returns from the back. Davey's squiggly at the return of Paolo, keeps looking at me for some reason. "What?" I mouth, Davey waves it off, never mind, Gary continues with Edward, "What kind of person would I be if I put money and business, over family?"

—Maybe the burn is a war wound?—
Vietnam? Korea? Cambodia? Iraq? Apartheid?

This place is weird
Where am I?

Gary looks over at me, releases Eddie's hand, rubs his face, examines mine, "Are you *Jewish*?" Gary asks.

"Yeah, why?" I ask, not sure where he's coming from. Gary turns to Paolo perched beside the window, "Your kinda guy." Paolo smirks. I agree big guy, that was kinda weird.

Gary turns back to me, Davey looks as confused as I am, "Don't mind me. My friend here has a fondness for, well you know."

"Not sure?" I'm not comfortable with his insinuation. Davey does not want me to start anything, but this is suddenly cutting it fucking close. Gary looks down at my crotch then right back into my eyes, "You know," and he snips the air with his fingers. I open my mouth, "That's fucking racist, you know that?"

-Pause for effect-

"Racist? No," Gary starts, "*Jew's* are just a religion; that's a choice. Me, you see, this," he presents himself, the gay, "I was born this way. This perfection is all I need. I don't need gods." Gary tries lessoning me, but I'm too offended to even think about his rational— "You're born *Jewish*, from your Mother's side," I correct him, clear the air.

"Yes, I've heard that before. So, okay, because you are so polite, and you're our new transport, I fold. You are right, you're born *Jewish* just like we're born *Homos*," Gary uses some knotted reasoning to make me comfortable.

o

—I can live with that—

o   o

.

Davey and Eddie look like they're going to kill me.
Chill out guys, I think Gary really liked me.
"You got enough gas to get us back?"
"Yeah. *Santa Rosa* next, right?"
"Yeah, *Santa Rosa*."
"Cool, cool."
"Drive."
"Ok."

.

○   ○

We cruise past *Petaluma*, north to *Santa Rosa*. No one has brought up the *Homo-Jew Debate* this whole time. "Gary's kinda interesting," I try to inspire some words, but they really don't want to talk about it.

○   ○

"Just be cool," Eddie finally says something as he fills up my car in *Rohnert Park*. "Hey, you tricked me," I tell him. Davey gets out of the car, "I'm gonna take a leak," walks off, leaves my car door open, the cab light on. I wander around *Little Red*, close the door.

"No one tricked you. You offered to drive," Eddie's version of my new sudden employment.

"Yeah, but you knew I'd do that."

"Look, Davey's your best friend, right?"

"Yeah?"

"Well he needs you right now. This is his only way out of here, this is the only thing keeping your buddy together ever since his sister blew her brains out."

"She didn't use a gun."

"Semantics."

The pump stops. Eddie replaces the nozzle, twists the gas cap back on, shuts the hatch, looks me right in the eye, "We good?"

○   •   ○

In *Santa Rosa*, I'm not allowed to go upstairs, I have to wait in the car; Davey waits with me.

"You're cool with all of this now, eh?" Davey asks as we watch Eddie disappear into the front yard, behind the trees, poof.

"I'm alright, but it's not that cool, man."

"Yeah, I know," he says, "But it keeps my Dad off my back and puts money in the pants," he shifts in his seat, "I don't know if you've noticed, but I haven't had to bum off my friends so much no more. Shitty bumming off your friends."

"I thought all was good with your folks, now?"

"My parents blow, that's the bottom line," he says, rolls down the window, lights a cigarette.

"And mule-ing drugs, that's keeping your head above water, right?" I say.

"Yeah, something like that."

•

○   ○

Eddie's coming back to the car. Davey tosses his butt. I break the silence, "I turn eighteen next week." Davey's response, "Maybe I should get a gun," does a bump. "No," I tell him. "Yes, totally," advices Eddie and I rest my case— Guns are dumb.

•

•

•

•

•

•

•

•

•

•

•

•
•
•
•
•
.
.
.

chapter 30-FIVE

i've rehashed my *Lysergic* tale at least twenty times by now. Told the story to my old school pals, my friends from *Junior High*, some of my oldest friends who are all studious in nature and straight edge by default. I rarely hang out with them, but after this weekend I'm in need of some tempered entertainment. I find no shame in spending some R&R around people who are not always teetering on the edge of life.

When you huddle around these cats your deepest concerns are with the coming *Fall* line up on *Television*. You're not deliberating on societies inconsistencies on race, riots, and the present dystopia. Here with this crew, dystopia is for the future, safely bound in *X-men* comics, and *Major Motion Pictures*. My memory of *Star Trek* has instigated this desire to calm the fuck down. My brief jaunts back to this clan of *Dungeons & Dragon* masters has not been without my own attempts to influence these minds. Fifteen to twenty minutes into a night of *Elves* and *Magicians* wandering our fictitious maps sketched out on graph paper, generally gets me spewing about my other world. I am their portal to the alternative and do my best to influence them through *Zap Comics*, but they prefer *Heavy Metal*, and music like the *Cramps* gets passed on with a preference for *Van Halen I, ZZ Top*, or on the extreme *Alice in Chains, "Here they come to snuff the rooster, aww yeah, hey yeah."* More or less I think that they need lyrics that include the word, "yeah," for their ears to digest the distortion of guitars.

This week I'm in a personal process of garnishing *Good Karma* where ever it may be found. I'm like a chipmunk, collecting and saving up *Karma* nuts in the preparation of a harsh winter. No one can control your *Karma*, but yourself. *Karma's* all yours. So, now that I've signed up for a stint at being a *Drug Mule*, it's all up to me to make sure that the *Karma-Bitch* doesn't flip around and bite me in the ass, rip up my ankle, or melt my wings as I soar towards the sun of high school graduation.

"Tyler, you rolled a 2," the *Dungeon Master* reads my throw of the *D20* die, "You've been casted right into the star's core. Relinquish your character to me." I hand him my character form. The table is silent, all eyes on the Master. "Tyler Goodman, your *Cleric* has a value of -10; he is dead." And with that, the *Master* of this domain rips my character form in half and drops it in the trash. *"Mountain Dew?"* offers the *Dwarf* to my left.

"No thanks."

○   •   ○

Still haven't called Sheena back in like three days. Mom took the message down on a *Post-It* and left it on my pillow. Time to cash in on my surprise— Ring, ring —"Yep," she actually answers.

"Yo," says I.
"Oh hey, what's up?"
"Nothing."
"You can vote tomorrow, huh?"
"You remember?"
"You wrote it on my calendar, dude."

chapter 30-SIX

*e*ighteen times seven equals one hundred and twenty-six. Eighteen times five is ninety, eighteen n' four = 72. Four rounds. I will turn 18 approximately 4 times in my entire life. If I push the 89'r line, I still won't reach five full rounds of 18 year bookmarks. Four. Only four in a lifetime. Seems short. I had hoped for a bigger number— six, maybe seven, but five? Sounds like a jip.

o   •   o

Mom & Dad? They're nowhere in the house. No sign of life; both cars gone. Birthday morning and I have been left, alone.

o   o
•

Munts has been invited over for dinner, cake n' candles, and our small family celebration with the folks and I. They ordered take out, BBQ ribs from *Jerome's*. So, good. Messy as fuck. We're all smackin' our lips, licking our fingers, ripping off the soft long cooked meat from the bones, suckling the salty fat, with spoonfuls of beans, corn on the cob, and fine fluffy yellowed cornbread. I'm gonna shit hard to-night.

Mom brings out the cake. She got me my fav, an ice-cream cake from *Baskin Robbins,* chocolate fudge. "Is there rum in it?" I ask. No, no rum. I'm eighteen not twenty-one. The man can vote, but the boy can't drink? For this alone I must now support illegal narcotics.

"Make a wish," Mom says. I take a deep breath.

—Simple...the girl from City Lights—
Maybe the gay Waitress from Dennys?

And the fire blows out. Yeah. The wicks reignite all on their own. No way out, childhood forever. My father laughs. Mom smiles. Munts is ready to get a move on. So am I. "Excuse me," I leave for a moment to take a toilet ride. Dad turned to Munts.

"How's my son?"

"Fine?"

"I don't want you to give him drugs anymore."

"Uh, okay, sorry," Munts was not ready for this.

"Good," Dad says, "I don't want his friends fucking up his future."

"Tyler's a good dude. You don't have to worry about him," Munts tries to help.

"I know that, but his friends are all screw ups—" Mom interrupts him, "Don't be like that. We like you very much Munts. Have fun tonight."

"Don't get him drunk either," Dad's last word.

•

•

•

•

chapter 30-SEVEN

*M*unts and I roll up to the curb of *Putnam Park*. Thursday night, summertime, everyone is here and no one at all. I couldn't care less, tonight we're headed out to *Salmon Creek*. B-day beach night. The Germ has got Davey caught in a chat trap. I honk. D waves for me to hold on, palms Jimmy a baggie of *Meth* and finally joins us. He sticks his shaved blonde head into the window. "Hair cut?" Munts asks, but it's the new pierced rook in his eyebrow that's really got our attention. "Happy Birthday, T," he says. "Thanks, nice pierce," I tell him. He taps it and cringes; the hole is still sore. "Where's Erin?" Munts inquires. "*Deaf Dog*," Davey points across the street to the new coffee shop just as Erin crosses with the Sheena. "Open," Davey insists yanking on the locked door handle. Munts opens, "Out," Davey says, "You're in the back with your sex-toy. I ride shotgun." Munts crawls between the seats. Sheena pops open my side, "Old fart," she greets me as she pushes my seat forward shoving me into the steering wheel, "Fat much?" she jokes, slides into her seat, "Cholesterol's really bad for men your age," and Munts has been caught in the center backseat as Erin squeezes in. I lean my seat back, Sheena's on a seatbelt search, Davey's still outside, about to light a cigarette, and Trish and a cohort of her sophomore friends are headed our way.

"Don't smoke in my car." He rolls his eyes, "Whatever," and tosses the stick, "You're a real bitch to your Dad's rules sometimes. Aren't you supposed to be an Adult now?" he asks. "Dude, get in, I don't want Trish bothering us." He looks down the block. They see each other. "DAVEY!" Trish yells. "Shit," he swears, gets in quick, slams the door, "Okay, go," but Munts has a complaint, "I don't like the middle."

"Really?" Davey scoffs.

"Really, I can't take it, I can't die like this."
Trish has hurried her steps. She looks mad.

"Come on we gotta get out of here," Davey's anxious now.

"Fine, I'll sit in the middle," Erin compromises, and Munts is fine with that.

"Great, so that's okay with you?" Erin starts, "Let your girlfriend be the one that flies through the windshield 'stead of you? Quite the romantic," and they start the switch. Trish is yards away, closing in, "DRIVE!" Davey yells in my ear. I peel out, stall, everyone in the park laughs, Trish starts banging on the passenger window, "You fucking shit!" Davey flips her off and I get the car going again and we're off. "So, what now?" I ask the pierced prick beside me.

"I fucked her Mom," Davey says, earnestly, truthful, and we are all sickened by the thought. I check the rearview mirror. Trish will kill my friend one day, this I am sure of now.

○   •   ○

"But we're wasting our time if we dwell on the past or fear what lies ahead, because without someone to call your friend, you'd probably be better off dead."

Day by day the *Conspiracy* lyrics of Davey's anthem become clearer and clearer. *Dave Young* may have been a psychic, wrote a song specifically for my pal, or just *Too far gone* himself. Young will take a bullet to his head years later. Pull his own trigger. I won't let that happen to my Davey.

○   •   ○

The drive out to Bodega is a memory. Sheena's got her hand on my shoulder. Keeps squeezing me. She has the memory too. I shove the ejected cassette back into the stereo, press play, *Country Death Song* from the *Femmes*, "Can we listen to something else?" Sheena asks, well aware I set her up. My Romantic Birthday plan has failed. "Yeah, totally, turn this pansy poetry off," Davey says, ejects the tape, starts searching for something else. Car is a silent killer. All you can hear through the emptiness of a non-playing radio is the chug hum of my *Little Red Civic*, accompanied by the wind against our windows, the deep thump of my lonely heart, and the plastic clatter of Davey rummaging through my tapes as usual. The tapes are really loud now that I had to trade down from my cassette tape briefcase after Carrie crushed it to hell giving me head in the *Denny's* parking lot; now all I got is a plastic bag from *Thrifty's* with the corners of the cassette cases punching through the skin of the bag.

I have a lump in my throat, a pain in my chest. Guess Sheena's memory is not as grand as mine, or maybe more so? The clatter has stopped. "You ain't got shit," he says, "Good thing I got," and he pulls a single cassette out of his flight jacket's inner pocket, shows it to me, "Happy Birthday *Speedo*." I look. In those boney fingers of his is a black and white Lamprey with block letters, *LARD*, he puts it in. "You bought me a tape?"

"Don't be an idiot, I swiped it. Thought that counts," and the tunes explode like a tandem bomb dropped on the hood of my car as we do not *slam into a massive cow lost on the road*, and its *Jello Biafra and Ministry* along the windy dark road out to *Bodega bay*, home of *Hitchcock's Birds*.

—Thought that counts?—
Sheena told me to mute those thoughts. To Eject them.
Happy Birthday, Tyler.

•

○   ○

The waves are shadowed curls of white virgin draperies crashing against the gazillion grains of sand of *Salmon Creek*. I'm alone. Munts has gotten everyone stoned. Said it was some good bud he scored from *Stepanoff* who's bussing at *Jeromes' BBQ* these days. "A theme," I said, a concept that even went over Munts who ate the birthday dinner. Now I am alone with the sea and myself. Few minutes back I had stepped away from my crew holed up in between the dunes with a bonfire. I want to be happy. What makes a person happy? My mind can tell me how to be sad, depressed, angry, or disgruntle, but how to be happy, that's become too abstract for me. If I was poet, would I be able to comprehend happiness? Maybe if I had siblings? Lived in a city? Rich? Famous? I won't think about having a girlfriend all the time. The sea has helped bury that thought in the dunes behind me. It's my biggest birthday since my *Bar Mitzvah*, I should feel happy, not blasé. What about God? Do I believe in it? Does it believe in me? Did it really make the stars as bright as diamonds? Did God bury the real diamonds deep in the earth so we would seek faith out? Turn black *African* babies into slaves to satisfy all the rich asshole's wives like *Ivana Trump*? Does baby *Eric Trump* have a cocaine habit now that he's ten years old? Does anybody even need to know about that gold plated apartment occupied by that scum-lord's family? Probably not. See, that's how you can be sad. Think about the entitled actions of trust-fund kids with racist parents, while urban homemakers are labeled killers, freeloaders, and useless. If the blacks rise up, burn more cities, would that make me happy? Davey and Sheena join me by the sea. They take a seat on opposite sides.

"You think *Oakland's* next?" I ask Davey.

"What about it?"

"Burn? You think they're gonna burn down *Oakland* next?"

"Don't believe the hype," he quotes *Flavor Flav*.

"You're stoned," Sheena states a fact.

"I don't think so," I say, "Ocean's amazing though."

"Dolphins live out there," says the stoned D.

"Dolphins? Really? Okay you're stoned," Sheena says.

"Drunk," he corrects her, offers me a swig of his *Wild Turkey*. I take it, fuck it, B-day, three more years to be an illegal drinker. Better start now or forever miss my youth. Davey continues his oceanographic observation, "Dolphins are fucked up. They are the *Anarchists* of the sea. Viciously attack other fish, gang rape she dolphins; don't underestimate the dolphin," Davey philosophizes.

"How 'bout the Sea Horse, do I gotta watch out for an

underwater stampede of alien shrimp?" I ask, take another swig, which Sheena takes away from me, "You're driving, kid."

"I'm an adult, bitch," I scorn.

"Balls drop yet?" Davey asks before tackling me down to wrestle. I take a swing at him, don't like to wrestle, creeps me out, not fun, then— Pop —Davey's fist playfully collides with my eye. "Oh shit, I'm so fucking sorry," half laughing, but it's cool and I am totally laughing. Barrel laughing. Guess I got happy. Alcohol. Hit me while toasty and I get happy?

—What's wrong with me?—
Repressed much, Goodman?

Sheena crawls over, "Let me see," takes my face in her sandy hands, "Oh shit, he really—" and now she's gotten sand in my eye. I jump back; rub my eye with my arm, also covered in sand. Bad move. Even more sand in my eye and in my recently split brow, "Oh, the shit hurts" and I gotta wash the sand off, out, go to the ocean, my boots get soaked in the tide, and just as I'm about to wash a bunch of salty Pacific H_2O over my face, Sheena pulls me back, "You crazy?" and she gently begins to wipe the grains away from my blinking red eye with the corner of her shirt. "Oh, salt water. Yeah, that would have been a mistake," I realize. "You're so fucking cute," she says.

—Really?—

o   •   o

Erin and Munts are making out at the bottom of the sand dune. Bonfire's gone out and now just smoldering ash, smoky, dying. "SHARK!" I yell from the top of the dune and then leap, do a half flip, land on my ass, slide all the way down instigating a...

...Hollywood Montage: Five cool, punk rock, alternative,

small town/urban minded teens that the Studio has casted with twenty-something year olds. *Paramount's* attempt at a new Nineties *Brat Pack*; more alternative, edgier, soberer, even more fake than *Robert Downey Jr.* casted as a coke-head turned prostitute in *Less Than Zero*. The cast takes turns sliding down the three-story sand dune. They double up, triple up. The Director gets a sudden idea, "Let's have them start an orgy," but the Producers won't allow it. Not real. Kids don't have orgies. Not in *California*, maybe in *New York*. Maybe if they were skaters. Nobody wants to see skaters on TV anymore. Maybe the girls can kiss? Did they do that on *90201* yet? Find out. Get me the statistics. *Brenda* and *Donna* maybe? Better not. Maybe they should all check into rehab? —And this is the industry I want to get into? No, an industry I want to change. Hope *Dorenfeld* doesn't beat me too it. *Harmony Korine* and *Larry Clark* will prove all that wrong with their *KIDS* next year, but this week, not a shot. Indywood's still gonna play it somewhat safe. Sheena blows me a kiss from the bottom of the dune. I'm gonna stay away from that; too many games.

—We're in the friend's zone now, darling—

o · o

B-52s on the way home is not boding well with the D sitting shotgun. The girls are screaming, Munts is nauseous, and I, well I got four people to drive home; I have plenty of time to change the tunes.

o · o

Pull my car over right before Davey's house. Best not to be seen. He has to sneak back in; still trying to look like a Saint so Papa Bear doesn't bother him. "Happy Birthday, old man. See you Sunday," flips me off, hops out, and closes the door on Munts before he can move to the front. "Oh sorry," Davey begs his pardon, reopens the door lets Munts out, "G'night," waves and disappears behind the brush. Munts has got his front seat back and I drive us back to the mainland of *Luma*, then all the way across town and deep into the never ending opposite countryside of the *North East*, to drop off my friend Sheena.

○   •   ○

I get out for S. She gives Erin a hug, "We should hang out more," Sheena tells her. "Yeah okay, I'll get your number from Tyler 'kay," Erin replies, best new friends. I'm a bit suspicious. "Night, Munts," and Sheena climbs out, closes the door, walks me to the gate.

"Happy Birthday. Three more and we can drink together at a bar," she says.

"I won't be around," my absolute prediction.

"College boy," she bats her eyes.

—AWKWARD SILENCE—

"Well, happy birthday. Maybe we'll hang out. You can take me to the *Gillman*," she makes a last attempt.

"Yeah, maybe. You're a good friend Sheena," slips from my chap lips. Is she going to cry? She looks like she might cry. Don't cry Sheena. People change, "No, they don't," she says.

"But the world does," and I give her a hug goodbye.

"I love ya, Tyler. *Stay gold, Ponyboy.*"

…and I don't see Sheena for the longest time.

And that's a real thought.

Horrible.

True.

Absolute.

Pray.

Hell.

.
.
.

•

We are all,
Too Far Gone

•

•

•

•

•

•

•

•

•

•

•

•

chapter 30-EIGHT

*d*avey, tweakin', tipsy, happy, not gay, has control of the radio, and he's flipping through stations; *KAMEL Rap/Top40, C&C Music Factory, Boyz II Men, Public Enemy,* "Ya know, I like *Public Enemy* now," he says. "True dat," says I.

"Rest of the Radio's shit; steroid junkies and commercialized tattoos," says he.

"Hairband's that think they're hard rock. Just pussies singing *Elton John Ballads,*" says Tyler the critic.

911 wears a late crown— szitztiaslkdj —Berkely Gardens...
Talk Radio

"Sunday's always talk radio."— *szitztiaslkdj* —"Find something man."— *szitztiaslkdj* —"I'm trying!!!" D's rolled all the way down to *89.9* on the dial. I tell him, "Go to *90.7,* that's the *UC Berkley* station," and I swipe his hand away, twist the knob myself— *szitztiaslkdj* —catch *90.7,* "the cue is the extension of the player. With a rectangular..." Davey does a bump from his bullet offers it to me. "No, duh? Are they talking about pool?" I ask him— *szitztiaslkdj* —D spins the dial, lands on *KPFA 94.1,* more talky-talk. "Sundays suck less, if you like classic rock," Davey complains, sniffs, rubs the drip from his nose, bends down, picks up my bag of tapes— *clackity-clack-clack-clack* —He's like a hamster sorting through a trough of nuts, "Find something," I say as he pulls out a *Butthole Surfers* mixed tape, pops it in, hits rewind,

"This'll do."— *Cunts, Cunts, Cunts,* delay, infinitely repeating. Davey fast-forwards >> "You got any of their fast stuff on here? *Wichita* shit?"

"*Cunts* is a classic," I defend the strange of strange.

"Yeah, don't get all cunty. *Cunts* is cool, but it's SLOOOOWWWW!!!!! as fuck," Davey yells as he fast-forwards >> play > listens, fast-forwards >> finds *Wichita,* lets it role, sings along, drop kicking my dashboard with his boots, and now we're havin' fun, *"Wiped-out wasted Wichita, Watch out where I am, Last time I's in Wichita I did not give a damn!"*

o　　　•　　　o

We pull off into *Sausalito*. "So, you know where we're going?" I ask. "Yeah, yeah, turn at the third light, ice cream store," he says as he picks at his eyebrow hair. He's picked at it so much recently that he resembles *Pink* in *The Wall*. We cruise, I'm counting blocks, ah, there's the ice cream shop across the street. Davey's patting down all of his pockets, again, and again. Slides up on his seat, checks his ass pockets. Looks on the floor, checks the back seat, shakes his head, rechecks his pockets. "So, now where?" I ask him as I turn up into the hills. "I don't know, maybe I lost it?" he says.

"Huh?"

"Bullet. I just had it," he's tweaking, looks up, "Turn there," says he, just in the nick of time. We make our way—*winding, winding*—Davey's keeping a tight eye on nearly every house we pass. "I know it by sight, ya know? Don't remember the street name." He looks down by my feet. "Hey, don't," I swat him away. "Not down there anyway," he justifies, and he's really starting to drive me bonkers. At the stop sign I look down at the ashtray. The bullet, half full of crunched *Crystal* is right there. I pick it up and throw it in his chest, "Here."

"Not cool," he says pissed, "Don't go hiding my shit, man. That's not cool."

"It was in the fucking ashtray tweaker."

"I know you got a broomstick up the ass about this stuff, but hands off."

"I'm over it dude. I'm, here, aren't I?"

HONK! The car behind us would like us to actually go now that we've stopped at the sign for an hour. Davey leans his head out of the window, spits at them, "Shit eaters!" I drive off. "How much farther?" because the sooner the better if he's going to start acting this way. Davey kisses me on the cheek, "You're a good sport, *Speedo*."

"Save it for Mike, ya fag," I tell him.

"Funny. Look, you'll come to a fork in the road, go left, then the trees change."

"Are you sure?"

"No."

"Davey?!"

"I'm sure, I'm sure. Look, I'll totally recognize the house right before the driveway. Keep going. Turn on your brights."

"You're gonna have to get a Driver's License before you get that car, ya know?" I mentor the kid.

"Later. So, you really ate that acid with Munts, huh?"

"Yeah, watch the road, dude."

○   •   ○

It is highly possible that we have driven farther than I remember. Davey's had me turn around twice now. We're stopped at the opposite side of the original Stop Sign. "Yeah, we must have missed it. Fuck," he's not funny anymore, now he's agro, "Turn around, and not so jerky, gives me a headache." We gone too far yet again, and he's digressed to beat-downs on my dashboard with his fists. "You gotta chill," I tell him, "You're gonna find it." D squeezes his face up, all up into the brow, creates wrinkles. Frustrated. His thoughts are triggering, but they're translating in gibberish. Words. Fragmented sentences. Prolonged punctuation. Incomprehensible.

"Sometimes the *Glass* makes me feel illiterate," he tells me. I'd rather he crack a joke, punch me in the face or something, not complain about a habit that I'm trying to ignore, and we get there, roll onto the gravel driveway, crunch, crunch, and I'm out of the car like a rabbit. I gotta pee.

•

○   ○

Mike answers the door. "Hey," I say, "I gotta," but he gets it, points down the hall, "Bathroom's that way," and I'm thanking him as I rush to the john.

○   ○

•

The pisser's nice, real high-end, fancy pants, black tiled from head to toe, everything else is basically stainless steel with a shine, not all wire spiraled like the other stuff, save for a porcelain shit bowl. The shower door is made of a cryptic black glass that matches the tiles. I press my face against the glass. Solid. Can't see through it at all. I got my nose grease on the glass. Wipe it with my hand and now I've made it worse.

—Do I hear music?—

I do. Real low, can barely notice it. I listen closer, *"What's going on,"* Marvin Gaye. There's a speaker above my head. They got this place wired. I open the shower door, peak inside, the knobs are studded in diamonds, and directly above, a matching diamond showerhead. Never seen a showerhead like this before. Looks like Paolo's fingers. I gotta turn it on. You haven't lived until you've seen a diamond shower sprinkle. I wrap my hand around the $5,000 dollars of earth glass on the knob and at the very moment I twist it, the diamonds of the showerhead literally light up as the water streams out in an illuminated rainbow of light. Now that is the gayest thing I think I have ever seen; that's until I'm watching myself pee in the mirror behind the toilet that has been perfectly angled down to show you yourself. I have a nice-looking dick, but what would I know? Shake, flop, zip, wash my hands, be sure to rinse the bar of soap off first, ya' know, to be sure. I tell myself how stupid, naïve, and nearly outright prejudice I am about this gay man's bathroom. I know that's not how you get *AIDS*, but I'm an idiot, I got the spooks, better safe than sorry.

—stupid—
How many Mini-Thins have you taken, Goodman?

Check the pack. One, two, three...They're all still in there? We didn't take any? We had opened it, but forgotten to pop any.

—Stop lying to yourself—
You're no good at that Ponyboy.
Too honest to even pretend to yourself.
Dad's not here. You can lie to him later.

| | REWIND <<—Davey has twisted the radio dial all the way down to *89.9* on the dial. I told him, "Go to *90.7*, that's the *UC Berkley* station," and swiped his hand away, twisted the radio knob myself, past *Marvin Gaye— szitztiaslkdj —* stopping at *90.7*, "the cue is the extension of the player. With a rectangular..." Davey did a bump from his bullet and offered it to me. "I'll take the wheel, just put it in your nose, close your other nostril, and sniff hard," he told me as he had taken the wheel after I took hold of the bullet. No time to think about it, had to put my hands back on the wheel going 70 on a 55 mph freeway. Up, in, close— SNIFF! — BURN — immediately grab the wheel again to weave us back into our lane. I dropped the bullet, Davey had a laughing fit, and my right eye wouldn't stop watering for a good couple of minutes and my nose leaked snot like a stream, but once that resided, my generally stuffy allergic sinuses felt clear and easy for the first time since I could remember, and I was suddenly wide awake >> *szitztiaslkdj* >

—Maybe I'll do a little more? —
I feel good. Clear-headed.
Everything's so crystal clear.
Shit, I gotta get out of this bathroom, been in here forever.
How's my hair? Growing in too much.
Need another Mohawk. Liked the cut. Empowering.

Sniff! Burn! Why'd he give me this to hold? Tear a piece of

ply, blow my nose, toss it; check the mirror. Eyes blood shot. Wiggling my nose like a bunny. Bite my lip. Clean. Bright. I feel amazing. Fire eyes. Power. I'm in control. Drugs. Good. Better. Better than I thought. Not as crazy as *Acid*. Clear. Me.

—TnT—
Sudafed. Methafed. Fuck Allergies. Chemistry Gods.

I stand by the door inhaling and exhaling over and over. It feels so good to breathe. I had gotten used to being nasally all the time. So much so, no one ever made fun of me for it. Kids aren't cruel all the time, sometimes. I've had my hand on the bathroom doorknob this whole time. Leave, dude. One more breath. Check your face, did you wash it? Probably would feel good. Okay, one time. I turn back to the faucet, splash water on my face, and rush out of the bathroom forgetting to dry off. Can't be late. I have to use my shirt to wipe away the water drip from my forehead as I stroll down the hall like nothing's up.

—What was that?—
Saw something out of the corner of my eye.
Just a shadow? Probably mine.
Ha. Cool. Guess I'm high.

。 ○ ○ ○   ○ ○ ○ 。

I step into the living room. Davey's by the windows overlooking the bay, nurses his beer, and Mike spooks me from the left. Didn't see him there, "Can I get you anything?" he's asked.

"No, I'm cool," I say, "Where's your Kaye?"

"I was just telling Davey here, he left me. It was petty, over a house," Mike turns to Davey, "After 30 years, and she's still mad I never moved us to the city."

"Fuck him, you can do better," Davey advises the guy.

"Sorry, man," I say, pat the Mike on the back, "*Love's a fickle thing.*"

"Sorry is for *San Francisco*, son, I'm better than sorry," he tells me and rubs my back.

"Totally," I say turning towards him, his eyes locking onto mine, his hand still on my back, and I step away from that strangeness, "I really like your place, why would he bitch about this place?" I talk as I walk towards my pal, for protection, "I mean I could totally live here forever. I'd make a ton of movies here," reach D, who offers me his beer, I take a sip, hand it back, turn to Mike, "And that shower? Dude, crazy. Your idea?" Mike nods, "Love it. Super cinematic." Davey's gives me a look I can only decipher as, "You're talking too much." Chatter, chatter, can't stop, have to speak, maybe I shouldn't have done that second bump at the Stop Sign? Oh shit, in the bathroom. I gotta give him that bullet back, I don't have any idea what I'm doing. Davey explains my behavior to the Mike, "I gave him Meth for the first time tonight." I'm tweaking on Mike's outfit of the night. A slim suit, probably *Armani*, no tie, top couple buttons remain open so you can see his thin silver necklace accompanied by his grey chest hair curling out of the crease. He's barefoot and wears a cold sore on the edge of his lip. His tongue creeps out, licks his sore. The detail of everything is just so crystal clear.

"Davey," Mike instructs him to follow him to the back.

"Hold this," Davey hands me his beer. I instinctually take another sip, regret that, and put it down, flashback to Mike licking his cold sore. I need whiskey. Whiskey kills everything, so I've been told.

　　　　。 。 ○ **O**　　　　　　　　**O** ○ 。 。

We're leaving the house; Davey's got the bags in his hand and still sipping that same beer.

"You can't bring that in the car, man," I insist.

"Don't be a prude, it's just a beer."

"We're only eighteen," I say well aware that I'll be tried as an adult and can't fuck up.

"Speak for yourself, old man, I'm still underage," Davey says, and spits his beer on me, soaking my *Alice Donut* shirt with the stink of yuppie, six-dollar suds. "DUDE?!" I'm pissed, but D-boy just laughs, tosses the empty bottle into the bushes, "Dude, what? Let's go," he orders me as he pulls on the passenger door handle, but it's still locked.

"Chill Davey. What happened? Mike statutory your tender ass in there?" I jest, and that makes me feel better about the beer. "Not cool," he glares at me, "Gimme my bullet back." I unlock my door, pop it open, and ask the D, "Can you mix *Mini-Thins* with *Crystal Meth*?"

"Probably, but I don't fuck dudes, 'kay?" he says getting in the passenger side.

"But you fucked Trish's mom."

"That was a mistake."

"Was it?"

"Absolutely."

"Was she good?"

"Can we go to the city already?"

"We need to get water for the *Mini-Thins*."

"Just do another bump," Davey suggests.

"Rather not."

"Good. Now give it back and drive," another order, and he's got his hand out, opening and closing his palm for me to give him back his goods. I dig into my pocket, slap the bullet into his palm, "You know this place used to be the Bootlegger capital of the West Coast?"

"Whoopee," Davey doesn't care.

"Rum runners too," I add.

D does another bump, checks the bags, "Are we going to drive anytime soon?"

"We're like *Meth* runners of the great *American* drug prohibition," I connect the dots for him.

"You talk too much," and he crinkles the paper bag closed, "Drive!"

"Balls hurt?" I ask.

"They do actually," he admits about the *Crystal Meth*.

"Thought so."

"Drive!"

Vroooooom, shift, reverse, crunch, crunch, and we're back to the mission at hand. Just two drug runners nearing the end of the 20th Century over a hundred years past the gold rush.

o o o O   O o o o

The *Golden Gate's* not very foggy tonight, and we did grab a *Pepsi* at the Deli in *Sausalito*, so I could pop a couple of *Mini-Thins*. Davey had some too. No pressure needed. "You see the *ghosties* yet?" he asks.

"What's a *ghosty*?" I ask as fog swishes past my windshield. Davey's watching the second red arch of the bridge pass over us through the skylight, "You probably need to do more."

"*Thins*?"

"No, *Crystal*," he lowers his head, "If you do enough, you see these sneaky spirits wandering around."

"I thought you only hallucinate on *Acid*?"

"You don't see them outright, just out of the corner of your eye," he looks at me, "I never believed in ghosts until I met Eddie," we glide through the toll booth, "The world's filled with them. Lost spirits; Anti-Heaven Souls who've attached themselves to limbo, by choice. Heavy shit. Feel like they want my attention," he turns to watch the nothing of trees out his passenger window, "Eddie told me not to talk to them."

"Why?"

"They can't be trusted. Says they ask for too much from ya, that they want you to talk them all the time."

"Do they talk to you?"

"No, they just want you to talk to them."

○ ○ ○ ○   ○ ○ ○ ○

D's finger can't stay out of his nostril. The *Gold Rush's* over, buddy. Not sure what Davey expects to find up there as he mines his facial cavities. He cringes each time. Must hurt. "Oh, fuck," he says as he removes a bloody fingertip, "You got a tissue?"

"I don't want to park on that fucking hill again," I warn him as we near the *Castro*.

"Yeah, park on the bottom, we'll find a spot. It's Sunday. Tissue?" he asks as he leans his head back, plugs his left nostril, and snorts up the coming blood river. "I don't think so. Use your sleeve." He gives me an evil eye, "I'll manage," he says.

—Tweaker—

₀ ₀ ₀ O   O ₀ ₀ ₀

After a harrowing twenty minutes of circling the *Castro*, we finally find a spot to park, three blocks from the bottom of the hill, but my agro-meth-head passenger has a complaint, "Fuck that, I ain't walking that far. Park on the hill, pussy," and he wipes his nose on his sleeve, does another bump. "Why you doing *Crystal* like its *Cocaine*?" He punches me in the shoulder, "What do you know about *Cocaine*?" I pop off my blinker and head for the hill. I know better. I could make him walk, but the drive home will be a non-stop conniption fit about why Eddie is a better driver or some other frivolous and combative train track of bitching, and then, a mile of apologies, excuses that the *Crystal* gets him all uppity by the end of the day. So, I oblige his lazy request. We find the same exact parking spot as last weekend. "You think these guys listen to the *Depeche Mode*?" Davey asks.

"How the fuck would I know?"

"Probably do," he says, and we get out, head to the carnal strongman carnival drug den of the *Castro*, only after Davey stops into a bar to use the john and tend to his nose bleed for the next fifteen minutes. I followed him inside. Ten to twenty men scattered around the bar, nursing their mixed drinks, have eyeballed me for the tender slab of *veal* I am. "You can't be in here," I'm told by the bartender. "You didn't even ask for ID?" He points me to the door, I leave, wait on the curb, imagine myself as a gay man in *San Francisco*, decide men probably have worse fights than heterosexual couples, seriously fucked up ones; domestic arguments that lead to fist fights, and wonder how much secret abuse occurs within' these homes. No one will ever know and even if they did, probably blame it on being gay, not because they're males. *Jews*, gays, blacks, and gypsies, we all shared the same showers.

₀ ₀ ₀ O   O ₀ ₀ ₀

Door opens— Paolo the key-master smirks at us. This time

Mr. Beefcake's dressed in a tight pair of acid washed blue jeans, a white, cotton tee, blue suspenders, with the same matching blue laces, but this time they're holding up a pair of shiny, white steel-toe *Docs*. "You got a blue beret to go with that?" my *Meth*-mouth jokes. Davey pushes me inside, "Ignore him, he's an idiot."

"You're no *Einstein*," Paolo retorts in that thick *Eastern European* accent, as Davey passes him. D leans into my ear, "You're a fucking comedian."

∘ ∘ ∘ ○　　　　　　　　○ ∘ ∘ ∘

I'm in the middle of the living room, standing, don't want to sit, want to come and go as quick as we can. This place gives me the heebie-jeebies. Someone's rearranged the apartment since last week. Fickle interior designers can't decide on the art. I preferred the last week's choices better. Seems as if they've really stereotyped themselves this time with a *Liberace* wet dream of a *Julie Andrews* four square *Warhol* styled print, an oil painting of *Bette Midler* the handicapped-mermaid, and a silver gelatin print of a naked *Javelin* athlete as he tosses his spear across a depressed skyline. The photo really gets under my skin. The image is so homoerotic I can only imagine it must be a *Mapplethorpe*; it is not, and I won't figure that out for a few more months. As for now, I'm chewing on my tongue like the D, and honestly, now my balls hurt. Feels like their being yanked up by my groin muscles. Is that the *Crystal* or the *Thins*? The *Thins* shrivel up my dick when I take too many; guess *Crystal* shrivels your balls. I adjust myself. I don't like it. Shouldn't have tasted the stuff waiting for D on the curb. I was curious. What's it taste like? Is it as strong as snorting it? How much should you eat? D had been all sketched out about bringing the bullet into the bar with him. Gave it to me to hold. "But I want it right back," he had said as if I was going to steal it forever, still paranoid about losing it in the car two hours ago. On the curb outside the bar, I had just poured a bullet hit onto my palm, took a lick. It was really sour. Twenty minutes later and I'm starting to think eating it is actually more potent than the quick jolt up a nasal cavity. Maybe now I'll see some of them *ghosties*?

"That's some *Mapplethorpe*," I say to Paolo. "What's a *Mapplethorpe*?" he humors me, not really interested in an answer, "Sit, I have to weigh your package," and presses play on the boom-box, with a CD player, very posh; *"KMFDM sucks."* Might as well make ourselves comfortable. I choose the baby blue, fuzzy, lounge chair and instinctually start rubbing the material with my palms; so soft. Davey plops his skinny, white-boy's ass on the couch, scoops up the *San Francisco Chronicle's Pink Section*, starts to browse. The pink section, for those who do not live in *San Fran*, is not the gay section of the newspaper, it is merely the entertainment section and has been pink, like, forever. I notice they don't have cheese and crackers for us this time, what's the big? Don't love us anymore?

 ₒ ₒ ○ **O**   **O** ○ ₒ ₒ

Moments later we are accompanied by yet another bald Beefcake from the back bedroom with Paolo. If I had thought Paolo wasn't pretty, this guy makes him look like *Nordic* perfection, and yet, to my absolute amazement, nearly twice the size of the giant Paolo. These dudes are so massive the floor reverberates under their boots. The new monster's dressed in black leather that is so constricting that his package looks like he's got elephantiasis of the ding-dong. On his torso he bursts from a tank top. *KMFDM* switches to *Soft Cell's Sex Dwarf*; talk about uncomfortable. This guy's biceps cut *Schwarzenegger* down to the lightweight division. The *Hulk* would be hard-pressed to compete against this ugly son-of-bitch. I don't want to stare, but the sight of his thick, welted scar that spans from his jugular up along his cheek to his forehead is truly impressive. Davey won't even look at the guy. This monster of a man is unable to wear an earing, all because he is actually missing a segment of his ear, and when he turns the corner of the couch, the back of his head is revealed and it's obviously been patched back together.

Hey, D, how 'bout we get the drugs

& get the fuck out of here?

"What's up?" my new tweak slinging mouth defies my logic as I address our new associate.

"This is Gustav," Paolo politely makes an introduction. I rise out of my seat, can't control it, gotta be social, reach my hand out over the glass coffee table to this Gustav. He just nods, says nothing, does not shake my hand.

— Okay? —

Davey says hello to the muscle, but this beast just takes a seat by scooting D to the other side of the blue couch.

— Does Paolo fuck this guy on that couch? —

I can only imagine, *Horrible Thoughts*. I want to go home. The whole apartment rattles a 5.2 when Gustav of the *Castro* drops his might on the fancy-boy couch. If Davey looked like a pick up stick before, now he resembles a toothpick beside this one. "Gustav likes you," Paolo says to me.

"Me?" okay that's super random, "He just met me." Why you gotta spook me like that? Bad enough I'm waiting for those *ghosties* to creep along the corner of my eye, but this monstrosity taking a liking to me at first glance, let's not get weird here, 'kay?

Paolo, shrugs his shoulders, as Gustav stares, hard, directly into my soul, and I fear those *Elephant Man* balls of his might be getting crushed under his growing hard-on. I look to my friend for salvation. Davey, with that shit-eating grin of his, kinda thinks it's funny, and that obnoxious fuck-shit-up twinkle in his teenie-bopper, tweaker eye is not offering any sort of security.

"I told he you a helmet head," Paolo clarifies Gustav's man crush, and the needle of equity skips out of the groove of life and scratches the *Abba* record we're trapped in.

"Ah man, really, that's not cool," I turn to Davey, "Dude, that's not cool, can we get outta here?"

"Chill out," Davey snaps at me, turns to Paolo, "That's cute, can we just do the thing?" Gustav pulls his own shoulders back, his chest stretches out the tank top, and his back cracks. That's not helping.

"What's the rush? You relax a minute. Spend time with us," Paolo insists.

—No, thank you—

"Where's Gary?" Davey asks. My buddy's knee won't stop shaking. Now he's nervous and that makes me even more apprehensive— *Please stop that* —I can't look at Davey anymore, he's not going to help me in this; I miss Eddie. My own disheartened anus has clenched itself up into my abdomen. If they only circumcised baby boys in Europe, then maybe my *Jew* pecker wouldn't be such a delicacy to these foreigners. I gotta stop looking at him. Look at the floor, look at his boots. He's got the same blue laces as Paolo. Look, I'm no lover of the police either, but you guys are asking for a quick deportation with that shit.

"Gary's with Mike. You not see him?" Paolo asks.

"Nah, he wasn't there," Davey tells him.

"Why are you wearing blue laces, you're not straight-edge," spews my uncontrollable mouth. I blame my Dad. He has no filter and now, thanks to my best friend and the wonders of *Crystal Methamphetamines*, I have no fucking filter.

"You, *kike*?" Gustav finally speaks and the accent is thick, a dark fog so very reminiscent of the typical *Austrian* sound— brutal on my senses.

"Whoa! No way, fuck that, I don't go calling you a f..." and I stop myself.

—TYLER! Are you fucking crazy?—
Look at the size of that guy, don't talk back.
You started this, you pissed him off.
This is all Davey's fault.
Wise up
Remember what Davey always says,
"You keep me from getting in trouble."
Do your job Goodman. Drop your agenda.
Save Davey.

"Come on, I finish with scale and you go," Paolo says to Davey and heads to the back. D gets up, turns right to me, he's pissed, "Eighteen's really gone to your head, man. Wise up."

"Sorry," and watch my fucked-up friend go deeper into self-service as he walks away from me, follows Paolo, and leaves me with the gay *Austrian* who seems to have a repressed desire to make sweet love to a *Jew*; *Austrian* guilt? I'm not all that surprised; I've heard about it before, didn't think I'd be privy to it, the subject of reconciliation, but yet here I am, scared as fuck that I'm gonna be taking one for the team. "Uh, so where you from?" I start the small talk in an attempt to mend our initial combativeness.

"*Austria,*" he admits, "You know *Austria*?"

"Yeah, yeah, I know about *Austria*," I say.

"They hate *Jews* and <u>Gays</u> like me in *Austria*," he explains the obvious to me, but with an emphasis on himself.

> —*Maybe he's just trying to relate?* —
> *Doesn't know what kike means?*
> *Probably thinks it's German for Jewish?*
> *Cool down. Crystal's got you paranoid.*
> *The dude is gay, gay as day, gay as they come.*
> *Probably got beaten up as kid, so he got big to overcompensate.*
> —*Empathy, T, Empathize with his plight* —

I lean forward, address him more properly, show interest, and respect, "Is that why you moved to the *States*?"

"Yeah, more here," he says.

"Well, welcome to *America*," I greet him correctly this time, "We don't discriminate against people like you here. We're not fascists, we have a *Constitution* that protects people like you."

    ₒ ₒ o O   O o ₒ ₒ

I follow Davey down the concrete steps of the hill, "Okay, next time I'm waiting in the car," I tell him.

"Good, cause you were a fucking asshole tonight," still

pissed.

"Screw you, Davey."

—that's not fair, I've never done Meth before, I couldn't help it—

We get to the bottom of the hill, turn the corner, and Davey's gotta lecture me about it all.

"Look, Eddie and I are already on thin ice 'cause of him quitting and shit. So, please, just calm down, no harm, nothing's weird, I've done this a million times before, it's always fine."

"Sorry, I," and he cuts me off, tells me what I already knew, what I was going to admit.

"You're a light weight, I get it. Next time don't do so much, 'kay *Speedo*."

"Don't call me that."

We've reached my car.

"I thought Eddie's Dad had a stroke?"

"Eddie quit, man. That was his excuse. You need an excuse to quit the drug trade; can't just quit."

"Why didn't you tell me that before?"

"None of your business?"

o o o O   O o o o

And we drive home. No music, no talky talk. We're both spinning in our own heads. I'm debating everything I saw tonight, and Davey, Davey's fantasizing about buying a car of his own and running away.

As we pass the old Drive-In off the *101 N* Davey finally tells me of this fine plan of his, "One more time. Next Sunday you take me again, then I can afford to get my own ride and you'll be off the hook."

"You're really getting a car?"

"Yeah," he says.

"Finally, someone who can drive my ass around," I try to lighten the mood, find a break in the fog, get our lives back to normal, but better.

"Not likely, I'm moving to *Oakland*," he says, "I'm done with this *North Bay* shit, D-O-N-E. Gonna get this last check and quit. I'm done with being Mike's bitch."

"Why?"

"I don't relate to anybody in *Luma* anymore."

"That wasn't my question."

"My point exactly," the disgruntle son of *Petaluma, California* specifies.

And *The Conspiracy's* anthem rings true once again, but this time I pay attention to all the lyrics.

"Too far gone, too far gone.
I went out last night to renew my faith in those I called my friends,
And to talk about the old days and all the fun we had back then.
I thought we'd share a beer or two, then wander the streets all night,
Reminiscing of our younger years and everything would be alright,
But now we're old and bitter from growing up to fast
In a world that doesn't wait while you're living in the past.

(Too far gone, too far gone)

Well it didn't take much time at all for us to notice all the changes.
This fucked up world's taken my best friends and turned them into total strangers.
We've lost sight of all our goals - Just given up or so it seems,
And now we depend on a new generation to realize our dreams
Cause now we're old and bitter. We're jaded to the bone.
We're turning our backs on each other and we're dying all alone.

Sometimes as we get older, and we look back on what we've done
We might regret our past mistakes and we might fear the days to come
But we're wasting our time if we dwell on the past or fear what lies ahead
Because without someone to call your friends, you'd probably be better off dead, oh yes you'd probably better off dead,

Too far gone is what we are, a fucking pitiful disgrace
Just a bunch of useless jerks amongst the human race

I don't want to be - It won't happen to me -
I'm not gonna be too far gone
Can't you all just see, we are all gonna be too far gone."

·

·

·

·

·

·

·

·

·

·
·
·

chapter 3-EIGHT AND 2/3^{rds}

*t*he glow of my TV
isn't keeping me up. The flickering light of the tube screen
has me tuned in, straight as an arrow, seeking clues,
predictions toward my friend's future. The digital clock
beside my mattress on the floor reads 4am and I've been
scribbling notes while *Suburbia* rolls through the *VHS* player.
I don't know what I expect to find, it's all pretty status quo
when it comes to the *American* punk scene. I need some
Death. There are not enough *African Americans* in *Petaluma*. In
general, not enough blacks in punk rock. So, Davey likes
Public Enemy now, guess that's progress? Maybe rap has
squashed all hope for a blossoming agro-afro punk or metal
scene. *Fishbone's* doing it all for everyone. *Fishbone's* got a
burden the size of the *South*. *Living Colour's* fallen into the
Mtv trap, but I don't know, they've always come off a little
Guns n' Roses to me, and less like *Bad Brains*. I guess the
Fisher brothers aren't totally alone, not like *Dimitri* the
adopted *African* baby *Jew* of *Petaluma*. And Davey pretends
he's adopted. Be *Dimitri* for a day, and then let's see who
feels adopted. Fuck, ya' know the holocaust was one
seriously retarded shit-storm—

—and the T passes out
right before the kid on the big wheel
gets run the fuck over.

•

•

•

•

•

•

•

•

•

•

•

•
•
•
.
.
.

chapter THIRTY-NINER

f *ugazi,* *Repeater,*
again...and again. Where the fuck is Davey? I've been waiting in my car for like 15 minutes. I'm over it, his folks like me well enough, think I'm a good influence, I'm knocking this time, want to get this over with. Eject the tape, *"Repeate—"* pull the key from the ignition, hop out, slam my door, take three steps, and look who's decided to show up. Davey wasn't even at home. He's strolling down the road towards me. Where was he? Who cares— he's here now, let's go. "Want a bump?" he asks. I do a line instead, right off the dashboard, way more intense, really burns, my right eye's blood vessels burst into a map of the *Red States*. "You'll get used to it," Davey the nasal-holic mentors my intake with a lisp and turns the ignition for me. Car sits idle. "Not an automatic, dude," I tell him. He rolls his eyes, reapplies his eyebrow pierce, sniff, "Just drive."

₀ ₀ O   O ₀ ₀

"Dad, I have swim practice again starting tomorrow, right?" I had asked before heading out to D's.
"Morning practice, 7am."

—Oh, fuck you, I quit—
Take this team and shove it, I ain't swim here no more!

And then I walked on out the door to do something worthwhile with my summer time roll; childish drug dealing.

                    ₒ ₒ ○ ○   ○ ○ ○ ₒ

"I was over at Aunt Ellie's," Davey's reason for being late. Aunt Ellie's this little old lady that lives a house or two down from him. He's always had a fondness for her. She was like the first lesbian in the history of time— at least it seems like that since she's the only old fart we know that likes to go muff diving without a swimsuit. She doesn't judge him, gives him cookies, lets him complain about his parents, and cry on her shoulder. Davey never cries, *Boys don't cry*, *The Cure* excuse. I've always found it strange that Davey's so into *The Cure*. Uses *Josh Staples* as his reasoning, "Someone that cool can't be wrong, right?"

I don't like The Cure. I do like that Davey likes them though, shows that he might actually has some feelings buried deep down inside. "I ain't going to get to see her anymore once I move," he says, "I think I'll miss her the most."

—Good, the guy's still goal orientated—
Progress.
I'm rubbin' my boy the right way.
That sounds so gay in my skull.
Rewrite that. I'm positively influencing my pal.
Better. Much better. Crystal. Crystal Meth. Crazy.
Brain sparks. Clarity. Fun. Jacked up. Driving.
Need some LSD? Maybe tomorrow.

"I hear ya. She good?" I ask.

"She's old, don't think she'll be able to take care of herself soon. Son's gonna probably put her in a home," Davey says.

"She has a son? Thought she was a lez?"

"It's not all so black and white. You have to be more open minded."

"Okay? Just thought."

"Personally, I'm not gonna let myself get that old," says the philosopher, "I'm jumpin' off the bridge before I'm forty, that's my plan."

"I'd rather you not."

"I'd rather you suck a dick, and shut up," he says, sticking his tongue out at me, revealing yet a new piercing. That explains the sudden lisp— *"REPEATER!"* he's popped the tape in and clacks his metal tongue rod against his teeth to the beat as we head to the bay, early, 4:30 in the afternoon, too soon for a *Moon over Marin*. Plenty of time for *Tom Waits* who, *"looks good without a shirt on."*

₀ ₀ ○ ○   ○ ○ ₒ ₒ

Mike is short on time, short on words, doesn't even invite us in this time, just opens the door and hands Davey the two paper bags. "I have a date. See you next week," he says closing the door in our faces. Davey, crunch, crunch, walks away. I'm left at the door.

—You gotta tell him Davey—
What's your excuse? Anal cramps?
How you gonna quit?
Huh?

"Davey!" I yell after him. He knows what I'm about, flips me off, crunch, crunch, to the car, turns back, yells at me, "Come on!" Fuck, well I'm not driving him next week. I'm done. Get that car fuck-face, you're on your own after this; crunch, crunch. Grow a pair. Get yourself outta trouble from now on; I'm going to college.

₀ ₀ ○ ○   ○ ○ ₒ ₒ

At the car, crunch, crunch, I walk around to the driver's side, look over the top at D and shoot him a reasonable reminder, "I'm not going in this time, remember?"

"God, you're such a pain in the ass, can we just go?" bump, snort, sniff, sleeve wipe, now who's wasting time, door closes, he looks at me, "Well?"

—Oh, he's in fine shape today, Dick—

₀ ₀ ₀ O   O ₀ ₀ ₀

Half way across the bridge and Davey snorts up a lugie and spits it out the window, except the window's up and it splatters against the glass, "Fuck!" and he punches my window, nearly shattering it and his hand. "What the fuck, dude!" I accidently swerve into the other lane, pull back, "Shit."

"What's your problem, T?" as he digs through his pockets looking for the bullet; I assume, and assume correctly as he does yet another bump, cringes, blows his nose into his shirt. "My problem? Fuck you dude, you're spitting in my car, punching the fucking window? And what the fuck was that with Mike back there?" I soar through the teller, agro driving, agro thinking, agro friends, agro, agro, agro, maybe I need some more speed, "I thought you were going to quit?"

"What do you care? You're not my Dad, you're barely a friend anymore," he bitches and yet offers me a bump, "Want one?"

"No," turn right towards *Castro*-land, "Fine," I decide to take the bullet, pop one before chugging up the monster hills. Maybe it'll distract my mind. Help me ignore my ignorant burden. That in its self is a fine reason to snort *broken glass* up my adult nostrils. "You're still a child, you know that?" I say to him.

"Very funny," he responds.

"But true."

Davey smirks, I drive.

₀ ₀ ₀ O   O ₀ ₀ ₀

Coming up to the *Castro Theater*, there's a line tonight, must be a good film. I try reading the marquee, but my car's too low and I just can't get a good angle on it. "Left," Davey's short with me. "Yeah, I remember dude," and I take a left. I don't see any spots on this block so I gotta circle again in the hopes we find something— nothing, and I'm getting testy, testier, kinda confused, keep squinting, dusk is hard on my eyes, my brow so tight, trying to make sense of the concept of thinking. My balls hurt from sitting and probably the *Crystal* again. I really have to find a fucking spot 'cause I am not doing that hill this time, no fucking way, this time things go my way not his. Today I got nothing to lose. Today I quit even if he's too much of a pussy to quit himself. "THERE!" Davey yells, and I slam the breaks, stall in the middle of the street, "Fuck!" My frustration is so on high that I can't get it started as my foot keeps slipping off the clutch too soon. *Varoom*, the engine finally revs again, okay, now, "Where?" and he points right beside us, "Uh, right there," he says, "But wait, let me get out," and just hops right out to nervously wait on the sidewalk for me to parallel park. Takes me three tries because I rather drop a nuke on the whole city than deal with anything at the moment. "You good?" he yells through the window, but I've seen a *ghostie*. It ran right by me, right by the left corner of my eye. I'm looking back, trying to see who it was, where it went, what it really was.

Davey taps on the window. I lean over, roll it down, "Wait here, I'll make it fast," he says and tosses me the bullet, "Hold this," and he's out. Prick. What am I supposed to do with this? Do more? No. Maybe one? Sniff, burn, why'd I do that? I didn't need it. Hope my heart don't pop. I take my pulse. Seems fine. Davey's gone. What do I do now? Wander I guess.

。 ○ ○ O   O ○ ○ 。

There is no way Davey is ever going to, "make it fast," so breathe, take this walk, a little tweaker tour of the *Castro*, check out the hoopla at the theater, sightsee the world of the gays. Good people these gays. They do seem generally happier than most people. Jubilant, loving, friendly, rambunctious; good people the gays. By the time I get to the *Castro* the line to the theater is moving. I can read the marquee now, "*Kenneth Branagh's Much Ado About Nothing.*" I'm pretty sure that's *William's* not *Kenneth's*, but whatever, I'm not going to see that one. You know it's been awhile since Mom and I had a movie day in the city. Next weekend. My treat. Love my Mom. "You need a date?" calls some lady boy in line. I turn, "Yeah, you cutes. You wanna shake a spear? Got an extra ticket," which he waves at me.

"No thank you," I say, wave, being cordial.

"Your loss, sweet cheeks," is all I hear as I make my way to the corner in a much better mood than earlier. I shouldn't blame Davey; he's got a problem. I know that now. It's obvious. I need to support him. Find a way to help him kick this shit, sniff, and I turn the corner— SMACK —right into some dude on accident, "Sorry," I say, look up into the eyes of this lanky, tall, shaved head dude wearing unstrapped red suspenders. The suspenders hang down beside his pants. He steps to the side of me, and then I see them, right there with my own *Jew* eyes; white laces to compliment the red straps. Laces strung through the holes of a pair of ox-blood, steel-toed *Docs*. This fucker is a full-fledged skinhead, a *Nazi-Punk*, one of the ones from TV, and he's cruising the *Castro*, and I can't fucking believe it, and he feels me eyeing him, turns, "There a problem faggot?"

"No problem, my fault," and I rush off, hopefully fast enough, pray he doesn't follow me.

—Baruch Atah Adonai, Eloheinu Melech haolam—
don't let me die at the hand of a Neo-Nazi
—Amen—

I turn back; he's not there, thank God. "He didn't have an accent. He's a *Californian*, not a *German*. Maybe he was a *ghostie* from my subconscious. Probably. I'm such an asshole," I talk to myself.

"You okay kid?" some guy asks me as I pass. He's heard me talking to myself. I wave him off, keep walking, gotta get to the car, get off the street. I've never seen a real *Neo-Nazi* before. Crazy. I didn't make it up. He was right there, in front on me, not out of the corner of my eye. He was real. *"Ted, just admit it."* The cops should be on that shit like flies. Didn't the mayor say they were taking care of it? Politics. Bullshit. Everyone's full of shit. I fumble in search for the bullet in my pockets, gotta ignore that shit. It worked for me in the car, should work again, just a little one, don't pop your heart, maybe better to lick it. Sure it was stronger that way, but came on slower, so maybe that's the way not to overdose? Probably the speed of the drug hitting your system so quick that kills you? Fuck it— SNORT —okay that was bigger than I thought, didn't burn as much though, where's my car? Bump into another guy, a little pussy, effeminate, rainbow child, at least it's not another fascist, "Watch it!" I snap at the lady-boy, unconsciously shove him aside and keep walking.

—The Skin was all alone—
I thought they roamed in packs?
Pile on an innocent victim.
Why's he alone?
Okay, I'm obsessing over this.
Bump didn't help, did the opposite.
Sweating. Hot. Back hurts.
I should get Gustav to beat him down.
That would be awesome.
Just what this town wants.
A beefcake curbing the jaw of a Nazi.
An Austrian beefcake, ugly as fuck,
ass raping White Power on the Castro.

—I reach my car, home base. Safe. Look around. The skinhead's not there, not down there, yeah, I think I'm in the clear. Not sure if I should wait inside or out? There is literally nobody on this street. Getting dark. Spooky. Strange...

—What if he comes back? —

If I'm in the car he won't see me, but if he does? Shit, this parking spot's too tight to get out in time. He probably thinks I'm gay. Gay and *Jewish*. Fucks like that can smell a dirty *Jew* from a mile away. My schnoz gives me away, always does. Jew nose and wavy, brown hair. I should have kept that Mohawk. Dad's fault. If I get a beat down then it's on Dad, he made me grow this pussified hairdo. If I just stand here, behind the cars, then maybe I'll see him first. I'll have the upper hand. I can run, or strike, probably run, but at least see him first. Yeah, that's gotta be the plan. Okay, breathe, get some nerve, do another bump? No, that's just stupid. I can handle this, sweating, picking at my eyebrow like the D; nervous, waiting, where is Davey? So much for making it fast— Holy shit, here comes the *Hitler American Youth*! Man, those shiny heads are like a beacon of hellfire. Where am I gonna go? I'm gonna go to Paolo's, that's the only safe place, *yeah that's the ticket.*

₀ ₀ ₒ O!!!O ₒ ₀ ₀
—*Can he see me?*—

I've crouched down behind my *Little Red Civic.* I can see him through my car windows, across the street, looking for something, someone———G   H   O   S   T   I   E   S . . .

O ₒ ₒ ₒ! ! ₒ ₒ ₒ O ! O ₒ ₒ ₒ ! !ₒ ₒ ₒ O

—G H   O   S   T   I   E   S . . .

. . . G H O s ᴛ ɪ ᴇ s—

To the left of me . .   .

     . . to the right of mE

aNNOYING, NOTHING's THERE, JUST HALLUCINATIONs
BᴏᴛH   SIDES

—*Crystal souls, lost in limbo, want to distract mE*—
Eddie's right, can't trust theM
ghosties just a joke
IN YOUR
town

Shit where did he go? —FLASHBACK— what Davey taught me, the night they marched on the *Phoenix*, made me stay home, said it was no place for a *Jewish* kid, not even in your hometown, we got *Neo-Nazi's* marching in *Petaluma*, crazy, anti-freedom, anti-trust, "They're gonna march this Saturday; probably already here. Be vigilant; don't going thinkin' that they're just here to spook us. These mutherfuckers want you to burn. They want to fight. It's the coming sun. The rapture. If they'll do this here, now, the nineties, then they're never going to stop, unless we stop them first. Just remember *Speedo*, if their red suspenders hang low it means they're looking to pick a fight—"

...and this guy, wandering *Gaytown*, whom I've lost because of the shadow freaks in my eyes, he had just that; had his suspenders hung low. Are there more? Where the fuck is he?
I
     stand

         up...
            ...He's right there,

                       crossing the street,

                              sees me, points,
                                        "
                                  Y

                           o

                 u

                .

          "

       and   I   hightail   it   as   fast.......

   ...as I

fucking
       c a n,
          never look b a c k,
                  n e v e r question my
actions,
      n e v e r
          wanted
             t o b e

in this

s i t u a t i o n, never

w   a   n   t   e   d
to die—
        —*I want to go home. ..*

                                                            .

                                        —and   I   cross
diagonally
            through the intersection to Paolo's hill.
                                                    Didn't

look both ways, could have died then...I have got to g e t u p

            t h e   h i l l

                                .

I'm sure he's following me— *Is he? Don't look T* —he is a
starved WOLF that smells the fear of this f a w n turnED D E ER

                                .

Chug up the cement steps, so many, but I'm in fine shape,
and finally, I'm at Paolo's apartment, house, apartment-
house, whatever, but before I can even get a foot on the first
the rainbow step I'm stopped by two skinny dollies just
leaving their first floor apartment, the only other apartment
of the house. "Where are you going?" one of them asks me. I
l o o k d o w n the   hill

                                        He did follow me,
                                    he's there at the bottom
                                    his eyes set on me
                                    he's not climbing
                                        the steps,
                                        he's waiting
                                    watching eyes
                                straps his suspenders

"Paolo, I'm going to Paolo's," I tell this downstairs neighbor.

My legs are shaking, but I can't go up, they're blocking my passage. "Who's Paolo?" he asks me.

"The guy that lives above you," I state the obvious, but they don't believe me, "Can I go, huh?"

"You mean Jake?" he asks as he curls his long hair over his ears.

"No, Paolo!" I holler at him, no time to be misheard.

"You must have the wrong address."

"What?" no this is the place, I ask, "I mean Gary?"

"Gary?"

His boyfriend just shakes his head, "You should leave."

"Fucking fags, come on, I know they live there, big, beefcake, super gay, hello?"

"What did you just call us?"

That's it, I gotta go, fuck them, and I rush up the stairs, shove right between them, nearly dump them down their own stairs, and I'm at Paolo's door, and I look back, and the neighbors are looking right at me, pissed, and I have to fix that, didn't mean to call them fags— *I can fix this* —Tell them about the hellfire they are about to walk into at the bottom of their hill, "I wouldn't go down there," I warn them.

"Why's that?" he asks, snide, untrusting, pissed all to hell about me.

"*Nazi* brotherhood all over the place," I say, "Fuck your shit up."

•

The two of them are totally shocked.

"Are you threatening us?"

"No," and I ring the doorbell, again and again.

"You better leave before we call the police!"

•

—THUD—
Behind the door, in the apartment?

—*What the fuck was that?*

Ghosties, ah, go away—

I pound the door, but it's unlocked, not even closed all the way, swings open from my fist's force, I rush the fuck into safety—

•

•   •

•

... • ● Davey's begun to crawl out the apartment window,

and

I see this, and I'm confused as I enter, stepping on broken shards of a
      J a   ck   D an   iel   s
                     b o tt le   on the floor,
"D   A   V   E   Y!"
but this confuses him, I'm not supposed to be here, I've interrupted something, and he loses his grip, slips, falls, vanishes out the window. I lunge forward, my hands wrap around the window sill, lean my head out, down, see if he's okay, but he's not; the D has fallen all the way down, all three stories, crammed himself between the lot wall and the dividing wall, that tight squeeze I remember so clearly. But I can't see him right. I try. Where's his head? He's twisted, bent, backwards, sideways, and I find his face, cocked up, incorrectly, rotated his neck, snapped back, eyes wide open, so sudden, so quick—

.Instantaneously   Lifeless.

—and the bags of

Broken Glass along with the hundreds of *Ecstasy* pills have burst against the pavement, spilt everywhere, and blood has gushed its way up Davey's throat from a massive internal hemorrhage, and it flows red, as red as that *Nazi's* suspenders hung low, a steady stream, pouring out of the side of his dislocated jaw, dousing the narcotics he had attempted to steal from Paolo, but Paolo isn't here, it's Gustav I spy standing at the front door, closing it behind him, standing there, only in his briefs, his underwear, barefoot, no shirt, crazy eyed, sniffling, a bloody nose, and replacing his false eye back into its socket...

—A glass eye?

...it's Gustav staring at me. Gustav, all alone standing in his underwear, barefoot, in the broken bits of glass; actual glass. He wipes the blood away from his nose with the back of his hand, his monstrous hand with a grip on the broken *Jack Daniels*, sniffs, and simply says, "Hello, *Jew*," and drops his drawers.

CUT

chapter 40

τhe handcuffs are freezing cold and the cops are rough with me. I am presumed innocent, right? The officers, must have considered that when they entered Paolo/Gary's, whoever's apartment this is, and saw me squatting on the overturned couch crying with blood soaked hands, shaking, scared, two thirds the size of the monster beside me. I was shooken not stirred, coiled, trying to disappear like Trish, ignoring my torn jeans that were soaked in blood, and avoiding the myriad of broken table glass everywhere. I immediately held up my hands, showed the police my thrashed palms that were riddled with shards of glass. The broken *JD* bottle was just inches away from Gustav's own hand, the same hand I had smashed into brittle fragments, but it wasn't the bottle I had used; the broken bottle of *JD* was his weapon of choice.

There was a lot of commotion once the police showed up. The downstairs neighbors made their best effort to see inside to get a look at the evil they had called *911* in regards of. There was a constant chatter from the walkie-talkies, a lot of back and forth by police, detectives, and forensics snapping photos after photos— PoP flAsh, PoP flAsh —so bright, blinding— PoP flAsh —They couldn't get a word out of me, I was frozen, I couldn't see anything, everyone swarmed around the room, too fast, all just a blur. More photographs of the room— POP FLASH —photos of the details; my hands, my face, my jeans, him, his head, his hands, the bottle, his nakedness, the window, out the window; everything.

They bagged items, *DNA* swipes of blood from my palm, from his palms, his face, my face, my jeans, the shattered coffee table, and the bottle. Rookie cops escorted the neighbors back out and down the stairs. I could hear the wooden steps thud and creak as the *SFPD* marched up and down doing their business—

X   X   X

—"Stand up," I'm told.

The officer pads me down, removes the *Crystal Meth* bullet from my pants, "What's this?" I shrug, he shakes his head, hands it forensics, they bag it. A paramedic takes me to the kitchen, cleans my palms, picks the shards out, and proceeds to wrap them in sterilized gauze. I'm lost, an empty shell, Tyler Gone-man.

—davey?—

Who are these people?   *Why are they doing this?*
                    —help—

Did something bad happen? Who's fault was it? I can't decipher between the past, present, and future. I vomited when the forensics assistant had asked, "Is this semen?" as he re-swabbed my jeans, my outer thigh. An officer is called over to attend to me after I've puked, "Hold it together, kid." Maybe this one presumes my innocence, "Calm down. This is all going to take a long time." How long do I have? Who am I? May I close my eyes? Is that allowed? But when I do, I only see brutality, terrible things. Terrible things have happened, and no matter how innocent I am, they'll still cover my head in a jacket and lead me out of the apartment. I don't want to leave. I struggle. I need to stay here. I need to wait for the D. Are you going to help him? He's stuck down there, in trouble, my fault, I left him alone, broke my own rule, let him down, got him in trouble; for real this time. "Calm down!" and I'm put in some sort of police hold, arms wrapped around my neck, struck under my arms, stuck, stuck, and lead down the rainbow staircase. I can see my boots take each step from under the jacket covering. Why did they cover my head? Red, yellow, blue, green, the colors of the sky that lower you down to hell, *Dante's* maze, deeper, farther, away from the original hell I had been victimized in, in the first place. "Watch your step," and suddenly— Snap, Snap —like firecrackers, and I'm shoved to the ground, someone's on top of me, "Stand back, BACK!" and I hear terrible cries, calls of justice from a crowd that has gathered on the street outside of the home—

"Gay Basher!"

"KILLER!"

"SEND HIM TO HELL!"

"Murderer."

"Lock him up! Rape him!" and someone whispers in my ear, "Die homophobe." Terrible commotion. The police remove the woman who has approached me, "Back off or we'll arrest you as well."

—Arrest? But I'm innocent?—

My wrists shake, try to release the metal that bounds them, but I've been picked up, lifted off the ground, from both sides, two officers grasp my armpits, control my movement, "Watch your head," but my skull bounces off of something solid, metal, and I'm shoved inside, into a car, a squad car, and the door slams shut, and the outside world is partially muted, but the screams have intensified, "Out of our city! No *Hitler Youth*! Die Scum! Send him to the gallows!" Someone else gets in the car, in the front, starts the engine, winds up the siren, and we're moving, in reverse, slow, makes a 3-point turn on the hill. Gravity slides me across the seat; I hit my head on the window. I want to die. Jump off the bridge before I'm forty; good idea Davey. Instead I curl into a ball in the back seat and weep.

PART TWO

I'm in the police station. I'm not as popular in here as I was outside the apartment. Here in the bustling station, I'm just another common criminal, a thug; a thug of white privilege, "but I'm not white," but they don't want to hear it, "Turn to the left,"— SNAP —Mugshot number one— "Turn to the right,"— SNAP —Mugshot number two— "Straight ahead." They had to have an officer hold the slate for me. My hands are too bandaged up, couldn't get any sort of grip. "We'll press his fingers later," I hear a female officer say, callous, annoyed that she will have to return to this process later. "Next time can you bandage them up after I get the prints?"— *I am so ashamed* —"Do I get my phone call now?" I ask, naïve, innocent enough, scared, young, yet charged as an adult. "After the detectives talk with you," says another guard who is completely cold, and delivers no eye contact. I've been shifted around so much that I'm under the belief they are cloning cops these days, and I'm escorted to a holding cell, empty, in the middle of the station. I stare blindly through the iron bars at the stir that is just another day at the *San Fran PD*. Then, for no reason, just like in the movies, a pig in blue taps on my bars with his baton and comforts me, "After *Moscone* took the bullet they tied our hands, kid. Can't treat your kind any better these days. It's *their* city now."

> *—Their means the gays.*
> *They have the wrong guy behind bars.*
> *You should be in here you bigoted pig fuck. Not me.*

"You should have killed one in *Kansas*," and he leaves making sure to drag his baton along the bars— CLACKITY- CLACK- CLACK- CLACK —just to annoy the shit out of me.

PART THREE

I sit silent on the chilling cement floor of the cell. There is no bench. I deserve no place to sit.

> *—Do I deserve the electric chair?*
> *I've only been an Adult for a few weeks.*
> *They'll consider that, right? Try me as juvenile?*

PART FOUR

They offer me a soda after cuffing me to the table in an interrogation room, "Yes, please?" This particular officer is kind enough to give me a straw as well; least they could do, I guess? I really want to call Dad.

—Maybe I'm still tripping?
Maybe I'm still just walking
Maybe still with Erin and Munts
Maybe living in a hallucinatory haze?

I turn to my right; call out for my friend, "Munts?" I can't do that shit, that shit looks crazy. You're not on *Acid*, Tyler, you're in jail, face it, you fucked up, you fucked up big time, and your best friend is gone, gone for good, not too far gone, but completely wiped off the planet. I begin to cry again.

X   X   X

A few minutes later the door opens. Two male detectives that I recognize from the apartment step inside, turn to the guard, share a few words, shut the door, turn to me, notice I've spilt the soda, accidentally knocked it over, sugar water puddled on the table, dripping onto the floor, "You want another?" the taller of the two asks me, and I think that's kind, appreciate it; kindness goes a long way in a time of trauma.

"I'm scared," I confess, but the other guy, not so liberal with his empathy, drags a metal chair from the corner of the room, all the way to the table, lifts it up, slams it back down, spins it around backwards, sits, and dumps out a file of *Polaroid's*. With his hands, he methodically lines them up for me to review.

The flash photos in their plastic *Polaroid* frames are more heinous than I remember. I can't believe it. I'm hypnotized by my own destruction. Don't want to look. Won't. The detective authoritatively taps his finger on the photos, "Look. I want you to see this." I shake my head, he slams his fist on the table, the photos shift, I wipe a tear from my eye with my shoulder, grimace, squeeze my brow, and look down at the mess I've made of my life.

X   X   X

The apartment is a disaster. Everything's been toppled over, destroyed, ruined, and there in the middle of it all, Gustav, dead, naked, with large shards of glass that have been jabbed into his belly, into his neck, and in his mashed-up face; I can't look at it— "Look!" —I turn back. I don't want to, I'm scared, scared that I have no choice.

Gustav has no face left. His head is merely a mess of collapsed skull fragments, mashed meat, blood, and shards of blue glass. So much blood. The solid brick of glass I had used as my weapon that had broken off of the coffee table when we had both collapsed upon it, lies just beside the pummeled mass of what used to be Gustav's face. I presume much of the meaty substance is brain matter. I gag, want to puke, "You puke and we do this later. Again." I swallow the rising bile. Burns my throat. He shifts the photos around, presents yet more of my not so mild-mannered destruction. Gustav's arm stops at the wrist. The hand that was once attached is now a red pulp of cottage cheese. I gag again. Detective-dick gives me that look, the look that forces me to swallow my stomach acid. Beside that photo is another, different angle of the non-existent hand, focused on the broken neck of the *Jack Daniels* bottle, the bottle he had threatened to shove up my, "*Jewish kike* asshole." That had been the moment I accepted that Gustav knew exactly what that word meant. That nothing was *Kosher* about that guy, that everything was a shield of some sort, a red herring, and a plot point in a *Hitchcock* film that has me floundering in my innocence in the real world. The other detective has returned. Brought me a *Sprite*, "All outta of *Pepsi*," he says, looks down at the photos, shakes his head, pops the can, drops in the straw, places it beside me.

"It wasn't my fault," I confess.

"We read you your rights, son," he says, "You don't have to talk to us yet."

"I don't?" I ask, but Detective-dick still has a few questions for me, "We just want to know a few small details; help us sort out some things we're not so sure of."

"Okay," I want to be cooperative, prove I have nothing to hide, prove my innocence.

—Innocence. Innocence. Visualize, Tyler. Innocence—

"Did you do it because he tried to jip you out of your drug money, or do you just hate homosexuals this much?" and he taps on the one photo I would not look at. The photo of Gustav's smashed testicles strung out along the floor.

"I don't hate gay people," I plead, with my voice, my eyes, and the nerves that shake my inner being— my <u>everything</u>.

"So, it was boy trouble; your boyfriend in the alley? Maybe he was cheating? Hurt your feelings. Made you mad?" he asks completely misinterpreting my words, "Maybe you threw your friend out of the window then attacked this man?"

"No, I'm not fucking gay!" a visceral reaction to the night's ever so confusing events, "That *Nazi* killed my best friend!"

"*Nazi*?" he looks at the empathetic detective.

"Ease up, Jack," the guy tells him, pulls up a chair, and sits at the end of the table. "What makes you think he was a *Nazi*?"

But I have no answer for that, besides him calling me a *kike*, besides him being a foreigner from *Austria*, besides being spooked from the skinhead that had chased me up the hill. I have no real answer for that. "He called me a *kike*," I say.

"What about your friend? He *Jewish* too?"

"No."

"So, what's his story?"

"<u>They</u> threw him out the window," I misspeak.

> *—Why did I say that? I just lied to the cops.*
> *What now? Don't forget.*
> *Keep that story. Keep up that lie.*
> *Can't take it back,*
> *they'll throw away the key for sure.*
> *I fucked up; again.*
> *I suck at this.*
> *Terrible.*

"Who's they?" the nice guy asks.

> *—Wait, Paolo wasn't actually there?*

Paolo's always there? I'm not lying about that.
He's usually always there, and Gary?
Where the fuck were they?
I don't know what to do.

So, I remember...
...how it goes on TV.

X   X   X

"I want my phone call. I want to call my Father so he can call a lawyer," and with that the dick scoops up the *Polaroids*.

"Tied our hands now. Good luck kid," and he leaves. The kind one just looks at me, at my puppy dog eyes, and gently asks, "Eighteen?"

"Yeah."

"Fuck. Okay, I'll get you that phone call," and he leaves.

PART FIVE

I'm in a phone booth at the police station. My swollen, gauze wrapped hands are still handcuffed. Some desk deputy drops the quarter in the slot for me, hands me the receiver that I cannot grab. "Figure it out," he rudely says and asks me, "What's the number?" I reel off the digits for him to dial as I cradle the receiver between my ear and shoulder, impatiently waiting as the phone rings and rings again, until Mom answers, "Hello, Goodman residence."

"Mom. Uh, um— *(breathe)* —Can I talk to Dad?" I'm trembling.

"Tyler? Is everything okay?" she asks, well knowing I only ask for Dad when I do something wrong, stupid, this time terrible, and besides, it's past midnight and I was supposed to be home five hours ago.

"Please," I beg of her, "Can I just talk to Dad?"

"It's Tyler," she tells Dad beside her in bed. He doesn't immediately pick it up, he goes to another room, to answer a second phone so they can both be on the call. "Tyler?" I can tell he is ready to strike in anger, "What's going on?"

"Dad," and I breakdown, weep, work on collecting myself, sniffle, snot sniffle, no more drugs, just snot, "Dad, I messed up."

"Tyler, calm down," he says, compassionate enough, possibly going to listen to me.

"I'm— I'm in the city. Been arrested," and the receiver slips from my grip. I fumble to get it back into my shitty hands, prop it between my head and shoulder again, "Sorry, dropped the phone."

"Damn it, Tyler! You better tell me what's going on."

"It was an accident. He tried to rape me."

"Oh my God," Mom is traumatized just by the thought.

"Stop. Listen to me. Tyler?"

"Yeah?"

"Where are you?"

"I'm in jail. I'm sorry, Dad."

"Don't talk to them. You can't trust the police," he advises me.

"I told them you would get me a lawyer?"

"Good. That's good. No more though. Say nothing. Do not, do not answer their questions."

"But—"

"Damn it, Tyler, don't argue with me!"

"I'm sorry."

"Mother and I are going to come now," he starts, "Do not talk to them."

"I understand," I say.

"I don't think you do. Just don't be a chatty shit like you always are, this isn't one of your movies," he's really pressing this gag order.

"Dad?"

"Yeah?"

"I'm scared."

PART SIX

The new cell they've moved me into is even colder than the

first. The guard told me they don't turn the heat on down here. A few cells down from me there is this guy who won't stop whispering to himself. Sounds like nonsense, nonsense that means the world to him. I rather he stops, but I have no authority about it. How long until I start whispering to myself? Tried covering my ears with my bandaged hands. That hurt. Tried to lay out on the cot, but that pulls at the tendons in my wrists, which in effect pulls at my palms, which hurts even worse. There is no comfort here. This is not the *Hyatt* hotel on the hill, this is hell frozen over and hell has no mercy. "You have a visitor," announces the guard. I turn from place in the corner. He unlocks the gate, makes me turn back around, re-cuffs me, and escorts me back upstairs.

PART SEVEN

Mom and Dad are in a windowless room. The empathetic detective holds the door, as I'm lead in. Mom rushes over, hugs me, but my cuffed hands are unable to return the gesture. "Can we uncuff him?" the detective asks the guard. "Your case," he says. "Uncuff him," the detective restates his request, with vigor, authority, and annoyance. "I'll give you all a minute," and the detective leaves with the escort. Mom hugs me again. I hug her back. Dad paces; upset, confused, disappointed in his only son. "I'm sorry, Dad," I just can't say it enough— ever.

PART EIGHT

Back in the cell I'm served beans, bread, and a chicken thigh, "Thanks," but the guard ignores me. The food is terrible. I take a bite of the chicken, a scoop of beans, but before I can get a solid slice of bread down I puke it all up, remembering Davey's twisted head, and the lifeless look in his eye from three stories up. This is not how *Suburbia* ended.

PART NINE

"obviously, my client is more than remorseful. He's willing

to be openly honest about all accounts," says my *Jewish* lawyer, Eli Eschowitz, a respected criminal defense attorney; he was a friend of a friend's uncle, he's sixty-five, short yet firm, grey hair, dressed in a dark blue suit complete with a light blue neck tie. We sit in a jail cell office with the District Attorney; my parents wait elsewhere. "So, pleased your client is willing to be *truthful*, but honestly, Eschowitz, his testimony reads like a paranoid teen with his nose burnt out by the same junk we found in his pocket and scattered all over the scene of the crime," lays out the DA. I'm not allowed to speak. Sit and listen. Gag ordered by my attorney. Forced to not verbally dispute this DA's petty visual truth, which is merely the sub-plot of the story, not the actual story, not the whole truth and nothing, but the truth. There is no discussion about the hateful actions of the deceased. No words about my motive, no defense by me.

"He didn't run from the scene, he confessed to the murder after his *Miranda Rights*. He was overtly cooperative. I wasn't here, you got lucky on that, so at the least let's start with a little leniency," Eschowitz defends me. I like him. Seems solid.

"Okay, so what? So, maybe he talked because he wanted to get on the front page? Everyone wants to be famous these days. Kid sees gay-bashers getting a lot of press, so kid sets out to become the story. We know he wasn't there for a good time, or revenge. You cleared that part up with our detectives well enough," and she presents Eschowitz with a transcript of my denial of their gay love triangle theory. He's not happy. He doesn't like that I spoke up about anything. "I know, I've seen it, but a *Hate* charge, on Tyler? I just don't buy it. You have no proof this was motivated by *Hate*. Drugs maybe, but *Hate*, come on? The kid's *Jewish*. When have you ever heard of *Jews* acting out a *Hate* crime?"

"Bible's full of them," says the ignorant District Attorney. "Is that going to be your defense? You're going to quote a book of fiction? We're pleading *Temporary Insanity*," and I guess I can go along with that, but really, it's not true. Gustav was the one *Hating* on me. I was defending myself.

"The investigation has just gotten started," claims the DA, "I'll wait for more facts, besides, that book of fiction?" and she turns to me, "You're going to have to swear on that book before the court, so I advise that you start believing."

"*Involuntary Manslaughter*," Eschowitz changes our plea.

"Did you see these pictures? This is no accident, this is not defending one's self. I'd rather chance the jury, than settle for that garbage."

"You can't prove that," Eschowitz looks like he's losing his grip, but what do I know, I'm out of personal options, I have no voice, I can only surrender to anyone who is willing to help me. The DA takes a moment before responding. She's put an eye on me. I tell her I'm sorry, with my eyes. Can she read them? Do you hear me? I'm really fucking sorry.

"Look, I don't like this case anymore than you do. This is problematic from every angle. I got a dead, under-aged kid crammed between two buildings, drugs everywhere, and upstairs, from the apartment he came from, I got another guy, gay, alone, brutally murdered and Tyler here on record admitting it was all done by his own hand," she takes a deep breath, exhales, flips through some papers, and ends the meeting with, "I can offer you a *Hate Crime*, and you go and prove me different, or *Voluntary Manslaughter with Cruel and Unusual Death Blows*, but I can't go lower, not without more specific evidence that paints a completely different story."

"*Voluntary Manslaughter*," Eschowitz, "But I want access to the investigation."

"WHAT?" my hands buckle, the handcuffs getting caught on my chair. I've startled them both. She packs up her briefcase, "Of course, but for a limited time. I'm not wasting taxpayer money on a wild goose hunt. Guard!"

PART TEN

I saw it all later, about a year later. I saw it, not all of it, twelve, thirteen, twenty-two different newspaper articles about me, my crime, not Davey's and my crime, not Gustav's actions, no mention of a Mike or a Gary. No commentary about the coupling of them all. No curiosity about Paolo and his million-dollar collection of finger jewelry; no, not their crime, just my crime, just me and the communal outcry that I would dare make a plea for *Temporary Insanity*. "Another *Hate Crime*? Or *Double Hate Crime*?" SF Chronicle; The Jewish Journal runs with, "*Young Adult Jewish Man on Trial for Hate: Pleads Temporary Insanity*." Misguided, opinion driven articles, and two peaceful protests in support of Gustav, a man nobody has ever met, that ended at the rainbow stairs of the *Castro* house where strangers have created a memorial for a man that threatened to shove a bottle up my *Jew* ass. *Jake Gilders*, the subletter of the *Castro* spot; the subletter who the neighbors thought actually lived upstairs, was even quoted, "This is a tragedy that echoes the days of *Harvey Milk*. May justice prevail."

> —*Where's the truth?*
> *Knotted up between two buildings?*
> *Being buried in the Petaluma cemetery,*
> *right beside his fallen sister?*

Why is it so difficult for people to consider a gay man may want to rape? That's a hard theory to come by, but the theory that a young *Jewish* man, a midget in comparison to his assaulter would come to the city to murder him with his bare hands? That they chew down like a *Flintstone's Vitamin*, but that monster threatening to rape me, that is an obvious untruth? Have the gay-bashing *Neo-Nazi's* of *Northern California* created such a stir of panic that anyone, or everyone is suspect of being them? Is that the Mayor's stance? Is that what I am being accused of? Is any of this real? Has society made this much of a lack of progress? What if I was black? How much worse would this all be if I had been a *post-American slave* instead of a *post-Egyptian slave*? Didn't anyone see the guy with the red suspenders hung low, sporting white laces, calling people faggots? I want out. Frustration. "Let me out! GUARD! GUARD!" but they never come, and I haven't hurt myself yet, so, why should they?

X　　　　　　X　　　　　　X

The police can't find Eddie. Can't find Eddie's car, have no address for Mike's house, can't question Davey, and as much as they've canvased the *Castro*, no one has ever heard of Paolo, and those who have claimed relations with Gustav have been unable to supply the police with any sort of proof of such relations, not even a snapshot. Eschowitz is really making them hustle. I credit my father for this. Sheena helped. She took the detectives to the *Santa Rosa* apartment. Heard she was remorseful. She had nothing to do with nothing; she shouldn't feel that way. The apartment had been abandoned. It was a month-to-month rental. No lease, no record of any tenant's identification; always paid in cash. Only match they got were Davey's fingers on the flusher.

I don't cry anymore, all dried up, feel heartless, a shell, a shell on a mental hunt for answers I have no control over anything, and yet here I am, hand and ankle cuffed in the back of the detective's sedan cruising the windy roads of *Sausalito*. We keep passing through the one stop sign I remember, turn around, and pass through again. "Fork in the road," I tell them, I remember that too, and finally we see a pedestrian out for a doggy walk. They ask him if he knows of any fork in the road that might lead to a house with a stainless-steel door, no handle.

X   X   X

"Mike?" asks the empathetic detective, but the guy who has answered the stainless-steel door isn't Mike, he's Bob, and Bob's a little nervous to see a sedan with a siren, totting a hardened boy criminal in the back seat.

"No, I'm Bob. Is there a problem?"

"Does a man named Mike live here?"

"Mike has lived here, on and off," Bob tells them, "Is he in some sort of trouble?"

"Would he be?" the detective asks.

"IRS?" Bob asks, "I'm in trouble with the IRS, aren't we all?"

"Is Mike here now?"

"No, he's been gone for a minute now."

"When did he leave?"

"Last Sunday night, had a date in *Paris*."

"*France?*"

"High roller— Mike has good taste in men."

"How can we contact this Mike?"

"Call his office?" and Bob gives them Mike's card, *EX-O-TICKLE IMPORTS*, and they look into it. Mike, Michael Olenstat, runs an import/export company registered out of *South Africa*. He did all his work from *South Africa*. Mike doesn't live here; everything Davey and Eddie were told was a lie, everything.

PART ELEVEN

ᴍy Arraignment—

No Bail. The judge has determined I was a walking target, feared for my safety. The general public wants my head. They want to finally get one of these gay-bashing *Nazis*, and I look good enough to them, at least to the homosexual extremists who are out to get me. I don't know how I'd see it from the outside. I'd probably hate me as well.

Eschowitz thought it best if I told the Judge my story, for face, for some level of empathy, and so I finally got to speak out, defend my actions, "Gay or straight, he was threatening me, and my ethnicity. My religious affiliation." My stomach knots up every time I think about it. Memories. Visions and sensations of that night. Gustav's monstrously huge arms reaching out for me, his crazy eyes, the bloody nose, his member, erect, rubbing up against me as we struggled, his pelvis thrusts, his— I can't. I can't think about it. It wasn't my fault, none of it. Won't someone finally believe me? The whole story, not just parts, not partial empathy, full empathy, please, "I'm not a bad person!" and now I'm shaking, and the courtroom is shaking, and my *Tyler Tantrum* vein pulsates along my skull, and I fear the worst from myself, as my own Mother has to be escorted from the court for emotional outbursts, "Believe him! GOD PLEASE BELIEVE MY SON!"

X   X   X

"And David?" the DA questions me after I've composed myself.

"Gustav pushed him," I lie.

"Why was David being pushed out the window?"

"I don't know, I came in and Davey fell. I don't know why," and I've fucked up, lost my verbal grip in the courtroom, on the tail end of a lie I've been so good at keeping all these weeks.

"So, Mr. Goodman, did you just admit that when you entered the apartment what you actually saw was Davey fall from the window, not that he had been pushed by Gustav?"

"Objection! That's semantics, my client is obviously under a lot of pressure."

"Over-ruled. That is not semantics. Answer the question," instructs the judge.

"I guess so?"

"You are under oath Mr. Goodman."

"No, I didn't see him get pushed, but that doesn't matter, he was waiting for me. Gustav. He was waiting for me because I'm *Jewish*. Davey was probably running to warn me; don't you get it?"

—Nope.
Because he wasn't trying to save me,
Davey was stealing from his suppliers.

PART TWELVE

"I don't know," I conclude my statement, "But I didn't mean to kill him."

Munts wore a suit to the hearing, so did Dad.

PART THIRTEEN

Erin came to court with Sheena on the day Sheena was called to the stand as a character witness, the only person alive that the police could find that knew something about nothing, but something indeed. Erin wore a black dress, waved to me from the audience with a solemn expression the entire time. Erin's never been anything less than overtly happy; today she was not. Sheena was a character witness to Eddie, Davey, and I. Sheena defended every word I had said, a real trooper, frustrated about her own lack of action. Her entire testimony was regret, after regret. Said she never felt she was a good enough person for me. Told the court Eddie and Davey were absolute mess-ups that had dragged a good man down. My father didn't appreciate the pun, but I did, I thought it was quite charming. She made me well up. Jury seemed to believe her. The DA didn't bother to cross-examine her, and Eschowitz did a fine job driving her to tears about Eddie's whereabouts. "I just don't know. I've called everyone. I've gone to every place we've ever been, and I went to places he's talked about. I just don't know. I'm so sorry Tyler, you don't deserve this," and then she was escorted off the bench, out of the court for her hysterics, and I finally understand the appeal of *The Cure*.

PART FOURTEEN

ᴍʏ father is so upset about the entire system that I am concerned he's going to show up with a gun during the verdict.

PART FIFTEEN

ᴀnd yet, Dad cannot understand how his swim team champion of son with a small temper could be such a brutal murderer. He blames the drugs. I don't. I blame history.

PART SIXTEEN

ᴛʜe courthouse swarms with protestors on the day of *Closing Arguments*. I get it. I understand the community is exhausted by the abuse being swept under the rug as a temporary fad. I'm with you on that. That in its self is the real injustice. That mistrust will fester and rear its ugly head in the years to come. People will be surprised when they learn the *Haters* have begun to organize underground, invisibly, only to be emboldened by some politician who will bark about nationalism. This lives deep in the *American's* blood. You don't have one of the most savagely violent wars in history on your own soil in defense of slavery without creating a culture of bitterness and hatred. When you repress those ideas, ideals, you will surely be designing a time bomb for the future. I'm still amazed it hasn't happened sooner, or yet even. It will, but today the protestors are barking up the wrong tree. You all should be preparing for something much worse than the murderous kid who is actually on your side. But the whole city is caught up in hating on *Hate*. Paolo's downstairs neighbors want revenge so bad they've started making things up to the press, "He was *Sieg Heiling* us before he went in the apartment. Threatened us. Said there were more of his kind waiting for us, waiting to beat us to hell."

Munts and Tenderloin tried to come to my defense; tried to sway public opinion. They made a photocopy *Kinkos* comic book about the entire incident, from my perspective. Probably got too creative with it, the violence, the language, all so very animated. That's the problem with the truth; minute you put it on paper, is the minute you exploit it on accident, and the public will interpret that worse than they already have. Art is a dangerous weapon that can backfire on the most innocent man. I don't blame them. I appreciate their efforts, but I never did as much *Crystal Meth* as they had drawn in their comic squares. I never smoked it like you have us doing at the bottom of the hill before the shit went down. I didn't have a habit like Davey. I just wanted to see what the fuss was all about.

PART SEVENTEEN

Tom Gaffey has done his part as well. Did me a solid at the recent *Greenday* show. On stage, in front of a full house, showed a photograph of Eddie, begged the audience to take part in the search, even set up a little hotline office in the *Phoenix*. No one ever called in. *Billy Joe* even chimed in a couple times during the set. "Never knew him, but if *Tom* vouches for Tyler, well then, that Goodman must be a good man." I'm not going to hate on *Greenday* anymore. I'm not going to hate on anything anymore, ever.

PART EIGHTEEN

closing Arguments: District Attorney
"Your Honor, Jury, even War has its limits," is how the dick Attorney opens. She's a real bitch about it all. No room for empathy, no giving a good kid a break. "Even if we were to assume, perhaps speculate that Mr. Gustav was an *anti-Semite* and <u>not</u> an innocent homosexual living in the well protected *Castro* district, and this was not *1993*, and was indeed *1942*, *World War II*, on the *European* frontline, and Mr. Goodman was an *American Soldier* confronted by a *German Stormtrooper* for hand to hand combat; Mr. Goodman's actions would merit a *Military Court's* review for the brutal magnitude in which Mr. Goodman, who, let me remind the jury, has pleaded guilty too, had inflicted upon Mr. Gustav."

My eyes are on fire, stomach in knots, pulsing urine in my bladder from the water they have forced me to drink. I had become dehydrated. Stopped drinking a week or so back. Stopped eating. I wasn't on strike, I was, am, losing my grasp on any form of optimism.

"This man, not this child, he is no child, he is a grown eighteen-year-old in honors classes, bright, aware, well knowing the difference between right and wrong, is not absentminded of his actions, they are not a blur, he did not *blackout*, he in fact, with his own words, remembers everything from that night, yet Mr. Goodman here suggests he suffered from some sort of anxiety attack, that he was not of sane mind at the time of the murder, and still, through a conniving set of storylines, has openly changed his tune on the death of his dearest friend."

I can taste the bile in my mouth. I must swallow. I cannot vomit here, not now.

"Maybe Mr. Goodman did have a panic attack, maybe he got in over his golden boy head by dealing drugs with his friends from high school, but does that condone such vile brutality? Tyler Goodman maybe troubled, but innocent, my fine jury, he is not."

PART NINETEEN

closing Argument: The Defense

—This is my last chance.

"Everything is relevant," Eschowitz pauses, waits for that to sink in, his hand gently pats the stained wooden rail of the jury box. He sighs, steps away, and continues, "The burden of proof of the homicide in question was the responsibility of the *Prosecutor*, but it was us the *Defense* who spoke, based on Mr. Goodman's own accord, admitting to the accidental homicide. So why have we spent weeks debating the issue? Because the burden of proof was not who killed Mr. Gustav, but why. Why was Tyler Goodman, a high school student, half the size of his aggressor, forced to defend himself with such severity? We have heard specifics from Tyler. We have heard his detailed account that lead up to that tragic evening. We have had striking, highly positive testimonies of Mr. Goodman's character. The *Prosecutor* herself, has supplied us with clear forensics that indicate the assailant, Mr. Gustav, was acting in an extremely inappropriate manner based on his lack of clothing, broken bottles, and drugs, before young Tyler even entered the home. We have another young high school student, seventeen years of age, deceased due to this outrageous behavior in the apartment." Eschowitz wipes his brow, he's nervous, he knows he's right, he knows this is a circus, he knows I'm a scapegoat for the people. "The state— The State has supplied no character witnesses for Mr. Gustav. If anything, the *Prosecution* has allowed *Public Opinion* to influence their case in the wake of a lack of evidence. *Public Opinion* does not belong in a courtroom, and I would hope you take Tyler's well being into account when you deliberate and decide whose story you would rather believe. Tyler's unwavering accounts of being a young *Jewish* man threatened by an undocumented foreigner, a *Neo-Nazi* posing as a homosexual drug dealer, from a country known for their bigotry towards the *Jewish* people, or the *State* that assumes Mr. Goodman here is just a common drug user out on a homosexual killing spree, for which there is no prior proof of such bigotry in his past. So, I ask the jury, if it was your son up here, on trial for defending himself, what would you want to be done?"

PART TWENTY

rhe *Jury* barely deliberated. One day. I'm probably free to go— obviously.

The *Judge* asks, "What is your verdict on the charge of *Involuntary Manslaughter in the First Degree*?" The *Jury's* spokesperson, a weathered thirty-something, stout, balding man rises, "Your honor, after serious deliberation we the jury must find the defendant guilty."

I heard that. The whole world heard it, if they were listening, which they are not. I am guilty as charged. My calf tenses up, cramps, pulls on the back of my knee, and rips at my tendons.

—Can I die now?

The Judge thanks the Jury, and proceeds to address me, "Mr. Goodman?"

—What?
What do you want from me now?
What's left, but to send me to hell?

I rise.

"Mr. Goodman, do you understand the severity of this verdict?"

"I do."

"Mr. Goodman, I will be frank with you. There is nothing in this case that I like as a *Judge of Law*. I do not like young people selling drugs. I do not like young people caught up in violence and dying over drugs, and I am definitely not fond of adults taking advantage of naïve young people for their own agenda. As for the court, and the press that has so spectacularly taken this trial into their own hands— *clears his throat* —the idea that the deceased was a homosexual is of no significance in such a travesty of actions on all parts employed in these activities. This was a crime about illegal substances. There is no factual evidence of *Hate* by either party involved. There is however, a mountain of evidence that all involved with the crime in question, were acting in insidious behavior that not only reflects poorly on the community, but also is in fact completely illegal in all states. Mr. Goodman, I highly suggest as you live out your sentence, that you watch fewer movies and stop being a victim. I sentence Mr. Tyler Goodman to an unwavering stay, institutionalized, with a release based solely on the institution's psychiatrists and psychologists, with a minimum of 5 years. Court is adjourned." —BANG goes the gavel.

PARTY TWENTY-ONE

"I'm not crazy!" I yelled, spittle spraying all over Eschowitz in the holding cell with my Father, "Calm down, Tyler," and I had swatted my own Father's arm off my fucking shoulder, and he hit himself in the nose, a little dribble of blood; I was forgiven, but the tantrum didn't stop there. I tore off my shirt, bared myself to Eschowitz, spit in his face, "You fucking fat, pathetic, piece of shit, I am not crazy, I am not going to a crazy place! You fucked me."

—Might I rather be electrocuted than punished?

X   X   X

PART TWENTY-TWO

Locked tight, drugged, "I'm okay, I'm not depressed, I'm not crazy," honesty is the best medicine. I'm not talking to anyone in this looney-bin. I'm not listening either. I've read this book before; seen the movie. I'm not liberating these other assholes. Fuck this cuckoo nest.

Sheena writes me letters.

I'm so fucking bitter.

PART TWENTY-THREE

Tyler,
    Nothing's changing out here. Gosh, I'm not sure what to write. I lost at poker the other night with Sandra and Kayla's brother. Kayla's brother won two pink lipsticks, a quarter butt of a cigarette, two buttons, and a fart. You don't know them, but they feel really bad about what happened to you. I'm still at the *JC*. Feel like I am always gonna be there. I'm learning, but like maybe I want to learn something useful, ya know, like a trade. My mom wants me to do accounting. I told her I'd try next semester; you don't care about that. How are you? Shitty, huh? I saw no good movies this week. You get *HBO* in there? Or is it all daytime talk shows? OK, next letter won't be lame. Wish they'd let us visit ya, bye! I'm so sorry this happened to you. Write me?

Shennnnna!

PART TWENTY-FOUR

Tyler,
    Saw your Mom. I'm really sorry about everything I did

to you. You don't have to forgive me. I just have to be better.

Sheena

PART TWENTY-FIVE

т-man,
  It's okay that you don't write back. I don't blame you. I guess I'm just trying to keep you connected to the outside world?
  Went square dancing in the mill the other day. I had so much fun. The *Phoenix* shows have been weak this year, so I got my cowgirl on instead. No creeps there either, just good old middle-class boys n' girls having a twirl. You would have hated it.
  So, whatcha doing? I'm not giving up on you Tyler, you will write back.

All the best,
Sheena

      X   X   X

Tyler,
  Munts and Erin are moving to New York, dude. Crazy huh?—

> *—I'm still not crazy.*
> *I am however,*
> *very sad.*

  —Guess Erin got into some art school out there, *SVA?* Munts probably told you all this? Man, he misses you bro. He can't say your name out-loud. He loves you so much, we all do, and we want you to know we're here for you, always.

Sheena

X   X   X

It wasn't because of Munts and New York, it wasn't because she called it crazy, I was sad because I let go of the rope a long time ago now; I just fell back into the crazy house's single twin bed and starched white sheets, flat pillows, pillows and pills, so many pills. Pills that were spills of pills, all over the pavement, under— him. I won't say his name. Don't make me; don't even ask.

PART TWENTY-SIX

The therapist has instructed me that it's time I open Munt's letter.

—Fine.

I open the letter in front of her. It's been two weeks since I've gotten this one in the mail. Munts writes me every six weeks or so, usually just a drawing or two, nothing sentimental, nothing about nothing, drawings of girls who have waists tied in knots, and a bunch of other weird shit, but this new letter, that I'm gently pealing open, is apparently actually a written letter. I could tell. That's why I haven't opened it. I don't want to know shit about nothing that I don't know. Rather lose everything then remember what I've lost.

At least my daily drug dose has been cut down drastically. I am thinking more clearly, not acting out, keeping my *Tyler Tantrums* at bay. The shrinks might believe me soon. "Honesty is the best medicine," so ask me again, "Who was Gustav? "

"Gustav was a fucking *Nazi*."

"You don't have to read it out-loud, Tyler," my shrink informs me. I do anyway. Maybe it'll make her feel bad too?

Tyler,

I should have been there. I guess maybe you're having some sort of life experience on the inside? You can write a

MINI THINS

book about it. Do that. Maybe it'll help? I don't blame you for hating all of us. I'd totally come and visit ya, but they won't let us for like four years or something? I still feel guilty buddy. I should have been there. I'm so fucking sorry. I let you and D down.

Um, Erin got into *SVA, School of Visual Arts*, in *New York City*. I'm gonna do it. I'm gonna get on the plane with her and just totally wing it. Never been on a plane before, is it scary? Figure she'll sneak me into her dorm for the first few weeks before I get my own room somewhere. Thinking *Alphabet City*, kinda close to her, and lots of art things to do that I read on the *Internet*. You gots the *Internet* in there? So rad. If you don't have it, when you get out you will be totally mind-blown, mind-blown...and there's this program out now that people are hacking called *After Effects*. Totally does animation on your Mac. Erin's got a copy, but you'd figure it out faster than her.

Are you doing anything creative in there? Writing? Art Therapy stuff? Sheena says you never write her back either. I'm going to miss you, man. *New York* would have been cool with you. Soon though, right? You can meet me there soon?

—I can stop reading at any time now.

"Tyler, you haven't made any friends here yet?" the shrink had asked me so long ago. My temper does not permit a roommate. I have hurt no one, yet they are all under the belief that I may if I had to share my room. So, go ahead ask me again why I am not making any friends in here.

*—Because I don't want any friends,
ever again.*

PART TWENTY-SEVEN

I found a textbook on architecture in crazy house library.

PART TWENTY-EIGHT

ɪ'm drafting buildings. Tall and immense. Impossible buildings. I spend all of my time doing this and only this.

PART TWENTY-NINE

ɪ've requested a compass for my blueprints a number of times to no avail, so I've rigged my very own using a pen tip as my needle. Their reasoning was that I might use it as a weapon. I have shown zero signs of violent behavior since I blew up on my attorney after court.

The compass has really helped. My drafting skills have taken a great leap forward this past few months. My next building will be 20 acres wide, 1,200 stories tall, and have no doors or windows.

PART THIRTY-ZERO

ᴅavey and I have been trailing the *Petaluma* river for like forty minutes now, farthest either of us have gone up stream. We found a busted fishing rod and we've jerry-rigged it with some twine as we sit beside the water.

Davey and I are just kids, eleven maybe, still awkward. He sports a plain white t-shirt; I got a *Van Halen* shirt covered by my jean jacket, patches of *Iron Maiden*, *Ozzy*, shit like that; pre-punk.

"I think I want to live on a farm," Davey says.

"Yeah what kind?" I ask, but Davey's growing up sheltered, raised in the country without any animals, without any garden. The country is a prison when you have no reason to be there. The big city of *San Francisco* is a mirage to him. My parents always took me to the city. They'd take me to museums, parks, bridges, they'd teach me about how it's okay that men hold each other's hands. "Love knows no color, no gender," they'd always say and I believed that; still do. When I met Davey, I told him all about the *Golden Gate Park*, the *Japanese Tea Gardens*. Those were the days. Those were our Rushing River Days. Those were the days we were in a headfirst rush to become teenagers who were rushing to become adults and get out of town.

"Probably sheep; I'd farm sheep for cotton," Davey says knowing nothing about sheep or cotton, "I just don't want to kill nothing."

"Wool," I correct him, "You going to be a vegetarian?"

"I don't know. I don't like meat," he says, "I like fish, though."

> *—Need bait to catch fish.*
> *That's still murder.*
> *Worm murder.*

And we've morphed into our teens. Davey, with his suffocated blue skin, dead as can be, his head twisted backwards, casts the janky rod towards the river.

"Why'd Eddie run?" I ask.

"Got spooked. Told me he didn't like Paolo. Said something made him uncomfortable, something he saw," Davey says as he tugs on the fishing line.

"What'd he see?"

"A tattoo; under the guy's lip," he says, "Gave Eddie the serious heebie-jeebies. Paolo told him he was reformed, but couldn't get it removed."

"What was it?"

"Words. One word."

"What?"

"Skinhead."

"So, Eddie could have helped me?"

"Cops should have found the tape. That's how Eddie found out. It was on a sex tape," Davey explains, "Some naked skinhead chick was rubbing her coochie on his baldness, and first he saw her *SS* tat, and then Paolo pulled his lip down and showed the camera his *Skinhead* tat." There's a tug on the fishing line. "He wasn't supposed to be watching the tape. He was waiting for them to weigh the *Glass* in the back, and Eddie got bored and shuffled through their *VHS* pile, found one called *Fuck Me Funny* so he stuck it in. Super spooked him and he confronted Paolo about it, but Paolo was all like, dude, that's history. I came out of the closet, look, see, suck it, and whipped out his dick for a blow job to prove it."

"You knew this and you didn't tell me?" I calmly inquire.

"Eddie was on a lot of drugs, my man; I didn't believe half his paranoid shit," Davey tells me as the fishing line tugs again, "Hey, I think I really caught something."

"AIDS?"

"Very funny," Davey reels the catch in. It's ridiculous, the fish is a shark and the shark is already dead, half rotten, and in its gut a myriad of *Jewish* paraphernalia.

"Why would you let me go back there?" I ask.

"I was scared; you've always protected me," Davey answers, sticking his hand into the jaws of the dead shark and removes a bottle of *Vodka*, pops the top, and takes a swig; swigs it all down, one long gulp.

"Did people hurt you?" I ask.

"People hurt everyone," my dead friend answers and disappears forever more.

PART THIRTY-ONE

Tyler,

I got your drawing of that building. How did you do that? It looks so real, like you could build something that big. I can't believe you actually sent me something. Thank you. I put it up in my room, but Jeremy made me take it down. He's a little jealous of you. He has no reason to be, but he is. I think he needs to meet you.

Love,
Sheena.

PART THIRTY-TWO

Halloween.

"So how much longer am I going to be here? I'm ready to

know," I ask my therapist.

"I'm happy to hear that, Tyler," she tells me, but doesn't answer the question.

"Okay? Do you think I was ever crazy?"

"No."

PART THIRTY-THREE

Thanksgiving. I don't care; I am a draftsman now. I draw tall buildings.

PART THIRTY-FOUR

Chanukah. We have a menorah here. They asked me to lead the prayers; I refused. I'm not the only *Jew* here, "Ask someone else." My father has mailed me *Subbota* to read. I have been in here for four years now, or so I am told.

PART THIRTY-FIVE

I wish they had a pool to do laps; the track has not been satisfactory, hurts my chest when I run. Hurts my chest muscles. The physician thinks it's residual pain from my fight with Gustav. Does Gustav dream in hell? I killed that man. I did that. Me.

PART THIRTY-SIX

New Years. Happy New Year, New York. I don't see Munts in the sea of people on the screen.

—Wonder if he's still with Erin?

PARTY THIRTY-SEVEN

My parents come to visit. They want me to know they've sold the house, they've moved to *Corte Madera*; got me a new lawyer. I've been vocal and participating in most all activities here in the hospital for the past few months. My therapist swears I am not taking *placebos*. I will always be medicated. Sentenced to drugs for a murder over drugs.

PART THIRTY-EIGHT

I've started sketching out an oval shaped building, eight city blocks in diameter, four city blocks deep, sunken into the earth in the middle of *Manhattan*. I still have every right to be angry, but my anger comes from reason, and they are both dead; this is what we have learned here together, "You understand yourself very well, Tyler."

—This I know.

PART THIRTY NINER's FOUND NO GOLD

I'm released; only because this is a novel, and it would be a novelty to write a happy ending when so many others will sit tucked away in here, hidden for years to come, lifetimes, falsely accused. It's probably because I'm not *Black*, or an *Arab*. They think I'm a white guy. I will never allow anyone to consider me a white guy. Never.

Davis, California, that's where I've been. Somewhere between *Davis* and *Sacramento*, just an hour and half from home, I didn't go anywhere. I haven't changed a bit. Everything still looks the same in *P-Town* except *Putnam Park* is now empty. "Where'd all the punks go?" I ask my Mom.

"A lot of your friends moved to *Santa Rosa*."

"Oh."

"Your friend Sheena got married," Dad adds, "Mailed the invite to the old house."

"Why are we driving through town, then?"

—I will be seeing a therapist until the end of days.
That's it, fuck off.

X   X   X

PART FORTY

The end of an era.

ABOUT THE AUTHOR

Tzvi Peckar the Third is a native born Northern Californian who has rested his head in Manhattan, Los Angeles, and the San Francisco Bay Area, along with extended stints in Puerto Rico and abroad. An observer, a researcher, a wanderer, self-proclaimed scuttlebutt, and extreme culturalist, Peckar has spent his young adult life on the cutting edge of society, celebrating the best of its art, music, film, and strangeness. His first published work was the psychedelically charged series "Tzvi's Trees: Short Stories About Weed," featured at SmokingCannabis.com, UK's premiere Cannabis Website. Along with being the twin brother of acclaimed writer/director Tawd b. Dorenfeld, Tzvi Peckar the Third has garnished his own identity amongst readers young and old in the psychedelic subculture. *Mini Thins* is his first of many novels to come. As wild his imagination and reflections are, Tzvi lives in a state of bliss with his wife in Detroit.

2

www.ingramcontent.com/pod-product-compliance
Lightning Source LLC
Chambersburg PA
CBHW051935240626
47153CB00005B/1495